With a Stroke of the Pen

With a Stroke
of the Pen

Kimbra Leigh

Kimbra Leigh, Inc.
San Jose New York Lincoln Shanghai

With a Stroke of the Pen

Kimbra Leigh, Inc.
Revised Second Printing
Paulhamus Litho, Inc.

For information, please contact:
Kimbra Leigh, Inc.
PO Box 113
Muncy PA 17756
www.KimbraLeigh.com

Editorial Consultant: ND Wiseman
Copy Editor: Dr. Melinda McKee
Author Photo: Ken Siems © 2001
Cover Graphics Design by ND Wiseman/Vinland Images © 2001
Cover Design by ND Wiseman/Wayne Clarke © 2001
Main Cover Photo by Kimbra Leigh © 2001

Library Of Congress Registration Number: Txu 995-469
ISBN: 0-9718851-0-9

Printed in the United States of America

Dedication

**This book is dedicated to my children,
Tyler, Collin, and Mackenzie.**

* * *

May you realize that it *is* possible to go after your dreams with hard work, sacrifice and determination. You all have such unique qualities and talents, let the world see what you're capable of. Or better yet, let *yourself* see what you're capable of. I love you, Tyler. I love you, Collin. I love you, Mackenzie. I believe in all three of you, and I thank you from the bottom of my heart for believing in me.

Epigraph

"I believe in going after your dreams, and no matter what the outcome, the fact that you tried is success in itself. If I can teach my children this by example, then I've got more success than anyone could ask for."

Kimbra Leigh

"A real friend is one who walks in
when the rest of the world walks out."
Author Unknown

"Everyone hears what you say. Friends listen to what you say.
Best friends listen to what you don't say."
Author Unknown

"We all take different paths in life, but no matter where we go,
we take a little of each other everywhere."
Tim McGraw

In Memory Of Joseph Dalrymple
(1976-2001)

My Last Letter From Joseph

"When I was twenty-three years old, I was told that I had a tumor growing behind my heart. At the time, they said it was small and I should be fine. Then, in November 2000, I was playing volleyball and passed out. I went back to the doctor and found out that the tumor had spread, and that it was cancerous. They said that at the rate it was growing, I would have a year left before it took over my heart. As the doctors told me this, I was trying to take it all in. I started to shake. I fell into a deep depression for three months just trying to figure out why this was happening to me.

"Then, my little brother stopped to visit and asked me what was wrong, but I couldn't tell him. Letting it go, he asked me to go on a fishing and camping trip, and I went with him. While I was there, I found peace in myself. As I watched my little brother kill a fish, I realized that dying is a part of living — and normal, no matter what age you are.

"I am afraid that when my seed dies with me nobody will remember me, but a few friends, my mom and dad, and bro's and sisters. I will never know things like what it is like to have a child, nor will I know the future, and that does make me sad.

"Well, I am very sick and in the hospital, and I know that any day now I will pass on. I am getting weaker every day and am now refusing my treatment, 'cause if I'm going to die, I want to go feeling like myself."

*   *   *

Joseph contacted me by e-mail in June 2001 after having read *With A Stroke Of The Pen's* preview on *The Vinland Journal*. After a couple of cordial correspondences, Joseph shared with me that his life was ending.

Without getting into too much detail, Joseph and I began 'talking' about his fears and the reality he was facing. I became his sounding board and his friend. I encouraged and 'talked' real with him, without giving him the 'you're going to be okay' speech. He seemed to appreciate my candid responses, and our friendship grew from there.

With all of his e-mails, he kept asking to read more of the book, and without hesitation, I sent it to him electronically. Sadly, one of the last things Joseph did was read and finish With A Stroke of The Pen, even reading it when he was in the hospital. I am honored beyond belief that he would choose his remaining time to read my work, but at the same time, it leaves an eerie feel. That's quite a responsibility to live up to, but one I wouldn't change for the world. I am deeply saddened by his loss, and my heartfelt sympathies go out to his family.

As you have read above, Joseph wanted to be remembered — leave his mark on the world. I made a promise to him that to the best of my ability I would help make that happen by having a page for him in my novel. Even if I had not made this promise, I would still have this memorial for him. He was my friend for four wonderful months.

Joseph's words in his letter may be simple, but words we can all learn something from. He taught me perspective in living, and I helped teach him perspective in death.

Joseph was twenty-five years old, and he will be my forever-young friend.

Acknowledgements

I never could have done this without friends by my side.

*   *   *

When someone goes after their dreams, there are always people to show gratitude to, and I am no exception.

My family and friends have been wonderful and supportive. My Internet friends have encouraged me, as well as strangers I've met at the park or at a store while waiting in line. But there's always that one special person who has helped beyond the norm, and that person for me is my editor ND Wiseman. Without his hard lessons, support, guidance and friendship, *With A Stroke Of The Pen* would not be in publication. Thank you, Neil, for believing in me, teaching me and helping me turn my dream into reality.

To everyone who has written me or will write me in the future with words of encouragement or words of constructive criticism, thank you.

To Michael, thank you for allowing me the opportunity to go after my dreams and giving me the space and time to do so. I appreciate your loving support. And to my children, Tyler, Collin, and Mackenzie, thank you for understanding when *Mom* was in her 'writing' mode and for the pride on your faces when you spoke of *Mom's* work. Your continued interest, support, and encouragement helps to keep me going.

To my mom, Dee, I had so much fun photographing you for the book cover. You're a real sport for letting me dress you up older than you are, not to mention how you dealt with the weather conditions during the shoot. Thank you for your support, enthusiasm, and for just being my mom and loving me.

To my sister, Alana, thank you for reading my novel's rough-draft and for your constructive feedback. I truly appreciate your interest, help, encouragement, and support.

To Bob and Cindy Murphy, thank you for allowing me to use your house as my book cover's backdrop, not once, but twice. I truly appreciate your generosity.

To Harry Sauerhafer, Kathleen Aiello, Mae Burrows, Darwin and Jane Shaw, Lynnie and Ed Powderly, David and Jean Snyder, Wayne Clarke, Bob Wilds, The Alley Cat Hair Shop, Anne Johnson, Amanda Hogan, Jane Sedell, Bertha Fry, Karen Dincher, Vivian Daily and The Luminary, Dan Farr and The Sabre Radio Group, Heather Longley and The Williamsport Sun-Gazette, Donna McNulty and Wegmans Food Markets, Joe Murphy and The Harrisburg News Company, Ken Sawyer and WRAK, Beth Emley and The Brighton-Pittsford Post, Lance and Eno River Media Productions, Michael Cooper, Cary Abbott, Fulya Saka, Amy Klapp, Stacey Breneisen, Bobbi and Phil Wells, John Evans, Scott Warner, Dale Smith, Matthew Campagna, Melinda McKee, All my friends at C.T.L., Alan Davies, Mike Gorski, Craig Hoffman, Dave Demascole, Bob Taylor, Karen Lehman, Robin Bingham, Tom Ryersbach, and last, but not least, Joseph Dalrymple and his brother Bill, thank you for your enthusiasm, encouragement, support and/or just asking how things were coming along. You helped keep me motivated.

And to all, thank you for believing in me, which allowed me to reach beyond my own personal goal, write a story I love, and be in a place I had only imagined. Whether this book is read by one person or by a million people, the friendships I have made and the personal successes I have had through writing *With A Stroke Of The Pen* have already made it a true success.

Letter To The Reader

I invite you to fix yourself a cup of tea, sit back, and let me take you on Kaitlyn Marie Frost's journey, through her eyes and memories as she recalls her first love. Whether you're eighteen or ninety-eight, male or female, you may just find yourself recalling your own.

Chapter One

The woman rocked in the antique chair, while the floorboards of the farmer's porch creaked in time. Her fingers strummed the arm in soundless tune as her head relaxed against the tooled headrest. She broke the rhythm to reach for a steaming teacup, lifted it as if to drink, but stopped short when she detected its temperature. Placing it back on the side table, she looked out into the early summer morning and welcomed the day ahead.

Her eyes were drawn up past the porch eaves into a deep azure sky. Something about the color prompted a distant memory, but she couldn't quite put her finger on it. Wagging her head with a ghost of a smile, she chuckled out loud, startling a pair of courting squirrels on the far porch rail.

The woman turned her attention to the teacup and took note of the intricate yellow rose design fading into the creamy china. Sliding her finger around the dulled gold rim, she felt the small chip left there so many years before. She raised her eyebrows, questioning why she suddenly felt so vulnerable on this beautiful June, 2000 morning.

Kaitlyn Marie Frost was a good-hearted woman, and the passage of sixty-eight years had been kind to her, leaving more than a memory of yesteryear.

Her green eyes added graceful maturity, yet still held the gleam and exuberance of a much younger woman, framed with a lifetime's experience. Her cheeks were rosy and bright, and her smile welcomed in a grandmotherly way. She had a simple, warm style that made others feel like they had known her for years, which in fact many in town had.

Kaitlyn was a native of Winter's Crest, New York. A prosperous town of moderate size, it still had that small town feel. But like any close community, there were few well-kept secrets.

Winter's Crest was nestled in a picturesque valley on either side of the Odessa River, which meandered from the southern Adirondacks. Pausing in the middle of town, the river lingered briefly, forming a small lake as though gathering strength to continue on to join the Hudson, down below Lake George. At certain times, it seemed the waters carried with it the embracing scent of northern pine to those who lived nearby.

A similar morning breeze delivered the aroma of Kaitlyn's English Breakfast Tea, and she smiled. "Finally," she thought, picking up a teaspoon. Watching the swirling liquid, she squeezed the lemon at just the right moment and witnessed it dissolve in a cloud.

Kaitlyn gazed into the day sipping her now-perfect tea between the rhythmic melody of the rocker and porch floor's harmony. She scanned the tree-dotted front yard of her rambling old farmhouse.

"Good morning," she said softly to the birds as they argued impassively over the well-stocked and strategically placed feeders. Kaitlyn let out a giggle. "I must be losing my mind. I'm talking to the birds," she proclaimed.

Her ears perked up at the sound of a droning engine from the background of chattering grackles and recognized it as her long-time friend and mailman coming down the street. Kaitlyn paused to take a sip of tea before rising to go and receive the endless sheaves of bills and junk mail.

Clutching at the step rail, she felt slowed by her aging body — a reminder of her daughter's plea's to move into a 'Senior

Retirement Community'. She chuckled dismissively at the political correctness of the phrasing as she shuffled down the drive.

Shaded by a few ancient Elms, Kaitlyn turned to look up at her home just as the sun pierced the canopy, letting dappled sun drops play against the roof. She admired the well-kept place and felt a curious pang of regret that her husband was no longer there to enjoy it.

Her attention was drawn to the truck pulling up to the box, and she met the mailman with a friendly smile and hello, telling him of talking to birds. "Rose'll have me ready for the home before you know it," she muttered humorously.

"Kaitlyn," he smiled, "You are just as beautiful and capable as you always have been. You aren't going anywhere."

"I talked to your wife last night," Kaitlyn said with intended sarcasm. "Seems she's having trouble with her knee again."

"She's been running away from me," he grinned. "Now, maybe I'll be able to catch up with her and get a kiss or two."

They both chuckled, knowing well that even if his wife were to be slowed down by a knee, he still wouldn't win the chase.

He wished Kaitlyn good day while handing her the mail. "Seems there's something special for you today," he added with a wry grin.

Kaitlyn's attention turned to the wad of envelopes. "What's so special about bills?" she asked, glancing back in his direction.

"Oh, you'll see," he replied, grinning and slowly nodding. "Would you like me to have the old ball-and-chain call you?"

Kaitlyn giggled. "Better be careful with phrases like that. She'll ring you for those."

He laughed and drove off. Kaitlyn could still hear him laughing as he delivered the neighbor's mail.

Kaitlyn was almost content in her childhood home. She didn't want to leave it. There were too many fond memories connecting her to the old place. She knew tasks took twice the time they used to, and yes, she was lonely too. But leaving it, for her, was not an option.

Kaitlyn's daughter Rose came by often to visit and to do for her, but for the most part, Kaitlyn handled things just fine on her own. Her long-time friend Allison would also visit frequently. They would sit together knitting, relaxing, drinking tea, and reflecting on their more youthful days. Sometimes they would even get a tad wild and enjoy cherry cola instead of tea.

Kaitlyn strolled back to the porch, strumming through the daily mail. "Bill, bill, another bill," she recited. "Nothing special here."

Dropping the mail on the table beside her, Kaitlyn picked up her tea, sniffed the aroma and sipped softly. Releasing the cup's rim from her lips, she admired the yellow roses intertwined with greenery that encircled the fragile cup. She studied it and traced her fingers gently over the design again, remembering when her mother had given it to her fifty-odd years before.

Letting out a reminiscent sigh, Kaitlyn reached for the mail and shuffled through it once more. Her eyes widened in shocked disbelief when she stumbled across a letter. Without seeing the return address, Kaitlyn's heart pounded. She knew whom it was from. Shaking her head to see if what was happening was real, Kaitlyn's unexplainable feeling from earlier that morning became clear to her.

"After all these years ... " she whispered.

Kaitlyn leaned back against the chair and closed her eyes, cradling the letter against her bosom, as memories began to flood and swirl. Through the miasma of intervening years, in an instant, she traveled back to June twenty-sixth, 1950.

*   *   *

It was the summer following Kaitlyn's eleventh grade year. She and Allison had hurried into town to celebrate, giggling about their nebulous summer plans. Passing under stately maples along the street and past the small shops that decorated the parkway, they didn't notice the pensive undercurrent permeating the town. Blithely unaware of anything but boys, hem lines and the never ending debate regarding cashmere sweaters, they arrived at The Soda Fountain, fumbling their way through a bad rendition of *Some Enchanted Evening*. Universally regarded as 'The Most', Perry Como was certainly the dreamiest of dreamboats.

"The Twins are here!" someone claimed with a laugh as the two erupted through the frosted glass doors.

Allison Perry was Kaitlyn's best friend in the whole world. With sandy blonde hair flavoring her emerald eyes, Allison effused a bubbly personality. Her hair, as usual, was arranged in a ponytail, giving her a much younger appearance for all of her seventeen years. A few insouciant curls escaped the clasping bow, giving Allison a fresh, breezy look.

The pair's well-known moniker as 'The Twins' belied the one noticeable difference between the two: Kaitlyn's light brown hair and the more sophisticated way she carried herself. They were well-liked and firmly at the cutting edge of all the latest trends — strictly bobby socks, poodle skirts and defining blouses. And let's not forget — pure silk scarves. Their magnetic smiles invited, and the ladies charmed their way into every boy's heart, leaving traces of envy among the other girls.

The Soda Fountain, the place most frequented by high school kids, was a unique little restaurant snuggled in the heart of downtown Winter's Crest. Recently remodeled, the shiny black and white checkered Linoleum floor brought excitement to the newly finished walls. Decorated with mementos of days gone by, a small dance floor welcomed any and all, while the brand new Wurlitzer jukebox invited music lovers to drop a nickel and cut a rug to the very latest seventy-eight. Black fountain tables trimmed in white, each with four turned back chairs, were placed in the middle of the café, surrounded at the walls by cozy red vinyl booths, each decorated with a fragrant white carnation.

High above the usual bustle, stately fans slowly turned, oblivious to all but the oft-painted silver filigree tin ceiling, left over from the turn of the century when the building had been a hardware store.

Just as Kaitlyn and Allison settled in to order their cherry colas, John came rushing into the shop.

"There's a war!" he bellowed and held up the afternoon edition of the Winter's Crest Gazette. "A war has started!"

A startled silence fell over the restaurant as everyone turned to listen. Holding the paper in front of him while reading from it, John explained that North Korea, with the help of a zillion Red Chinese, had attacked our friends in South Korea. He looked up at his captive audience. "War has begun!" he ended dramatically.

John Fenderson was going to be a senior that fall and had planned on enlisting in the Army as soon as he graduated. Standing six feet tall and with eyes that matched his ash brown hair, his sharp facial features gave him a look beyond his seventeen years. His stature was confident, but with undertones of cocky arrogance — much like most of the other blue-collar boys in town. John, while popular enough, lacked several of the natty social skills necessary to be included in the rarefied realm of Kaitlyn and Allison's circle. While this lack was not lost on John, he still felt compelled to include himself whenever the occasion arose. John was tolerated by the Queen and her court with humor and good spirits.

Neither Kaitlyn nor Allison understood politics or worldly matters well, though the announcement did bring Kaitlyn's father, Captain James Allen Frost, to the forefront of Kaitlyn's mind. Captain Frost was a well-respected man in the community, having served our nation in World War Two — not to mention, he was the youngest president ever of Winter's Crest First National Bank. Kaitlyn clearly recalled the endless months of waiting for her father's return. She and her younger brother Alex would sit as door wards every night in the parlor as if expecting Daddy to come charging through the door at any moment.

Their mother Kathryn would silently fret about perhaps another officer baring only a telegram. The stark anxiety of him leaving to fight this new war shivered bleakly through Kaitlyn, leaving her in an uncharacteristic cloud.

All the kids scurried to their tables to discuss John's announcement, as Kaitlyn, with a hand raised to the side of her head, excused herself to freshen up. John came over to Allison and asked if Kaitlyn was all right.

"She's upset," Allison said a bit brusquely. "Have you forgotten her father was in the last war? Maybe he, or even Alex, will have to go straighten this mess out, too."

John sat down quietly in the chair next to Kaitlyn's. Chagrined by Allison's gentle rebuke, but grateful she didn't shoo him away, he eyed Kaitlyn's seat. His own father had been unable to serve, and though the reasons for it were perfectly legitimate, there remained the stigma of an unrequited duty to perform.

Allison cast a momentary sympathetic glance to John before returning to more important things. She raised her glass as if to sip from the straw, while scanning the room in an artful cover she'd learned from Bette Davis. "Same old crowd," she thought, and then took notice of a boy sitting against the far wall. "Interesting."

Without removing her eyes from the newcomer, Allison interrupted John's silence to ask if he knew who it was.

John peered across the room. "Oh, that must be the new kid," he chimed, happy to be of service. "He just moved here a few weeks ago, from what I've heard. Maybe I should go introduce myself."

Allison tore her gaze away from the boy to glance sharply at John, her brow knitted. "I expect a full report," she stated regally, but with a friendly smile.

Hopping to his feet like a marionette, John grinned ruefully at Allison and excused himself, making a beeline across the room.

Kaitlyn came out of the ladies room and noticed John approaching the boy. "I wonder who that is?" Kaitlyn thought with a whirlwind of interesting ideas. With her eyes transfixed upon the shadowed figure, Kaitlyn didn't notice the spill in front of the low counter stools. So when she slipped, she spun around and plopped right square in the middle of the dance floor. Landing with a bump on the behind, her legs were splayed and her poodle skirt was hiked all the way up to her waist. In an age where proper girls barely showed their knees, the expansive sight of Kaitlyn's creamy thighs was the absolute definition of racy.

Kaitlyn's sudden squawk and red face had all eyes sharply focused on her, and all chatter amongst the kids stalled.

"Oh my gosh!" Kaitlyn whispered in utter humiliation. Quickly yanking her skirt back down, she hid her face in her lap, trying to conceal the threatening onset of a full-blown sob.

John, seeing all, immediately captured the room's attention. "Okay everyone, excitement's over," he called out, flinging his arms in the air and drawing all eyes to him. Although exhilarated from seeing Kaitlyn sprawled out in her bloomers, he came across as if he had felt guilty for being insensitive to Kaitlyn earlier. John, being his normal overbearing self, demanded everyone continue with what they had been doing. "Show's over everyone," he finished.

The kids had all but forgotten what they were *doing* and looked at each other with red faces, giggling as silently as they could. The girls were saying things like: "Kaitlyn, of all people, poor girl." They were also secretly relieved it wasn't them.

"Everyone saw her underwear," they whispered. "Oh my goodness. How embarrassing for her," they said, under the sound of hidden giggles.

The boys huddled together were saying: "Hey, did you get a load of that? Whoa baby!"

No one noticed the new kid rising to his feet the moment Kaitlyn hit the floor. Hearing the footsteps approach, she peered up as the boy offered his hand. Drawing Kaitlyn to her feet, he craned to peer into her eyes.

"Are you okay?" he asked.

Kaitlyn looked wordlessly into the piercing cobalt eyes. Holding his hand a little longer than necessary, Kaitlyn felt warmth there, unlike the clammy fervor of her own.

8

The stranger helped Kaitlyn to her feet and let Kaitlyn hide her embarrassment in his chest. He gained the interest of the others, as John secretly burned with jealousy.

The boy helped Kaitlyn to where she and Allison had been sitting. "Is this your table?" he asked in a waiter's tone.

"Yes," Kaitlyn answered sheepishly. "Thank you. What's your name?"

"My name's Ray. Ray Niles to be exact."

Never missing a beat, John stepped up, speaking expansively. "Thanks for helping out, Ray. I'll take it from here," he exclaimed as if Ray had somehow crossed an unseen line on the floor.

"Ray," Kaitlyn interrupted. "Please sit down and join us."

Ray Niles had just moved north from Savannah, Georgia with his parents Jaycee and Nicholas. He had only been in town a few days when he entered The Soda Fountain, and no one had known who he was. Winter's Crest, although friendly, was a trifle hard on newcomers. Everyone had history with one another, and the people were not particularly welcoming to strangers.

The four sat quietly not knowing what to say, till Allison broke the silence. "Hi, Ray," she said, extending her hand. "I'm Allison, and this is Kaitlyn."

"Nice to meet you," Ray said with glowing eyes. "Nice to meet you, too, Kaitlyn."

Kaitlyn could only mutter: "Hi." She smiled, gazing at him.

"Thanks for taking care of our little Kaitlyn," John said with a certain misplaced propriety.

"No problem," Ray quipped, and waived his hand dismissively. "Are you okay, Kaitlyn?"

"Yes, Ray. Thank you."

Ray stood from the table. "Well, I must be on my way," he said breezily, keeping one eye on John. He nodded at the seat across from Kaitlyn. "It was nice to meet you, Allison." Allison's face lit at the attention. "See ya 'round, John," he added thinly as his attention returned to Kaitlyn. "It sure was nice to meet you,

Kaitlyn," he offered with a lowered voice for her alone. Ray gave Kaitlyn a private smile before excusing himself.

"Thanks again," Kaitlyn whispered as Ray stepped towards the door.

John walked Kaitlyn home, being that he lived in the neighborhood up the road from her, while Allison went and joined other friends. John was feeling oddly intruded upon and envious that Ray had received Kaitlyn's attention. He had come across as though he'd been looking out for Kaitlyn, but there always seemed to be something amiss when it came to his actual intentions.

John and Kaitlyn arrived at Kaitlyn's parents' large two-story colonial. Located in an upscale neighborhood called Oak Grove, their house sat on a one-acre lot, surrounded by maple trees that offered shade in the summer and sugary sap in January. Her house was trimmed in antique blue against a tan face, with a wrap-around farmer's porch. John helped Kaitlyn to the porch swing while waiting for her mother to come to the door.

Kaitlyn's mother Kathryn was beautiful, and she had such charm, grace and intelligence that Kaitlyn had only hoped she could be like her one day. Kathryn's beauty was not only outward in appearance, her inner beauty shined through as well. She came to the door with a bright smile, enhancing her deep brown eyes and hair, only to have her smile turn to worry when she saw Kaitlyn resting on the swing.

"What happened?"

John took it upon himself to explain.

Listening, Kaitlyn was perturbed at his over-bearing manner, but let him go on with his attempt at being a gentleman. Kathryn offered both some homemade lemonade, (she made the best in town), and John accepted, knowing it gave him an excuse to stay longer.

As Kathryn brought out the drinks, Alex came rushing up the steps. "What happened to you? Somebody beat you up?" he asked laughing. Alex didn't wait for an answer. "Hey John, how ya doing?"

"Fine, Alex. Did you hear about Korea?"

"No, what's Korea?" Alex asked as Kathryn brought out more lemonade and a plate of cookies. Alex grabbed a fistful and forgot he'd asked a question.

"Never-mind," John replied, shaking his head. "I'm sure your dad will fill you in later."

Alex was sixteen years old and would be entering eleventh grade that year. He was taller than Kaitlyn by four inches, reaching the scale at five foot, ten. His hair was dark like his mother's, and he had her eyes, too. Beginning to develop defined muscles, his face was becoming mature, giving him a stern look. This captivated the younger girls in town as well as some of the older ones. Alex would sway back and forth from being a bratty kid to a nice young man, depending on his mood of the day.

Kaitlyn had always been a mothering sister and had been even more so when their father was away at war. But Kaitlyn had begun to realize he no longer needed the looking after he once might have.

Grabbing another cookie and shoving it in his mouth, Alex disappeared into the house.

John's attention turned to Kaitlyn, and he asked if they still had the tree swing in the back yard. "Remember when we were kids, and I'd push you for hours on it?"

Kaitlyn remembered fondly. "Those were some fun times."

Putting his arm around her in an attempt for any attention he could get, John didn't miss Kaitlyn's questioning, sidelong glance toward him as the two made their way around the back of the house.

On their way to the swing, they came upon the decorative wishing well Kaitlyn's parents had put out on the side lawn. John reached in his pocket for a penny.

"Make a wish."

Kaitlyn took it, and with an indulgent shake of the head, closed her eyes and made a wish, throwing the coin into the well.

"What'd you wish for?" he asked with more than a little hope.

"Not telling," she replied impishly. "It won't come true."

John nodded sagely as if he understood.

On reaching the tree-swing, John took Kaitlyn in his arms. "Come on, Kaitlyn. Tell me. What'd you wish for?"

Kaitlyn looked at John with aversion. "I thought we were coming out to swing, *John*?"

"Yes," he said, quickly releasing her. "You're right. Hop on up there, and I'll push you like I did when we were kids."

Kaitlyn held onto both the ropes and hoisted herself onto the swing. John gave her a push, and Kaitlyn yelled, "Higher ... I want to fly," and let out a playful laugh.

When John and Kaitlyn were younger, Kaitlyn would always say that to him when he pushed her.

"Up to the clouds and back again!" John called, slipping into the old role.

They tittered in the delight of re-enactment.

When Kaitlyn came back from her *trip to the sky*, John stopped her short in mid-air, wrapping his arms around her waist. He quickly kissed her on the cheek, as he had done so long ago, but this time, Kaitlyn wasn't laughing.

She enjoyed the feeling of being held and kissed, but the feelings Kaitlyn had were not toward the person who was with her at that moment.

She wriggled free from John's grasp and scurried back towards the porch.

John didn't understand her reaction. "I was just playing, Kaitlyn."

"I know, John," she said, bothered. "We're not kids anymore, though. I think you'd better go."

John stood there with his mouth open as though about to say something. Then a shameful red colored his face. He hung his head, turned and walked toward the street.

Kaitlyn stomped into the house looking for her mother, finding Kathryn in the kitchen peeling potatoes. "You'll never believe what John just did!"

"Oh John," Kathryn purred. "What a nice young man. He looked after you and made sure you were okay. Your father will be very pleased."

"He just tried to kiss me!" Kaitlyn cried in outrage.

"Mind your tone, young lady!" Kathryn advised sharply. "I'm sure he was just trying to be friendly. After all, you two have been friends for so long. He's such a nice boy, and you shouldn't be showing spite after what he's done."

A disgusted Kaitlyn swept up to her room. "John, a gentleman! That'll be the day," slamming the open closet door.

Making herself comfortable on the four-poster bed while calming her anger, Kaitlyn smelled the rose scent of the quilt from grandma's house. The breezes of summer whispered through the floral curtains, embracing her. Turning her head towards the nightstand, Kaitlyn's eyes fell upon her diary. Snatching up the bound book, she let out a long, tired sigh. Opening it, she found the next clean page of the copiously written tome and began to write.

"June 26, 1950." The only words she entered were: "I'm in love!"

Kaitlyn laid her head back to rest with the opened diary across her chest, falling into a late afternoon slumber.

Chapter Two

*   *   *

Kaitlyn had awaken to the echo of her mother's call to dinner. Realizing it was not part of some dream, she rose with a stretch, only to fall back onto the pillow. After closing her eyes for a moment, Kaitlyn opened them in half-remembered irritation. A leftover dissonance of John's stolen kiss erupted in her memory, and trying to forget, Kaitlyn turned her thoughts to Ray.

"Now *there's* a gentleman," she thought, recalling those cobalt eyes.

Dragging herself off the bed and walking towards the antique vanity, Kaitlyn reached for the hairbrush, catching a glimpse of a womanly appearance in the mirror. She studied her body with a new eye while softly sliding her fingers over her curves. Releasing a sensuous smile, Kaitlyn's mind wandered into wishful daydreams of Ray, only to be interrupted by the repeated calls from her mother. With a startled turn toward the door, Kaitlyn hurried out and down the stairs.

Kaitlyn was almost embarrassed by the old photographs displayed proudly in the stairwell leading down, but did enjoy reminiscing about her and Alex's more youthful days. Pausing at a picture of Alex as a young boy, she drew her fingers along the portrait with a mothering touch. Recollections of caring for him during their father's absence came forward reminding Kaitlyn about the talk with Dad she'd planned.

She scampered down the rest of the wooden steps, with each step seeming to call out: "I'm coming, Mom."

Kaitlyn went about the mahogany table, setting ivory china plates, matching cloth napkins and gold-rimmed glassware. She retrieved the silverware from the velvet-lined buffet and placed each of the six items before filling the water goblets. She eyed the table to be sure all was proper, then headed toward the living room where her father relaxed from his work day.

Still wearing a business suit, James Frost sat with his ankles crossed and tie loosened, scanning the evening paper.

Kaitlyn recalled the times when she could run to her daddy and jump on his lap, exchange butterfly kisses and laughter. She absorbed the scent of his pipe, wishing she could once again feel the innocent security of those arms, knowing she was too big for that now.

He gazed over the glasses resting on his nose, aware of Kaitlyn's presence. "Hi, honey."

"Dad, may I talk with you for a minute?"

Mr. Frost folded the paper on his lap and motioned for Kaitlyn to join him. "I understand John was a regular gentleman today," he commented. "He helped you home after some *tragedy* at The Fountain?"

Kaitlyn affirmed.

With obvious approval for John, Mr. Frost told Kaitlyn of his intent to show gratitude and expected her to go along.

Kaitlyn, still disgusted with John's ulterior behavior, tried to conceal her emotions. She nodded head at her father's expectation.

Jim Frost was, for the most part, a kind and giving man ... the kind of person who would stop to help a stranger fix a flat tire without giving his attire a second thought. Always full of laughter, he gave both of his children special attention and involved himself in most everything they did.

As was true in many families, there was a 'pre-war' dad and a 'post-war' dad. In a way, Kaitlyn felt she'd lost the father she'd known and loved from before the service. And although his experiences were unshared with his kids, there was little question that they had changed him, both visibly and internally. In some ways, it was almost as if Jim had left a part of himself overseas.

It had taken several years for a semblance of the 'old dad' to return. This recollection made Kaitlyn even more fearful of him leaving again.

Jim detected the turmoil in his daughter as she sat near him. "What is it, Kaitlyn?"

Kaitlyn had a strange sense come over her as if she were seeing the world through his eyes, witnessing the heartache and suffering he had seen. She spoke in a whisper. "Daddy, I wanted to know if you're leaving again? I mean ... you know ... this *war* thing. John came running into The Fountain today yelling something about 'Korea'. What happened? Is Korea a place somewhere?"

Jim couldn't contain a crooked smile. While he'd certainly done his share to try and ensure that his children would never share his horrible war experiences, it still concerned him that, just maybe, they should be more aware of the world and its doings. It was still a dangerous place, after all. Clearly Mr. Truman had his hands full.

"Sweetheart," he said soothingly. "You don't know where Korea is? Why don't you get the globe from the library and we'll have a look."

Kaitlyn scuttled off, returning shortly with the beautiful thirty-inch globe. Kneeling down beside Jim on the Oriental rug, he traced his finger around the Pacific Rim, making sure she had some points of reference for the 'geography lesson'. Pointing out the little appendix-like peninsula dangling from Mainland China, he carefully showed Kaitlyn North and South Korea.

The country had been politically divided at the thirty-eighth parallel, Jim explained. Previous to this, the North had come under the tutelage of Mao Tse Tung, the tenacious Chinese dictator. The people of the South had wished to align themselves with America. The saber rattling had come to a head this very week, and the North had invaded the South in an attempt to impose their communist will on our friends.

"As the United States," Jim went on, "it's our duty to protect our friends against the godless reds. It's the proper and honorable thing to do. I would be proud to serve this nation again, but I'm too old now," he said almost wistfully. "However, if this thing drags out, it is possible Alex could be drafted."

Kaitlyn's mouth dropped on hearing those words. Unlike Allison, she'd never thought this might affect Alex in any way. Underlying her thoughts about the possibility of Alex having to go to war, she was dying to ask what communism was.

Jim smiled and put his hand on Kaitlyn's shoulder, squeezing with affection. "I have a feeling that Doug MacArthur will have things well in hand long before he needs to call on another Frost."

"Thank-you, Daddy," Kaitlyn said as she leaned against her father's arm. "I feel better."

Jim briskly hugged his daughter, assuring her everything would be fine, sealing it with a peck on the forehead. He asked Kaitlyn to return the globe to the library and to finish helping her mother in the kitchen, returning his attention to the paper.

Walking towards the library, Kaitlyn glanced back.

Although she loved and respected her father, sometimes he made her cringe. The way he could turn-on and quickly shut himself off from people, (*especially* her), made him seem abrupt and aloof to many. While warm and caring when it suited him, there were times when he just seemed unapproachable.

There he was, perched in his maroon leather wing chair, surrounded by mahogany paneling, while sunlight streamed through the window, lighting the cloud of pipe smoke above his head. The elegant drapery that hung from the cathedral windows framed the sunlight around him, like some kind of red carpet to

'His Majesty'. She rolled her eyes, making sure her gesture was unseen, and returned the globe to the library.

Just as Kaitlyn entered the kitchen, Alex popped in the back door. "Hi, Mom. Hi, Kaitlyn," he greeted sarcastically, "how's John?"

Scolded absently by Kathryn, he was told to clean up for dinner. "You too," she added as an afterthought to Kaitlyn.

Jim could smell the roast beef, baked potatoes and buttered corn, and it drew him to the dining room.

"Smells delicious, Kathryn," he said on entering. "You've really outdone yourself this time."

Kathryn smiled, enjoying her husband's compliment.

They all joined in the dining room, decorated elegantly in ivory and gold. The chinaware on the table matched the room, with each glass reflecting the sprays of light prisms from the chandelier. They joined hands in prayer, beginning the dinner ritual.

Kathryn spoke of her PTA plans for the upcoming school year, while Jim asked her questions. Kaitlyn and Alex tried to look politely interested.

Before the war, Jim usually spoke very little during dinner, or at anytime for that matter. A man of few words, he usually spoke only when necessary. But after his return, he was suddenly interested in everything anyone had to say. He listened intently to Kaitlyn and Alex, as well as Kathryn, as though everything they said were of value. This was an acute turnaround from the time before the war. Taciturn and aloof, it seemed as though he had little time for anyone. The sharp contrast manifested itself in peculiar ways sometimes, with the lines between the two occasionally becoming muddy.

Alex talked about his own summer training program, intended to get him ready for football season, while Kaitlyn sat quietly observing the subtle body language between her mother and father. Now that she had herself been 'smitten', she was curiously interested in what had brought her parents together.

Kaitlyn studied them unobtrusively as she watched them simply pass dishes to each other, always using proper manners. There was nothing out of the ordinary that struck Kaitlyn as a solid reason for them being together, until she caught a glimpse from the corner of her eye.

Noticing her mother send a soft smile towards her father, she turned her gaze to him, seeing him on the tail end of giving a private smile. Her thoughts turned to Ray as if she were experiencing a similar moment shared between them, realizing now what her parents saw in each other. Kaitlyn's cheeks abruptly turned red when taken suddenly from her thoughts. She'd heard her father mention paying John a thank-you visit.

"Kaitlyn loves John," Alex sing-songed at the other end of the table, mistaking his sister's face for blushing.

"That will be enough, Alex," Jim said calmly; he bemused by false assumption.

Kaitlyn returned to picking at her food, ready to burst out of her skin, while Jim gave Kaitlyn instructions as to what she was to do after dinner, and what time she was to be ready to leave.

John lived a couple blocks over from Kaitlyn in a different neighborhood, with his house located on a wooded lot overlooking a small pond. Actually, when they were kids, Kaitlyn and John used to enjoy watching the mallards floating and waddling about, while they tossed out small pieces of corn or bread to them. They used to do a lot together, like riding bikes, swimming, skipping stones and jumping on the large rock trail behind his house.

There was an old tale that went along with those rocks. The story went that the trail used to be a secret Indian pass used during the French and Indian War. John and Kaitlyn would play on those rocks and pretend they were the warriors; John always won the *battle*, no matter what side he role-played. But that all stopped when the two reached twelve and their relationship changed. With the advent of World War Two, Kaitlyn had been called to care for Alex and help run the household while their father had been away.

When Jim and Kaitlyn arrived at the Fenderson's, John came to the door and greeted them with a hello and a firm handshake to Mr. Frost, making Jim like him more. "Nice to see you again, Kaitlyn," he said, stiffly formal.

"Nice to see you, too," Kaitlyn replied. "Thanks for the help this afternoon," she added as if by rote.

Jim mistook his daughter's reserve for bashfulness. "Thank you for taking care of her," he beamed expansively. "I like that kind of character in a man. Please feel free to call upon Kaitlyn any time."

Kaitlyn could hardly contain herself. "Great," she thought. "Just marvelous. Now he'll *never* leave me alone." She smiled, hiding her revulsion from both.

"Thank you, John, and good evening," Jim said with a polite smile.

"Thanks, John," Kaitlyn forced between clenched teeth.

"I'll see you soon," John replied back with hidden sarcasm.

The only thing Kaitlyn felt like seeing was her hand slapping him across the face.

Walking back to the house, Kaitlyn did remember liking John as a little girl. She would chase him around, and they would tease each other. He was friendly and caring; his kindness never had an ulterior motive then. She missed *that* John and the sweet little boy he used to be. Now he was just a snake in the grass who could fool anyone and everybody — everyone but her that is.

Kaitlyn needed to get away from everyone and talk things over with her best friend. She called, and Allison answered the phone in her cheery voice. Kaitlyn asked about meeting at The Soda Fountain, and Allison agreed enthusiastically.

Unfortunately, her few moments of solitude were not to be. As she stepped out on to the sidewalk, a recent familiar face almost immediately met her.

She heard: "Where you going, Kaitlyn?" from behind her and turned to see John following in the glow of a streetlight.

Kaitlyn sighed. "I'm going to the Fountain to meet Allison."

John stepped up with her as she turned to continue on. "I bet you're going to see if that new kid is there, aren't you."

"No I'm not," Kaitlyn replied smugly.

"Well, maybe I should come along to keep an eye on things anyway," John said flatly.

"Do what you want, John. It's a free country," Kaitlyn replied, irritated by the intrusion.

"That's right!" he said loudly. "It *is* a free country. Your dad saw to that, and so will I come next August."

"That's nice, John." Kaitlyn was trying to sound bored.

That stopped him short, and he stood there, watching her recede down the street.

When Kaitlyn arrived at the restaurant, all thoughts of the pesky John had fled, and she wore a smile as she walked through the doors. Although still showing a few signs of the day's earlier embarrassing event, she spotted Allison sitting at their usual table and started singing 'Some Enchanted Evening' while swooning up, pretending to dance like Gene Kelly.

Allison joined in when the line of the song reached: "When you find your true love." She rose from her chair and joined Kaitlyn's overworked caperings. They giggled and then got down to the serious business of talking about Ray.

"He's just dreamy, and his accent is enough to drive you crazy," Allison blurted out.

"I know. I know," Kaitlyn said as she drifted into a moment of thought.

"I think I'm in love, Allison," Kaitlyn said. "I've never felt like this before. I can't stop thinking about him. His face, his eyes, his smile ... I can't get them out of my head, and I don't think I want to."

So wrapped up was Kaitlyn in her own feelings about Ray, she never realized that Allison secretly had a crush on him too. That was until Allison blurted out: "Me too."

"But you saw him first, so he's yours," she told Kaitlyn, collecting herself. "Maybe he has a best friend, an identical friend, for me?" Allison wishfully asked out loud.

Kaitlyn, thankful the waitress had come to take their order, ordered their usual cherry colas and changed the subject as quickly as she could, changing it to John.

Kaitlyn filled Allison in on John's behavior at the house, while Allison tried to convey to her that John was just being John and that he probably didn't mean any harm by it.

As she finished John's defense, Allison spoke softly, "Speak of the devil," while slanting her eyes in the direction of the opening doors.

"Hello, ladies," John said, sauntering up to the table. Inviting himself to sit down, he wrapped them both in his arms with a tight squeeze. "How are we tonight? Did you miss me?" John smiled and peered into their eyes.

"Oh yes, John," Allison replied sarcastically. "We just can't live without you."

"Aren't we sassy tonight," John replied with a sneaking grin. "I like them sassy you know?"

"Remind me not be so sassy next time, Kaitlyn," Allison laughed.

An odd feeling suddenly overcame Kaitlyn, and she looked up to the doors just as the handle turned.

Her sudden trance was broken when John yelled, "What is it with you? You in love with him or something?"

"I don't know," Kaitlyn replied in a drifting tone, not taking her eyes off of Ray.

John broke Kaitlyn's view by approaching Ray and asked him to join them. Kaitlyn, snapping out of it, couldn't believe her ears. She had already figured out John was bothered by Ray being near her. As to why, she had no idea.

Ray eagerly accepted, while Kaitlyn and Allison giggled in delight. He greeted them with a smile. "Nice to see you again, ladies." His voice melted both girls in their seats.

"Nice to see you too, Ray," the girls replied in unison. "Please join us."

The girls' smiles were from ear to ear, and they were dying from embarrassment inside. Ray took Kaitlyn's hand, asking her how she was doing. All Kaitlyn could reply was an unspoken *'wow'* as her mouth dropped.

Now not knowing what to do or say, Kaitlyn started chattering with Allison about how excited she was being a senior, and about her birthday that was forthcoming. Kaitlyn was going to be eighteen on August fourteenth, and Allison's birthday was the day after Labor Day. Allison suggested having a joint party at The Soda Fountain and inviting all their friends. "If the place's big enough, that is," she said expansively.

Kaitlyn looked to Ray and asked him if he'd like to come.

Ray's eyes lit up. "Yes, I'd love to."

"What about me?" piped in John, feeling ignored for the moment.

"Of course, John," Allison said laughing. "You always come, whether you're invited or not."

"Ha ha. Very funny," John replied in faux hurt.

"We're just kidding you, John," Allison said, while Kaitlyn only agreed halfheartedly.

"You know, *my* birthday's coming up, too. In October," John said proudly. "I'm going to be eighteen."

"Well, John, turning eighteen doesn't make you a man," Kaitlyn said, examining her fingernails.

"What's that s'posed to mean?" John insisted.

"Never-mind, John," Kaitlyn sighed dramatically. "I hope you'll understand what I mean *someday.*

"Kaitlyn turned back to Ray, locking her fingers together under her chin and gazed at him with a wispy smile and half-closed eyes. "Ray," she asked, knowing the answer. "What grade are you going into?"

Ray said that he'd be a senior that fall and planned on joining the service after graduation.

John said, "Me too," excitedly. "Are you going in the Army, Navy or Air Force? I'm going in the Army myself."

"I've decided on the Army," Ray answered. "Maybe we'll be in boot-camp together."

23

"We can be the girls that wait for you after training," Kaitlyn blurted out uncharacteristically.

Allison looked on in shock; not believing those words came from Kaitlyn's mouth. She made it sound like they were trailer girls or something.

Kaitlyn laughed, saying she was kidding. John's eyebrows rose with interesting thoughts running through his head. The same could be said for Ray. They all let out a tension-relieving laugh.

Kaitlyn and Allison found themselves engaged in talk about their senior year, as Ray and John discussed the Army and the events taking place in Korea.

"They'll probably have it all mopped up by the time we get there," John was saying. "But I'd sure like to have a chance to teach them gooks a thing or two."

Ray looked at John with surprise, wondering where on earth John had heard that dark expression. For himself, he looked to the Service as an opportunity to learn about life, himself and maybe have the chance to help others. He had known that war meant killing, but he kept his feelings on that distasteful part of it to himself.

"They'll probably have it all cleared up by then. Sure," he said. "We'll wind up in Iceland or somewhere, guarding oil cans." His laughter was glibly forced.

John's wasn't. "Nah! They'll take a couple of tough G.I.'s like us and maybe just make some trouble somewhere, so's they can send us in and teach a lesson." He lowered his voice. "I've heard that they do that stuff. Special teams. All hush-hush." He put his finger to his lips and glanced over his shoulder as if old Joe Stalin were eavesdropping.

A pensive quiet descended, but not for long. Again, John chimed in with more prattle. He knew Alex would be seventeen at the end of November.

"Kaitlyn, do you think your brother realizes he could be drafted?" he asked. "He might, you know, if this war is extended."

"I don't know," Kaitlyn replied. "My dad said it was possible if this thing drags out. I assume he's speaking with Alex about it. I hope not. It was hard worrying about Daddy when he fought in the big war. To have to go through that again, I'm not sure I could handle it all over again. War changes a man, you know."

"I'm sorry, Kaitlyn," John said sincerely. "I didn't mean to upset you."

"Thanks, John," Kaitlyn spoke softly. "There's no need to apologize. I appreciate it though."

"Maybe there's hope for him yet," Kaitlyn thought during the quick silence that came over the table.

John might have gotten something in his eye, or maybe not. He dragged his hand across his face and then hopped up quickly from the table. "Hey guys," he called. "Let's check out this new dance floor!" He made a beeline towards the jukebox. "Let's get this place rolling," he said, dropping a nickel into the Wurlitzer.

Ray stood and offered his hand to Kaitlyn. "Let's go."

Kaitlyn took Ray's hand while grabbing Allison's. Allison grabbed one of the other kids there, and everyone in The Fountain soon joined in. They sang and danced with smiles and laughter until it was time for curfew.

One last song was played, and Kaitlyn and Ray were able to dance in each other's arms. Not speaking a word, they held each other while enjoying their first true embrace, with both feeling as if a flame had been ignited.

When the last note played, Kaitlyn said goodbye to Ray with a sweet smile, not wanting the evening to end. Ray took his hand in hers to say goodbye, and the grip of their hands slowly faded as they released. With the remaining two fingers touching, Ray gave her his private smile before letting go.

John walked Kaitlyn home without teasing or making her angry. He even apologized for his behavior. Kaitlyn looked at him, confused, not understanding the sudden change. She welcomed it though; it reminded her of the John she'd known when they were little.

They arrived at Kaitlyn's house, and John smiled as he waved. "By the way, you looked nice tonight," and faded into the night down the road.

John was bothered by Kaitlyn's comment earlier. He had somehow thought that when you turned eighteen, you were automatically a man. Kaitlyn had him questioning himself, and he was not so sure he liked that, or his answers.

Kaitlyn entered the house to find her father's arm wrapped around Alex in serious conversation, explaining the events taking place in Korea. Kaitlyn eavesdropped, hearing the explanation of what Alex might be called upon to do, and Jim telling Alex to pay attention to what was happening in the papers. She walked quietly into the living room and waited for them to finish before leaning into her father, hugging goodnight. She turned to her mother, sitting on the couch, and gave her a hug and kiss too. Then Kaitlyn scurried up the stairs.

The soft ambiance in Kaitlyn's room welcomed her with security and comfort. While standing in front of the mirror, Kaitlyn began unbuttoning her blouse, removing it sensuously as she stared at her reflection. Tracing the outline of her womanly curves and closing her eyes, she lightly slid her fingertips over her chest, down to her navel. Closing her eyes in a self-embraced hug, she swayed back and forth, recalling her first dance with Ray as the last song, 'All My Love' by Patti Page, played over in her mind.

Chapter Three

The sun shone bright through Kaitlyn's eastern window as warm summer breezes danced by in a whisper. Waking with a smile and releasing a yawn, Kaitlyn rose from the bed. Strolling to the window, she took note of the finches fluttering outside.

With the joy she always felt when watching her window birds, Kaitlyn raised her hands above her head and yawned, "Good Morning," to her little friends. Kaitlyn's presence didn't slow their morning routine as they continued tending their nests, taking only brief notice of her as though she were singing out of tune. She giggled, imagining what the birds thought and knowing it couldn't be anything good.

Kaitlyn smelled a trace of her favorite tea and homemade jam. Slipping on her robe as she walked out the bedroom door, Kaitlyn had no idea her mother had something special planned when joining her in the kitchen.

"Morning, Mom," Kaitlyn greeted through a final yawn.

"Good morning, Kaitlyn," Kathryn replied, motioning for her to sit. Pouring tea and fixing toast, Kathryn sat down across from Kaitlyn, handing her the toast and placing tea in front of her. "It's time for you to have this."

Kaitlyn's eyes widened like she was a young girl receiving her first present. "But, Mom, this is yours. I can't accept this," she replied, even though she had always wanted it.

Kathryn looked at Kaitlyn. "I've been waiting for the right time to give you this, and today's the day."

"Why though," Kaitlyn asked. "Why *now*?"

"Did I ever tell you the story behind this teacup?" Kathryn asked with squinted brows, ignoring the question.

"No," Kaitlyn replied trying to recall. "I don't think so."

"Well, let me warm my tea, and I'll tell you the story."

Kathryn walked towards the stove and poured hot water over a fresh tea bag. "You're going to like this story, Kaitlyn," she said, making her way back to the table.

Kaitlyn sat wide-eyed looking at her mother, anxiously waiting to hear the tale.

Fussing needlessly with her cup while trying to organize her thoughts, Kathryn began. "My grandmother used to have a cabinet filled with all sorts of china cups," she said whimsically. "Collecting them was her passion, and every cup had a story all its own. Some were given to her, and others she found herself, with each having some significance. *This* particular cup had a special place in the cabinet, separated from all the rest. It sat on a cloth doily with two yellow satin roses crisscrossed at its base, with mirrored backdrops highlighting it."

"Each time I went to visit Grandmother as a young girl, she would take me by the hand and walk me to the cabinet. 'Out of all these cups,' she'd say, pointing to this one, 'this is my favorite.'"

"She'd ask me if I knew why, and I would always tell her no, even though she had told me many times before. She'd hoist me onto her hip and cradle me in her arms, showing me the design on the cup."

Kathryn's eyes misted and she looked away at nothing, warmed with the distant memory. She smiled stiffly and turned back to Kaitlyn.

"'Do you see the small yellow roses?' Grandmother would ask. I, of course said *yes*. 'Yellow roses have always been my favorite,' she'd continue. 'They remind me of sunshine and happiness. And you, Kathryn, are _my_ yellow rose.'"

Kathryn's voice cracked slightly with the words, and she drew her hand to her chest before going on. "This cup not only represents her love for me and the special times we shared," she said, "it also represents my love for you. For _you_, Kaitlyn, are '_my_ yellow rose'."

Kaitlyn rose quickly from the table and hurried around to her mother, where they embraced in a loving hug. Silent tears were the order of the moment.

"I love it, Mom," Kaitlyn whispered as she wiped a tear from her cheek. "I'll treasure it always."

Kathryn broke the moment with a smile and a giggle. "I feel like I've been a child holding a secret, just ready to burst for the last eighteen years." She hunched her shoulders and grinned sidelong at Kaitlyn. The two laughed together like schoolgirls before Kaitlyn calmed and looked into her mother's eyes. "What do you mean?" she asked pointedly.

Kathryn smiled and let out a long breath. "There's a whole history behind this cup," she said slowly. "It dates back to ... several great Grandmothers ago." She flagged her hand at the possibility of having to recite so many '_Greats_'. "I've never told you the story because it's traditional to tell it _only_ when the cup is handed down."

Kaitlyn paused in thought. "That would mean this cup dates back to ... the 1840's." She looked down at the cup in new wonder, now cradling it protectively with both hands.

"Yes," Kathryn replied decisively. "You'll need to pay close attention to this, as some day you will have to tell your own child."

Mother and daughter warmed their tea, deciding to take the conversation into the library. Both took a seat in high backed brown leather chairs against paneled walls, with their legs curled beneath them. Kathryn kept the tradition alive by unfolding a long tale of love and adventure before her rapt daughter.

Kaitlyn was amazed by the history of the teacup and realized the significance of what she was holding in her hands, carefully etching every detail into her memory.

At the end, Kaitlyn looked at her mother curiously. "Why now though? What's so significant that it's time for me to have this?"

Kathryn looked at her with furrowed brows. "You don't know? Haven't you been listening to the stories? The stories are all about first and true love, dear."

Kaitlyn shook her head in furtive misunderstanding.

"Kaitlyn," Kathryn said with gentle reproach, taking her daughter's hand. "*You've* fallen in love for the first time. This feeling will be remembered in your heart forever. This is why I chose to give it to you on this day."

Kaitlyn's eyes locked with her mother's; a mix of horror and curiosity blended on her face. "How'd you know?" she whispered, eyes now sagged to the carpet.

"Kaitlyn, I was a young woman before becoming a parent. I know what love looks like. Honey, it's written all over your face."

Kaitlyn blushed and looked away. "I guess I don't hide it well, huh?"

"Nope. Not well at all." Kathryn swallowed a sip of tea and let out a smile. "So, are you going to tell me who this young man is?"

"Yes," Kaitlyn replied with the color remaining in her cheek. "His name is Ray Niles. I met him at The Fountain when he came to my rescue after I fell. He and his family moved here from Savannah, Georgia a few weeks back."

"I thought John helped you?" Kathryn interrupted.

"No," Kaitlyn corrected. "John just made it out as if he had."

"Interesting," Kathryn said, saying no more.

"Ray was such a gentleman. And, Mom, his eyes, you should *see* his eyes," Kaitlyn gushed. "I saw him at The Fountain last night and ... " Kaitlyn paused, "we danced," she snuck in with a grin.

"Oh, *really?*" Kathryn replied with a smirk. "Well, he sounds like a nice young man, Kaitlyn. I'll have to make up a welcome basket for his family. Maybe you'd like to help?" she asked, standing.

"Sure! I'd love to," replied Kaitlyn, jumping to her feet.

"So, he's cute, huh?" Kathryn asked as if her daughter were a teenage friend.

"Oh, yes," Kaitlyn replied giggling. "He's *definitely* cute."

As Kaitlyn and her mother began working on the basket, the phone rang. Kaitlyn answered it to find Allison on the other end. And after listening to the convoluted and elaborate teen sub-text, Kathryn determined that the two were making plans for the beach; she thought at around eleven. With further decryption, she decided that "wheels" meant that Kaitlyn would be borrowing the car.

Hanging up and continuing to help with the basket, Kaitlyn filled her mother in on the day's plans. "What are you doing today, Mom?" she added as an afterthought.

"I have to go to the ladies auxiliary to take care of a few things, then head over to the school to arrange schedules for PTA meetings for the upcoming school year. In between the two, I'm going to meet your father for lunch at The Chamberlain."

"Wow, this is going to be a busy day for you. Are you sure you don't need the car?"

Kathryn snickered to herself, realizing that her daughter and friends might be a tad too self-absorbed. She didn't recall having been asked for the car; Kaitlyn obviously assuming that her mother had overheard. She let it go.

"No, everything's in walking distance," she answered. "Besides, it's a beautiful day. And you know me, I love to walk."

"The Chamberlain, huh?" Kaitlyn asked with a grin.

Kathryn raised her eyebrows with a smile in her eyes. "Uh hmmm."

The Chamberlain was the preferred restaurant in town, where a social pecking order was strictly maintained. The Frosts kept perennial, standing reservations.

Kaitlyn stopped what she was doing. "Mom," she began timidly, "may I ask you something?"

Kathryn nodded.

"Are you still in love with Dad after *all* these years?" Kaitlyn asked out of the blue.

"Yes," Kathryn replied simply, fussing with the bow on the basket. "He still gives me butterflies." She raised her eyes to look at Kaitlyn. "What brought that up?"

"Oh, I don't know," Kaitlyn whimsically replied. "I hope I'll be as happily married as you two are when I'm that old."

Kathryn stifled a shocked snicker at her daughter's blithe remark. She hadn't thought of her thirty-nine years as 'old' before. "You will be," Kathryn replied. "Just don't rush anything. Take your time and get to know everything about the man you fall in love with."

Mrs. Frost looked at Kaitlyn with raised eyebrows, knowing what Kaitlyn was thinking. She remembered thinking similar things about Jim when she was her age. "My little girl's growing up," she thought. "I'd better keep an eye open," recalling her dates with Jim. "If she's anything like I was, I'm in big trouble."

Kaitlyn and her mother put the finishing touches on the Niles' welcome basket. Kaitlyn then helped clean up and put her special teacup in a safe place. "I've enjoyed this morning, Mom," she said.

"Me too, Kaitlyn," Kathryn replied. "Guess it's time to get going," she said, suddenly aware of how much time had gone by.

The two of them scampered around, getting ready for their separate, but equally important day ahead. Kathryn was faster than Kaitlyn by a few minutes and started for the door, gathering her purse and fixing her hat in the front hall mirror.

"I love you, Kaitlyn," she called up the stairs. "Have a fun day. And don't forget we have to deliver the basket tonight."

"Okay. Love you, too," Kaitlyn called back, bobbing down the stairs just as Kathryn closed the front door.

As if on cue, Kaitlyn heard the slam of the kitchen screen door, and seconds later, her brother came racing through the parlor towards her. A deft backward step prevented a collision.

"Where've you been, Alex?" Kaitlyn asked, not bothering to say hello.

"What are you," he asked sarcastically. "My keeper?"

"No," Kaitlyn replied, "just wondering where you've been this morning."

"Oh," Alex said, leaving it at that.

"Well, got to run," Kaitlyn said. "See you later."

"Bye," Alex said as he went racing up the stairs past her, wishing his sister would mind her own business.

Kaitlyn finished packing the picnic lunch, adding a little extra than she normally would. And making sure she had everything, headed out the door.

The beach, located at Valley State Park, fifteen minutes from her home, was one of the most popular teenage hang outs in the summer, and Kaitlyn had made sure she was ready to see anyone who was *anybody* there.

Packing her things into the family station wagon, she started on her journey and picked up Allison before heading out to route seventy-four.

Route seventy-four was the only highway that led to the beach and was famous for its Burma-Shave road signs. All travelers, young and old, got a kick out of them. Burma Shave split up roadway advertisements and used them as a ploy to help increase sales - successfully too. They were fun to read and made driving more interesting. As Kaitlyn and Allison drove along chattering about anything and everybody, they took notice of one set of signs.

Kaitlyn and Allison read in unison: "She Will" on the first red and white sign. Then, a hundred yards down the road, the sales pitch continued with: "Flood Your Face". Further on: "With Kisses 'Cause You Smell". Kaitlyn and Allison broke out in squeals of laughter till they came upon the punch line: "So Darn Delicious."

"They must be talking about Ray," Kaitlyn proclaimed. "'Cause he's 'delicious' all right. Hmmm, I wonder if he uses Burma-Shave," she thought out loud.

Allison looked at Kaitlyn with her eyebrows raised. "Maybe," she replied through a devilish grin.

The girls and all the other route seventy-four drivers always knew what the last sign would say, and as they approached it, together shouted, "Burma-Shave Lotion!"

Before they knew it, they had arrived at the beach. Parking and unloading their beach bags, the girls set themselves up on a nice sandy spot near the water, but not too close.

Kaitlyn donned a strapless pink bathing suit that accentuated her already bronzed skin, bringing many eyes upon her as she settled in. The bow placed strategically at the bust-line enhanced her already well-endowed appearance, with the pleated skirt showcasing her long legs.

Allison, being an attractive girl too, sported her new navy strapless suit with white lines running at angles, complimenting her shapely curves. The two of them turned some heads, catching the special attention of two onlookers: John and Ray.

John came over and planted himself right next to the girls, acting as if he were supposed to be there. "Look who I brought with me, Kaitlyn," John announced while jerking a thumb at Ray, then focused his eyes on what sat beside him, scanning the girls head to toe.

Ray approached the girls. "Hello," he greeted politely, waiting for an invitation before joining the group.

Kaitlyn had to turn her head away; Ray's hard body transfixed her. The sparkling reflection from the water intensified Ray's eyes, making Kaitlyn melt.

Ray also caught Allison's attention, but Allison for some unknown reason seemed to be drawn towards John. For the first time, Allison took notice of him, thinking, "He doesn't look too shabby himself. Hmmm, he actually looks 'delicious'. That's the word Kaitlyn used, right? Yes, John looks delicious." Allison thought quietly to herself as she examined him from head to toe with her eyes. "What am I thinking? This is John. Stop it! Stop it!" she reprimanded herself, with cringing shivers. But she continued with her thoughts, comparing John to Ray in their bathing suits. Their touch tempting muscles brought thoughts popping into

Allison's head, while at the same time, thoughts of her being crazy wrestled inside her mind.

John took notice of Allison that day too, observing the blonde hair framing her soft face while the summer winds playfully danced with it. Inching his way closer, John brought out all the charm he could muster, while Ray and Kaitlyn lost themselves in unspoken conversation.

Kaitlyn broke the silence. "How do you like it here, Ray?" she asked shyly.

"I like it. Everyone seems nice, and it's beautiful here. I know I'll be happy here though, because ... you're here."

Kaitlyn smiled and lowered her head in delight. "I'm happy you're here too, Ray. I want to know everything about you. Tell me about yourself and your family."

Ray went on to tell her that he planned on joining the Army after school, with Kaitlyn nodding in remembrance. "After I serve, I'd like to attend The University of Southern California and major in engineering. They got this new "GI Bill," and the government pays for everything. On graduation, I want to find a job in my field while I start my own business. I want to travel the world and have a family someday, too."

Ray had a lot of hopes and dreams, and from what Kaitlyn could tell, Ray seemed to be the kind of person who would realize them. He continued with another dream he has had since he was a young lad; he wanted to sail around the world. Ray had such passion when he spoke and seemed to have everything planned out, that he left Kaitlyn awestruck.

Ray interrupted her wandering thoughts. "What about you?"

"Me?"

"Yes, what do *you* want to do?"

Kaitlyn was anxious sitting there trying to answer his question, realizing she had no idea what she was going to do after graduating high school. A few ideas floated around in her head, like becoming a teacher or working at her father's bank, but she didn't have any direct plans. Feeling completely inadequate, she opened her mouth with an "I have no idea."

Ray smiled and let out a laugh; Kaitlyn was unappreciative.

"Here you are telling me all your dreams and goals," Kaitlyn pouted, "while I sit here without knowing what I'm going to do, and you ... you laugh at me!"

"Kaitlyn, I'm sorry," Ray spoke softly. "I wasn't laughing *at* you. I laughed because the look on your face was so cute when you said that. I didn't mean to hurt your feelings."

Ray sat across from Kaitlyn looking at her face. He raised his hand, extended his finger and bent it with a 'come here' gesture.

Kaitlyn slithered over towards Ray with a hurtful look in her eyes muttering, "What?" as she gave a girlish frown.

Extending his arms, he took her in a hug — a look of apology in his eyes.

Time stood still for Kaitlyn as she lay her head into Ray's neck. And closing her eyes, she felt at that moment she had truly fallen in love — without a doubt in her mind. When the reality of their first loving embrace hit home, Kaitlyn released her arms slowly and backed away from Ray, with her head bowed in shyness. Ray put his palm under her chin and raised her head until their eyes met. "I'd like to kiss you?"

Overwhelmed with emotion, Kaitlyn's body trembled as he brought his lips to hers. And as she felt the warmth of his lips press against her, unfamiliar sensations ran wild, continuing to leave the feel behind when their lips lost touch. Wanting more, Kaitlyn leaned into him, and with her eyes wide open, she asked him to kiss her again. Ray placed both hands gently on her cheeks and brought their lips to a touch, leaving a shimmer of warming chills.

Kaitlyn and Ray cradled each other as they sat together viewing the waves break on the water's edge. Completely self-absorbed, they hadn't noticed that John and Allison had gone to the shore, playing in the lake like little kids; Kaitlyn never thought that seeing those two together would bother her, but it did. Dismissing the thought, she brought her lips to Ray's, and kissing with smiles in their eyes, the two fell back into one another's arms.

After a few silent moments, Kaitlyn looked up to Ray. "You didn't tell me about your parents. Do you have any brothers or sisters?"

"No, but I used to have a Yellow Labrador named Sandy," he replied with a big smile.

"Ahh," Kaitlyn sighed happily.

"I love animals," Ray went on. "Especially dogs. Sandy had been with me since I was five years old. She got old and couldn't move around like she used to, so we had to ... you know ... She was like a sister to me."

Kaitlyn smiled affectionately, but with sympathy.

"My mother's name is Jaycee," Ray continued, shaking off the sad moment. "She's a beautiful, kind, gentle and caring woman. She has auburn hair, green eyes and a great smile. Many of the women back home were envious of my mom's outlook on life as well as her striking facial features. She's got perfect cheek bones."

Kaitlyn chimed in. "She sounds wonderful, and beautiful too."

"She is. She's a great mom, and my dad seems to like her okay," he replied with a laugh. "My dad, his name is Nicholas, but everybody calls him Nick. People say I take after him, so I guess he looks a little like me."

"What do they do?" Kaitlyn asked.

"My mom works at The Diner, and my dad works for the city," Ray answered. "We live over in the Pine Crest neighborhood, number 227. You know where that is?"

"Yes I do," Kaitlyn replied. "I have a few friends that live over that way. Why'd you move here?" she asked, wanting to know more.

"Well," Ray replied, "my mom and dad wanted a change of scenery, no particular reason, just thought it would be nice to live where you get a change of season.

Kaitlyn nodded, knowing exactly what he was talking about. Winter's Crest was known for its color in fall, drawing many photographers, hoping to catch the perfect shot.

"My mom," Ray continued, breaking Kaitlyn's drifting thoughts, "used to live near here. She missed the autumn colors and the feeling she got with the first snow of winter. So, here we are."

"I know that feeling; I like it too. I'm glad you came, Ray; I'm absolutely thrilled", Kaitlyn said, turning her head to steal another kiss.

"I am, too."

Kaitlyn sat against Ray on the beach taking in the view of the mountains' horizon. Seagulls flew through the air, not caring where they landed or how closely they flew to the beach goers, while children laughed, played and built sandcastles. Couples walked hand in hand as a few clouds drifted in the sky, bringing occasional relief from the radiant sun. Kaitlyn closed her eyes and absorbed every moment she and Ray were together, both feeling all warm and bubbly inside.

Suddenly, John and Allison came running over and dumped a pail full of ice-cold water on them, daring Ray and Kaitlyn to join the fun.

"What'd you do that for?" Kaitlyn bellowed while rising to her feet. "I'm gonna get you."

"It's war!" Ray yelled.

Kaitlyn and Ray began chasing Allison and John, tripping in the beach sand that seemed to swallow their feet. Catching up, they challenged the two to a chicken fight. John took up the challenge on behalf of Allison, while Ray was already headed for the water with Kaitlyn in tow.

Kaitlyn laughed as she climbed on Rays' shoulders, while John hoisted Allison onto his, ready for anything. The two girls grappled to get each other to fall, with Kaitlyn in the lead most of the time. But the battle shifted in Allison's favor, and Kaitlyn almost took a tumble. Slyly, she called to her friend: "Hey! Look at that hunk over there!" A distracted Allison turned her head, and Kaitlyn toppled her into the water, declaring her and Ray's victory.

John, being none-too-pleased with losing, grabbed Ray's legs from under the water and brought the two winners tumbling down. Spluttering to the surface, all four laughed in fun.

Wading back to the beach, all smiles and affectionate, laughing hugs, John got Ray's attention over the girls' heads. With high eyebrows and a cock of the head to the water, his meaning was clear. Ray nodded solemnly. With a silent 'one, two, three', the two of them picked the girls up and pitched them, squealing, back into the water. The laughter from those close at hand echoed through the air, with the girls taking it all in good humor, accepting they were 'that day's entertainment'.

The four strolled back to the beach blanket, dried off and began to eat their lunch. Kaitlyn leaned over to Allison. "This is going to be a great summer," she whispered.

"Oh yeah! It's going to be a *great* summer!" Allison confirmed.

They spent the remainder of the afternoon tanning, holding hands, and playing in the water. They didn't want the day to end, but eventually the time came to pack up and leave.

Ray and John helped the girls get their stuff into the car, and with Kaitlyn against the driver's door, and Allison on the other side, the boys took them in their arms for a goodbye kiss. Kaitlyn and Rays' was long and sensual, giving them both chills, while Allison and John laughed through their first kiss in disbelief.

"Ray," Kaitlyn asked for his attention. "My mother wants to stop over to your house after dinner tonight. She has one of those corny 'welcome baskets' for your family." She rolled her eyes at the old-fashioned idea.

"That'd be great!" Ray excitedly replied with a laugh, but with the excitement of seeing Kaitlyn again so soon; the notion of any old idea was good enough for him. "I can't wait to see you then."

With all four smiling ear to ear, the girls waved goodbye and drove towards home.

John and Ray got their beach supplies together while talking about their girls and how much fun the summer was going to be. Once packed, and ready to go, they left for home too.

A minute of quiet went by before John filled it. "Ray," he began, "I'm sorry I was such a jerk to you. You know ... in the beginning. I've always been a little protective of Kaitlyn."

"That's okay, John. No problem," Ray accepted, with a chuckle. "It sure is easy to figure out why."

"Hey, you wanna swing by The Fountain tomorrow night?" John asked.

"Yeah, that'd be great. I'll meet you there at seven. We'll invite the girls?"

"Oh yeah, we're inviting the girls all right," John replied, with a big smile.

Meanwhile, Kaitlyn and Allison were high-spirited from their day at the beach, and didn't even bother with the Burma-Shave signs. They were too busy talking about how dreamy their new beaus were and were flying high with the excitement of summertime romance.

"Allison," Kaitlyn confided. "I'm in love."

"I know, Kaitlyn. I can see it all over your face." She let out a giggle.

"What's all this with *you* and John?" Kaitlyn asked.

"I have *no* idea," Allison joked. "Who'd of thought it: me and *John*? I like it though. He's a great kisser." She laughed as if she had some plan in her head.

"I know what you mean. Ray too."

Both squealed in unison: "Delicious!"

Kaitlyn dropped Allison off at her house and went home, and as Kaitlyn entered, her mother asked if she had had fun.

"I had a great time. Ray and John showed up. We had a blast."

"Great, honey. Go wash up and give me a hand, okay?"

"Okay, Mom. Be right there."

Kaitlyn joined Kathryn in the kitchen and helped fix dinner. As Kaitlyn sliced lettuce for the salad, she hummed sweetly to herself. Kathryn looked up.

"I guess you *did* have a good time," she said with a secret smile.

"Oh yes. Good time," Kaitlyn droned from far away.

Kathryn peered in Kaitlyn's eyes. "Kaitlyn," she reminded slyly. "Don't forget, we're paying the Niles' a visit after dinner."

"That's right, Mom. I haven't forgotten," Kaitlyn said, with a tone that wondered if there was anything *else* going on in the world tonight. Kathryn gazed back, seeing her daughter with new eyes. She smiled again to herself.

The family sat down to their Saturday dinner of hamburgers, french-fries and salad, with the topic of conversation being the news from Korea and what was happening there.

After dinner, all four helped clear the table and straighten out the kitchen. Alex dried the dishes as Jim put them away, while the ladies, listening to Alex, wrapped up the leftovers. Kaitlyn seemed slightly distracted.

" ... oh, c'mon, Dad." Alex was saying. "Richey's dad went out and got one. Why can't we have one too? I mean ... it ain't like we can't afford it."

"A Frost doesn't use the word 'ain't', young man," Kathryn piped in sharply.

"Alex," Jim said, closing the cabinet door and looking indulgently at his son. "It has nothing to do with *cost*. It has to do with having ... this 'device' in our home. What's wrong with the regular radio?"

"Dad," Alex whined. "Radio is for squares! Television is ... scientific!"

Jim and Kathryn laughed out loud. "Well then," Jim chuckled, "we should leave it to the scientists. I'm sure Mr. Einstein and Mr. Teller *love* theirs. Besides, if everyone has one of these contraptions in his home, no one would get any work done. The next thing you know, the Chinese will walk right in and knock on the door!"

"Land sakes," Kathryn added. "The way you talk, Alex, we'd eventually be having dinner in front of the thing, on trays or something. Listen to your father. This is just a passing fad."

"Next thing you know," Jim said, shaking his head with a smile, "you'll be talking about rockets to the moon or something."

Alex fell to silence, but he wasn't too happy about it. He'd never thought of Mom and Dad as 'L-7' before, but it was obvious that they were living in horse-and-buggy times.

Kaitlyn and her mother finished cleaning up and went to visit Ray and his family, but not before Kaitlyn fixed herself up a bit.

Ray lived on the other side of town in a nice, well-kept development. Like many communities after the war, Winter's Crest hosted its share of real estate developing as low and middle-income families had started spreading out across the land. The Pine Crest neighborhood wasn't exactly low-income, and it certainly wasn't laid out like Levittown on Long Island, with that decidedly utilitarian feel. But it was still very new, and most of the landscaping in it reflected that 'just built' feeling.

Kaitlyn and her mother drove slowly down the street looking for 227, finding the number posted on a white cape-cod style house with red shutters and flower boxes. A patch of garden decorated the lamppost's base, and neatly trimmed youthful shrubbery graced the front of the house. They pulled in behind the Niles' gray '49 Desoto and got out. With the welcome basket in hand, they sauntered up the walkway to the red front door and rang the bell.

Kaitlyn and Kathryn were drawn to a beautiful auburn-haired woman when the doorbell was answered. With kind eyes and a friendly smile, Kathryn introduced herself as well as Kaitlyn.

"Nice to meet you," Mrs. Niles said as she pulled her hand from a dishtowel and stuck it towards them in greeting. "I'm Jaycee. Ray told me you might stop by tonight."

Kathryn glanced at Kaitlyn with a slant. "Oh, *really?*" she whispered suspiciously.

"Come on out to the back porch for some tea and cookies," Jaycee invited them as they followed her through the tidy little house, through the spotless kitchen and out again into the back yard.

Kathryn, Jaycee and Kaitlyn settled onto colorful aluminum-and-web lawn chairs, only to have a handsome young man join them shortly.

"Hello, Kaitlyn," he said, extending his hand to greet her. "This must be your mother. Nice to meet you. I'm Ray."

"Nice to meet you too, Ray," Kathryn said in delight, taking notice of his eyes.

"Oh here, Jaycee. I almost forgot," Kathryn said, looking past Ray. She handed Jaycee the basket. "Kaitlyn and I made this for you and your family."

"Thank you both so much," Jaycee said. "That's very kind of you. Folks 'round here are so friendly. It's lovely."

"Where's your dad, Ray?" Kaitlyn asked.

"He had to work late today," he replied. "Problems at the Highway Department or something."

"Oh okay," Kaitlyn replied. "I'll meet him next time."

The women exchanged pleasantries as Ray and Kaitlyn made googly eyes, trying to hide their affection from the mothers. Of course, Kathryn and Jaycee picked up on it, exchanging smiles with each other.

After forty minutes or so, they wrapped up their visit with smiles and handshakes. Kathryn and Jaycee made plans to get together soon for tea, before Kathryn and Kaitlyn said their goodbyes and left for home.

"He's a fine young man, Kaitlyn," Kathryn commented on the way. "Nice looking too. I see what you mean about those eyes." She paused. "What about John though?"

"John?" Kaitlyn squirmed. "I don't like *John*. However, John and Allison like each other."

"John and *Allison*?" Kathryn exclaimed with a wag of her head. "Really? Who'd of thought? Kids today." Then she thought again of herself and Jim, and looked at Kaitlyn from the corner of her eye.

"Well, honey," she said. "Ray seems like a nice young man. Just keep it light, okay?" she added, with a pat to Kaitlyn's knee.

Kaitlyn nodded with understanding and an unseen roll of the eyes. "Okay, Mom. I will," knowing that would be hard to do.

Chapter Four

*   *   *

Kaitlyn opened her wearied eyes to the afternoon sun sprinkling through the trees. "Oh my, what happened to the morning?" she thought, realizing she had actually dozed off in the rocker. Kaitlyn's rumbling stomach brought attention to the now-cold tea, and she leaned forward to rise, only to notice the small envelope tumble from her lap.

Kaitlyn's own name stared back defiantly from the porch boards, and her heart pleaded with her to open it. But the fear of uncovering some painful wound held her back, and Kaitlyn closed her eyes, releasing a defeated sigh.

Frustrated, she rose from the chair, picked up the teacup, and placed the letter inside her housecoat pocket, before heading inside to make lunch.

Each step Kaitlyn took through the hallway echoed with memories of youthful days. Her eyes caught the stairwell, decorated with rows of photographs taken over the years, which brought a distracted smile to Kaitlyn's face as she walked by.

In the kitchen, the cabinets, table, and countertops screamed to be repaired from scratches and wear left from too many years of use. She knew they should be maintained, but never got around to it. Today though, Kaitlyn was particularly bothered by their appearance.

Retrieving some leftover turkey and half a loaf of bread, and putting them on the butcher-block, Kaitlyn reached for the

44

teakettle on the stove. As she turned around to make her sandwich, she bumped the teacup, carelessly placed on the edge, and sent it spinning towards the floor, barely catching it in time.

"Damn it!" she screeched in complete irritation. "Why does *he* still do this to me?"

Frustrated and no longer hungry, she dawdled through the sandwich making, knowing she had to eat something. Kaitlyn then sat down and waited for the kettle to boil. All the while, a war raged within her mind as her feet kept pace in a march.

The kettle whistle blew, momentarily ending her inner turmoil, and brought Kaitlyn to her feet. Seeing the chipped rim of her treasured teacup again made Kaitlyn's heart ache. Having one last thread to hold onto, Kaitlyn patted the side of her housecoat's pocket, making sure the letter was safe and secure. It was.

Going back to the table with tea and sandwich in hand, she then settled in and took the letter out of her pocket, putting it behind the plate in front of her. Kaitlyn stared at the handwriting, and as if time were standing still, she drifted back again to the summer of 1950 with Ray, Allison and John. An emotion-mixed tear ran down Kaitlyn's cheek as she went to take an unwanted bite of her sandwich.

*   *   *

The morning after Kaitlyn's escapade at the beach welcomed her with bright blue skies, whispering trees, and soft breezes, allowing the smell of summer to waft through her room. Rising from the bed and straightening her cotton nightshirt, Kaitlyn stretched with a big yawn before going to the window, again saying "Hello" to her chirping friends. "I must be getting old," Kaitlyn giggled, before reaching for her diary on the nightstand. Getting cozy on the bed and with pen in hand, she made a notation:

"I've never felt like this before. I can't stop thinking about Ray. I love the way he looks at me with those eyes. I love him."

In the bottom right-hand corner of the diary she wrote: '*K & R Forever! S.W.A.K.*' Then she drew a heart around the words with an arrow piercing through it. Locking the diary and putting it away for safekeeping, she gathered her bathroom items and headed for a morning shower.

Closing the door behind her, Kaitlyn began to undress in front of the full view mirror that hung on the back of the door. Kaitlyn studied her body's image and traced her fingers over her curves, face and hair. Kaitlyn liked what she saw. Closing her eyes while passing one hand through her hair, Kaitlyn floated her fingertips over her breasts. She became aware of her own sexuality, while new sensations traveled through her body.

"What's happening to me?" her eyes seemed to ask. Kaitlyn answered with a smile to herself, holding thoughts of Ray. She touched her breasts, feeling the fullness of them, seeing her nipples become erect with pleasure. She slid her fingers down her chest towards her navel and a little ways past, feeling the tingling within as she stared at her reflection with a tilted head. Kaitlyn allowed herself to enjoy what she was feeling and what she was thinking.

Containing her thoughts, Kaitlyn turned on the water and stepped into the shower, letting the beating water caress her body. Running fingers through her hair and wiping the water from her face, thoughts of Ray's embrace swept her into a daydream. As Kaitlyn's mind wandered with each drop of water, a frenzied pounding on the door broke her trance.

"Kaitlyn," Alex called. "Hurry up! What's taking you so long?"

Kaitlyn didn't bother answering, but assured Alex she'd be right out. She hurried through the rest of her shower and exited wearing only a towel.

"There you go, *Your Majesty*," she said sarcastically, sweeping the long wet hair to one side, spraying Alex with a few drops as she strode past him, going to her room.

Just as Kaitlyn closed the bedroom door behind her, she heard the phone ring. With a miffed smirk, she barged back down the hall to answer it, calling: "I'll get it!" Being the hypocenter of the social world certainly had its drawbacks, and Kaitlyn was thinking that Allison *really* needed to start picking up the slack, just as her hand grabbed the black plastic.

"Hello?"

"Hi ... Kaitlyn?" said a voice. "This is Ray."

The instant silence in the hallway was deafening, and Kaitlyn's bath towel slipped from around her, landing unnoticed in a heap at her ankles.

"Hello?" came a tentative voice from the receiver.

Kaitlyn snapped back and mouthed 'hello' wordlessly a few times before getting it right.

"I was wondering," Ray continued nervously, "if you would like ... like to meet me at Crestview Park this morning. Maybe we could have a picnic brunch or something."

"I ... I'd love to," Kaitlyn stuttered. "What time?"

"Ten?" Ray offered.

"I'll meet you there. Should I bring anything?"

"Just your smile, Kaitlyn."

Kaitlyn happened to glance into the little hall mirror set into the phone alcove to discover that, indeed, the only thing she wore was a smile.

"I'll be there," Kaitlyn said, trying to sound calm as her hand darted to the floor, scrambling to snatch at the towel. Getting it partially wrapped back around her while juggling the phone between shoulder and chin was no mean feat. Securing it just in time before Alex barged out the bathroom door, making silent mocking kissing faces as his sister swatted at him irritably.

Kaitlyn rushed around her room, throwing underwear, shirts and slacks everywhere, trying to find the perfect outfit to wear. After an hour of important decision-making, Kaitlyn settled on a pair of Capri pants and a Navy style shirt. She found the right color sneakers to wear before going downstairs.

Rushing around the kitchen to get cereal and milk, as Kathryn looked on in wonder, Kaitlyn slopped milk off the rim of the bowl and stood shoveling the mess into her mouth.

"What's got you in such a tizzy?" her mother asked, amazed to see Kaitlyn move so fast in the morning.

"Ray invited me for a picnic brunch at Crestview Park," Kaitlyn said, in between spoonfuls of corn flakes. "Is it okay if I go?"

"I think it'd be alright," Kathryn replied. "But, don't you think you should have asked me first?"

Kaitlyn knew she should have asked, but hadn't wanted to come across as a little kid to Ray. She finished her breakfast and ran back upstairs for some last minute details. Checking her hair in the mirror before brushing her teeth, she decided to leave it in a ponytail, thinking it worked better for play. (Not to mention, she was hoping Ray would kiss her neck.)

She ran down the stairs like a stampede of horses, calling, "I'm leaving, Mom," as she was half way out the door.

The knell of Kathryn's voice rang from the kitchen. "Kaitlyn. Wait a minute."

"Oh, *Mom*," Kaitlyn said as her mother's head appeared around the corner.

"Be careful and watch out for yourself," Kathryn insisted with a wagging finger. "Remember what we talked about. Keep it light, okay?"

"Okay, Mom," Kaitlyn replied impatiently, hovering at the open door.

"And another thing," Kathryn reminded. "Why don't you invite Ray and his folks over for a barbecue sometime? Your father should meet him if the two of you are going to be dating."

"Okay, Mom. I will," Kaitlyn called as she bolted out the door.

"Be back in time to help with dinner!" Kathryn called to no one.

Crestview Park was located well within walking distance from Kaitlyn's house. Decorated with walking paths, picnic tables, a small duck pond, and patches of woods, it was popular with young and old alike. 'Sweetheart Lane', the unofficial name of the main walking path, wandered through the large copses of trees surrounding the park.

Kaitlyn walked the tree-lined streets of downtown Winter's Crest, being greeted by what seemed like everybody. As she passed Wertmann's Hardware Store, a group of older gents looked up from an intent game of checkers. Several tipped their hats, beaming at their princess apparent.

Kaitlyn greeted the men she'd known since childhood with a radiant smile. "Good. morning, gentlemen."

A few doors past Wertmann's was Sweet Treats, a bakery owned by Mrs. Peterson, a friend of Kaitlyn's late grandmother. The aroma from the breads, hot cross buns, and cinnamon rolls made her mouth water.

Up a little further was the five-and-ten-cent store, the children's favorite. Among other things, they sold jacks, chalk for hopscotch, and jump ropes. And of course, there was the 'penny' candy, with which kids, (and some adults), could fill a whole lunch bag for a nickel. The sidewalk outside the store doubled as a proving ground for all the latest toys.

Passing the five-and-ten, Kaitlyn turned left onto Mulberry Street, named for the many mulberry bushes planted long ago between the oak trees that led the way to Crestview. And up ahead in the distance, Kaitlyn saw her destination.

She arrived at the opening of the park, where an embossed granite arch welcomed visitors. On either side of the arch, bronze plaques dedicated to fallen World War One and Two soldiers were set in the stone, and well-groomed rhododendrons encircled the base of the arch's legs, with an attractive floral apron surrounding them.

Kaitlyn entered the park, and her attention was drawn to the many children frolicking in the sun. Some held balloons sold by vendors in the park. Others played Red Rover and Kickball. Some were crying as they watched their balloons sail away over the treetops, while other games like Double-Dutch, Roly-Poly and Red Light/Green Light went forward in the background. Kaitlyn smiled as she passed by, remembering her own childhood games.

Some kids happened to throw a ball nearby, startling her. They came running over to get it, and as the kids scrambled at her feet, she looked up to see Ray. Kaitlyn's face turned beet red when their eyes met, and she just stood there gazing at Ray, causing her smile to widen like a small child getting her first lollipop.

He wore blue jean cut-offs and a spotless cotton tee, and looked downright 'delicious'. Ray called Kaitlyn over with a wave, and Kaitlyn walked towards him with her eyes never straying.

"Hi," she said simply, still trying to focus.

"Hey, Kaitlyn," Ray greeted her. "I'm glad you could come."

"Thank you, I'm glad I could come, too," Kaitlyn replied nervously. All she could think of was touching him, holding him and kissing him. She leaned into Ray and closed her eyes for a hello hug, hoping for a kiss.

He felt good against her, and Kaitlyn felt her body awaken with excitement, while those newly discovered sensations showed their face once again. Kaitlyn, melting inside, composed herself enough to sit down with Ray on the red and white checkered cloth blanket, taking a few calming breaths while she tried to be mature.

"Kaitlyn," Ray asked. "May I call you Kait?"

"Sure," Kaitlyn answered enthusiastically. "No one's ever called me 'Kait' before. I'd like that."

Kaitlyn was brought up using her full name, and it never occurred to her to have a nickname. "Wow," she thought, "this is kind of naughty," feeling a bit special.

Ray produced a bottle opener and deftly flipped open a cola bottle, handing it to Kaitlyn before opening one for himself. He lay down on his side facing her, and then he took her hand as they sat staring into each other's eyes, unsure of what to say, or what to do, for that matter.

Ray started talking to Kaitlyn about little things, like how life was when he was a young boy. He told stories about school and spoke of his grandparents that lived half an hour away. With his grandparents getting on in years, he explained to Kaitlyn that his mother wanted to be near them — another reason for the move. Ray paused and looked to Kaitlyn. "What about you?" he asked.

Kaitlyn began telling Ray about being born and raised in Winter's Crest, and about her friendship with John when they were younger. She talked about how she had to help handle things in the house when her father went off to war and how she was almost like a mother figure to Alex, explaining that he didn't need her as a mother anymore, but as a sister.

"Well, now you can take care of *you* and enjoy life," Ray chimed in.

"This is true, Ray," Kaitlyn agreed. "I never looked at it that way before. I somehow felt like I wasn't needed anymore. I guess I got caught up in the mothering role, forgetting I had a life of my own."

"I need you," Ray said flirtatiously, capitalizing on her comment. He leaned over for a kiss, with Kaitlyn obliging.

"Ray, I need you, too," Kaitlyn said as she sat back. "To be honest, I can't stop thinking about you."

"Me too," Ray replied as they both looked again into each other's eyes. "Want to go for a walk before we eat?" Ray asked with a questioning brow.

Kaitlyn grinned and nodded quickly.

Ray stood up and offered his hand. They headed in the direction of Sweetheart Lane, striking up another conversation, with Kaitlyn telling Ray of her mother's proposal.

Ray thought Kathryn's idea of a barbecue was a good one and said he would check with his parents. "When did you want to have it?"

"How 'bout this Sunday after church?" Kaitlyn suggested. "I'll check with my dad, but that seems like a good time."

"Great! Should be fun," Ray replied, feeling a little nervous about meeting James Frost.

He'd heard of Mr. Frost's reputation for being strict, but also knew that meeting him would mean he could spend more time with Kaitlyn. Something he was more than willing to do.

As they approached Sweetheart Lane, Kaitlyn and Ray toyed with the idea of holding hands, gently sweeping the other's as they walked side by side. Eventually, they let go of their inhibitions, and their hands locked together.

Smiling from ear to ear with first romance, the warm breezes whispered by them as squirrels hurried through the trees and chipmunks popped out to see who was coming. Birds tended their nests, and the sun filtered through the treetops, giving the wooded area a warm glow.

Kaitlyn and Ray approached an open glade within the thick brush and made their way to it. Off to the left, smaller saplings surrounded a huge maple, and Kaitlyn went to release her hand from Ray's, but he wouldn't let go. Smiling, Ray led her towards the tree with a firm grasp, releasing her hand only when he leaned back against the maple.

"Come here," Ray teased, with a crooked index finger gesture. Kaitlyn moved towards him with a 'maybe I will, maybe I won't' motion, laughing as she took each step. He held out his hand, and as Kaitlyn reached for it, Ray pulled her in, bringing her body to his. Ray brought his lips to Kaitlyn's before she could react.

Kaitlyn didn't fall away from Ray this time, no longer afraid of her feelings. She welcomed them as both their smiles turned to those of want and new love. They stayed in each other's arms, kissing, hugging, and enjoying each other, being careful not to over-step any boundaries.

Kaitlyn's secret wish came true when Ray kissed her neck, bringing chills spiraling through her. She reached up, wrapped her arms around Ray's neck and kissed him. "I love you," slipped from Kaitlyn's tongue, leaving her mortified.

Ray looked into Kaitlyn's eyes and smiled, saying, "I love you, too, Miss Kait."

Kaitlyn breathed a sigh of relief, having felt that she had prematurely revealed her true feelings. They also both realized their spoken words had now brought their playful relationship to a whole other level. Time stood still.

Ray had his arms wrapped around Kaitlyn's waist and while pulling his head back, he asked, "You getting hungry yet?"

Kaitlyn replied with a nod as if she hadn't eaten for days.

Ray invited Kaitlyn to take his hand, and the two strolled back to the lane swaying their arms back and forth.

Back at the blanket, Ray pretended to be a waiter, offering Kaitlyn an early afternoon meal. Kaitlyn got into the act with replies like, "Why, thank you, sir," and "That's lovely, sir."

Ray had brought fried chicken, homemade biscuits, and macaroni salad, all of which his mother had made. Kaitlyn's mouth watered. Ray reached his hand in the picnic basket and brought out some honey. He licked his lips as he draped the gooey stuff over her biscuit and then hand fed her the first bite, while a playful grin appeared.

After enjoying their conversation and meal, they relaxed in the sun and held hands, while a few words crept in every so often. Smiles and rapid beating hearts were the theme of the hour.

As 'all good things must come to an end', or so they say, it was time for them to pack up and call it a day. Gathering their items into an organized heap on the ground, Ray stood and asked Kaitlyn to come to him with his eyes.

She went to Ray's arms, and they kissed as if they were the only two around. Saying goodbye made it hard to leave, but Kaitlyn slowly backed away, letting their hands glide against each other until their fingertips lost their last touch.

Kaitlyn turned and walked slowly towards home with her head hung low, saddened by having to leave Ray's side. As she went to cross through the park's entrance, Ray came behind her, hugging Kaitlyn around her waist and kissing her neck. Kaitlyn turned around to face him, and they hugged with desperation. She reached up for one more kiss and whined, "I don't want to go."

"I know," he said. "I don't want to go either. I love you, Miss Kait."

"I've got to go," Kaitlyn said as she buried her face in his chest.

"Oh," Ray said, getting her attention. "You want to meet at The Fountain tonight after dinner? I'll be there with John, and he'll be asking Allison?"

"Yes, I'd love to," she replied. "Hey, Ray," Kaitlyn said sweetly and with a smile, "I love you, too." She turned away, waving goodbye, still not wanting to go. But Kaitlyn was happy knowing she would see him again later.

Ray watched Kaitlyn walk off for a few moments before picking up the picnic supplies and heading home himself.

Kaitlyn walked home humming and with a smile that wouldn't quit, as if she were walking through the pages of a fairytale. *Cloud Nine* wasn't high enough for the delight she had in her heart.

"How was your picnic?" Kathryn asked as Kaitlyn walked through the door.

"It was great. Had a wonderful time," she replied. "We're all going to The Soda Fountain tonight. John, Allison, Ray and I. Is that okay?"

"Sure," Kathryn replied.

After Kaitlyn took some time to clean up and put things away, and after strumming through the pages of one of her mother's novels, Kaitlyn helped get dinner ready.

Jim arrived home precisely at 5:15 p.m., his usual time, and by 5:30, they were all sitting down at the table and exchanging small talk, while eating their evening meal.

Kathryn raised her eyebrow with a look to Kaitlyn, implying she should bring up the barbecue.

"Daddy," Kaitlyn said, catching her father's attention. "I've met a nice young man who's just moved here from Georgia. His name is Ray Niles, and I was wondering if we could invite he and his parents over for a barbecue after church on Sunday?"

"Yes, that would be fine," Jim answered. "Actually, I've met Mr. Niles at the bank. Nice man," he added, then thought, "What happened to John?" while continuing with the meal.

After dinner, Kaitlyn and Alex helped clean up, and when all was done, Kaitlyn went upstairs to get ready for her date.

She wanted to feel sensual, yet confident in her appearance, choosing a light green poodle skirt with a matching blouse. The green in the skirt brought out her eyes, making them smile without trying. She then took her hair out of the ponytail and brushed it out, letting it fall onto her shoulders. She chose some matching bobby socks and put a pair of white sneakers on, remembering how slippery the dance floor can get. When Kaitlyn was ready, she went downstairs and let her parents know she was leaving.

Kaitlyn walked to The Fountain, and John joined her on the way. They talked about their newfound 'loves' as they passed by the old library, the local post office, and the food market.

The food market, also known as Westman's Market, was owned by a family which Kaitlyn had known since she was born. The Westman's have a son named Bob, who had always been kind of a big brother to Kaitlyn. She had always looked up to Bob, but didn't get to see him as often as she used to. However, every once in a while, he'd show his face around town. Bob had been busy with summer classes at the college nearby, girls, and holding down a part-time job at his parents' store.

As Kaitlyn and John walked by the market, Kaitlyn couldn't help but think of Bob. Kaitlyn and Allison always used to go in the shop to see him when they were younger, being thirteen and having their interests turn from playing jacks and skipping rope to boys. Since Bob was the only older boy they knew, they would practice their flirting skills on him. He indulged their harmless teases by never laughing out loud at their girlish advances.

"I wonder how he's doing," Kaitlyn thought as she and John continued towards The Fountain. "I wonder if he'll get drafted for the war?"

John interrupted Kaitlyn's thoughts. "You're in love with Ray, aren't you?"

Kaitlyn was surprised by his nonchalant manner. Her embarrassed silence answered him.

"I knew it. I just knew it," John said. "I can see it in your eyes and in your face when his name is even mentioned." He paused, and with query in his eyes asked, "How come you never look at me that way?"

"John," Kaitlyn said matter-of-factly, "because I'm not in love with you. Never have been. Never will be."

"Oh," was all a deflated John could mutter. "Well, here we are," he said, opening the door for Kaitlyn.

"Aren't *we* the gentleman tonight." Kaitlyn curtsied graciously in sarcasm. "Why thank you, sir."

"You know I like them sassy, Kaitlyn," John replied.

"Oh yeah, that's right. I'd better stop that," as she let out a playful grin.

The two entered The Fountain, and Ray and Allison rose to their feet, greeting them. The two couples exchanged quick hugs before Kaitlyn and Ray began their predictable silent conversation.

"Hey you two! Hello?!" John tried to get their attention. "I thought this was a double date?"

"Yes, sorry," they said together.

Allison broke the uneasiness. "Kaitlyn, we *must* discuss our birthday bash. It's coming soon, you know."

"Yes, a couple weeks to go." Kaitlyn agreed, "You're right, we'd better get moving on this."

The four made themselves comfortable and ordered cherry colas before working out the plans for their eighteenth birthday. They chose a theme, what kind of food to serve — including the cake and who to invite. Since they knew almost everybody, they just figured they would invite their closest friends, and if anyone else showed up at the party all the better.

"Anyone hungry yet?" John broke the discussion for a moment.

"I could go for an ice cream sundae with hot fudge, caramel, and almonds." Kaitlyn replied, while the four looked on as if she were a pig.

"*What*?!" Kaitlyn whined. "Best sundae there is!"

"Yum! Me, too," Allison said, agreeing with her.

"Why don't we get two sundaes and split them?" Ray suggested.

"I like that idea, Ray!" John replied. "How 'bout it, girls?" John asked with his ever-so-graceful charm.

The girls looked at each other and then Kaitlyn answered, "Yes, that's a *delicious* idea," as they glanced at each other devilishly before breaking into roaring laughter.

Ray and John looked at them, not having a clue as to what *that* was supposed to mean. The girls didn't bother to explain.

Peggy the waitress came over, and they ordered their sundaes, then continued on with their party plans.

John spoke out of the blue. "You're both going to be legal adults now, and soon, I will be, too."

"That's right, John," Allison replied. "Your birthday's in October, right?"

"Yes it is," John said proudly.

"When's your birthday, Ray," Kaitlyn asked.

"I turned eighteen last month," Ray answered.

Kaitlyn thought quietly to herself for a moment, wishing she had known him before his birthday so she could have given him a gift or at least celebrated it with him. Kaitlyn turned her thoughts back to the current discussion.

"Remember what I said, John," Kaitlyn said in a parental tone. "Turning eighteen does *not* make you an adult, or even a man for that matter."

"I still don't get what you mean, Kaitlyn," John replied. "But, that's okay. I don't get what you mean half the time anyway." He laughed.

"Sundaes are here!" Ray announced.

They leaned back to allow Peggy to serve the ice cream, and although each sundae had two spoons, they seemed to only need one per couple.

Ray took a heaping spoonful of vanilla ice cream, doused in caramel, hot fudge, and sprinkled with almonds, and brought it to Kaitlyn's mouth. John picked up on what Ray was doing and did the same with Allison, with both girls ending up with the sweet, sloppy mess all over their faces. Being proper young ladies, they carefully tried to clean themselves up, but Kaitlyn missed a spot at the tip of her nose. Ray lightly wiped it off with a napkin as Kaitlyn scrunched her face in embarrassment.

"You seem to be doing a good job of getting yourself into some *sticky* situations lately, Kaitlyn," John commented in a southern tone.

"Thanks for noticing, John. You don't miss a beat, do you?" Kaitlyn replied snidely yet joking ... or maybe not.

As they were eating their sundaes, one of the restaurant's patrons dropped a nickel in the jukebox, pushing "C-4", the number for the girls favorite Perry Como song: *Some Enchanted Evening.*

"Kaitlyn, come on!" Allison called out to her. "Our song is playing! Come on guys! Dance with us."

They all went to the dance floor, and Ray bowed to Kaitlyn, asking for her hand, while John approached Allison with an extended elbow. Each girl pretended to be Ginger Rogers as they accepted their escorts' invitations.

They held each other dancing, while Kaitlyn and Allison sang out of tune, laughing their way through the song. When the song ended, Ray dropped another nickel and played "I Can Dream, Can't I?" by the Andrew Sisters. The two couples, now joined by others, moved softly to the music, while the girls rested their heads against the boys' chests, every so often sneaking in a kiss or two.

The final note played, and they returned to their table as if on cue. And with their thirsts quenched, the girls continued to work on their birthday plans.

Excitedly, Allison suggested they try to get in touch with Bob Westman, to see if he would like to come to their party, and Kaitlyn thought that was a great idea. "I was just thinking about Bob on the way here," Kaitlyn replied. "I'll keep my eyes open for him."

Finishing their detailed plans, they all decided it was time to get a move on. Exiting the restaurant and walking to the side of the building, Ray and Kaitlyn embraced in a sappy hug, careful not to cause too much of a scene. Meanwhile, Allison and John exchanged kisses, this time not laughing through them.

Saying goodbye, each couple left hand in hand, with Kaitlyn and Ray walking together in silent love.

Chapter Five

Inside the old Saint James Episcopal, the service was uneventful — even boring, compared to the double date the previous night. Kaitlyn gazed over the room, not paying attention to what the priest was saying, instead studying the high, stained glass windows lined up on both sides of the room.

The detailed glass depicted stories from the Bible and was magnified by the presence of a midnight blue carpet that vibrantly showcased the likeness of Jesus in the Narthex that Kaitlyn admired so much. High above in the back of the church, voices filled the air with song every Sunday, and the one thing Kaitlyn loved about going to church was the singing. She couldn't carry a tune, but in church, that never seemed to matter. *Amazing Grace* was Kaitlyn's favorite church song, not only because of the rhythmic beauty and heart touching words, but because it was the one song she could actually stay in tune with.

Quietly surveying the room, Kaitlyn spotted Bob Westman across the aisle and a few seats back. Her eyes lit up, and she slowly raised her hand to wave a covert "hi". Catching Bob's eye, she put a hand to her ear pretending she was on the phone.

He mouthed back, "Okay."

Bob Westman was a good-looking young man of twenty years. His dark brown hair and matching eyes accentuated his eyelashes, which were the envy of all the girls, and his smile melted them to their feet. Being a kind person, he stood tall with a muscular build at five foot, eleven, and was the type of guy who could be counted on in a pinch.

When the parishioners began filing out to join the post-sermon social, Kaitlyn caught up with Bob. Excited to see her long-lost friend, Kaitlyn gave Bob a big hug before inviting him to she and Allison's birthday celebration. He was happy to accept the invitation.

Kaitlyn and her family arrived home and changed out of their Sunday clothes before preparing for the barbecue. With Kaitlyn shelling peas and Alex shucking corn, Kathryn began making salads, while Jim read the Sunday paper, relaxing in his favorite chair. When all was almost complete, the doorbell rang, and Jim rose to his feet to answer it.

Kaitlyn came out from the kitchen wiping her hands on a dishtowel and introduced her father to the Niles. Just as Jim extended his hand to greet their new friends, Kathryn came out, saying hello to Jaycee, before introducing herself to Nick and saying hello to Ray. "We're so glad you could come," Kathryn welcomed. "Please come in."

The Niles entered and immediately felt comfortable, exchanging pleasantries, before Jim turned his attention to Ray.

"It's a pleasure to finally meet you, son," Jim said sincerely. "We've heard a lot about you."

"It's nice to meet you, too, sir," Ray replied nervously.

Alex came downstairs and thought he was helping Ray out of the uncomfortable situation by introducing himself. "So, *you're* the one who's got my sister all riled up?" Alex said as a joke. "Hi, I'm Alex," extending his hand to Ray, and then to Jaycee and Nick.

"It's nice to meet you," Ray deflected with a smile, with his parents sharing in the sentiment.

The tension wore off a bit for Ray as he saw that Jim was not as gruff as he had heard, or expected. And as for Alex, he let his comment go.

The men went out to the backyard and cracked a couple bottles of Carling Black Label while firing up the grill. They offered one to Ray as he and Alex threw the football back and forth. Ray accepted.

Jaycee, Kaitlyn and Kathryn joined the festivities by sipping Chablis and talking 'ladies' talk at the shaded picnic table, all acting as if they'd known each other for years.

Kathryn didn't allow Kaitlyn to drink wine often, but during social occasions, Kathryn felt she needed to teach her how to drink socially. And besides, she *was* almost eighteen.

When the stone barbecue pit was hot, Nick and Jim began cooking the steaks, while the ladies went into the kitchen to finish last minute macaroni salad. Alex and Ray set the picnic table, and when things were ready, they sat down to their feast. They enjoyed easy conversation and plenty of laughs, until no one could eat another bite.

After their meal, Ray pushed Kaitlyn on the tree swing, while Jim and Nick sat down to a cribbage game. Alex watched them intently. Jaycee and Kathryn cleaned up together, telling the kids and men to enjoy themselves and to give the two an opportunity to enjoy their new friendship and get to know each other better.

When the afternoon came to a close, the men shook hands, and the ladies hugged each other goodbye, with both families having enjoyed themselves. The Frosts stood in the doorway, waving goodbye, as the Niles drove off in their Desoto.

"Nice young man, Kaitlyn," Jim commented, watching the car drive down the street. "Nice family."

Kaitlyn smiled, knowing she had her father's approval, and knowing this meant she could spend more time with Ray. Her heart raced with the mere thought.

Over the next couple of weeks, Kaitlyn spent a lot of time with Ray at Crestview Park, visiting their special place by the majestic maple and hanging out at The Fountain with Allison and John, dancing, chatting and visiting with school friends, while Ray made new ones. On August fourteenth, Kaitlyn's birthday arrived, and she celebrated it with her family, with Ray attending as her guest. After the small celebration, Kaitlyn and Ray took a long walk, talking and just loving one another. They were waiting for the big birthday party to arrive so they could celebrate more in style.

The twenty-first of August did come, bringing the long awaited bash. Kaitlyn and Allison were excited, and with plans completed and Allison spending the night at Kaitlyn's, the two readied for the evening activities, going to extra lengths to brighten their faces.

Kaitlyn wore an emerald green, floral print, button-down dress with a full skirt, and Allison chose a soft pink floral dress, similar to Kaitlyn's style, but with a little less detail. Both were streamline at the bodice.

When Ray and John came to pick up the girls at seven o'clock, their eyes widened, and they suddenly had to swallow, not believing the radiance and sophistication they saw before them. For the first time, they saw their girls as young women, not the giggling teenagers they had been spending time with.

Jim and Kathryn showed the four to the front door and handed Kaitlyn money to pay for the food, drinks, and jukebox. Kathryn reminded Kaitlyn that she had already dropped the cake and other items off, and both girls showed their gratitude. Jim and Kathryn hugged their daughter goodbye and told the kids to enjoy themselves as they headed out, ready for a fun-filled evening.

Hand in hand they all walked to The Fountain under a moonlit sky, arriving to find a few added decorations of balloons, extra white carnations, all the friends they had invited, and one very special friend.

"Bob, you made it!" Allison enthusiastically called out, running with her arms out towards him, wanting to give him a bear hug.

Bob opened his arms out. "Hi, Allison. Great to see you," Bob said, wrapping his arms around one of his favorite girls. "Happy Birthday!" Looking over towards Kaitlyn, he expressed the same sentiment, leaving John with his 'being intruded upon' feeling.

John had known Bob his entire life, too, but he has always been *just Bob* and never considered him to be a threat — until now.

Feeling a tinge of jealousy squirm inside, John acted on it, breaking up the intimacy between Bob and Allison.

"Hey, Bob, how ya doin'?" John interrupted, plopping his arm around him and pulling Bob in his direction.

"Great, John ... you? I hear you're joining the Army in August. Good for you," as he patted him on the back.

John replied, thrilled that he had turned Bob's attention towards him, "I'm scheduled to leave August nineteenth."

"Well, I'm happy for you," Bob reiterated. "Good luck, man."

Kaitlyn and Allison joined their girlfriends and talked about the latest fads, gossip, and *dreamboats*, while Ray and John hung out with Bob and the guys, talking football as well as other *important* issues.

The party got under way when Bob dropped a nickel into the jukebox and played *Some Enchanted Evening*, having heard it was their favorite. Bob got down on his knees with begging hands and pleaded with the girls to sing it for him.

"Only if you'll sing it with us," the girls insisted while looking at Bob with teasing, dominating eyebrows — demanding him.

"Okay," Bob replied, laughing his way to the dance floor and shaking his head from side to side, knowing what he had gotten himself into and kicking himself for it.

After the first couple lines were belted out, Kaitlyn called out for all to chime in, and everyone who had come to The Fountain, whether invited friends or visiting townsfolk, got up on the dance floor and sang — most of them laughing their way through. Applause rang through the small shop, mixed with peals of laughter when the tune came to a close.

The next song to play was *Goodnight Irene* by The Weavers, with Gordon Jenkins. After that, Allison played If *I Knew You Were Coming, I'd 've Baked A Cake* by Eileen Barton, dedicating it to Bob with a smirk on her face. Songs like, *I Can Dream, Can't I* by The Andrew Sisters and *All My Love* by Patti Page brought couples, young and old, to the dance floor, swaying back and forth in summertime play — or not.

Closing their eyes and feeling their love for each other, Kaitlyn and Ray held one another close in dance. John and Allison embraced to the music and enjoyed their rather new feelings as well, with the simple swaying giving them permission to actually stay on the dance floor in a hug.

Bob interrupted both Kaitlyn and Allison to say goodbye. "I have to get going; parents need help with the books tonight."

The girls looked at Bob with pouting lips and puppy-dog eyes.

"Happy Birthday, girls. You both look wonderful tonight." Raising his hand in a waving gesture, Bob called out, "Ray, it was nice to meet you, and John, take care of yourself. Great seeing you, and good luck in the Army."

"*Bye, Bob,*" both girls teased in unison. "Thanks for coming."

Bob looked back at the girls, knowing they were making fun of their thirteen-year old flirting days, and winked at them. John caught a glimpse of it and sneered in Bob's direction.

Deciding to take a break from dancing, since the song was almost over, the four sat down at their table and discussed their back to school plans, with all of them looking forward to their senior year. John, realizing he was the *baby* in the group, brought up his birthday, excited he'd finally be of legal age.

"What are you going to do for your birthday, John?" Kaitlyn asked.

"Well ... I was hoping to have an intimate birthday dinner with Allison," he replied, looking over in her direction and asking if that would be fine with her. Allison nodded, with her body jumping in, feeling the excitement.

"That seems like a wonderful idea," Kaitlyn commented. "Why don't you two meet us here afterwards?"

John looked at Allison for her approval before he said, "Yes, that'd be great."

Kaitlyn, changing the subject, asked, "Allison, do you know what you're going to wear the first day of school?"

"I haven't made up my mind yet," Allison sadly replied as if it were the most important decision in the world to make. "I was thinking of my peach day-dress or my brown, floral print skirt and my silk blouse. I just don't know. What 'bout you?"

"I'm not sure yet either," Kaitlyn answered. "I want to look and feel good though."

"Kaitlyn, you look and feel good in anything," Ray flirted.

"Why thank you, sir," Kaitlyn replied in a sarcastic manner, laughing.

"Why do you girls do that?" John asked.

"Do what?" both questioned.

"Why do you worry so much about what you wear, how you look, or how your hair is done?"

"Well, we want to look good for the cute boys," Allison replied in her sassy tone.

"I shouldn't have asked," John commented out loud.

"That's right, John," Allison said laughing, while Kaitlyn joined her. "You shouldn't have."

Ray looked at John and replied to the conversation. "Women!"

The invited guests began to come over and wish Kaitlyn and Allison each a happy birthday, bidding them a fond farewell and also making them aware of the time.

Deciding it was time to end the party, the four chipped in to clean up. When the place was spotless, Ray dropped in a nickel, and both couples enjoyed one last birthday dance, replaying *All My Love* by Patti Page.

Ray stopped short and reached into his pocket, pulling out a small velvet box with a yellow bow on top. Kaitlyn's eyes widened with excitement, and an embarrassed shy smile erupted.

"Happy Birthday, Kaitlyn," Ray said, handing it to her.

Kaitlyn opened the box, and her eyes lit when she saw the glimmering shine of a charm bracelet with one yellow rose charm dangling from it. "I love it, Ray. I love you," she said, jumping up and down in a hug. Stopping her excitement, Kaitlyn spoke softly in his ear. "Thank you," then gave him a slight kiss on his cheek.

"I love you, too, Kait," Ray replied before helping to place the bracelet on her wrist.

Hugging again as the last note played, Kaitlyn again whispered her appreciation to Ray, giving him a bright smile and a wide-eyed look.

Ray took Kaitlyn's hand and led her off the dance floor. "You're welcome. I'm glad you like it, Kait," he replied before reminding all of the time.

Ray and John walked the girls back to Kaitlyn's house, bringing them to the front porch and wishing them both happy birthdays before embracing each other's date. Making sure she was out of her parents' sight, Kaitlyn kissed Ray, and Allison, being careful not to be seen as well, took the opportunity to kiss John. They all said their final goodbyes, and as the boys trailed off, the girls hovered at the front door waving goodnight.

Kaitlyn and Allison walked inside with dreamy-eyed, teenage delight and filled Kaitlyn's parents in on the evening, saying goodnight and thanking them before heading to Kaitlyn's room for the night.

"Allison," Kaitlyn called her attention. "How's things going between you and John?" she asked, removing the charm bracelet and placing it in her jewelry box. Noticing John hadn't given Allison anything, Kaitlyn decided not to carry on about her gift, sparing Allison's feelings.

"Fine," Allison replied. "Hey, Bob looked good tonight, huh? He looks better than I remember."

"Yeah," Kaitlyn replied. "He looked 'delicious'," letting out a laugh.

"That was a lot of fun," Allison commented.

"Yeah, I had a great time. Goodnight," Kaitlyn replied yawning. "I'm tired."

"Me too," Allison agreed, turning out the light. "Goodnight."

*   *   *

Kaitlyn looked at the kitchen clock and realized she had been sitting at the table for over an hour nibbling her lunch and recalling times with her friends. She picked up the letter, first staring at it, and then cradled it in her arms as if she were hugging Ray, bringing a certain misplaced joy to her face.

Knowing what the letter could bring, Kaitlyn was not strong enough to overcome her desperate fear of opening it, even though Kaitlyn's heart fought every second with her common sense. Feeling she should listen to her head, Kaitlyn decided it best to put it in her pocketbook for the time being, until she felt she was ready to handle what, if any, emotional turmoil the letter might bring.

Kaitlyn put the kettle on and awaited its steaming water before heading back to the porch to enjoy the afternoon's sun and sip her favorite tea from her special cup.

"You know," she thought, looking at the cup from an arm's length, "I really should pass this on to Rose sometime soon," but dismissed the thought; she wasn't ready to give it up just yet. Relaxing back in the rocker, listening to the sounds of summer and blowing on the tea to cool it, Kaitlyn's memory drifted back to her first day of twelfth grade.

*   *   *

An Indian summer announced Kaitlyn's first day back to school, which usually started shortly after Labor Day each year — this year being no different. The temperature hovered in the high seventies, while the sun tried to peep through the haze of the morning fog. Kaitlyn awoke singing, and cheerfully greeted the finches outside the window as if she had suddenly become Snow White.

Placing one hand on each knob of the doublewide closet doors, Kaitlyn flung her arms out to the sides and stared in fright. "I have nothing to wear!"

Being a typical teenager, she had plenty of clothes piled high, with shoes to match almost every outfit. Still though, in her eyes, she had *nothing to wear*.

Kaitlyn rummaged through the clothes, making faces as to which outfits were possibilities and which ones were not. Spotting a pink satin day dress stuffed in the back of the closet, she carefully reached for the dress and draped it in front of her. Getting a good look at it in front of the full view mirror in her closet, Kaitlyn thought, "Hmmm, this just may work." She slowly unbuttoned the dress and slid it on over her slip, liking how it looked on her. Feeling it was the perfect dress for the first day of school, Kaitlyn made her decision. She picked out a nice pair of summer casuals, foregoing the nylons, as the forecast was calling for high humidity.

Kaitlyn walked to the vanity while she finished buttoning the front of the dress and looked in the mirror, tilting her head in wonder about the buttons. Her breasts had matured over the summer, and she played with the idea of accentuating her more womanly appearance, deciding to leave one button undone.

Raising the hairbrush to her hair, she began to pull it back into a ponytail, before releasing it and letting it fall upon her shoulders, choosing to keep it down for the day. It gave her that more sophisticated look. Kaitlyn applied a little rouge to accent her cheeks and dashed her lips with a light pink lip-frost.

Continuing to look in the mirror, Kaitlyn turned to the right glancing over her shoulder and repeated the same movement with her left, then carefully checked her backside. Standing in front of the mirror for one last glance and making sure she felt comfortable with her chosen attire for the day, Kaitlyn smiled in acceptance before making her way downstairs for breakfast.

Kathryn was busy in the kitchen preparing lunches for Kaitlyn and Alex while also placing their meals on the table and getting James his coffee. Feeling a bit taken for granted, she secretly enjoyed the fact that she was needed. "What would they do without me?" Kathryn thought with a confirming smile of what she already knew, while spreading butter on the kids' bread.

Looking over her shoulder to glance in Kaitlyn's direction, Kathryn commented, "You look nice today, Kaitlyn. That's the dress my mother made for you, isn't it?" Kathryn asked, continuing on with her morning scurry, saddened her mother couldn't see Kaitlyn in it.

"Yes it is, thanks," Kaitlyn proudly replied. "I'm going to get going."

"You're going to eat breakfast first, young lady."

"Yes, Mother," Kaitlyn succumbed, sitting down to the oak kitchen table to a plate of French toast and tangy sausage.

Kaitlyn finished her breakfast and brought her plate to the sink. "All set, Mom. I'm going now, love you."

"Love you, sweetheart. Have a great day," Kathryn said as she went to kiss Kaitlyn's cheek and then headed to the bottom of the stairs. "Alex, get a move on or you're going to be late," she called up to him. "Your breakfast is getting cold."

Kaitlyn began her walk to Mackey High School, meeting up with John on the way. The two enjoyed casual conversation about Allison and Ray as they caught up with them entering the property.

With the beautiful park-like landscaping making up the school grounds and surrounding the old stone building, Mackey High had a college atmosphere, with the four white pillars standing at the front entranceway adding to that feeling.

On one side of the school there were two football fields and a concession stand building painted in blue. The other side held tennis courts and soccer fields, as well as a running track for the athletes or local townsfolk to use.

Kaitlyn and Ray, with Allison and John, walked to the stone steps of the main entranceway.

A moment of silence passed as they each stared at the school with a look of *here we go again* on their faces.

"Our last year as high school kids," John said. "Let's make this the best year of our lives."

"Yes, let's," Ray replied. "You girls up to it?"

"Oh yeah, we most certainly are," Kaitlyn responded, while Allison agreed, "This *is* going to be the best year of our lives."

Their first day of school was met with the normal excitement of traveling back to school after a long summer's break, and each student's anxiety walked inside with them.

Walking through the entranceway, rows and rows of blue and white lockers lined the white hallways, sticking out as if they were greeting the students and screaming to them *there is no escape*, and making reality sink in a little faster then *most* were ready for.

The cold ceramic white tile, sprinkled with droplets of blue, echoed the sounds of scurrying feet from lost lower classmen, and each wooden door to the classrooms, looked like prison doors, giving a trapped feeling to those who wished to hang on to summer a bit longer. The now lost smells of summer were replaced with antiseptic, chalk, and bad perfumes, worn by a few not so up-to-date teachers.

As Kaitlyn and Ray made their way through the halls, they caught up with their many friends they'd seen over the summer and also with the ones who had vacationed in far off places. It seemed like everyone was coming over to meet Ray, having heard about *the new kid* and wanting to meet him.

There has always been something intriguing about a new kid coming to town. Maybe it's because the person is different and refreshing, or maybe for the girls, it's one more guy to check out. Or maybe it's to be a part of something so trivial that it's made into something big just because everyone is talking about *it*. Regardless of the reasons, Ray seemed to be the first on the students' lists for the first day of school rumors, and anyone who was *anybody* made sure they had met Ray.

Everything went fine, and the students all found their classes eventually, with some of the new lower classmen being sent to bathrooms by their superior upper classmen — the typical taunt, *a right of passage* — if you will. The new high school kids knew to expect this, but some forgot the rule about asking the more experienced students for directions.

Over the next few weeks, Allison, John, Kaitlyn and Ray were all busy adjusting to their new schedules, not having much time to socialize. Once things did settle down and they were able to get organized, all four began to get together more often. Nothing major happened during the adjustment time, except the time apart made

Kaitlyn and Ray feel stronger for each other. It took a little work for John and Allison to reconnect, however, they did hook back up in time for Homecoming, allowing the four to share in the festivities together.

It was the biggest thing that happened in Winter's Crest besides the holidays, and this year meant more to the locals. With The Korean War going on and the constant worrying of the local soldiers that had gone to serve, the Homecoming festivities helped the townsfolk take their minds off of it for a short time; the people needed it.

During the opening ceremonies at Town Hall, Principal Mr. Petry began the festivities by saying a prayer, asking for their local soldiers to return home safely. Most everyone bowed their heads and joined him when he said, "Amen."

Mr. Petry stood six feet, with black hair and black wire-rimmed glasses. His hair was graying on the sides, giving him a distinguished yet authoritative look. No one could pull anything over on him. It was as if he had *eyes in the back of his head,* and some students were starting to believe that it was a possibility. He was kind and gentle, firm when he needed to be, and he commanded respect at all times — receiving it too. Even some of the parents were a bit intimidated by him. Although, it's possible that these were the same students that Mr. Petry caught with *those* eyes.

The opening ceremonies concluded when Mr. Petry shouted proudly, "God Bless America," with his rejoicing arms raised in the air. And with the crowd joining him in the cheer, the seventh and eighth grades band instructor struck up the band, and the parade down Main Street began.

Class representatives stood on their homemade floats, throwing out candy to the parade watchers, as the young children scurried in the streets, making sure they got each and every piece thrown out. They smiled in delight from their newfound treasures, while their parents tried to keep them from getting run over by the other oncoming floats.

World War Two veterans, town officials, Winter's Crest Finest, and The Hook and Ladder Company honored Main Street, while parade watchers lifted their hands in salute. The fire engines rolled down the lane sounding their horns, and the police cars sounded their sirens, making some children squeal with excitement, and leaving others crying in fear.

The cheerleaders, also called *The Rah-Rah's,* walked together chanting cheers, and the football and soccer teams walked behind them, drawing prolonged applause and cheering. Behind them, the Mackey High School Band, dressed in their parade best, played *It's A Grand Old Flag,* and continued on down Main Street, following with *God Bless America,* and then *The Star Spangled Banner.*

As the musicians passed, several older ladies swung the arms of younger kids in an impromptu dance on the sidewalk, while others belted out the well-known tunes. More reserved people watched the display with varying degrees of indignation, but with secret wishes of joining in. Aging First War veterans stood stiffly at attention as the songs played, some wearing their faded uniforms, others with service ribbons dangling from their lapels. Street vendors plied the enthusiastic crowd, hawking popcorn, colas and candied apples.

Pretty Irene Tibbets and Warren Compton, the Homecoming King and Queen, rolled regally behind the band, sitting in the jump seats of a shiny blue Cadillac convertible limousine. Dressed in a crinoline gown and formal tux, the popular couple played the crowd to the hilt. Behind them in the rear seat, the Parade Marshall, Captain James Allen Frost, in the full regalia of his Captain's dress uniform, created a rolling wave of cheers and applause as they passed each section of the crowd. Kaitlyn, standing with Ray, his parents, Kathryn, Alex, Allison and John beamed with pride as the limo passed by.

Allison leaned in to Kaitlyn while clapping wildly. She nudged her chin towards the car. "I thought I told Irene *not* to do her hair in a bouffant. Look how she has to keep fussing with it in the wind."

Kaitlyn nodded vaguely, shining eyes for her father alone.

Known to all but a few, Kaitlyn had been overwhelmingly regarded as the obvious choice for Queen. Much to everyone's surprise, she'd taken herself out of the running in a gracious nod to Irene.

When the last float drove by, a final wave of cheering erupted before the throng headed towards the field to watch Winter's Crest challenge their perpetual Lake George rivals to a football game.

After the parade, the Frosts, Niles, along with Allison and John, went to watch the game. After seeing the plays shift back and forth for a while, Kaitlyn and Ray excused themselves, leaving for a more private location under a tree that was out of view from the others.

Kaitlyn sat down against Ray. Ray wrapped his arms around Kaitlyn and leaned his head over her shoulders, and whispered, "I've missed you," as he kissed her neck.

Kaitlyn shuddered delightfully and looked back at him. "I've missed you too." They kissed.

Kaitlyn turned around, and he placed his hands gently on her cheeks, bringing his lips close to hers. Kaitlyn closed her eyes, and they engaged in a powerful kiss of passion, leaving both of them wanting more, but both knowing it was not the time, nor the place.

"I'm dying inside, Ray," Kaitlyn confessed. "I can't seem to get close enough to you. I want to hold you, kiss you and be with you every second of every day."

"I love you," Ray replied. "Every little thing reminds me of you. I think about you night and day, too." He squeezed her tight and smiled.

Kaitlyn and Ray sat under the tree holding each other without the need to speak, for they had everything they needed — each other.

While Kaitlyn and Ray were resting in each other's arms, Allison and John spied them. Tiptoeing up behind the tree and at an unspoken count of three, they jumped out, scaring the living daylights out of the lovers.

"What you lovebirds doin'?" John asked with a laugh.

"Ha ha, very funny, John," an irritated Kaitlyn replied.

"We're just teasing, Kaitlyn." John said. "So, you know my birthday's coming up? You guys meeting us after our dinner or what?" John asked.

"Sure, we'd love to, John," Ray answered.

"Next weekend, October first," Kaitlyn said. "That's next Saturday."

"Bingo," John replied. "You're bright today, Kaitlyn."

"Keep that attitude and you can forget it, John," Kaitlyn responded annoyed.

"You know I love you," John said sincerely.

"You love me?" Kaitlyn asked bewildered.

"Yeah, in that brotherly, fatherly, kind of way," John replied.

"Well, that's good," Kaitlyn laughed. "Can't have you falling all over me now."

"We'd better get back to the game before people start talking about us," Allison reminded them, feeling unsettled with John's *I love you* to Kaitlyn.

The four returned to the stands just as the last touchdown was scored. Winter's Crest prevailed over Lake George with a score of thirty-four to six, and cheers echoed through the stands.

The band members sprang to their feet playing for the victory, and the rustle of people packing their things and stepping down the bleachers resonated with those cheers. Young toddlers were oblivious to the commotion, with their heads buried in their mothers' necks asleep for the night, while the football team was excited and jumping as well as tackling each other with enthusiasm. The Rah Rahs jumped, did splits and did cartwheels while screaming their high-pitched squeals as people politely tried to make it seem as if they were interested.

When the commotion of victory began to settle, people began filing out of the stadium, and John and Ray walked their girls home.

Kaitlyn and Ray held hands while strolling through the streets, passing under the green wrought iron park lamps. They watched the parents scurry to get their little ones home to bed, and watched the moon fall behind clouds, only to pop out again a few moments later. They'd pull each other towards one another, then extend their arms as if they were dancing in the streets, never letting go and loving every minute of their play.

They passed by a patch of trees on the way to Kaitlyn's, and Ray led her over to them. Bringing Kaitlyn in close and allowing his breath to fall on her, Ray showed Kaitlyn how much he loved her with a strong kiss. He brought her hand to his heart. "Do you feel it, Kait? That's how much I love you."

"Yes," as she brought his hand to hers. "And that's how much I love you."

Words were unnecessary for the remainder of the walk. All they had to do was to look at the other to know what they were thinking. They had become soul mates — two of a kind in love.

Chapter Six

* * *

Deciding to head inside for an afternoon nap, Kaitlyn cuddled up with her torn quilt on the couch, as she has done so many times before. This time though, Kaitlyn smiled while laying her head against the pillow, thinking about how much she had loved Ray. She enjoyed being able to be carefree with him and express her exact thoughts, without fear of ridicule. She missed it. Kaitlyn closed her eyes while remembering all the silly talks they used to have, and she even let out a slight giggle as one memorable conversation came to mind that had taken place on Saturday, October first, in the year 1950.

* * *

John was excited all week long in anticipation of his birthday, and he was even a bit bossy, as if he had earned some *right* to be that way. When the big day came, John walked with his head held higher, and his cockiness grew in stature as well.

He and Allison went through with their plans, enjoying a fancy dinner out before joining Kaitlyn and Ray at The Fountain.

Kaitlyn and Ray huddled in a private booth, conversing about everything under the sun. Views on life, world politics and social issues were at the top of their list, along with a few not so worldly discussions like how much they loved each other and how they felt being with one another, or being apart. Ray would become quiet every so often, bringing Kaitlyn to ask the ages-old question, "What you thinking about?"

Ray would appease her with his answer: "You," when in fact, his mind had traveled completely off subject, such as the happenings in Korea.

Kaitlyn didn't care much about worldly matters, figuring that when she needed to know the information she could find it out then. Kaitlyn did however enjoy discussing matters of the heart. She liked to know what made people tick and enjoyed sharing her views on some rather simple, or not so simple passages.

One phrase that intrigued Kaitlyn was: "To each door closed, a window is opened," with another being: "Everything happens for a reason." These selected sayings ordinarily got Kaitlyn going off on some long conversation, usually completely confusing the person she was speaking with. That night, Ray was her audience, and had been since the two began dating. Before that, Allison customarily was on the receiving end of Kaitlyn's tail-spinning views.

Kaitlyn was funny. She'd be talking to Allison about how she was going to do her hair or what she was going to wear, and the next second she would bring up a topic totally off base. It's one of the things Allison loved about Kaitlyn. It's also one of the things Ray loved about her.

During their conversation that night, they discussed some rather trivial matters, and then in the next breath, Kaitlyn changed the subject. Starting in with one question followed by another and never expecting to hear the answers to any of them, Kaitlyn brought Ray into *her* world.

Beginning a lengthy dialogue, Kaitlyn brought up those two quotes that bothered her so much. "Why does there have to be a reason for everything? Why can't things just be — for no reason at all? Why does a window need to be opened just because a door has been shut? Who said I wanted the door shut in the first place? And what if I didn't want a window to be opened when a door is shut?

What if I wanted the door to stay shut for a while? Or what if I wanted the door opened and the window opened too?"

Ray, trying not to laugh, looked at Kaitlyn in incredulity that so many questions could come pouring out of her at once, without her taking a breath in-between — or waiting for an answer. Not that Ray had the answers, but he would have at least liked to try. So, he sat, leaving Kaitlyn to believe he needed an explanation.

Kaitlyn began clarifying what she meant and how she had come to her conclusions, making it harder for Ray to understand where she was going with her views in the first place. Kaitlyn, picking up on Ray's confusion, tried to help him understand. More often than not, her attempts were unsuccessful.

Ray sat back in his seat, smirking as he sipped from his straw. He enjoyed this talk with Kaitlyn, even though he had only spoken a few words. Without knowing what to say, he just looked at her and said, "I love you."

Kaitlyn liked the stimulating conversation for the simple reason that she actually understood what she was talking about, even if no one else did. She also enjoyed the surprise element, taking people completely off track — one of her favorite things to do.

Ray was about to bring up his own take on the subject, when John and Allison arrived. Actually, John announced their arrival in a rather abrupt fashion.

"It's 8:02, let's get this place moving," John bellowed, slightly losing balance. "It's time to celebrate!"

Allison looked to Kaitlyn, almost begging for help, and Kaitlyn looked back, rolling her eyes in parental type disgust.

"What's that look for, Kaitlyn," John slurred obnoxiously.

"Nothing, John," Kaitlyn replied annoyed.

"Ahh, you missed me, Kaitlyn," John said, flopping his arms around her in a hug, and telling Kaitlyn how much he loved her.

Kaitlyn, feeling extremely uncomfortable, escaped John's arms just as he went to lay a kiss on her, while at the same time Ray approached John, protecting his girl. Kaitlyn scurried over to join Allison, who had retreated to the soda bar, while Ray stayed with John, trying to get him to calm down.

Allison broke out into a sob the second Kaitlyn placed her hand on Allison's shoulder, trying to console. Allison looked up to Kaitlyn as tears fell from her eyes. "This isn't the first time, Kaitlyn. I'm really getting sick of it."

Kaitlyn, disgusted with what she was hearing, took control. "You stay here, I'll be right back."

"So, John," Kaitlyn started. "I see you decided to have a few drinks tonight."

"Yup," John said with his head held high, standing in a military position.

"You're proud of your behavior?" she asked.

"Most certainly am, my love," John sarcastically replied.

"Well, John. I'm not," Kaitlyn said. "Remember what I said?"

"Yes, *Mother*," he said as if he were a little boy being scolded for touching the cookies. He then let out an annoying laugh.

At that point, Kaitlyn was completely repulsed and beside herself with anger and frustration. Ray, noticing Kaitlyn was ready to burst, took over, asking her to go tend to Allison, while he handled the *John* situation.

Kaitlyn and Allison stayed at the counter for a while, letting things simmer down. Meanwhile, Ray got some food into John and tried to keep him occupied talking about their joining the Army.

Allison regained her composure, and the red blotches and swollen eyes began to fade. Unfortunately, John left behind an open wound in her heart, stinging with resentment.

After some time went by, John settled down enough that Allison and Kaitlyn could rejoin them, and the girls hesitantly rose from their seats. Allison started to walk back to John and Ray, while Kaitlyn walked beside her as *the bodyguard*, with her eyes and ears alert to all potential hazards.

As they returned to the boys, John looked over to Kaitlyn and apologized while glancing over to Ray asking forgiveness from him too. Allison put her head down in humiliation, wondering why she was going back to him in the first place. John, surprisingly taking notice of his insensitivity, looked at Allison with sincerity and puppy dog eyes as he begged for her mercy.

Allison, flooded with inner turmoil, stared at him as if she could see right through his skin. John *fell* off the seat and landed on the floor. "I'm dying. You've killed me," before he got to his knees, pleading with the palm of his hands together. "Please, Allison, forgive me. I love you. I beg of you," he spoke as he leaned towards her feet to kiss them. "I can't live without you."

Allison chuckled out of embarrassment *for him,* and although still angry, she said, "Get up, John. You're making a spectacle of yourself," and only said, "I forgive you," to get him to calm down.

The four sat in the booth trying to make the best of a ruined evening, chatting about non-confrontational subjects and trying to keep the peace. They stayed as long as they could to make sure John was under control before calling it a night.

The owner of The Fountain called for the last dance, and they joined some of the other patrons on the dance floor for the occasion.

Kaitlyn and Ray embraced in their usual loving way, whispering sweet nothings into each other's ears, while they playfully kissed one another and kept an eye on John out of the corners of their eyes. Allison swayed in John's arms, looking extremely uncomfortable in her position, with the distant look in her eyes confirming it.

The song ended, and John went to kiss Allison, only to find his lips fall on Allison's cheeks. He matter-of-factly offered to take her home, and she refused, saying she felt like being alone. So, John left, saying goodbye to everyone at The Fountain as if he were some celebrity deserving their attentions. He had no idea he had contaminated his relationship with Allison.

Ray and Kaitlyn offered to walk Allison home as well, and although she appreciated their offer, she really *did* want to be left alone to figure out her feelings. Kaitlyn hugged Allison goodbye, telling her to call if she needed to talk. Ray placed his hands on Allison's shoulders and asked, "Are you sure you're okay?"

Allison smiled. "Yes, I'm okay. Thanks, Ray," and she left The Fountain with her head hung even lower than when she had arrived.

Ray took Kaitlyn home, and he began to discuss John a bit, with Kaitlyn getting perturbed at the mere mention of his name. Deciding he should change the subject, he asked what her plans were for the week.

Kaitlyn had forgotten to mention to Ray that she had accepted a babysitting job down the street from her for the week, and that she would be tied up with that most the time.

"Do you have to sit Thursday night?" Ray asked.

"Yes, why?" Kaitlyn questioned.

"Oh," Ray said with disappointment in his tone. "I was hoping you could come to my grandparents' fortieth wedding anniversary party with me."

"Ray," Kaitlyn said, also displeased, "I wish I had known. I would have loved to go. I'm sorry."

"That's okay," he said. "I forgot about it until last night. Another time though, I'd love for them to meet you."

"I'd like that," Kaitlyn said as they pulled into her drive.

Ray made sure he was out of the light as he leaned into kiss and hug Kaitlyn goodnight, before getting out of the car to open the door and present his hand in a gentleman-like fashion.

Walking Kaitlyn to the front door, Ray winked and then whispered, "I love you," as she opened the door and walked in. Before closing the door behind her, Kaitlyn peeped her head out and mouthed back, "I love you too," with a big smile on her face. "Goodnight."

*   *   *

Kaitlyn began stirring in her sleep, recalling through a haze the days following John's birthday. Having trouble making out a clear picture in her head, Kaitlyn heard Ray clearly say to her, "I'll see you on Friday."

Still in a light sleep, she tried to figure out if what she was hearing was real or imagined. Her breathing became heavy, her pulse pounded, and she tossed and turned. Then Kaitlyn suddenly sat up in bed with her eyes wide open, sweat soaking her clothes and her hands gripping at her chest. Feeling dizzy and wanting to push her stomach out of her throat, Kaitlyn tried to catch her breath, realizing she had just lived through the entire nightmare once again.

As she lay there, vivid memories came flooding back, with thoughts unable to keep up with the torrent. Shocked that the feelings she'd had fifty years ago were just as strong today, Kaitlyn realized what she had to do.

Taking some calming deep breaths and trying to lull herself back to sleep, she realized that her recollections were far too intense to allow it. Sitting up, she twisted to work out the kinks, rose from bed, changed into dry clothes, and went down to the kitchen to put the kettle on the stove.

Slumping at the table, she reached for her pocketbook to pull out the letter as her mind and heart went into full battle mode — unsure which side would prevail.

Saved by the whistle, Kaitlyn poured herself some tea, only to sit back down again and toy with the idea of opening the envelope. She teased herself, fanning the letter over the hot steam rising from her cup, while questioning herself about reopening *that* door, even though she had already opened it a crack by calling up the old memories.

Deciding that enough was enough, Kaitlyn's pulse quickened as she began unsealing the envelope, fumbling to grasp it with trembling hands. Anticipation, anxiety and dread battled it out, leaving her in a relentless cold sweat.

*   *   *

Thursday after school, Ray walked Kaitlyn home in an effort to spend a little extra time with her. With the babysitting job all week and Ray's plans to celebrate at his grandparent's that night, there was little time for the two to be together.

There wasn't anything out of the ordinary about their walk. They held hands, talked and swung each other's arms, bumping their hips together when their arms flowed inward. They were just happy to be together, as being apart had begun to drain them.

They reached the front steps of Kaitlyn's house, and Ray kissed Kaitlyn goodbye, telling her he'd call when he got back. Kaitlyn smiled and went inside looking forward to his call later that evening, while Ray, feeling revived, turned with a click of his heels and headed for home.

Later that evening, when eight o'clock arrived, Kaitlyn's babysitting job ended and she returned home a short time after. Walking in the door, she grabbed her homework, sat down and completed any assignments she had left to do, while her parents read in the library and Alex tended his studies. Thirty or so minutes later the phone rang, and Kaitlyn jumped off her seat and raced to kitchen phone, knowing Ray would be on the other end.

"Hello," Kaitlyn answered brightly.

"Kaitlyn," the voice said flatly.

"Oh, hi, John," Kaitlyn said disappointed.

"I have some bad news," John said. "I need you to listen carefully." He paused. "Ray's been in a car accident."

"*What?*" Kaitlyn said in disbelief. "No, that can't be," "He's at his grandparents' house. This is one of your sick jokes, and I don't think it's very funny."

"Kaitlyn," John said in a tone she'd never heard from him. "He and his parents were in an accident tonight."

Kaitlyn was speechless. John's voice belied any such joke. She felt her heart pound through her chest and brought her hand to her mouth. "No!" she screamed, falling to the floor. "Mom!" Kaitlyn cried out in overwhelmed anguish.

John, with the phone to his ear, stood quietly by letting the news sink in. "Kaitlyn?" he spoke as if she were still there. But it was Kathryn on the other end asking who it was.

John told Kaitlyn's mother what he had told her daughter, what hospital they had been taken to, and a few other details of the accident.

"Thank you, John," Kathryn said, hanging up the phone in a daze.

Just as Kathryn put her hand on Kaitlyn's shoulder, Kaitlyn shrugged it away, crying, "No, this isn't real! This isn't happening!"

Kathryn let Kaitlyn gather herself for a moment.

"Okay, calm down," Kaitlyn said to herself. "I've got to get to Ray!"

"Kaitlyn," Kathryn said, bringing her hands to her daughter's cheeks. "I'll take you. You're not driving anywhere by yourself this upset."

Kaitlyn nodded silently, while her father and Alex, having come to investigate the commotion, agreed.

Kaitlyn sat in the passenger seat; her feet tapping furiously in place, feeling as though it were taking forever to get to Crestview Memorial. She kept craning her neck to check the speedometer, seeing if her mother was driving the speed limit and hoping she was over it.

Kathryn gave Kaitlyn some words of advice, having experienced this with her own grandmother when she was ten. Kaitlyn, not able to take in any more information, only half-listened

There were two hospitals in town. One was Winter's Crest Community Hospital and the other was Crestview. Crestview was the hospital used for serious emergencies and was located near the park, while Community was essentially just a 'fix and patch' station on the outskirts of town.

Arriving at Crestview, Kaitlyn and her mother exited the car as Kaitlyn froze in mid-step. "I can't," she said. "I can't do this. I'm scared."

"Yes you can, Kaitlyn," Kathryn said forcefully. "You *have* to do this."

Getting her senses back, Kaitlyn resumed the frantic race to the doors, trailed closely by Kathryn. All sorts of horrible visions were conjured in her head. She saw Ray dead, lying on a gurney with a white sheet over his head. His face was mangled — his body bandaged from head to toe. Having no experience with these kinds of situations, anything was possible, making her more fearful as she stopped short and hesitantly walked in.

Entering the main doors, the astringent, institutional smell of the hospital assaulted their senses, reinforcing Kaitlyn's ennui, and they quickened their pace to the white information desk. Trying to keep their composure, they approached the smiling, gray-haired woman, whose nametag read: 'Dolores'.

As soon as Kathryn mentioned the Niles family, the woman pointed towards a stairwell to the left of her. "Up one flight and then ask at the nursing station," Dolores said, her cheerful face now somber.

Kaitlyn and Kathryn knew something was terribly wrong and hurried towards the stairs. Taking the steps two at a time, Kaitlyn and her mother felt the cool breeze meet them. Dampness seemed to penetrate their bones, bringing additional shivers to their trembling insides.

Opening the heavy fire doors, they were met by bright lights and a scurry of uniformed nurses. Wheelchair bound patients sat off in the dull white hallways, while wails echoed from the rooms behind other walls.

Zeroing in on the blue nurses' station, Kaitlyn and Kathryn waited only a few seconds with their hands resting upon the counter, tapping fingers. A sandy-blonde nurse named Alice looked up. Kathryn explained who they were and who they were looking for.

An expression came over Alice's face that didn't hide a thing. It was a look Kaitlyn had never seen before, yet knew she didn't like. Kathryn asked Alice for a private word.

The two headed to the end of the desk area, and Mrs. Frost investigated what was going on. "Ray Niles," Kathryn queried, "is he okay?"

. "Yes," Alice said happily. "He's in room 211," Alice explained, pointing down the hall in Ray's direction.

Kaitlyn, overhearing their whispers, took a deep breath. Relieved and feeling calmer, Kaitlyn headed to his room. "You coming, Mom?" Kaitlyn asked.

"I'll be down later," Kathryn replied. "I'm going to check on Jaycee and Nick."

"Okay," Kaitlyn said as she started down the hall.

Kaitlyn didn't know anything about Ray's condition. She didn't know how or why it happened. All she knew was that her Ray was hurt, and she was scared with what she was about to see — not to mention Kaitlyn didn't know how she would react seeing him the way she imagined him to be.

Each step Kaitlyn took on the cracked linoleum grew louder as her pulse raced faster. The fear seemed to age her twenty years as her eyes caught '211' engraved on the door in front of her. "God give me strength," she prayed, bringing her hand to the knob and taking a few more deep breaths. She turned the knob and stepped into Ray's room.

A pungent, antiseptic smell overtook her on entering. She peered in the dim lighted room to see Ray lying on the hospital bed, facing the other direction. Raising her hand to her mouth, she took a few more quiet steps towards him. Not wanting to scare Ray, Kaitlyn carefully maneuvered her way to the other side of the bed before softly saying, "Hi."

With all her might, she hid her reaction from seeing the agony in his eyes as he struggled to greet her. The white sheet draped over his body matched the paleness of his skin while highlighting the purple and red bruises. His swollen cheeks partially obscured his blackened eyes, while the hard black stitches resembled centipedes crawling in several places.

Kaitlyn pulled a small wooden chair near Ray's bedside and took a hold of his hand. She spoke quietly, telling Ray she loved him and that she would be there for him every step of the way.

Ray tried to respond, finding it painful. He blinked to let her know he had heard.

"I'm going to stay with you until they kick me out," Kaitlyn said. "Close your eyes and rest, Ray. I'll be right here."

Ray fell back asleep, which seemed like it was only for a few minutes, when he suddenly woke in fright. His eyes moved from side to side in fear, his face clenched. Awakening to Kaitlyn whispering his name, Ray calmed. Kaitlyn held his hands, trying to comfort him, but not knowing how.

Kathryn came into the room with a solemn look on her face. "Hi, honey," she whispered. "How's he doing?"

"He's in a lot of pain," Kaitlyn said ready to burst into tears. "It's so hard to see him this way."

Kathryn went to her daughter and tried to console. "It's hard to see someone you love in pain," she whispered. "It's even worse when you can't fix it."

"I hurt for him, Mom," Kaitlyn confided.

"I know you do," Kathryn validated.

"Mom," Kaitlyn called her attention. "How are Mr. and Mrs. Niles?"

"Kaitlyn … we should be going," Kathryn hedged.

Just as Kathryn was about to tell Kaitlyn that visiting hours were well over, Alice came in the room. Telling them it was time to leave, Alice went to check Ray's intravenous fluids and add more Codeine to his I.V. drip.

Kaitlyn carefully leaned into Ray, trying to figure out how she could hug him, realizing it wasn't possible. She gently kissed his cheek, being careful not to upset his position and told Ray she'd be back tomorrow.

Ray opened his eyes just as Kaitlyn lifted her head. "I love you, too," he mouthed, squeezing her hand weakly.

Kaitlyn held his hand a moment longer, before being eyed by Alice. "I have to go, babes. They're kicking me out." She let her hand slip away from his.

Kaitlyn and her mother left Ray's room, making their way out to the parking lot. Kaitlyn mentioned that she wanted to stay with Ray tomorrow, saying he needed her, and he was more important then going to school.

"I don't know, Kaitlyn," Kathryn said. "You can visit him after school and stay until closing, but missing school is something I have to discuss with your father."

The two walked to the car in silence, letting what they just saw and heard sink in. Kathryn started the engine, but instead of backing out, she stared sightlessly straight ahead. After a moment, Kathryn covered her face with her hands and bowed her head on the steering wheel.

"What is it, Mom?" Kaitlyn asked with worry in her voice. "Is it … Mr. and Mrs. Niles?"

Kathryn could only look at her with tears. Choked with emotion, Kathryn was unable to make audible sounds, her voice coming across as broken syllables.

Kaitlyn began crying, fearing the worst. "Mom, you *have* to tell me. Are they okay?"

Kaitlyn listened to her mother as the story came tumbling out.

"Oh my God!" Kaitlyn cried out in total disbelief. Does Ray know?" her wailing question beckoned.

"They're telling him tomorrow, Kaitlyn," Kathryn warned. "It's best you don't go to the hospital during the day tomorrow. It's best that you let him handle the news by himself and then be there for him after."

"But, Mom, I want to be there for him NOW! I can't leave him all alone for this!"

"Kaitlyn, you're going to have to trust me. Please. I'm doing this to protect you *and* Ray too. Trust me on this. I know what I'm doing."

Kaitlyn couldn't reply. Somehow, she knew her mother might be right, but it didn't make her feel any better. She wanted to be there every second for Ray.

"I'm sorry," her mother was saying. "But I have my reasons. You may not understand them now, but someday you will. You can go tomorrow after school, and then on Saturday you can spend the day. Okay?"

"Okay," Kaitlyn agreed meekly, trying to understand.

Mother and daughter arrived home to Alex and Jim running out the front door to hear what happened. Jim saw that the two of them had been crying, and he immediately put his arms around his wife in comfort. He held his hand to Kaitlyn's chin and asked if she was okay.

"I'm okay," Kaitlyn replied. "I have to go upstairs."

Kaitlyn escaped to her room, still smelling the hospital's scent trapped within her clothing. Changing, she looked at herself in the mirror, seeing a scared stranger peering back. "I can get through this," she said, trying to convince herself. "I have to help Ray get through this. I must be strong for him."

Emotionally and physically exhausted, Kaitlyn curled up in her quilt and into the safety of her bed. Behind the protective walls of her room, she recited Reinhold Niebuhr's *'Serenity Prayer'* as her head rested on the pillow.

"'God grant me the serenity to accept the things I cannot change, the courage to change the things I can, and the wisdom to know the difference.'"

Chapter Seven

Kaitlyn woke Friday with bags under her eyes and filled with worry. All she wanted to do was to get to Ray. She didn't care about anything else. She flung the pillow over her head and hid beneath it, not wanting to face the day and knowing she had no choice. Kaitlyn forced herself to get out of bed. Showering and then throwing on a crumpled poodle skirt with an old sweater that didn't exactly match, Kaitlyn went downstairs for tea looking positively dreadful.

The daybreak brought with it an eerie silence as everyone immersed themselves in their own thoughts. Still trying to grasp that the events were factual and not illusory, few words exchanged in the kitchen as they all went through their morning rituals.

Discontented, Kaitlyn sipped her tea with her feet feeling her restlessness as they tapped the floor. Her legs trembled with turbulence. Picking at the scrambled eggs with a fork and moving them around, few bites were taken before Kaitlyn excused herself to brush her teeth. Tossing her hair back in a ponytail, she left for school.

Walking alone, feeling as if she were somehow separated from the outside world, Kaitlyn tried to get herself into the mindset of school. She focused in on making it through the day as she approached the grounds. Allison and John were waiting for her at the front steps, along with a slew of other kids expecting to hear word of Ray.

She was met with questions that were far too intense for her to answer, making her breakdown in a runaway cry. "I can't do this right now, please," Kaitlyn begged her friends. "Please, I just can't … " as her voice withered, gaining distance from the countless questions.

Kaitlyn walked through the halls of school, mindful not to make eye contact with anyone or draw attention, afraid doing so would bring on more questions. Staying to herself all day and doing what she had to do, Kaitlyn held vigil with the classroom clocks, watching the seconds pass by — feeling as if each second were a minute, and each minute was an hour.

All of the students seemed immature to her as Kaitlyn began to see everything that was so important to her yesterday was of absolutely no significance to her today. Observing the girls giggling in the hallways or crying over a broken nail made Kaitlyn suddenly understand that there was more to life than bobby socks and poodle skirts. She couldn't help but think how childish they were being. These thoughts continued throughout the day, while the constant unintended torment of queries came at her, until she had had enough.

It was her last class, and all it took was one well-meaning kid to say one thing about Ray's accident, and Kaitlyn blew up. She completely lost it, lecturing the entire class in a powerful tone focusing on one particular girl.

"Why do you want to know?" Kaitlyn asked, not waiting for an answer. "You want to know because you care or because it's the *hot* rumor everyone's talking about? My boyfriend's in the hospital right now fighting for his life," she said over-dramatizing, "and the response at school is *not* whether he's okay, but who knows the most information. Do you have any idea how angry that makes me?" Kaitlyn screamed, flailing her arms in the air. "I've had it!"

Kaitlyn's teacher and all the students around her came to a sudden hush, aghast with Kaitlyn's outburst. Noticing the time was 2:59, the class stared at the clock fumbling with their hands, keeping an eye on the long hand as the short hand clicked towards the top of the hour. It was the longest minute of everyone's day.

The clock finally struck three, signaling the bell to ring, just as the teacher said, "Class dismissed," thankful to have ended the day.

As Kaitlyn tried to get out the door, her teacher, Mrs. Dolan, called her back.

Mrs. Dolan was a kind woman in her late forties, with graying brown hair and hazel-brown eyes. She was one of the many well-liked teachers, popular with the kids as well as the faculty.

"Are you okay, Kaitlyn," Mrs. Dolan asked with concern, putting her arm around Kaitlyn's shoulders.

Kaitlyn was going to give her a standard response of: "Yes, I'm fine," but decided to actually be honest with her answer. "No," she said. "I'm not."

Mrs. Dolan was surprised with Kaitlyn's candid reply, having expected the *normal* response. She encouraged Kaitlyn to continue.

"My boyfriend and his family were in a car accident last night," Kaitlyn explained. "He's in a lot of pain and his parents ... Anyway, all of a sudden, everything seems so trivial to me. Things I worried about yesterday have taken on a whole new meaning and basically are of no importance. So when all these kids come running over to me asking about Ray as if he's the latest rumor, it gets a little unnerving. Then as I've gone through this rotten day, all I've seen and heard is frivolous stuff the kids worry about, and well, it's getting on my nerves."

Mrs. Dolan gave Kaitlyn a hug and smiled. "Kaitlyn," she said, then paused, "welcome to adulthood."

"If this is adulthood," Kaitlyn replied," then I don't want it."

"It'll be okay," Mrs. Dolan comforted. "You'll be okay, too. I can tell."

"Thanks," Kaitlyn said. "Sorry I lost control in your class."

"Understandable," Mrs. Dolan replied. "Get going. I don't want to keep you."

Kaitlyn hugged her favorite teacher and left the classroom briskly, stopping quickly at her locker before high-tailing it out of school. She was thankful the hospital was close by, only running two blocks to get there.

She didn't take notice of the small street shops decorated with fall celebration, nor did she notice the hardy mums blooming in the town planters lining Main Street. Her focus was on getting to Ray as fast as she was able.

Arriving at Crestview, she ran past the information desk, through the stairwell doors and took steps in twos, arriving on the second floor.

She said hello to Alice between her labored breaths and asked how Ray was doing. She told her he was in a lot of pain, but that he was improving. "We have him on some medicine, so he may be a bit groggy, possibly even incoherent."

Kaitlyn nodded with understanding and prepared herself to deal with it. "Alice," Kaitlyn called her attention nervously. "Does he know?"

"Yes," she answered. "He was told this morning."

"And?" Kaitlyn asked, wanting more information. "How's he handling it?"

"Not good, Kaitlyn," Alice replied. "One of the medicines we had to give him was Valium, to calm him down."

"Oh," Kaitlyn replied, thinking that wasn't good news.

"Thanks," Kaitlyn said as she turned to go to Ray.

Pausing at the entrance, Kaitlyn closed her eyes and gave herself a pep talk. While trying to force her hand to turn the knob, simultaneously swallowing her anxious heart back down, Kaitlyn opened the door and took a careful step in. Approaching Ray's bedside, Kaitlyn felt as if she were intruding, realizing her mother *was* right.

"Hi," Kaitlyn greeted Ray, ill at ease.

"Hi," Ray muttered in a distant tone, not focusing in on anything.

Kaitlyn was unsure what to make of the situation, and feeling as if maybe she shouldn't be there, asked Ray if he wanted her to stay. Ray nodded as he scrunched his face in pain from doing so.

Kaitlyn sat down beside Ray and held his hand in silence. Except for their breathing, nothing else could be heard. Kaitlyn found her main purpose that afternoon was just to stay with Ray. He needed the comfort of a friendly recognizable face.

Kaitlyn obliged, staying with Ray until visiting hours ended. Then, tearfully she had to say those few words she dreaded. "I have to leave now," she said in a whisper, hoping that maybe if she didn't say them too loud, it wouldn't have to be true.

Ray's eyes met Kaitlyn's, and no words were necessary to convey his thoughts. "Don't go. I beg of you," cried out from his tearful eyes, pleading as if he were on his knees.

Kaitlyn's heartstrings pulled in a tug of war between what she had to do and what she wanted to do. Hating to tell Ray she had to leave, she grasped his hands tightly and assured him she'd be back tomorrow. "I'll be here first thing in the morning and stay all day," Kaitlyn assured. She kissed him, gave him a light hug and whispered, "I love you."

Ray hung onto Kaitlyn, using all his strength to try and keep her from leaving. Kaitlyn had to remove his hands from hers as if he were a two-year old child hanging onto his mother's pant leg as she tried to get out the door. Taking both his hands, Kaitlyn confirmed her plans with him, nodding as she opened her eyes a bit wider, making sure Ray understood she'd be back. "Goodnight, babes," she said. "I'll see you bright and early tomorrow." Kaitlyn walked out of the room, looking back once to say, "I love you."

Stepping out into the hall, Kaitlyn collapsed against the wall to the side of the door, inching her way to the floor in a squat, overcome with emotion in an uncontrollable sob. Alice came and knelt down next to Kaitlyn and embraced her with consoling arms. "Let it all out," Alice said as she rubbed her back. "Let it all out," she said in a whisper.

Once Kaitlyn felt in control of her emotions, she stood, and Alice gave her some tissues. Kaitlyn gave her a thankful hug before she left for home.

Arriving at the front steps, Kaitlyn was met by John.
"How's Ray doing?" he asked.

"Not too well, John," Kaitlyn replied, not in the mood to be talking with anyone — _especially_ John.

"You doing okay?" John asked.

"I'm doing the best I can," Kaitlyn replied expressionless.

"What happened to Ray?" John asked, not sure what injuries he had.

"Well," Kaitlyn began to reply, gathering her thoughts. "He's got bruises — almost everywhere, and he's still hooked up to an I.V., but he's starting to get better. He does have a problem with his knee, something having to do with ligaments or tendons. I don't know, something like that."

"Oh," John muttered. "Does he know about his parents?"

"Yes," Kaitlyn replied lowering her eyes. "They told him today, but he and I didn't discuss it."

"I'm sorry, Kaitlyn," John said. "I'm going to get going. Thanks for your time," he said as he began walking away.

Kaitlyn entered her home on a mission. She wanted to find a particular book she thought would be good to take to the hospital tomorrow. "Hi, Mom. Hi, Dad. Do you know where that red book of phrases is?"

"Yes, Kaitlyn," Jim replied. "It's in the Library by the Charles Dickens collection.

"What's it doing _there_?" Kaitlyn thought, not bothering to ask.

Jim was an avid reader. Against the far walls of the library, there were piles of numerously read novels lined up on the bookshelves.

The library was done in a tasteful manner, with a braided area rug on the hardwood floor in the center of the room. Colonial blue draperies hung from the cathedral windows offsetting the mahogany desk, sitting outward from the wall, with a matching liquor cabinet nearby. A large matching table they called the 'study table' sat against the opposite wall near the two leather high back chairs. It was used to organize Jim's papers, the kids' larger school projects, and Kathryn's PTA work.

All the books were alphabetized according to the author's first name. How this book ended up with Charles Dickens, no one will ever know. Looking for the 'C' category, Kaitlyn spotted the small red book tucked between Charles Dickens', "The Christmas Carol" and "Oliver Twist." Excited to find her special book, she blew the dust that had settled on top and read the cover: "Words To Live By." The author's name was scratched off and a few of the pages had been torn, but the main thing Kaitlyn wanted it for was still there: the words.

Kaitlyn brought the book upstairs and put it on the nightstand next to her diary, so she wouldn't forget to bring it with her in the morning. She went about her normal evening routine, having dinner and spending time with the family, before saying a prayer and going to bed, her thoughts continuous with Ray.

*   *   *

Kaitlyn took a sip of tea at the precise moment the phone rang. Hurrying to swallow, she wiped the few drops that had fallen to her chin as she answered the phone. With a quick hello, Kaitlyn heard Allison's voice.

"Hi," Kaitlyn said, happy to hear her best friend's voice. "Would you like to come over for awhile and visit?"

"Yes," Allison said, "that'd be great. I'll be over in an hour."

Thinking she must look frightful, Kaitlyn looked in the mirror by the phone and confirmed her belief. With only an hour to freshen up, she went upstairs to shower.

Stepping into the bathroom, which hadn't changed much since she was younger, except a fresh coat of paint and new plumbing, Kaitlyn began undressing in front of the mirror. Perking her breasts up to where they *should be*, she spoke out loud. "Not what I used to be," she laughed. "I've still got my eyes though, time can't take that away from me," she comforted herself.

Turning the spout to full blast, Kaitlyn showered, feeling refreshed from the warm water massaging her. Washing her body, she noticed that her once defined curves were now lowered, loosing their well-formed lines. Kaitlyn frowned briefly before shrugging her shoulders and thinking, "Oh well ..."

Although Kaitlyn missed her youthful appearance, she enjoyed having the wisdom of sixty-eight years behind her — taking knowledge and prudence over outward beauty anytime. Besides, Kaitlyn was beautiful inside and out, regardless of the wrinkles and gray hair. Inside her aged body remained the eighteen-year old girl, with just a lot more experience under her belt.

Kaitlyn dressed and applied some light foundation, trying to hide some of the wear and tear from the day. She went downstairs to put the kettle on and waited for her best friend in the world to arrive. Kaitlyn enjoyed Allison joining her for afternoon teas.

As Kaitlyn was taking a teacup out for Allison, she heard the doorbell chime. Kaitlyn opened the door saying, "You, silly, what are you doing ringing the bell? Just walk right in," as she gave Allison a hello hug.

Sitting down at the kitchen table, Kaitlyn, wearing a sneaking grin, poured the English Breakfast Tea. Allison, wondering what was up, questioned Kaitlyn about the grimace.

"I've got something to show you."

Allison anxiously asked, "What?"

Kaitlyn's eyes smiled and then with a look of uneasiness, she slowly pulled the letter from her purse and held it in front of Allison. Allison, in shock, brought her hands to her mouth.

Allison held it to see if the letter was for real. "Oh my, Kaitlyn," she said in disbelief. "After all these years ... "

"I know," Kaitlyn said, relieved she could share it with someone.

Allison studied the envelope. "You haven't opened it yet?"

Kaitlyn clenched her face and half smiled before she answered, "No."

"Why? Aren't you dying to?" she asked with a confused chuckle.

"I started to," Kaitlyn replied. "But then, I just couldn't bring myself to do it."

Kaitlyn held out her hand in gesture asking for the letter back. Placing it in her purse, she asked Allison if she'd like to hear about the visits she had with Ray at the hospital, after his accident.

97

Allison, being a bit sketchy with the details, perked her ears, ready to hear all.

Kaitlyn remembered everything as if it were yesterday, right down to the conversations and little things that took place. Excited to be able to talk with Allison, instead of recalling everything alone, Kaitlyn reminisced, beginning with the Saturday following the accident.

*   *   *

Kaitlyn left the house early Saturday morning and headed over to the hospital, walking as fast as she could to get there. She worried about Ray being alone for too long. Arriving and making her way upstairs, with a bright smile and cheerful walk, Kaitlyn went towards Ray's room.

"Kaitlyn, wait," Alice called out urgently, unable to catch Kaitlyn before she walked into the room.

Ray was sleeping when Kaitlyn touched his shoulder. "Ray?" Kaitlyn questioned, noticing a disconcerting aura.

"Who are you?" Ray asked incoherently.

"What?" Kaitlyn asked confused.

"Mom, is that *you*?" Ray asked.

"No, it's me, Kaitlyn," she replied, scared out of her mind. "You okay, Ray?"

Ray seemed disillusioned to Kaitlyn as if he didn't know where he was or *who* he was for that matter. "What happened?" he mumbled, Kaitlyn barely able to understand his words.

Kaitlyn choked up with tears. "You're in Crestview," she answered as a tear fell to her cheek. "You had a car accident Thursday night. You're going to be okay," she said, wearily.

"Oh," he replied.

Kaitlyn had to leave for a few moments and went into the hallway, puzzled as to why Ray was acting so strange. She couldn't believe what she was seeing and hearing, and took a few moments to try to figure out how to handle Ray's strange behavior.

Once she felt more prepared to deal with Ray's condition, she walked back to Ray's side.

"Hi," Ray said as if he had just seen her for the first time.

"Hi," Kaitlyn replied, dumbfounded.

"Were you just in here a few minutes ago?" Ray asked.

"Yes," Kaitlyn replied in wonder.

"I'm sorry. I think I was half asleep," Ray said, still a little woozy.

"Kaitlyn, my parents," Ray began. "Where are my parents? Why haven't they come to see me? Why do I feel like I'm in a nightmare?"

Ray's question stabbed Kaitlyn like she had just had a dozen dulled knives thrown at her. She didn't know what to do or what to say. She left the room, again assuring Ray she would be right back. This time, she wanted to find out what the heck was going on. She went down the hall to the nurse's station in tears.

"Alice," Kaitlyn called her attention. "Ray's asking about his parents. I thought he knew."

Alice took Kaitlyn aside and explained that they had to give Ray a sedative earlier.

"I tried to warn you. It should wear off soon though," Alice said. "He may or may not make sense when you speak with him. He's a little out of it right now. Just go in there and be with him. He needs you."

Kaitlyn contained her emotions and took a few relaxing breaths while re-approaching Ray's room. Taking one deep solemn breath, she placed her hand on the knob and slowly entered, avoiding any eye contact with Ray, fearing he would see the truth in her face. She went to the bedside and took a hold of his hand. Looking briefly at him, Kaitlyn saw tears well in his eyes, as tears had already been formed in hers. She lowered her head.

"Kait," he cried out softly, "my parents ... "

"Ray," Kaitlyn said, fighting back the tears, "Your dad's going to be okay. He's in the intensive care unit recovering from a heart attack. He had it during the accident — but he's going to be fine."

Ray began sobbing, compounded by tears of pain from his body. "Oh my God, Kaitlyn." He raised his hands gently and motioned that he needed a hug.

Kaitlyn sat on the side of the bed and carefully put her arms around Ray. He held onto her for dear life as the memory of the car accident came flooding back to his consciousness.

"We were driving home from my grandparent's house," Ray began. "Out of the blue, this car ... this car hit us. We spun around before coming to a halt. Oh my God! Help me." Ray took a moment.

"The doctor told me, but I didn't believe him. "Is it true?"

Kaitlyn lowered her eyes answering him.

"It is true." Ray accepted the truth, taking a moment to himself.

"The next thing I remember was hearing alarms and the roar of engines approaching us. I was locked in the car with twisted metal all around me. My dad ... my dad was being worked on in the street. They were pounding on his chest. I was scared and looked away, looking back to see him being carried to the ambulance. I didn't know he had a heart attack. I looked around for my mom when the firefighters were trying to free me. I caught a glimpse of her laid out on the pavement, just as they pulled a white sheet ... "

Ray couldn't continue. He held onto Kaitlyn with such intensity, his knuckles turning blue from his grasp. Kaitlyn and Ray held each other in a death grip, crying tears with such magnitude, too heart wrenching to describe. Pain was written all over his clenched face, trying to hold back from bursting into an emotional breakdown.

"Stay with me, Kait," he pleaded. "Please, hold me and stay with me."

"I'm not going anywhere," Kaitlyn replied through her broken tears. "I love you."

Ray and Kaitlyn stayed in their embrace for an hour, without speaking a single word. Tears flowed down their cheeks as Kaitlyn hugged Ray in comfort. His emotions now breaking down as he sobbed on her shoulder.

Alice came into the room a short while after to see how Ray was doing. She smiled with compassion as she placed Ray's breakfast tray on the bed-stand. Since Ray was eating okay, it was time to take the IV and catheter out. Alice asked Kaitlyn to excuse herself, while she helped Ray into a chair.

Kaitlyn hugged Ray and kissed him lightly on the cheek. "I'm going to go visit your father while Alice tends to you, okay?"

"Okay," Ray replied. "Please tell my dad I love him."

"I will," Kaitlyn said.

"Come back soon, please," Ray begged, for fear of being alone.

"I'll be back. I promise," she reassured.

Kaitlyn went to the nurse's station and inquired as to where Nick's room was. The nurse politely signaled the way to go. "He's in room 279, right down that hall and through those glass doors," she said.

"Thanks," Kaitlyn replied as she headed in the pointed direction, walking by a few wheelchair-bound patients out in the hall. She greeted them with a slight hello smile and continued to room 279. Finding the right room, she knocked on the door gently before hesitantly letting herself in.

"Mr. Niles," Kaitlyn said meekly. "It's me, Kaitlyn," introducing her presence.

Nick turned his face in her direction and smiled gently.

His room was dreary like Ray's, and Nick looked like he had aged thirty years. Looking gaunt, his face was struck with grief, overtaking his once semi-youthful appearance.

"How are you?" Kaitlyn asked timidly.

"I'm okay," Nick replied, both knowing well he wasn't.

"How's Ray doing?" Nick's whisper cried out in worry.

"He's hanging in there," Kaitlyn replied. "They're removing the IV and catheter right now. And they're helping him get into a chair. He told me to tell you he loves you.

Nick began crying, realizing his wife would never hear those words again — from anyone. Kaitlyn had never seen a grown man cry before and had no idea how to handle it. Feeling uncomfortable, but forcing herself, she hugged Nick. "I'm so sorry. Is there anything I can do for you?" Kaitlyn asked, hoping there would be.

"I'm okay," he said quietly. "I'm just worried about Ray. Can you help look out for him, take care of him for me? I'm going to be in here for awhile."

"Yes, of course, Mr. Niles," Kaitlyn replied. "I was planning to do so anyway. Has my mom come to visit you yet?"

"No, not today," he replied.

"She said she was going to come up after she took care of a couple things," Kaitlyn said. "I'm sure she'll be up soon, and the two of you can discuss arrangements."

"I'm going to go back with Ray and let you get your rest."

"Okay, honey," he said. "Give Ray a hug from his dad okay? Please tell him I love him," Nick reminded her.

"I will. I promise."

Kaitlyn returned to Ray's room, arriving to find Ray sitting in a chair, eating his breakfast. His right leg was bandaged with a brace, and he looked fifty percent better.

"How you feeling?" Kaitlyn asked.

"Okay," Ray replied. "It feels good to get out of that bed," he said, glaring in its direction as if he hated it.

"What actually happened to your leg?" Kaitlyn asked.

"I pulled some ligaments and tendons," Ray replied. "They're keeping the brace on for support. It doesn't hurt as much as it did, but I do have a numb area, and they can't figure out why."

"Could be worse, I guess," Kaitlyn said. "Your dad said, 'Hi'," she relayed to him. "He says to say, 'Hello and I love you'."

"How's he doing, Kait?" Ray asked. "Honestly, how is he?"

"Well," Kaitlyn paused, "he's doing okay."

"Kaitlyn ... " Ray reprimanded, letting Kaitlyn know he could handle the truth.

"He's pale and weak," Kaitlyn continued, "but he's coming along. He looks tired, sad and he's in a little pain. Mainly though, he's more concerned with you. My mom's coming up to talk with him today," Kaitlyn informed. "Your dad's going to be in here for awhile."

"I know," Ray replied, saddened.

"I think they're going to discuss you coming to stay with us while he recovers," Kaitlyn added.

"Oh, really?" Ray said with a grin on his face.

"Maybe," Kaitlyn said, sharing the same grin. "Guess you're starting to feel better. The medicine they gave you earlier has worn off now, hasn't it?"

"Yes," Ray replied. "I was having terrible nightmares, and they gave me a sedative earlier this morning so I could rest."

"Kait," Ray said as a frown came upon his face. "I miss my mom," beginning to cry. "I can't believe she's gone."

Kaitlyn put her arms around Ray and held him close while rubbing his back in a soothing manner. "I know you do," she said as she stroked her fingers through his hair in a loving, almost motherly way. Holding his head against her bosom, Kaitlyn rocked him gently as if she were comforting a young child.

Kathryn came in as Kaitlyn was consoling Ray. "Hello, Ray," she greeted him. "How are you doing, honey?"

Kaitlyn replied for Ray. "He's having a hard time, Mom."

Ray wiped the tears from his eyes, greeting Kathryn with a bow of the head and a clearing of his throat. "I'm okay, better than I was earlier," he said, beginning to pick at his breakfast again. "Feels good to get out of that bed," again sneering in its direction.

"I'm sure it does, Ray," Kathryn said, hesitating before saying something she wasn't sure how to say. "Ray, honey, I need to talk with you about a couple things. They're not going to be easy to review either, but we have to discuss them."

Ray nodded with understanding because he was expecting this talk.

Kaitlyn sat next to Ray and held his hand, while Kathryn said what needed to be said.

"The night of the accident, Mr. Frost made some phone calls. He was able to get a hold of your grandparents and let them know what happened. He also helped arrange for the funeral home to pick up your mother. Do you remember your grandparents coming to see you that night?" Kathryn asked.

"No," Ray replied. "No, I don't."

"They did," she said before continuing. "Mr. Frost has taken care of funeral services for your mother, and they will be Monday at four o'clock. We're going to try and get you discharged by then, so you can attend the service."

"I want to be there," Ray begged. "I *have* to be there."

"I know," Kathryn replied. "There's something else I need to tell you," she said pausing a moment. "Ray, your father will *not* be able to go. He's too weak, and he has to stay here for two, possibly three weeks."

"Oh, man," Ray replied, realizing the significance of what Kathryn had just said. "He can't go to Mom's funeral? That right there's going to kill him."

Ray became quiet. He was sad and taken back by her words, understanding why his dad couldn't go, but not believing it at the same time. He brought his hand to his mouth in a circular motion and bowed his head, trying to fight back the tears. He looked up to Kaitlyn with a tear rolling down his cheek. "Help me," cried out from his expression.

"Ray," Kathryn regained his attention. "I have to tell you one more thing, rather ask you something."

Ray looked up to Kathryn with questioning, glossy eyes.

"I just spoke to your father about you coming to stay with us while he recovers here," she explained. "Is that okay with you?"

"Yes, thank you very much," Ray replied appreciatively. "Are you sure? What about my grandparents?"

"Your grandparents aren't strong enough to take care for a young man. It'd be too much for them."

"Yeah, I guess you're right," Ray said understanding. "Are you sure it's not a bother?"

"We'd love to have you," Kathryn conveyed. "We have a guest room, and Kaitlyn and I will get it prepared for you. Mr. Frost will be there to help you shower, and Kaitlyn and I will be able to help you with your other needs."

"Okay," Ray said. "Thank you, I'd like that."

"Kaitlyn will stay with you the remainder of the day, and Mr. Frost and I will work on the arrangements," she ended, leaning over to give Ray a motherly kiss on the forehead. She gave Kaitlyn money for lunch, gave her a hug, and said, "Goodbye."

A few hours passed, and Alice came in with Ray's lunch. He enjoyed his meal of having turkey in spiced gravy, mashed potatoes, corn, and of course, gelatin.
Kaitlyn laughed. "What's a hospital meal without gelatin?"
Ray laughed, agreeing with her sarcasm.
"It's nice to see you smile, Ray."
"Kaitlyn," Ray questioned, "You okay with me staying at your house?"
"Yub yub," Kaitlyn replied in a silly voice. "Most indubitably."
"What's that language?" Ray asked laughing.
"It's my own secret language," Kaitlyn answered, giggling. "It's sort of a goofy, love language. Seriously, Ray, I'm thrilled you're coming to stay," Kaitlyn said, smiling ear to ear. "I want to nurse you back to health," as she let out a giggle that was laden with a hidden agenda.
Ray chuckled, reading into her words and facial expressions. "Hmmm, do you give sponge baths?"
Ray and Kaitlyn started to laugh, helping to break the tension, but also leaving Ray 'crying' in agony.
Although Jaycee's funeral was ever so present on both their minds, it was nice to escape reality — even if it were for a few seconds.
Kaitlyn excused herself to go buy a cafeteria lunch and then brought it upstairs with her to Ray's room. She chose the same food as Ray and enjoyed it just as much — even the gelatin.
After lunch, Kaitlyn took the trays out to the nurses' station and returned to Ray. She opened her pocketbook and took out the red book, showing it to Ray. She asked Ray if he wanted her to read it, and he nodded.
Kaitlyn, resting on her elbows, lay down on the side of the bed and began to read a few sorted passages. After each excerpt read,

they would have a slight discussion about it. Ray sometimes understood where Kaitlyn was going with her thoughts and other times, he would appease her. During those times, he'd just smile and chuckle softly.

She came across one passage that read: *"If one goes through life with anger and pain, than one has not lived. When one goes through life with forgiveness and peace, then one has led a full life."*

"Now, that's interesting," Kaitlyn relayed. "I like that one."

"Yeah, so do I," Ray harmonized. "It says a lot. It kind of puts everything wrapped together in two small sentences. I'll have to remember that one."

"Kaitlyn," Ray said. "I'm getting tired. Can you call Alice for me, so I can get back in bed?"

"Yes," Kaitlyn replied, already to her feet the minute he said, "I'm ..."

Kaitlyn went into the hall and found Alice. She followed Kaitlyn back to Ray's room.

"Ray, you're going to have to do this yourself if you want to get out of here," Alice stated with clear intentions, maneuvering Ray to the bed. "You will have crutches to use, to help you out with that knee, but you should only need them for a couple days, if that."

"Okay," Ray replied. "I understand. Thank you."

Ray laid his head on the pillow, and Kaitlyn leaned from the chair, resting her head on his bed. Ray's fingers caressed Kaitlyn's hair as they both drifted off to sleep, only to be awakened by the doctor an hour or so later.

Wiping the sleep from their eyes, they greeted him, letting out a slight yawn.

"How are you feeling, Ray?" the on-call doctor, Dr. Miller asked.

"I'm okay," Ray replied. "Do you think I can get out of here by Monday? I don't want to miss my mom's funeral."

"I understand," Dr. Miller replied. "Can you get out of bed by yourself?"

"Yes, I believe I can. Let me try it."

Ray slowly shifted his weight to the side of the bed, dragging his legs over. His brace was not restrictive, making it easier for him to maneuver his injured leg. Ray was careful not to moan, as he didn't want anything to interfere with him going 'home'. He placed both feet on the ground and with the use of his arms, slowly lifted himself to a standing position. He walked carefully to the chair with the aid of miscellaneous furniture, and then went back to the dreaded bed.

"Good," Dr. Miller said. "Real good. Do you feel secure enough to do that outside the hospital?"

"Yes, sir. I do."

"Well, you seem to be eating okay and your input and output levels are fine. Your rates are fine and everything's looking good," he relayed. "I think it's possible for you to leave Monday, but we'll have to wait and see, okay?

"Yes," Ray said with appreciation. "Thank you, sir. May I go and see my dad?"

"Yes," Dr. Miller replied. "Let me have Alice get your crutches and teach you how to use them."

"Okay, thank you," Ray replied.

"You're welcome, son," he said as he walked towards the door to leave. "Take care now."

Alice came into the room holding a pair of crutches. "You ready to give these a try?" she asked.

"Yub yub," Ray said laughing and looking at Kaitlyn, while Alice looked confused.

Shrugging it off, Alice helped Ray get situated, giving him a quick lesson. Ray stood up, and holding the crutches under his arms, he began to slowly move in the direction of the door. Once Ray was in the hallway, nothing could stop him. He was an 'old pro' in no time. Kaitlyn tried to stay up with him, but his strides were too long. They made it to Nick's room and entered.

"Hi, Dad," Ray said with delight, thrilled to see for himself that his father was truly alive.

Ray went over to Nick and sat down beside him while trying to figure out what to do with the crutches and configure where his hands were to go. "Oh, Dad, I'm so glad you're okay." They hugged.

"I'm glad you're okay, son," Nick said.

"I miss Mom," Ray began to sob.

"So do I," Nick said through his choked up voice.

Kaitlyn realized she had no business being there and decided to wait outside. She peeked through the small door window and could see Ray and Nick embraced in a strong tearful hug. She then backed away and waited for Ray to come out.

Ray's mood had changed from excitement of seeing his father to a solemn, tired one. He slowly walked with his crutches back to his room, with Kaitlyn following closely behind. Once he was situated in bed, Ray looked at Kaitlyn and sobbed insurmountable tears.

"Do you want me to stay or would you like some time to yourself?" Kaitlyn asked when Ray's tears began slowing.

"Stay and hold me for a bit, Kait," Ray cried. "I need you."

Kaitlyn stayed with Ray, and the two embraced. Words weren't needed as the unspoken silence spoke volumes. After an hour passed, Kaitlyn told Ray she was going to give him some time to rest, seeing that he had overdone it a bit.

"I love you, Ray," Kaitlyn said, with stronger conviction than she had ever said it before. "I'm here for you."

Kaitlyn left the room. Looking back once, she waved a slight bye and went home to help Kathryn prepare his room.

As Kaitlyn was leaving the hospital, she saw John approaching the entranceway and approached him.

"You going up to see Ray?" Kaitlyn asked.

"Yes," John replied. "How's he doing?

"He's doing okay," Kaitlyn replied. "He's resting right now, so don't stay too long."

"Oh, okay," John said. "I'll stop and say hello to his dad and stop by Ray's quickly."

"You've met his dad?" Kaitlyn asked, thinking he hadn't.

"Yeah," John replied. "I've met him a couple times. Remember the parade?

Kaitlyn recalled.

"Take care, Kaitlyn," John said as he turned back towards the hospital's entrance.

"You too, John," Kaitlyn replied, glad that John finally had the courage to visit.

John had detested hospitals since Kaitlyn had known him. She never knew the exact reason for this hate, only guessing it were more fear than anything else. Regardless, she was happy he was there.

Kaitlyn walked home and took notice of the change in seasons, this time noticing the blooming planters. The autumn foliage was in full bloom, and the mountains surrounding Winter's Crest were brilliant with colors. Kaitlyn loved the fall season. As she was walking home, she picked up a deep red maple leaf and held it in her hands, studying its beauty, admiring the power of nature and the miracles it creates. By the time she made it home, Kaitlyn had collected a bouquet of deep red, bright orange, and golden yellow leaves in the grasp of her hand. She placed the leaves in a wicker basket on the front porch before entering her home.

"Kaitlyn, is that you?" Kathryn asked. "Can you give me a hand?"

"Yes, Mom," Kaitlyn replied. "I'll be right there."

Kaitlyn went upstairs to help her mother tidy up the guest room. It had been a long time since anyone had used it, and it needed a thorough cleaning.

The room was decorated in a country pattern, with vintage green broadcloth curtains and an Amish style print bedspread that was simple, but nice. The hardwood floors accented the oak full-sized bed, and the braided Vermont green area rug added warmth to its ambiance. The room received the afternoon sun, which would make it that much more comforting for Ray when he came to stay.

Finishing up, Kaitlyn began to yawn excessively.

"Honey," her mother said, "why don't you go take a nap."

"Good idea, Mom. I think I'll do that."

The emotional strain of the day had caught up with Kaitlyn, leaving her physically exhausted too. Laying her head on the pillow, incapable of having any stimulating thoughts, Kaitlyn fell into a deep, much needed sleep.

Chapter Eight

Monday morning came with a fury. Thunder roared through the hills, and rain slammed against the windowpanes as whistles from the wind escaped through the tiny cracks in the window's seal. Kaitlyn threw her head back onto the pillow, tossing the blanket over her head and sarcastically thinking, "Great! A perfect start to an already rotten day."

She hesitantly dragged herself out of bed, showered, dressed and went downstairs to the kitchen.

"Do I really have to go to school, Mom?" Kaitlyn whined.

"Yes, Kaitlyn," Kathryn insisted. "You have to go, plus you need to pick up Ray's studies."

Kathryn looked at Kaitlyn with a mothering look of *don't give me any grief today* before saying, "I'm picking Ray up at noon. Before that, I'll be going to get Ray a suit. Do you have something to wear to the funeral?"

"Mom, I didn't even think about that," Kaitlyn replied worried. "I don't think I have anything."

"Okay, I'll pick you up a suitable dress," Kathryn replied.

As the storm subsided and moved easterly towards Lake George, Kaitlyn ate her breakfast. She then left for school, with Alex following a few seconds behind. Alex shouted while running to her. "Wait up!"

Alex approached Kaitlyn and put his arm around her. "You okay, sis?"

"Doing the best I can," Kaitlyn replied. "Thanks ... it's going to be a rough day."

"I'm here for you if you need me," Alex said maturely.

"Thanks, Alex," Kaitlyn replied, surprised at her brother's uncharacteristic generosity.

"I guess the old saying holds true, Kaitlyn," Alex said.

"What saying's that?" Kaitlyn asked, shocked that her brother could think of anything besides football.

"About making your last words to someone kind and loving," he replied. "So, you never have any regrets. Things can happen so fast and once the words are said, you can't take them back."

"You're right, Alex," Kaitlyn said, scrunching her face. "When did you get to be so smart?"

"I've been smart all along," he replied. "You've just been too busy mothering me to notice."

"I'm sorry, Alex," Kaitlyn said sincerely. "You don't need mothering now."

"No, I don't," Alex agreed wholeheartedly. "If you need me, though, I'm here for you."

"Thanks, Alex," Kaitlyn said pleasantly surprised. "I may take you up on that."

Kaitlyn and Alex arrived at school, where Allison and John were waiting for them. John was in a strange mood, being distant and not his usual obnoxious self, while Allison was absorbed in her own thoughts. "This day is getting worse as it goes on," Kaitlyn thought as she headed for classes. "God, please help me get through this day."

Kaitlyn went through the school day, occupied with everything *but* schoolwork. Her mind drifted all day as she played out what lay ahead, and she kept looking at the clock, waiting for it to turn three.

While Kaitlyn and Alex attended school, Kathryn made final preparations for Ray's arrival to their house, and completing her list, she went to the hospital to await Ray's discharge. Before his release, Ray and Kathryn went down to Nick's room, and Ray gave his dad a hug, having a private father to son conversation, while Kathryn waited respectfully outside in the corridor.

Nick handed Ray a sealed letter and asked him to place it on his wife's casket, relaying to Ray a verbal message for his beloved as tears fell to both their cheeks. Wiping away the tears, Ray said, "I love you, Dad," then hugged him one more time.

"I love you too, son," he said. "Take care of yourself and mind your manners at the Frost's house."

"I will, Dad," Ray replied. "I'll be up to visit in a couple days. You going to be okay?"

"I'll be okay," Nick assured. "I'll be home before you know it."

"Okay. Bye, Dad. I love you."

"Bye, son. I love you, too," Nick said as he went to rest his head. "Don't forget to do what I asked. And Ray, please don't open the letter. It's personal."

"I won't," as he walked with a limp out the door. His father left behind with a tear rolling down his cheek, his hands masking his face.

Kathryn and Ray went back to Ray's room. They gathered his items together and waited for the nurse to come with the discharge papers. By noon, they were on their way, and Kathryn took Ray back to the house, getting him situated on the couch in the living room. Providing a pillow and blanket for Ray, Kathryn told him to get some rest.

Ray slept until 2:37 p.m., waking up when Jim came home. Saying hello and telling Ray it was time to get ready, Jim helped him upstairs to assist him with showering and getting dressed.

"May I ask you something?" Ray asked Jim.

"Sure, what's on your mind?"

"Will I ever get over this empty feeling I have?"

Jim stood quietly and reflected on his own feelings he had had when his mother passed on. Standing with his head slightly bowed, he looked up and said, "No, but, you fill it with happy thoughts and memories. It just takes some time."

Ray looked solemnly to Jim. "I think I know what you mean. You know the old saying about *you don't know what you have until it's gone*?

"Yes," Jim replied, knowing where Ray was going with his statement, and allowed him to continue.

"I know what I'm missing," Ray said quietly. "I never realized how much I needed my mom, and now at a time when I really need her ..." Ray couldn't continue.

"I know," Mr. Frost said, wrapping his arms around Ray. "Just try to remember how much she loved you, and think of how she would want you to be now. She'd probably want you to feel at peace, go on with your life, remembering her spirit and filling your emptiness with treasured memories. Basically, Ray, she wants you to be happy. Moms don't like it when their children are sad."

"That's true," Ray agreed, nodding, reminiscing how his mom always tried to make things better for him. He remembered the look she had on her face during those times. "I understand. Thank you, Mr. Frost. You've given me some things to think about."

Jim accepted Ray's gratitude. "I'm going to get ready. You all set?"

"Yes. Thanks again," Ray answered. "I'm just going to take a few minutes."

School let out right on time. Kaitlyn and Alex scooted home, and Mrs. Frost met them at the door with their clothes for the funeral.

"Kaitlyn is this dress okay?" Kathryn asked, holding it up.

Kathryn had bought Kaitlyn a refined, black rayon dress with a scooped neckline and swing bottom. It was sophisticated, yet proper for its purpose.

"Yes. Thanks, Mom. It's perfect," Kaitlyn replied, accepting the dress and going upstairs to get ready.

Kaitlyn knocked on the guest room door. "How you doing in there?" she asked calmly.

"Doing okay," Ray answered. "I'll be out in a bit."

Kaitlyn went into her room and began undressing, her nerves full of anxiety as she prepared for a tough afternoon. Finishing up, she went downstairs and viewed Ray sitting apprehensively on the couch, seeming tired and worn as he twirled his fingers in a nervous frenzy. Dressed in a black double-breasted suit, with a white dress shirt, and shiny black shoes, Ray looked elegant. He was handsome for his mom.

Jaycee had always jokingly, yet, half-heartedly, talked about her funeral *some day*. She would make comments like: "I want to have a service and be buried on a hilltop, close to the heavens. I want everyone to sing "Amazing Grace," joined in a circle holding hands, and I want everyone smiling — no tears for I'll be in a better place — just celebrate my life."

Nick and Ray would laugh at Jaycee when she talked about her dying wishes, thinking she was off her rocker. Ray and Mr. Niles never thought they'd have to rely on Jaycee's intermittent comments over the years to commensurate her funeral in the prime of her life — neither did Jaycee.

The funeral was held in Winter's Crest Town Cemetery on top of a hill. The spot chosen for her burial was soothing, scenic and *exactly* what Jaycee would have wanted. Old maple trees, showing signs of autumn's presence, pranced with the winds, while their leaves fell to the soft, bright green grass below, and birds sang their sweet melodies. The winds carried the fragrant smell of stargazer lilies that graced Jaycee's casket in the direction of the mourners. The sweet smell brought soft mourning smiles to their faces.

The stormy morning had turned into a beautiful fall day. Temperatures hovered in the high sixties, and the sun shown through the light scattered clouds as if sunbeams were dancing their way down from Heaven. Jaycee was there in spirit; they could feel it.

Jaycee's childhood minister held a small service for the family's friends and relatives, as well as Ray's classmates and friends who congregated there. When the minister ended his final blessing, he asked all to hold hands and sing Jaycee's favorite song. Each person took a hold of his neighbor's hand. It took all the strength people could muster to get through a tearful rendition of *Amazing Grace*. Their cries wailed throughout the small cemetery, yet seemed to be soothed with a peaceful embrace.

Ray was gripping Kaitlyn's hand for dear life, and Kaitlyn kept her arms around Ray while they continued with the song. When the last note faded, he dropped to his chair with tears of immeasurable pain screaming through his countenance. Covering his eyes with his hands, he sobbed uncontrollably, his body jerking with overcome emotion. Kaitlyn, by his side and doing her best to help him, joined Ray in his horror.

Family and friends lined up one by one and placed single white tea roses on her casket while trying to force a last requested celebrating smile of Jaycee's life and said their final goodbyes. Jaycee's loving spirit seemed to hover above her final resting place, and a certain solitude was found there.

Ray pulled himself together enough to silently thank people for coming with a handshake and a forced half-smile, before seeking privacy by his mother's side.

"I love you, Mom," Ray whispered. "I miss you," he said, trying to find the courage to say his last farewell as he pulled out the small note from his pocket. "This is for you," he said, placing the unopened letter on her casket, " from Dad."

Ray paused for a moment before continuing.

"Dad said to say he loves you," Ray said with tears escalating. "He wishes he could have been here, but knows you are with him in spirit. He said to tell you he will miss you, and he will carry you in his heart for the rest of his life. His love for you will go on, as will mine. Goodbye, Mom," Ray wept in agony.

Jaycee's casket began lowering as Ray said goodbye, and seeing her descent into the ground became unbearable. He threw his arms onto the casket in a tight grasp, pulling upward as if he were trying to stop the nightmare. "Don't go, Mom!" Ray cried out in desperation. "No! No! I want my mom back!" He started to shake — his emotions engulfed him, and Kaitlyn rushed to his side, forcing him to sit down —keeping him back from falling. Getting Ray to a chair, she placed his head against her bosom and tried her best to soothe his pain.

"It's okay," Kaitlyn said to Ray in a tearful whisper, trembling herself. "I'll help you through this."

Ray's grip on Kaitlyn's waist screamed with fright as she continued to contain him, rock him and love him.

Looking up at the horizon and continuing to comfort Ray, Kaitlyn noticed a shadowy figure on the hillside. "Is that John?" Kaitlyn thought. "What a coward. He's scared of hospitals, scared of funerals — when is that boy going to grow up?!"

Allison came over and hugged Ray. "I'm so sorry, Ray," Allison gave her condolences. "If there's anything I can do, please don't hesitate to ask. Kaitlyn, that goes for you too. You both have a few hectic weeks coming up. If you need me, I'm here."

"Thanks," Ray tried to reply.

"Thanks," Kaitlyn said as she gave her best friend a one armed squeeze. "I'm glad you came."

Kaitlyn leaned towards Allison to whisper. "Tell John, if he's so excited about being an adult, than maybe he should start acting like one."

"I know," Allison replied. "Trust me, I know. I don't know if it will do any good or not, but I'll tell him."

"Unbelievable," Kaitlyn exclaimed quietly to herself. "That boy is simply beyond belief."

Kaitlyn stayed with Ray as he leaned on her for support, confounded with insufferable emotion. He tried to compose himself, but all he wanted to do was just scream at the world. Most of all, he just wanted his mom back and to turn back time.

Ray lingered by the graveside until the last person left.

"May I take a minute, please?" Ray asked Jim and Kathryn, somewhat calmed.

"Take all the time you need," Kathryn said, with a sympathetic heart, imagining Jaycee being she.

"Kaitlyn, stay with Ray and help him if he needs it," Mrs. Frost directed her.

"Of course, Mom," Kaitlyn said with sympathy. Kaitlyn kept at a close distance.

Ray moved his chair closer to the plot and talked to his mom privately. Looking as if he were in prayer, he looked up to Heaven and said, "I love you, Mom. Don't worry ... I'll take care of Dad. I'll make you proud."

Taking a few more moments, Ray said, "I'm ready," as he rose from his seat and softly tossed a remaining tea rose onto her casket. "I'm ready," he said again and headed towards the car. Kaitlyn joined him by his side. Both stopped briefly to look back and saw the first shoveling of dirt tossed onto the casket. Ray had to turn away.

Driving home, not one word was spoken, each dealing with Jaycee's death in his own way. Arriving back to the house, Alex helped get Ray to the couch, while Kaitlyn and her mother prepared for the onslaught of mourners, who would arrive any minute. Jim made a few phone calls, while Alex hung out with Ray, offering him moral as well as physical help.

Before their friends arrived for the post-funeral gathering, Kathryn sat down with Ray for a moment.

"It was a beautiful service," she said, unsure if she should speak it or not.

"Yes it was," Ray agreed. "It's exactly what my mom would've wanted."

Kathryn gave him a reassuring hug, whispering, "Everything is going to be okay. It's just going to take some time."

Friends and family members began arriving, with everyone approaching Ray as each one entered. Giving him their condolences, they asked Ray to convey their sympathies to his father. After they offered their support, the mourners helped themselves to some hors d'oeuvres and held idle privy conversations, while Alex overheard a few saying they were going to stop and see Nick before they went home.

Kaitlyn noticed that Ray seemed to be getting wearied and asked him privately how he was doing.

"I'm tired, Kait," Ray answered. "This is a bit much for me. I don't feel like having a *party* right now. It's just not right."

"I'll get my dad," Kaitlyn replied, motioning for him to stay put.

Kaitlyn interrupted her father from a frivolous conversation, and Jim, relieved from the interference, excused himself to assist Ray upstairs.

"It's okay, Ray," Jim said. "You've had a rough day. Go to sleep for a while, and then I'll have Kaitlyn come up to keep you company."

"Thank you, Mr. Frost," Ray said with sincerity. "Thank you for everything."

"No need to thank me," Jim replied. "Get some rest. We'll get things wrapped up downstairs, and get these people out of here," with a sense of uncharacteristic urgency in his expression.

The gathering started to wind down shortly after Jim came back downstairs, and Kaitlyn, Alex, Jim and Kathryn all chipped in to help clean up. When the cleaning was complete, Alex and Kaitlyn worked on their studies, while Jim and Kathryn relaxed in the library for a short time before visiting Nick later that evening. About an hour after Kaitlyn tended her studies, she went upstairs to be with Ray. Alex went to throw a ball with the neighborhood kids, first asking if he was needed for anything. Alex needed respite from it all, too.

Kaitlyn knocked gently on Ray's door, announcing her presence before entering.

"I brought the book with me," Kaitlyn said, showing it to him. "Would you like me to read some passages to you?"

"Not right now," Ray replied. "I don't feel like thinking anymore today."

"Yeah, you're right," Kaitlyn said. "I can understand that."

"Will you sit here with me though?" Ray asked.

Kaitlyn took Ray's hand and held it, then lowered her forehead to the back of his hand. "I love you, Ray. I wish I could help."

"You are," Ray said smiling. "Just having you here helps. Your family has been so generous to us. I don't think we can ever repay your kindness."

"Ray," Kaitlyn replied, "there's nothing to repay. We're happy we can help. Not to mention, I'm thrilled you're here. I just wish the circumstances were different."

"Me too, Kait," Ray said with a grin. "Yub yub," he said with a slight chuckle, trying to break the tension.

Kaitlyn and Ray passed the time with each other, making small talk and talking very little about the funeral. Ray was trying to cope with things, needing someone to just listen. Kaitlyn did so attentively, without taking her eyes off him — hearing every single word and seeing each facial cast.

Ray felt everything from anger to hurt — to joy, knowing his mother didn't suffer and knowing she was in Heaven. He felt alone and scared of how his life would change, yet took comfort in Kaitlyn's love, feeling safe in her arms.

"I'm scared, Kait," Ray confided. "What is my life going to be like without my mom? All the plans I have for my life included my mom in the picture."

Kaitlyn couldn't answer his question. She could only glance at Ray with empathetic eyes.

"Whether it was my prom," Ray continued, "my graduation, my wedding or having my own kids someday, they all included my mom being there. I don't think I could handle losing someone I love so much again. This is killing me," he said closing his eyes as he lay his head back on the pillow.

Kaitlyn still couldn't reply, as she had been wondering the same things. Not so much with Ray and his mom, but trying to put herself in Ray's situation. For once, Kaitlyn was speechless and truly could not relate.

It became late, and Ray as well as Kaitlyn, yawned incessantly. Kaitlyn realized it was her cue to leave so she gave Ray a bell to use before heading to her room to rest.

"If you need me, just ring the bell," Kaitlyn told him on her way towards the door.

"Thanks, Kait," Ray yawned, then sleepily said, "I can ring this bell *whenever* I need *you*?"

"Yes," Kaitlyn replied, looking back. "If you need me in the middle of the night, ring the bell, and I'll be here. I love you, Ray. Goodnight."

"I love you, too," Ray replied. "Goodnight."

Kaitlyn turned to leave Ray's room, and just as she placed her hand on the doorknob, she heard the bell ring behind her. She looked back at Ray smiling.

"Yes, Ray?" She said laughing.

"I need you," Ray said as he gave her the *come here* gesture with his finger.

Kaitlyn went to Ray's side, and he pulled her in for a kiss. "Goodnight, Kait," Ray said with a chuckle.

"Goodnight," Kaitlyn said as she left the room, grinning ear to ear, laughing.

The next morning, Kaitlyn rose from bed, feeling drained and emotionally exhausted. Having to get ready for school, she threw on a pair of Capri pants and a matching blouse, and pulled her hair back into a ponytail.

Peering into Ray's room to see if he were awake, (which he wasn't), Kaitlyn said, "Good morning," telling him she was getting ready to leave for school.

"Okay. Bye, babes," Ray said as he closed his eyes, still half asleep.

Contemplating how school would be during her stroll there, Kaitlyn figured she'd arrive with classmates and friends greeting her and asking how Ray was doing. She assumed it would be a somewhat decent day, even though she was thoroughly worn out. But Kaitlyn didn't come close to what she was expecting and was completely unprepared for what *did* happen.

Walking into the school, Kaitlyn eyed a portrait on the wall of Jaycee, with "In Memory Of Jaycee Niles" written underneath it, along with "Scholarship Fund" below her name. Below that, it read: *"Contact Winter's Crest First National Bank,"* and it continued on with the phone number and the specifications about the new scholarship set up in Jaycee's name.

Kaitlyn was touched by the sentiment and proud, knowing that her father had to be the one responsible for setting it up. She stood there for a brief moment and took a deep cleansing breath. Starting to walk towards her first class, she smiled — something good was coming out of this terrible mess.

As Kaitlyn walked further down the hall, she noticed huddles of students whispering and saying things like: "Did you hear?" She walked a little further down, and with the same sentence she had just heard, Kaitlyn made out the sound of a name, then caught the remainder of the gossip and gasped.

Time halted as Kaitlyn put the words together, incapable of accepting what she had just learned. She walked further down the hall with quickening steps. People hushed themselves when she approached, making her uncomfortable, as if she were naked with all eyes on her. Feeling as if the corridor walls crept in closer, she began to run, not knowing where she was going, and only seeing where she *was* going through tear-clouded vision. Continuing to run, she came to an abrupt halt, dashing right into Allison.

"You knew, didn't you?" Kaitlyn screamed in a furious manner, with her hands on Allison's shoulders, shaking her. "You knew! And you didn't tell me!" Kaitlyn exclaimed hurt and enraged.

"Yes, Kaitlyn," Allison said in shame. "Yes, I knew."

"That's why you showed up late for the funeral," Kaitlyn asked with hostility.

"Why didn't you tell me?" Kaitlyn voiced, not sure if she wanted an answer.

"I promised not to," Allison said.

"You promised not to?!" Kaitlyn yelled. "And why would you do something so stupid as to make a promise like that?!"

"Kaitlyn," Allison cried. " He's my boyfriend. What was I supposed to do? I wanted to tell you, but I made a promise."

"I can't believe you would do something like that Allison," Kaitlyn cried angrily. "We've been friends long before *John* was *ever* your boyfriend!"

"I'm sorry, Kaitlyn," Allison said through her tears. "I'm really sorry."

"I thought you were my best friend!" Kaitlyn replied distressed. "Where is the bastard?" Kaitlyn asked, demanding an answer.

"He's in jail," Allison replied. "He was arrested last night for vehicular manslaughter."

"Good, perfect place for him," Kaitlyn said feeling satisfied.

"Kaitlyn," Allison said meekly. "There's something you need to know."

"What?" Kaitlyn asked in an angry tone.

"John was drinking that night." Allison lowered her head.

"Figures! I got to go."

Kaitlyn left feeling betrayed by Allison and John, upset, hostile and downright furious. "How could John come to *my* house and cry on *my* shoulders ... How could he have done that to me? How could he have done that to Ray? How could Allison keep this from me?"

Kaitlyn, hurting and in tears, was beside herself and ran out of school towards Crestview Park. She ran and ran, till she couldn't run anymore, stopping at she and Ray's spot — crouching down against the tree sobbing.

One of the kids at school reported Kaitlyn's reaction to the principal, and Mr. Petry called Kathryn.

Kathryn was worried by the news, but kept it to herself until she could go over things with Kaitlyn. She asked the school to call if Kaitlyn showed back up, explaining that Kaitlyn probably just needed some time to let it out.

A half an hour or so later, the school called Kathryn back. "Kaitlyn's here now," the receptionist informed. "We're going to have her talk to the school guidance counselor."

"Thank you," Kathryn replied. "Please tell Kaitlyn I will pick her up today."

Kaitlyn was a wreck at school. She talked with the guidance counselor for a long while before going back to classes. She then drifted through the rest of the day in a cloud, not paying attention to anything that was going on around her. All she could think of was how she was going to tell Ray. Thoughts like: "He's going to hate me," and, "He doesn't need this" kept popping up.

At 3 p.m., the bell rang, and Kaitlyn went to the front of the school to meet her mother.

"Kaitlyn," Kathryn said. "You okay?"

"No," Kaitlyn said in a short tone. "No, I'm not okay."

"The school said something about John causing the accident?" she questioned.

"Mom," Kaitlyn explained, "he was drinking, and he drove. He killed Mrs. Niles."

"Oh, dear," Kathryn said. "Oh my goodness. Where's John?"

"He's in jail where he belongs," Kaitlyn replied, still angered. "Mom, what am I going to tell Ray? How am I going to tell Ray?"

"Kaitlyn," Kathryn inquired. "Do you want me to tell him?"

"No, Mom," Kaitlyn said. "No, I think it has to come from me."

"Okay, but listen, you're going to have to be totally honest, and tell him everything you know," Kathryn went on to explain. "Tell him everything, no matter how hard it is for you to say, and no matter how hard it is for him to hear."

"You're right, Mom," Kaitlyn agreed. "I know you're right. Does he know about what happened at school?"

"He knows you had a rough morning," Kathryn answered. "He doesn't know why."

They arrived home, and Kathryn told Kaitlyn she would leave the two of them alone. Kaitlyn went into the living room to find Ray reading from the book of phrases.

Putting the book down, Ray worriedly asked, "What happened?"

Kaitlyn started sobbing. "I can't tell you this. Oh my gosh, I can't tell you this."

"Kaitlyn what's wrong? Come here. You've got to tell me."

Kaitlyn switched positions to move closer to Ray and buried her head in his chest, while tears began to run down her cheeks. Her throat choked up in tears of hurt, betrayal and fear, and her words came across in broken syllables as she tried to speak.

"Ray," Kaitlyn started, "John ... Accident ... Your mom ... John ... killed your mom."

Ray took Kaitlyn away from his chest at arm's length. "What?!"

"He's in jail," she replied. "He was arrested last night for vehicular manslaughter."

"Oh, my gosh!" Ray said, not believing what he was hearing.

"Ray," Kaitlyn said with her eyes wide open. "He was drunk. The bastard was drunk!"

Ray's veins protruded from his neck and his face turned fire red.

"Ray," Kaitlyn continued, "there's more."

"More?" Ray questioned angrily. "How can it get any worse?"

"Allison has known since it happened."

"What?" Ray asked, not wanting an answer.

"John visited me here the day after the accident, looking for consolation, I thought," Kaitlyn said. "It seemed weird when he thanked me for his time, but I just figured he was upset and worried. Now, I'm just angry."

"You're angry?" Ray said, ready to burst. "I'm beyond angry. I don't know what it is that I am, but whatever it is that I am, that's what I am!"

"You're starting to sound like me," Kaitlyn said inappropriately, letting out a slight giggle.

Ray giggled too. "Oh-oh, that's not good."

"Come here," Ray said, gaining strength.

Kaitlyn went to Ray, and they embraced. Half of the hug was the two of them loving each other, and the other half was for comfort. Ray squeezed Kaitlyn tight. "We'll get through this together. We can. We will, and we have to."

"You're right," Kaitlyn agreed. "We will get through this."

Kaitlyn rested next to Ray on the couch, cradled in his strong arms, until they heard the footsteps of Mr. Frost coming home.

Jim came into the living room and greeted the two.

"Hi, Dad. How was your day?"

"It was fine, dear," he replied. "How was yours?"

"You don't know?" Kaitlyn asked, questioning why.

"No, did something happen I should know about?" Jim asked.

"Yes," Kaitlyn replied. "Do you mind if Mom tells you?"

"No," Jim said, a bit puzzled. "I'll go see your mother. Ray, how are you feeling?"

"Fine, sir. Thank you," Ray responded. "I would like to try to get back to school on Thursday.

"Let's take it one day at a time," Jim said sympathetically.

"Yes, sir."

Jim went into the kitchen to see Kathryn.

"Nice young man, Ray is," Jim said.

"Yes," Kathryn concurred. "He's quite a gentleman."

"Kaitlyn said you have something to tell me?" Jim questioned. "What happened?"

"Did you know?" she asked. "Did you know John was drunk and caused Jaycee's death?"

"No," he replied. "I'm not surprised, though. I've heard some comments at the bank about John and his drinking. I feel terrible for the kids though."

Alex walked in the kitchen just as his father said he wasn't surprised.

"Where have you been, Alex?" Jim asked.

"I had football practice, Mom," Alex answered. "Did you forget?"

"Yes," she said. "Yes I did. I'm sorry. It's been a rough day here."

"That's okay," Alex said. "So, Dad, what *aren't* you surprised about?"

"Didn't you hear, Alex?" Jim replied.

"I heard a rumor about John, but I didn't believe it," Alex replied.

Mr. Frost looked at Alex and said, "Believe it."

Alex went straight to the living room. "You guys okay?"

"Yeah, we're doing okay," Kaitlyn replied.

"I heard the rumor, but didn't believe it." Alex replied in shock. "John ... *our* John. I can't believe it. I'm going to kill him!"

"Well, he's at the jail. If you go there now, you can kill him, and then they won't have to transport you back there. It will save them some time and probably some money, too," Kaitlyn said with a grin, trying to break up the intensity of the day, and liking the idea at the same time.

"Kaitlyn Frost," Alex reprimanded. "How can you make light of this?"

"Alex," Kaitlyn 'replied. "I've been dealing with some pretty dreadful issues the past few days, and my brain is tired. I just need a break from the doom and gloom. Sorry it was at your expense."

Ray started laughing. "You know, it was pretty funny."

Alex chimed in with a grin, beginning to laugh. "Yeah, I guess it was."

"I can see you now," Ray said. "You go into the jail, kill John and then hold out your hands to be handcuffed."

They all started laughing.

"I'm still angry," Alex said.

"We are, too," Kaitlyn exclaimed.

"Imagine how I feel," Ray suggested. "My best friend killed my mom! Don't you think I want to kill him and hurt him? I am so angry right now, that it's eating me up inside. I feel like climbing a mountain and screaming at the top of my lungs, and having a tantrum like a three-year old child. I can't though. I am a man, and I have to act like one. So, instead, I'm going to calm down and try to be somewhat reasonable about all of this, remind myself to breathe and take this one day at a time."

"Good plan," Alex said. "I'm not so sure I could be so calm."

"Alex," Ray replied. "I have to be. My mom would have wanted it that way. Besides, being angry all the time isn't working."

"I respect you for it, Ray," Alex said as he went to shake his hand.

"So do I, sir," Kaitlyn said, extending her hand for a shake, leaving the three chuckling. Then they broke out into a roaring laughter, wiping tears away from their eyes.

Chapter Nine

Kaitlyn's and Allison's reminisces brought back fond memories, but also released painful ones they'd just as soon forget. Feeling tensions rise, they retreated to the living room, and Kaitlyn took out one of her old Perry Como records, and fixed it on the phonograph.

A familiar melody spread through the air, and Kaitlyn and Allison went to the braided rug to dance with one another and to sing their rendition of *Some Enchanted Evening,* making their youthful attempts of this particular song seem almost professional.

When the last note faded, the two sat down laughing. After refreshing their tea, they decided they were ready to travel back through once treaded waters as their eyes fell to the letter staring back at them from the coffee table.

* * *

The winds had begun picking up outside, signaling another storm as they all sat down for dinner. Outside the dining room window, squirrels and birds scurried about, returning to their nests for protection, while the trees swayed, turning the foliage upside down — a sure sign of an advancing storm. Within moments, rain began to pelt against the glass, turning quickly to slaps, as the wind picked up in fury.

"Wow," Kathryn said, looking behind her. "Where'd that come from?"

"Mother Nature's angry tonight," Kaitlyn replied. "Maybe she's had a rough day."

Ray and Alex looked at Kaitlyn in gross confusion. "You okay?" Ray asked.

"Yeah," Kaitlyn replied. "I'm okay, *why?*"

"Well, that's kind of a strange answer," Alex said. "Don't you think?"

"No," Kaitlyn replied firmly. "She's having the temper tantrum I feel like having, only ... Mother Nature can have one of this magnitude — I can't."

Ray and Alex, along with Kathryn and Jim, gave each other baffling looks. Then, the four stared in Kaitlyn's direction, thinking she had lost her noggin.

Kaitlyn stopped talking. Instead, she concentrated on picking at the roast turkey and mashed potatoes while anger slithered through her veins, causing her to hostilely blurt out: "I'm angry! ... I'm angry, and I'm hurt! May I *please* be excused?"

Without waiting for a response, but knowing her family would understand, Kaitlyn stood and barged out of the dining room. Perhaps the others heard a sob escape her as she hurried off upstairs.

She sat on the bed with her head propped up against the wall, and with notebook and pen in hand, she began to write. Kaitlyn tried writing poems about how she was feeling, only to crumple them into small balls and throw them towards the wastebasket, with most of them ending up on the floor around it. She tried writing again and again, until she finally gave up on the idea.

She placed the notebook on the desk and returned to the bed. Curling up in a comforting quilt, she hugged her pillow, incapable of thinking anymore. All she wanted to do was to escape - escape from the world, escape from the turmoil, escape from herself. After forty some odd minutes, Kaitlyn's 'vacation' was interrupted by a knocking at her door. She didn't bother answering it.

"Kait," Ray called through the door. "You okay?"

"Come in," Kaitlyn said. "Yeah, I'm okay. Just sick of thinking."

"Me too," Ray replied, coming in and sitting carefully on the bed. "So, how about that sponge bath?" he suggested, a grin appearing on his face.

Kaitlyn laughed. "I think you'll end up dead or in jail if I did that."

"You're probably right," Ray giggled, with naughty thoughts running through his head. "I still wouldn't mind though," he said as he smiled with half-joking eyes.

"Why don't you come downstairs with me?" Ray recommended, motioning for her to come. "Let's go talk things over. Your dad started a fire in the living room, and we can sit and talk — or not talk."

Kaitlyn considered for a moment before taking Ray up on the offer.

Ray left to go downstairs. He didn't need his crutches anymore. He only had to use them at the hospital and with his 'homecoming'. He still wore the support for his knee, and most of the pain had subsided, but the numb area remained. The doctor was keeping an eye on it, but, other than that, he was healing nicely. His facial bruises were slowly fading, turning from black and blue, to light green. His strength was coming back, and he was starting to feel like himself again. Especially after his 'centipede' stitches were removed. Although he was angry and hurt by John and Allison, he was handling it okay. Mostly, he was preoccupied with missing his father, and he sorely missed his mom.

The funeral seemed to help bring closure for Ray, and he was able to accept his mother no longer being alive, even though there were times he could still not believe it. He took comfort in the fact that her death was quick, and that she didn't suffer. But he worried about the future, only knowing one thing for sure: He loved Kaitlyn with all his heart.

Kaitlyn came downstairs holding two pillows and a quilt. She dropped off the items and went into the kitchen to make some tea. "Do you want some tea or hot cocoa, Ray?" she called behind her.

"Hot cocoa would be great!" Ray answered.

"I think I'll have some cocoa too," Kaitlyn said, changing her mind.

Kaitlyn popped her head in the library. Seeing her parents and brother in there, she asked them if they'd like something to drink. Alex looked up briefly from his studies, giving her a quick shake of "no", and her father, with eyeglasses resting on his nose, was deeply involved in some bank work, waving a brief "no thanks". Kathryn had her eyes glued to some syrupy-sweet romance novel. She didn't notice that Kaitlyn had even asked a question.

Kaitlyn came into the living room. Placing the hot cocoa on the coffee table in front of them, she then sat down beside Ray. She peered around to see if anyone was looking, and seizing the moment, she leaned into Ray with a kiss. "I love you," she whispered softly.

Kaitlyn curled up with a blanket and put a pillow in her lap. Laying her head on the back of the couch, her eyes trailed in Ray's direction.

Ray made himself comfortable in a similar fashion and an evening of soul searching and shared moments began.

Ray spoke first. "Kaitlyn, you know that verse you read to me at the hospital?"

Kaitlyn answered with a puzzled look, "Yeah."

"I've been thinking about it," Ray said. " 'Going through life with forgiveness and peace ... leading a full life'. I'm going to have to try to forgive John, and you're going to have to try to forgive John, too — and Allison."

"You're right," Kaitlyn agreed. "I know you're right, but it's going to be hard to forget."

"I don't think we need to forget it," Ray continued. "We'll remember it always, but we need to try and find a way to make peace with it. Kaitlyn, if we don't, we'll be miserable. It will eat at us and destroy us. I see two ways to go about this."

"What's that?" Kaitlyn asked.

"We can walk around with hate and hurt for the rest of our lives, or we can be the better people and try to forgive them. Allison should never have promised not to tell us, but she *did* make a promise. Regardless of whether it was right or wrong, maybe Allison values her word. And that's a good trait."

"Yes," Kaitlyn agreed. "I see your point. Don't like it, but I see it."

"Kaitlyn," Ray continued, "John has to live the rest of his life with the fact that he killed my mother. Not to mention, he'll have to live a social and judicial punishment. Would I be a better person forgiving him, or would I be a better person having anger build up inside me for the rest of my life?"

"Go on," Kaitlyn said, wanting to hear more.

"What John did was wrong," Ray said. "There's no question about that. I do know my mom would want me to try to forgive and not have hate in my heart. I'm not saying it's going to be easy; it won't be. But I know I have to at least try though — if not for me, then for my mom."

"Wow," Kaitlyn replied after some thought. "I don't know if I *can* do that. I know I'm angry, and I know it's eating me up inside. I can see myself forgiving Allison, because what you said makes sense. But John? I don't know if I can forgive John."

"I don't know if I can either," Ray admitted. "I don't even know if I want to. I still can't stop thinking about that passage though, and what my mother would have wanted. All I know is that I feel like beating him up, but instead, I'm beating myself up."

"I guess we take this day by day?" Kaitlyn asked while trying to figure out how to go about healing such hurt and anger.

"I guess so," Ray replied, himself unsure.

Kaitlyn leaned in for a hug and a quick peck, and didn't look around that time to see who was watching. "I'll talk to Allison tomorrow and see if we can smooth things out," she said as she backed away from her stolen kiss.

"Just remember," Ray said. "It's not Allison's fault. Allison *didn't* kill my mom — *John* did.

"Hey," Kaitlyn changed the subject, "how are you feeling?"

"I'm feeling a little better," Ray replied with a smile. "I'm anxious to get back to school and go visit our spot."

"Oh really?" Kaitlyn said mischievously. "Me too."

Kaitlyn and Ray talked for about another hour, discussing matters of the heart, school and what it would be like once Ray returned. They talked about Nick, Ray missing his mother, and they talked about their feelings for one another.

"One last thing, Kait," Ray said. "We're in this thing together, right? Through thick and thin?"

"Yub yub. Most indubitably," Kaitlyn replied giggling, but with seriousness in her eyes.

The hot cocoa became cold cocoa, and the fire died down — their cue to retire for the evening. Kaitlyn brought the empty cups to the kitchen and then went to the library to kiss her parents goodnight.

Ray followed behind, thanking Kaitlyn's parents, and giving Kathryn a kiss on the cheek. "Thank you for everything," he said, leaving the library and saying goodnight.

Kaitlyn and Ray went upstairs to prepare for bed, and when Kaitlyn finished dressing, she went to Ray's room, saying goodnight just one more time. Ray motioned to her with his trademark *come here* gesture, and Kaitlyn smiled, inching her way towards him. He held out his hands, and as she took them, Ray pulled her to his chest for a hug. Ray took his hand and lifted her chin, and with their eyes gazing into one another's, Ray kissed her with such passion that Kaitlyn was left tingling all over. It was the most passionate kiss the two of them had yet shared, and Kaitlyn was swept into another world.

Finishing her 'goodnight', Kaitlyn craved Ray's touch as she lay in bed. Sliding her fingers gently over her soft skin, causing tingles to penetrate throughout her body, she had him touching her through her hands and caressing her into a deep, relaxing slumber.

Wednesday came with a quiet hello, awakening to a brisk, beautiful day. The deep blue sky sparkled in the background of bouncing clouds as Kaitlyn's chirping friends were going about their morning routine. Kaitlyn was certain to say hello to them before showering and starting her morning.

Before heading downstairs for breakfast, she stopped in Ray's room to say good morning, kiss him goodbye and say, "I love you."

"I love you, too," Ray replied, haif-asleep. "Bye, babes."

Kaitlyn went downstairs, had her breakfast and gathered her books for school. She and Alex walked to school, catching up with Allison on the front steps.

Alex left, only saying a brief "hi", as he was still too angry to be around Allison.

"Allison," Kaitlyn said, scared as to how she would react to talking to her.

"Hi, Kaitlyn," Allison replied in a monotone voice.

"Allison, we need to talk," Kaitlyn said, looking seriously into her eyes.

"I know," Allison agreed. "I don't know what to say. I know I shouldn't have promised John, but I did. I was dying to tell you, but I didn't want to break my word."

"Allison," Kaitlyn said sorrowfully. "I know. I'm sorry for how I reacted with you. I'm not happy that you didn't tell me, but I understand. Ray and I discussed it last night, and he said some things that made me realize the position you were in. I don't want to lose my friendship with you; we've been friends all our lives. Do me one favor, though..."

"Anything, Kaitlyn," Allison replied. "Anything."

"Don't keep something so serious away from me again," Kaitlyn said with a pleading smile.

"I won't," Allison agreed. "That's a promise."

Kaitlyn stretched her arms out for a hug. "Friends?"

"Forever," Allison said as the two embraced. "And you know I keep my promises."

"Yeah, no kidding," Kaitlyn said as the two of them broke into laughter.

"How's Ray doing?"

"He's doing better," Kaitlyn said. "He wants to come back to school tomorrow."

"Really?" Allison asked shocked. "So soon?"

"He wants to get back to reality, and I think he's bored being around my mom all day."

"How's his dad?" Allison asked.

"I guess he's okay," Kaitlyn said, though unsure. "Ray's going to see him today, I think. I'll know more, later today. We'd better get to our classes."

"Kaitlyn," Allison said quietly. "I'm really sorry."

"I know you are, Allison." Kaitlyn replied. "I am too. Let's try to forget about it."

"Okay," Allison said. "I'll see you at lunch."

Kaitlyn and Allison went to their classes, had lunch, and did their normal school day activities.

Ray went to visit his father at the hospital and was pleased to see him looking better. Nick's color had improved, and he was able to sit up in bed. The nurses had washed his hair and bathed him, making Nick feel better and look healthier. Ray and his father sat together for a few hours talking, playing checkers and hanging around, while Kathryn took care of some long-neglected errands.

When Kaitlyn arrived home, she found Ray studying in the library, catching up on his missed schoolwork. Ray looked up and said, "hello," excitedly, telling her about his visit, and then handed Kaitlyn a piece of paper.

"What's this?" Kaitlyn asked.

"Just open it."

Kaitlyn unfolded the paper and was startled to find a doctor's permission slip allowing Ray to return to classes. "How were you able to get this?" Kaitlyn asked, showing it to him.

"I saw the doctor who treated me at the hospital and asked him it if would be okay if I went back to school. He said, 'Fine,' and gave me this slip."

"That's great, Ray?" Kaitlyn said.

"How about we go visit our tree tomorrow?" Ray asked quietly, being sure no one could hear.

"That'd be wonderful," Kaitlyn said with her devilish, scheming smile.

Ray continued with what he was doing. He still had schoolwork left to complete, but Kaitlyn had other plans. She leaned into him, and Ray puckered up to kiss her. Kaitlyn smiled as she neared his face, reached her hand up and tweaked his nose.

"Cute, real cute," Ray said. "Come here and give me a real kiss."

"My parents, Ray," Kaitlyn said worried.

"Ahh, they won't see us," Ray replied. "Just a quick kiss, please."

Kaitlyn leaned into Ray to kiss him. He brought his hand up as if he were going to touch her chin and tweaked her back. Laughing, Ray sat back down to complete his studies.

Kaitlyn joined Ray to work on her studies as well, while making googly eyes at each other every so often. When they were deep into their studies, the doorbell chimed, and Kaitlyn went to answer it.

"Hi, Allison," Kaitlyn said, happy to see her.

"Hi, Kaitlyn," Allison said distantly. "I brought someone with me," as she motioned for John to show his face and tried to hide her own.

Kaitlyn couldn't react. She was frozen with every kind of emotion one could think of. Fear, pain, nervousness, dread, disgust, hate, love and shock went through her body like a train curving a mountain's edge. She didn't know whether to cry, scream or punch him in the face.

Kaitlyn took Allison aside and whispered, "What's he doing here? I thought he was in jail?"

"He was just released on bond," Allison whispered back. "He wants to talk with you and Ray.

"Kaitlyn couldn't bring herself to speak with John. She couldn't even look at him. She motioned to Allison to go into the living room with John and await her and Ray.

John and Allison strolled behind Kaitlyn as they approached the living room. Kaitlyn prepared Ray, telling him someone was here. Ray looked up when he was about to ask whom and saw John standing by the living room entrance with Allison.

Ray didn't know what to do either. He looked at John and then looked away, as all he could see was a killer standing in front of him. He then tried to remember what he wanted to try to do and looked back in John's direction.

Tension was high. No one knew where to start or if they even wanted to as they sat down in the living room, staring at nothing. John looked dreadful. His face was filled with sorrow, remorse, guilt, fright and shame, and as they tried to get comfortable, the room suddenly became cold and dark, even though the sun was shining bright through the cathedral windows.

Kaitlyn and Ray took deep breaths. It took every ounce of courage and self-control the two of them could muster. It took every ounce of courage for John to even be there. Allison just stayed in the background emotionally paralyzed.

John couldn't look at Ray, as his shame was too deep. John started crying before speaking.

"I know that I'm the last person you want to see right now," John said through broken syllables, with his head bowed towards the floor.

"You're right, John," Ray replied in agreement.

"Kaitlyn," John said, looking up to her, "I'm sorry. I was planning on telling you the night I visited, but I couldn't. I couldn't bring myself to admit it. I couldn't even admit it to myself."

Kaitlyn sat there listening as tears began trickling down her cheeks, her heart pounding and her hands shaking.

John continued. "You were right, Kaitlyn. Turning eighteen doesn't make you a man. Being able to drink beer doesn't make you a man either; it made me a killer. I don't know if you can ever find it in your heart to forgive me, but I beg of you — please forgive me."

Kaitlyn sobbed, and Ray sat still, listening to every single word said — his emotions now frozen.

"Ray," John said, "What can I say? What I have done is reprehensible and does not deserve your forgiveness. If I could trade places with your mom right now, I would. I'd do anything to bring her back to you. The sad thing is, is all I can say is that I'm sorry, and I know it's not enough. It's never going to be enough."

John was in a full-blown sob, as were Allison and Kaitlyn. Ray sat on the couch staring as if he were in another world, trying to escape the one he was in.

"John," Ray said, breaking his trance. "I'm angry. I'm hurt. I'm in mourning, and I'm struggling with how I feel. Part of me wants to try to forgive you, and the other part wants to beat you senseless. I don't know what to say. Do I forgive you? No. Do I accept your apology? Yes, I believe you are sincere. Can I forget what you have done to my family and me? Never!"

"Ray," Allison interrupted. "I'm sorry for not telling you what I knew. I'm truly sorry."

"Allison," Ray replied, "as much as I think you should have told us, I also understand you made a promise. You were true to your word, and I don't hate you for it. I'm not happy that you didn't tell us, but I understand why. I forgive you."

Ray turned his attention to John. "When's your inquest?"

"Next Wednesday," John answered with fear in his expression.

"Oh, okay," Ray replied as if he were in deep thought about something.

John asked for a moment with Ray alone, and the two girls excused themselves to freshen up. John looked at Ray with questioning eyes and whispered, "Ray, was your mom given the note?"

"What note?" Ray asked. "The one from my dad?"

"Yeah," John answered. "Although, it wasn't from your dad. It was from me."

"My dad knew?" Ray asked miffed.

John answered. "The day I went to the hospital and saw you, I also went to see your dad. I apologized and gave him the letter."

"You wrote my mom a letter?" Ray asked.

"Yes," John replied. "I plan on keeping my promise, Ray."

"What pro ...?" Ray started to ask before the girls interrupted him and John.

"I think we should call it a night," Allison said, egging John on to get going. "We don't want to overstay our welcome."

"I'm glad you both came by," Kaitlyn said, while Ray stood in confusion, with a dismissive hand, waving goodbye.

Kaitlyn hugged Allison and waved a slight goodbye to John. She closed the door and went in the living room to be with Ray. Ray raised his hands, pleading for her comfort, and Kaitlyn was more than happy to oblige.

"You okay, Ray?" Kaitlyn asked.

Ray told her it was nothing and that he'd be okay. "Please, just hold me."

*   *   *

The phonograph began making that terrible skipping noise, which today is so often used in rap music. Back then, though, it was annoying, (still is), sending shivers up your spine.

Kaitlyn and Allison began to file through her records from fifty years ago, coming across one from The Andrew Sisters. Deciding they'd like to listen to it, Kaitlyn took the record out of the cover and placed it on the player, carefully placing the needle to the beginning of the record. As the music began playing, Kaitlyn brought out an old box for her and Allison to sort through.

Wiping the dust off from the cover, Kaitlyn opened it, viewing old photos of her parents, her brother and Allison with John, and of course, Ray. There were a few in there of Bob Westman as well.

They started going through them, smiling and remembering when the shots were taken, going through each one until they came to a blue book at the bottom. *Mackey High School, 1950* was written in gold lettering across the top. "Wow, I haven't seen this in years," Allison commented.

Kaitlyn took the yearbook out, and they started strumming through the pages, seeing names and faces from their childhood, recalling some in delight and others, well — they skipped over.

They came to the end of the book where there was a photo of Jaycee Niles. The book had been dedicated to her, and it had the names of scholarship winners listed below her photograph.

They went to the very last page, where friends left their autographs and saw a drawn heart, with the words: *Ray and Kaitlyn Forever*. Ray signed a loving, short message underneath the heart that read:

"I love you Kaitlyn. I will love you forever and will be yours forever. You're the best thing that has ever happened to me. I look forward to loving you for the rest of my life. All my love and adoration, Ray"

Kaitlyn smiled reading the old passage while disappointing thoughts filled her mind. "It was wonderful," she said to Allison. "He was wonderful. *We* were wonderful."

Kaitlyn got up for a moment and went to the coffee table, picking up the letter. She sat down while The Andrew Sisters' record played sweet songs of yesteryear in the background.

"Am I ready?" Kaitlyn asked herself out loud, with Allison sitting next to her, secretly wanting her to be. Kaitlyn teased herself for a moment as she began separating the glued flap from the envelope, stopping half way through. "No, not yet," she said, placing the letter next to the yearbook on the coffee table. Kaitlyn and Allison sat back on the couch with their legs crossed — no longer able to tuck one leg under them and recalled more of their youthful days.

                              *   *   *

Kaitlyn and Ray had prepared themselves for school the next day. Ray was a little nervous going back because he knew people would be reminding him all day of the nightmare he was living. He seemed to have just put John's news under the pile of mess he was dealing with and concentrated on what lay ahead tomorrow. He and Kaitlyn talked about ideas on how to handle things and what to expect before sitting down to the nightly family dinner.

After dinner and chores, Ray and Kaitlyn went back to the living room to finish their conversation. Mr. Frost came into the room.

"You two okay?" Mr. Frost asked.

"Yes, we're fine," Kaitlyn replied.

"Okay, good," Mr. Frost said. Your mom and I are going to take an evening walk. "Will you be okay while we're gone?

"Yes, Dad," Kaitlyn answered. "We'll be right here."

"Okay," Mr. Frost replied. "We'll be back in a bit."

"Have fun," Kaitlyn said. "Where's Alex, by the way?"

"He went to throw a ball with his buddies," Mr. Frost said. "He should be back soon."

"Okay," Kaitlyn replied. "Bye."

"Bye," Ray said. "Enjoy your time together; you never know when the time will be up."

Mr. Frost looked back at him with a surprised look, yet understood exactly what he was saying. "You're right, son. You're so right." Mr. Frost had a fresh reminder of how lucky he was and took his wife's hand. With a loving one-armed hug, they started their evening stroll.

Kaitlyn and Ray looked at each other when they heard the door shut. "We're alone," Kaitlyn said with a sneaking grin.

"Yes, I know," Ray replied. "Come on over here."

Kaitlyn laughed as she nudged closer to him.

"A little closer," Ray encouraged Kaitlyn. "That's better. May I kiss you, Miss Frost?"

"Why, yes you may, sir," Kaitlyn said in a teasing tone. "You can kiss me whenever you want to."

"*Oh really?*" Ray said back in the same teasing tone. "*Then come here.*"

Kaitlyn and Ray embraced in a deep feeling hug. Ray brought his moist, warm lips to Kaitlyn, pressing them against Kaitlyn's wanting lips. He brought his fingers to her hair and strummed his way through, massaging as he moved his hands.

Their eyes were closed as they felt sensations run through each and every vein in their bodies, and momentarily forgot they only had a short time alone together.

He brought his mouth to her neck, brusquely kissing Kaitlyn as she moaned in pure delight. She shivered from the pangs running through her; they were too intense not to make her shudder. She briefly looked into Ray's eyes and said, "I love you," then tilted her head downward, bringing her lips to taste Ray's neck.

Ray set his hands on Kaitlyn's shoulders and pulled her back. Looking for permission, he slowly brought his fingers downward towards her chest. Kaitlyn looked to him with naïve wonder and allowed Ray to study her as he carefully unbuttoned the first few buttons while tracing his fingers underneath the soft fabric.

Kaitlyn caressed Ray's chest, neck and cheeks as he continued on with his exploration and loving touches, unbuttoning a few more buttons, allowing his eyes to fall upon her voluptuous cleavage. He brought his lips to her while asking permission with his eyes, and she gently held his head in her hands and brought him to her bosom.

He slid his fingers from her navel up towards her chest and gently massaged his hands in a circular motion under Kaitlyn's blouse as Kaitlyn let out a gasp. Wanting his lips to meet hers, the two entangled in a deep passionate kiss as they touched each other and loved one another. Their few sharing moments came to a sudden halt when they heard the turning of the doorknob.

Kaitlyn jumped away from Ray and scurried to fasten her shirt, and fix her attire. Her cheeks were red with a look of guilt written all over her face.

Ray hurried to get his shirt buttoned up and tried to straighten up the couch before making himself look like he was deep into his studies as a devilish grin transpired upon both their faces.

"Well, well, well. What have we got here?" Alex said as he walked into the room. "Hmmm, ammunition, I think this is called," Alex said sarcastically.

"Please, Alex," Kaitlyn begged, "Please don't tell Mom and Dad.

"Well, Kaitlyn," Alex replied, "I won't have to."

"Why?" Kaitlyn asked inquisitively.

"Because they're right behind me," Alex answered. "I just passed them on the street. You'd better go upstairs Kaitlyn and freshen up. You've got that *naughty look* happening."

"Oh, dear," Kaitlyn said, completely embarrassed as she started upstairs. "You're not going to tell are *you*?"

"No, Kaitlyn," Alex confirmed. "No, I'm not going to tell. Get upstairs though, or they'll know."

Kaitlyn scurried upstairs, while Alex sat down and chatted with Ray, trying to help the awkward situation. "You like my sister, huh?" Alex said matter-of-factly.

"Yes, I do, Alex," Ray replied. "I love her."

"That's great," Alex said. "One thing though."

"What's that?"

"Don't hurt her," Alex said with conviction.

"I won't, Alex," Ray promised. "I would never do that to her."

Ray and Alex changed the subject to football, just as Mr. and Mrs. Frost came in the door.

"How was your walk?" Ray asked.

"It was wonderful, Ray," Mrs. Frost replied smiling. "Absolutely wonderful. Where's Kaitlyn?" she asked, looking around.

"She went upstairs to use the bathroom," Alex replied. "She'll be down in a minute.

"Oh, okay," Kathryn replied. "Why don't you boys get ready for bed. Ray, you have a tiring day ahead of you tomorrow and you should get your rest."

"You're right," Ray said. "I've got one more thing to finish up here, and then I'll call it a night. Is that okay?"

"Yes," Mrs. Frost answered as she excused herself to tidy up too.

Kaitlyn came downstairs and asked her father how the walk was, and Jim told her it was wonderful. He didn't notice the slight mark on her neck. Neither did Kaitlyn.

Jim went into the library, and Alex motioned to Kaitlyn with his hand. While mouthing the words *your neck* to her, he pointed his finger to the area she needed to know about. Kaitlyn was mortified and turned around to go upstairs again. Ray let out a slight giggle and returned to his studies.

Kaitlyn went back to the bathroom and indeed, noticed a mark on her lower neck. She took out some make up and covered it up, and although she was able to disguise it, she remained self-conscious for a couple days to follow. "Oh man," was all she could think, along with … "I liked it."

Kaitlyn came back downstairs to kiss her parents and to say goodnight to Alex, and to Ray. She went upstairs and retired to her room, taking a breather from what could have been a bad scene.

She heard a knock at the door and answered with, "Come in."

Ray opened the door and peeped his head in the doorway. "Goodnight, babes. I love you."

"Goodnight," Kaitlyn said smiling and wanting more of the earlier events. "I love you too."

Ray made a puckering face with his lips, pleading for a goodnight kiss.

"You're going to get me in trouble," Kaitlyn said as she inched her way towards him."

Ray and Kaitlyn kissed goodnight as they exchanged their feelings of love for one another. They both retired to their rooms, with smiles in their heart and lust on their minds.

Chapter Ten

The morning came too early.

It was a brisk autumn day, the kind of morning where staying curled up in a warm bed was so much better than getting up. Regardless, Kaitlyn, Ray and Alex had to get ready for school, leaving them no choice but to get up, get dressed, and be on their way.

Ray was nervous about going back, knowing what he would have to contend with. He took some comfort in the plans he and Kaitlyn devised: Ray smiling and thanking the well-wishers, while keeping talk about or with John to a minimum.

Alex left a few minutes before Kaitlyn and Ray, catching up with his buddies on the way, while Kaitlyn and Ray stayed behind gathering everything needed for school before walking out the front door. Once the house was no longer in view, Ray asked if he could see Kaitlyn's neck. She angled her chin and raised her eyes in an upward stare, showing it to him. The mark, for the most part, was covered, but Ray apologized anyway.

Kaitlyn half-smiled.

"Are we visiting our tree today, Miss Frost?" Ray asked with a bow.

Are you asking me if I *want* to or asking me if we *are*?"

"Both."

"Then the answer is yes," Kaitlyn replied grinning. "Yes. Definitely yes! No more marks though, okay?"

Ray looked at Kaitlyn. "I love you," he said softly, then let out a giggle.

"Me too," Kaitlyn replied, and then brought up another subject. "Did you know my parent's have a social engagement tomorrow night?"

"No," Ray replied, now interested. "They *do*?"

Ray could see Kaitlyn's mind churning. "They have a benefit dinner and dance. They'll be out until almost eleven o'clock."

Ray raised his eyebrows with naughty thoughts. "Oh, really? And Alex?"

"Alex is going to his friend's house for awhile," Kaitlyn answered, sneaking a grin.

"We'll be all alone?"

"All by ourselves, Ray," she replied, grinning wider.

"Well, well, "Ray said laughing, "what *will* we do?"

"I just *don't* know," Kaitlyn replied, with both knowing well she'd already planned out the evening.

"Hmmm, this could be interesting," Ray said, putting his arm around Kaitlyn and pulling her in to a side hug. "May I kiss you?"

"By all means, please do."

Ray peered around to see if anyone was looking. He turned her rosy cheeks to a full-blown blush.

"You don't hide things very well, do you Kaitlyn?"

"Why do you say that?" she asked.

"You have that *naughty thing* happening again," Ray replied with a chuckle.

The two were still smiling when they arrived at school.

Entering, Ray saw the "In Memory Of Jaycee Niles" portrait, with the announcement of a new scholarship. "That's nice," he thought. He also saw a large banner that read: "Welcome Back Ray!" He was touched by the sentiment and it brightened his spirits, knowing there were many caring friends around him.

Kaitlyn's girlfriends came up to her to say hello and then turned their attention to Ray, greeting and welcoming him back.

Ray and Kaitlyn walked through the hallways, and all they could hear were kids shouting out, "Welcome back!" and "Good to see you." Their words were kind and considerate, leaving out mention of the tragedy. Ray and Kaitlyn were relieved.

The two met for lunch. They chose a quiet place in the cafeteria away from the other kids' chatter, and sat together quietly near a windowsill. But the peace was interrupted when John and Allison came near.

"Hi," Allison said, nervous about John being with her.

Ray and Kaitlyn returned the greeting, with the same uncomfortable feelings.

"Sorry to bother you," John uttered, lowering his eyes.

"You're not bothering us, John," Ray responded.

Then there was too much silence. A hush had fallen in the cafeteria as the other students noticed the four together. The wings of a ladybug could have been heard through the white walled hall. Tension filled the room, as all ears seemed to be aimed in their direction.

"Join us," Ray said, looking at Kaitlyn for permission.

Kaitlyn nodded at the empty seats.

"I just wanted to know if you were doing okay?" John asked.

"Yeah, I'm okay. I guess," Ray replied. "Thanks."

Allison turned to John and lowered her voice. "We should go," she said. "It's too soon."

Allison and John waved good-bye to Ray and Kaitlyn, aware of the scores of eyes staring at them. John looked back at Ray and said, "I'm ... really sorry. If it's any consolation, I'm never going to drink again."

John left before Ray could respond. He didn't want to hear Ray's reply, afraid he would think it was an empty promise. But in reality it wasn't. John meant every word.

Kaitlyn and Ray felt the onlookers' eyes disappear. Instead, the students chattered amongst themselves, coming up with every possible outcome of the encounter they'd witnessed.

Kaitlyn and Ray finished their lunches, barely speaking to each other, both feeling like they were in one of the dreams where you imagine yourself forgetting to put clothes on before going out in public. Finishing their lunch in silence, they then continued on with their school day and met at their lockers afterwards.

"You ready?" Ray asked.

"Yes, sir. I am," Kaitlyn replied as she gathered her assignments together. "Let's go."

Ray held Kaitlyn's books while walking to the park, exchanging light conversation. As they approached the entrance, both noticed the bright red Mulberry bushes. The colors adorning the bushes and trees made the park that much more inviting. Walking towards Sweetheart Lane, their eyes smiled in delight of what was to come.

Ray tucked their schoolbooks under his right arm and took hold of Kaitlyn's hand — both tingling at the touch. They spotted their special tree in front of them and excitement grew. "I'll race you," Kaitlyn said, releasing her hand from his.

Ray looked at Kaitlyn with fretful eyes. "I can't run, Kait. My knee isn't ready for that."

"Oh, I'm sorry, Ray." Kaitlyn replied, frowning embarrassment. "I forgot."

"Don't worry about it, Kait," Ray said. "I think I should take it easy and stick to walking for right now. And anyway, we're here."

Ray rested against the tree and pointed his 'come here' gesture as a grimace came across his face. Kaitlyn followed Ray's instructions and fell into his arms with an enthusiastic embrace. "Gosh I've missed you, Ray," Kaitlyn said, gazing into his eyes.

Ray held Kaitlyn and agilely stroked her shoulders with penetrating massage, while Kaitlyn brought her fingers to Ray's face, drawing his lips in to touch hers. They exchanged a few tentative pecks before turning them into full kisses of passion and want.

Their breathing became both harder and shorter, feeling their bodies ache for more as their hands found places to touch and discover. Ray kissed her neck gently, tasting her skin, and moving up, he kissed her ears, letting his warm breath fall on her. Kaitlyn trembled blissfully.

Kaitlyn explored his aching body with her hands as he continued kissing her. Continuing to touch, Kaitlyn snuggled close into the nape of his neck, kissing him with hunger and gliding her lips and tongue over, tasting him.

"You feel good, Ray," she spoke softly through shortened breaths. "Hmmm, you taste good, too."

Ray kissed Kaitlyn while bringing his gentle hands to her face. "Oh yes, you feel *real* good, Kait," he agreed, not truly wanting to take a moment to *talk*.

"I want you to hold me," Kaitlyn said, motioning for them to sit.

Ray didn't want to *sit* either, but did so against the tree. Kaitlyn made herself comfortable, leaning against his chest. She tilted her head upward and to the right to view Ray's eyes. "I love you. I can't believe how much I love you. It almost doesn't seem real."

Ray massaged her arms and smiled, knowing what she was talking about, but not letting on that he did. And bringing his hands to her shoulders, Ray gave Kaitlyn a caring caress before slipping his hands downwards, towards her upper chest. Kaitlyn moaned with pleasure.

"Touch me, Ray," Kaitlyn whispered, her breasts longing for more.

Ray began stroking and cupping her breasts through the loose-fitting blouse, and Kaitlyn rested against him, tilting her head back in delight. Moving forward suddenly, Kaitlyn turned around and positioned herself in a straddle across his lap. Both could feel their urges through their clothes. Their eyes locked in yearning, and with craving countenances, the two engaged in more passionate kissing.

Kaitlyn pulled away from Ray, and one by one began unbuttoning her blouse. Bringing his lips to her bosom, Kaitlyn brought his hands to her soft delicate skin. Ray teased Kaitlyn with his fingers as he slipped them under the fabric supporting her breasts. Kaitlyn felt shivers run wild.

Kaitlyn kissed Ray and pulled back from him. Releasing her breasts from their bondage as she sat slightly back away from Ray, she began to gently touch her firm breasts, her nipples hard with desire. Ray enjoyed the visual masterpiece in front of him. Bringing her hands to her side, Kaitlyn allowed Ray to touch her with the tips of his fingers, as she gasped with pleasure, tilting her head back and closing her eyes, taking in the moment. Ray took hold of Kaitlyn's shoulders and pulled her in closer. Kaitlyn peered into Ray's eyes with pure love, enveloping him. His pleasure was shown with his smile.

Kaitlyn's hands found their way up inside Ray's shirt, and she pulled the clothing up towards his chin. He was warm and felt good. She cradled into him, allowing both to feel the warmth. They looked into each other's eyes with love, joy, and lust, and as they continued exploring each other's bodies, sensations excited them while bringing a little fear. Both wanted more.

"We'd better go," Kaitlyn said, realizing resistance was getting tough.

"I know," Ray said with a 'pleading for it not to end' kiss.

Kaitlyn put her hands on Ray's cheeks and kissed him with hunger. "We really should get going," she murmured, trailing her tongue towards Ray's chest.

"Yeah, I know," Ray had to agree while beginning to massage her breasts again, then firmly grasping her bottom.

Kaitlyn began kissing Ray's neck while slithering her tongue towards his ears. Stopping, she leaned back and slid the back of her fingers in a teasing sensual away over her breasts and down towards her navel, giving Ray another nice visual. She stopped and cuddled up to Ray as if she needed comfort. "I don't want to go. I want to stay here in your arms, holding you, touching you, kissing you forever."

"I don't want to go either," Ray said, his thoughts still on Kaitlyn's breasts, wanting to finish what had begun. "But you're right. We should."

Kaitlyn let out a whimpering "No," as if it were Ray's idea to leave in the first place, but continued kissing his neck, lips and face while touching him below his navel through his clothes, teasing him and exciting him even more.

She stopped herself and sat up straight, beginning to button her blouse. She looked him straight in the eyes as if she hadn't whined for it *not* to end. "We've got to go. It's getting late, and we'll get in trouble." All the while, not letting Ray know that her loins ached beyond measure.

"You're right," Ray said, taking Kaitlyn into a hug and closing his eyes in disappointment.

Kaitlyn cuddled her head into Ray's chest as her heart cried to stay. She closed her eyes, and they held one another for a few moments until their beating hearts returned to normal rhythms. They left their special place, holding hands and feeling on top of the world, while their bodies still yearned for satisfaction.

Arriving home before Kaitlyn's father, Kaitlyn and Ray tended to their studies before Kaitlyn helped her mother with dinner.

Shortly after the family meal, Ray *suddenly* felt exhausted and went to bed, while Kaitlyn, not quite ready for bed herself, relaxed by the fire with one of her mother's lovesick romance novels. Growing tired, but resisting the common sense of going to bed, Kaitlyn only did so after she had read the last page, knowing she wouldn't be able to sleep until she found out how things ended.

Friday came and Kaitlyn woke with she and Ray's evening plans in the forefront of her mind. She knew her thoughts would keep her occupied throughout most of the day, and it wouldn't be long before she could put her revised plans into action. After dressing and brushing her teeth, Kaitlyn joined Ray and her family for breakfast in the kitchen — Jim read the morning paper and drank coffee, while Kathryn sipped her tea.

Ray looked 'bright-eyed and bushy-tailed' as he too was excited with what lay ahead. Or maybe he just *slept* well. Alex was his normal self, chowing down on toast in a hurry, trying to get out the door to meet up with his football buddies. And when Ray and Kaitlyn were done, they too headed out the door.

"So, Mr. Ray Niles ..." Kaitlyn began sarcastically, "we going to the tree this afternoon?"

"Would you like to, Miss Frost?"

"Yub yub, most indubitably," Kaitlyn replied, laughing.

"Then consider it a date!" Ray said, pulling Kaitlyn into a side hug. Both slightly lost their balance. "I'll meet you at your locker after school."

Kaitlyn and Ray went about their day and even had a good time. There were no staring eyes in the cafeteria, and things seemed to have returned to normal. When the last bell rang, Ray met Kaitlyn at her locker, and the two headed to their tree for a little more quiet time.

Kaitlyn and Ray made it home just before Jim and exchanged their usual discussions with him before doing their studies and sitting down to a light dinner. Jim and Kathryn joined the three kids during their meal before going upstairs to get ready for their dinner/dance.

Alex rushed through dinner so he could go to his friend's house faster, having his own plans for the night. But before Alex was allowed to leave, Jim lay down the rules. All three nodded in understanding.

Jim and Kathryn went upstairs to get ready, and when they came back down, they reemphasized the rules and left for their evening out.

Kaitlyn and Ray had their pleasant evening worked out to the smallest detail, and as soon as Alex left the house, their sortie began.

Kaitlyn came across as being so sweet and innocent, yet her mind was always churning, devising scenarios with Ray. She wanted more than anything to finish where she and Ray had left off. Ray, it seemed, had similar ideas.

Unfulfilled aches were coursing through Kaitlyn's mind as she went upstairs to freshen, leaving Ray to start the fire and light candles — both knowing a fire had already been ignited earlier that afternoon. He brought the lights down low, and romance filled the room like soft music.

As Ray sat on the sofa, his eyes were drawn to Kaitlyn descending the staircase. The fire's glow picked up the glint in her eyes, and flickers of light illuminated her hair. His eyes traveled lower to her black satin, button-down dress, noticing how it hugged her curves. Ray was in a trance watching Kaitlyn glide towards him — her mere presence a seduction. He rose to meet her.

Taking Kaitlyn in his arms, Ray felt the soft fabric slide against her back as his touch sent shivers through Kaitlyn's body. He put her hand in his and led her to the sofa.

"You're beautiful," Ray said as they sat. "You look ..."

"Delicious?" Kaitlyn finished innocently.

"Yes," Ray chuckled. "You look delicious." Pausing for a second, Ray asked, "Why were you and Allison laughing about that word at the beach?"

Kaitlyn replied. "We'd been talking in the car on the way to the beach and saw a Burma-Shave sign. It said "delicious" and I made the comment that you were ... delicious. You definitely are *delicious*," Kaitlyn said smirking and licking her lips.

Ray just replied, "Oh."

"Come closer," Ray said, patting his lap.

Kaitlyn inched her way towards him.

Kaitlyn turned to face Ray, held his cheeks and gazed into his eyes, drawing his lips to hers. She closed her eyes and let her love for Ray escape through the tender touch as Ray held her in his arms, kissing back with intensity. His hands slid downward, and he brought her closer, pressing against her. With longing eyes, they engaged in passionate, pleading kisses, while Ray's hands massaged Kaitlyn with urgency as she clutched his collar, pulling him in even closer. With his kiss, he traveled down to her neck, tasting her sweet skin, and Kaitlyn tilted her head gently, allowing chills to escape, while her heart ached with love. Both squirmed with pleasure.

Kaitlyn leaned back as she had done earlier that afternoon and began to unbutton her dress, enough to allow much exploration. As she pulled the now two sets of fabric apart, Kaitlyn's breasts showed their delight. Ray had his first full view of Kaitlyn's bosom, without any contraption getting in the way of the vision before him.

"You do realize that we shouldn't be doing this?" Kaitlyn commented softly as she straddled Ray, wanting him to touch her, wanting him closer than is humanly possible, and wanting to feel his warm skin against hers, regardless of the risk.

Carefully situating herself on Ray's lap, Kaitlyn felt Ray's want pressed hard against her, exciting her. Feeling herself become wet with relentless craving, Kaitlyn began to gently roll her hips against Ray's lap, surprising him, but enjoying the *gift*. With Ray's shirt now off and pant buckle loosened, Kaitlyn increased the intensity of her circular movement, applying more pressure, relieving the intensity of pressure only as she completed the circle. With each choreographed movement, Kaitlyn rolled her head gently back while closing her eyes, with both enjoying the titillating thrill spreading throughout their bodies.

Continuing to rotate her hips in a mutually satisfying manner, Kaitlyn and Ray kissed hard with passion, while their hands, fingertips, tongues, and lips found all the right places to explore. Excitement burned through Ray's body as his touches and grasps became more urgent. His aching want was outlined in the beads of moisture on his face.

Neither one had felt this kind of exciting emotion or want before. The sensations were almost overwhelming, and when they became too intense, Kaitlyn buried her head in Ray's chest as though she needed comforting. They almost couldn't believe their feelings were this intense and real.

After a short while of thorough enjoyment, Kaitlyn pulled back. "We've got to stop," she whispered, lips stilled pressed against his, beginning to feel an almost tingling sensation in her loins that scared her.

Ray put his arms around Kaitlyn and held her. "I know," he said through short breaths. "But I don't want to."

"I don't want to either. But, Ray, we have to. We really do have to."

Discussing the matter further while still fondling, kissing, and rubbing against one another, Kaitlyn and Ray continued on with their 'conversation', feeling their urges becoming even more hard to resist, their loins overwhelmingly wet with desire, their hearts beating with urgency, and their love crying out for release. The two came to a point where they knew they had to end it, even though their bodies pleaded with them to continue.

Kaitlyn remained straddling Ray, her face pressed into the nape of his neck, with both trying to calm their crying bodies. Once they did settle and realized that their time had run out, Kaitlyn slowly rose from his lap with her hands in his, releasing them until only the tips of their fingers touched. She looked at him and smiled before going upstairs to change back to her previous clothes.

While Kaitlyn put Plan 'B' into action, Ray blew the candles out and put them back in their original spot. He straightened out the couch and himself, and then put his own plan 'B' into action, racing quickly upstairs.

Kaitlyn came downstairs before Ray, and when he rejoined her, she was placing another log on the fire. Both were trying to avert their attentions from the previous events, so Ray suggested they read from their book. Kaitlyn liked his idea.

Kaitlyn went into the library and returned with "Words To Live By." They settled on the couch next to one another and began flipping through the pages. They took turns reading the many excerpts and became entwined once again.

Another passage that seemed to awaken Ray was: "Changes in life occur. Make the right choices and you'll get through."

Ray was going to be facing many changes, as was Kaitlyn. Choices were going to have to be made to do the right thing, instead of doing what they wanted to do. The choices facing them were their desires. They had to figure out what they would allow to happen and what they would need to abstain from.

Ray was going to have to make choices regarding John, and he needed to figure out how he wanted to deal with him. On one level, he wanted John to rot in jail, but on another, he felt John's remorse was sincere.

Ray grew quiet. He didn't tell Kaitlyn what he was thinking about. He wasn't sure himself. It was as if he were still trying to figure out how to put the pieces together that had been thrown into a jumbled pile in his head.

"I need to see my dad tomorrow," Ray said quietly. "I need to talk to him."

"You should," Kaitlyn answered, "Do you want me to drive you?"

"No," Ray said, unsure of his answer. "I think I'll walk and take the time to sort through stuff."

Kaitlyn and Ray sat for a while and continued reading their book, not paying too much attention to whatever words were staring back. Ray asked to see the forgiveness passage again, wanting to study it. Kaitlyn flipped to it and handed the book to him. He held it while reading the phrase to himself. He read it three times and then nodded. "I know what I need to do."

Just then, Alex came through the front door, announcing his arrival. "I'm home. You two decent?" he asked with a laugh.

"Yes, Alex," Ray said snidely. "We're in the living room."

"So, kids ... What ya been doing?" Alex sing-songed in teasing. "Let me guess ... " Alex laughed, tossing a smile in Kaitlyn's direction, pretending to count his fingers while craning his neck to inspect Kaitlyn's neck for evidence. Turning his attention to Ray and pointing his finger to him. "You be careful there, Ray," he warned, throwing a teasing grin.

Ray smiled. Kaitlyn did not, giving her brother a dirty look.

As fast as Alex came into the room, he left and went about his business. And for some reason, Ray just excused himself and went to his room without explanation. Possibly, something came to the top of his pile.

Kaitlyn sat in the living room alone, wondering how Ray could go from loving her with hot passion to chilling her with distance. It was strange. Although she knew that he had a lot to be bothered by and respected his privacy, she still felt somehow slighted. She left him alone, having her own thoughts to ponder. Strumming through the book again, Kaitlyn reread a few passages and came to some of her own conclusions.

As she sat in the dimly lit room, Jim and Kathryn walked through the front doors, laughing and looking as though they had a good time.

"Hi, honey," Kathryn greeted her daughter. "How was your evening?"

"It was fine," Kaitlyn replied distractedly. "How was yours?"

"Wonderful! We had a great time," she replied, beginning to look around. Where's Ray?"

"He went upstairs," Kaitlyn said. "He's upset."

"Did you two have an argument?" Kathryn asked.

"No, no … nothing like that," Kaitlyn replied. "It has to do with John."

"I'll have your father check in on him," Kathryn said, always wanting to fix everything. Kaitlyn thought her mother's suggestion was a good idea.

Kaitlyn knew that she was not the person to go talk with Ray, as she wasn't exactly thrilled with him at that moment. She knew if she went up there and asked: "What are you thinking about" or "How do you feel?" she wouldn't get an honest answer. And asking those questions could balloon an already tense feeling. "Yup," she thought. "Best to let Dad handle this one."

Kathryn excused herself and went upstairs to her room, where Jim was changing out of his formal clothes. She explained the situation and asked that he have a word with Ray. Jim gave his favorite girl a peck and a wink, and went to Ray's bedroom.

Knocking on the door, Jim asked through it, "You alright, Ray?"

"Yeah, I'm okay," Ray replied while Jim entered. Neither made eye contact.

"Tell me what's on your mind, son," Jim insisted as he took a seat on the bed

"I don't know," Ray replied uneasily. "So many things, I guess." He took a moment and gathered his thoughts.

"I miss my mom. I'm angry with John, yet at the same time, I need to forgive him. I miss my dad too. I have so many mixed emotions, and I'm having trouble sorting them all out. I'm going to go visit my dad tomorrow though, if it's alright?"

"Yes, of course," Jim said sympathetically. "It's more than okay. I'd be worried if you didn't visit him. Listen to me carefully, Ray."

Ray gave Jim his full attention.

"I know you're scared. I know you miss your mom. You're always going to miss your mom. What you need to do right now is remember all the good things about her and smile with those memories. Keep her spirit alive by talking about her and loving her. Be there for your dad the way your mom would have been for him. Honor her memory by making decisions in your life that would make her proud. Be the man she taught you to be. And most of all, Ray, try to find happiness. I told you, moms hate it when their children are sad."

A tear rolled down Ray's face. "You're right. You are *so* right." Ray stood up and gave Jim a big bear hug.

"Everything's going to be okay, son," Jim said, patting his back. "In time, things will get better." He paused. "There's one thing that you have to know though."

"What's that?" Ray asked with questioning eyes, pulling back.

"You'll never get over the loss of your mother. You'll always miss her. But you will be able to come to grips with it. I promise."

Jim turned toward the door and then looked back at the young man on the bed. "I'm speaking from experience."

Ray appreciated Jim's advice, and he also knew what he needed to do, but still had a few minor details to work out.

A short time later, Kaitlyn came upstairs to bed and knocked on his door. "May I come in?" she asked.

"Yes," Ray answered.

"You okay?" Kaitlyn asked while trying to avoid the questions she truly wanted to ask.

"Yeah, I'm okay," Ray replied. "Come here."

Kaitlyn went to Ray, and he held her in a hug that confirmed his love for her.

"Goodnight, Kait. You know I love you, right?"

"I know, and I love you, too," Kaitlyn replied kissing him on the lips. "I'm here for you," she reminded him as she left his room. "Goodnight."

Kaitlyn turned off the light and climbed in bed. With her favorite quilt warming her, thoughts of Ray drifted through her mind as she gently floated her fingers over her breasts, lulling her into a deep sleep.

The following morning, Ray woke up early and left for the hospital, planning on spending the day with his father. Kaitlyn got up and enjoyed some tea with her mother, exchanging small talk and pleasantries.

Kathryn told Kaitlyn the story of her first love — Jim. She told her how and when they had met, and what kinds of things they did together. She didn't mention anything about kissing, Kathryn not being the type to discuss such flagrant matters. She told Kaitlyn about the butterflies she had when she was with him and how she missed him the minute he left her side.

As Kathryn reminisced about her first love, Kaitlyn's mind went a million miles a minute, comparing her feelings for Ray with those of her mother's. When the daydreaming stopped, they looked at each other and smiled.

Kaitlyn looked at her teacup with fondness. "I love this cup, Mom."

"So do I, Kaitlyn, " Kathryn said with a motherly smile.

"The intricate design and details of the yellow roses are exquisite," Kaitlyn said as if she were a designer.

"Yes, it is lovely," Kathryn chuckled. "I should never have packed it away for so long.

"Thanks again, Mom," Kaitlyn. "It's very special to me."

Kathryn took a sip from her too hot tea. "What are you up to today?"

"I think I'm going to call Allison and see if she wants to go to The Soda Fountain."

"That seems like a good idea," Kathryn replied. "It's been awhile since you went out with *just* Allison."

"Yeah," Kaitlyn replied. "I think she and I need to get together — I'll give her a call now."

Kaitlyn excused herself to use the phone, catching Allison as she was just getting out of the shower. They decided to meet at 11 o'clock.

Kaitlyn sat back down with her mother and finished their conversation and tea before going upstairs to shower and dress. Kathryn went to the library to delve into another sappy romance novel.

Kaitlyn showed up at The Soda Fountain and found Allison sitting at their usual table waiting, having ordered two chocolate sodas for both of them.

"A little daring today, aren't we?" Kaitlyn said, laughing and pointing to the sodas.

"I thought we should expand our horizons," Allison laughed.

Allison and Kaitlyn took the time together to work out their disagreement and catch up on what's been happening in their lives. The only problem was, they were both dealing with the same issue — just different ends of it. Kaitlyn was concerned with Ray and his father, and Allison was concerned about John going to jail. Kaitlyn was concerned about John as well, but it was not her primary worry.

"Kaitlyn, I don't want John to go to jail," Allison said.

"You don't think he should be punished?" Kaitlyn asked.

"I didn't say that," Allison said defensively.

"You might as well have," Kaitlyn replied. "He killed Mrs. Niles, Allison. He should be punished."

"I thought you were his friend too?" Allison said angrily.

"I am his friend," Kaitlyn said. "But he's the one who chose to drink and drive. It was *his* decision, *his* mistake, and now *he's* going to have to pay for it."

"I can't believe you would want to see John in prison," Allison said hurt.

"Listen, I don't want him to *rot* in jail," Kaitlyn came back, guarding her intentions. "He's got to be responsible for his actions though. He was a supposed *adult* when he got into his car. Hello! Welcome to adulthood!" Kaitlyn said sarcastically.

Just as Kaitlyn finished her words, John came from behind, hearing every word. "How can you be so callus, Kaitlyn?" he asked. "We've been friends ... forever."

"Yeah, Kaitlyn," Allison chimed in. "How can you be?"

"Because you killed someone, John," Kaitlyn replied with anger. "You killed my boyfriend's mother.

"Come on Allison, let's go," John demanded.

"Don't bother," Kaitlyn said in disgust. "I'm going," she said, already at a stand.

She walked home feverishly, angry thoughts and words screaming in her head. Stomping in the house, she slammed the door behind and went straight to her room.

Ray came home shortly afterward and asked for her. Kathryn pointed upstairs and told him she was angry. "Something happened between she and Allison. That's all I know."

Ray went upstairs as fast as he could and knocked on the door.

"Kaitlyn," Ray called to her. "What's wrong?"

"Nothing," Kaitlyn yelled. "Nothing at all."

"Kait," Ray pleaded, "talk to me. Can I come in?"

"Do what you want to," Kaitlyn said with anger in her voice.

"Come here," Ray said, extending his arms.

Kaitlyn rose from her bed and was rescued in Ray's arms. Tears turned to sobs when she buried her head in his chest.

"What happened?" Ray asked, holding her away from him to see her face.

"I don't want to talk about it," Kaitlyn said. "Just hold me."

Ray held Kaitlyn until she calmed.

"How's your dad?" Kaitlyn asked through teary eyes, changing the subject.

"He's okay," Ray said. "It was good to see him."

Ray held Kaitlyn away from him again and wiped a tear from her cheek with back of his finger. "Everything's going to be okay."

Kaitlyn looked at him and buried her face in his chest again. She wanted the comfort of his love. She wanted him to hold her and protect her. "I feel like running away and hiding from the world."

"Well then," Ray replied, "I'll just have to go with you," smiling at her.

Kaitlyn's lips turned slightly up.

"There's my smile," Ray said. "I see it. There it is."

"You sound like my mom when I was little."

"My mom used to say the same thing to me," Ray said fondly. "It's funny how little things that used to irritate you, you find yourself treasuring when that person is gone."

Kaitlyn looked at Ray, understanding his sentiment. "You're right. We do take things for granted, don't we?"

"I think we all do," Ray agreed. "Then one day when it's gone, you realize what you're missing. I know I sure am."

"Don't ever leave me, Ray," Kaitlyn begged. "I know what I'd be missing."

"I'll never leave you, Kaitlyn," Ray spoke sincerely. "I don't think I could live without you — I'm in love with you now. I'll be in love with you tomorrow. I will be in love with you for the rest of my life."

Kaitlyn held Ray as she whispered, "Me too."

"I'm going to take a nap," Kaitlyn said. "I just need to get away from the worry, the hurt and the world for a bit."

"Okay, babes," Ray replied. "Maybe I will too. Get some rest. I love you."

Ray kissed Kaitlyn and shut the door behind as he left, deciding to take a nap as well. His day had been equally draining.

Chapter Eleven

*   *   *

Kaitlyn saw Allison's face cringe and hands shake as they talked about their argument from fifty years before. "What's wrong, Allison?" Kaitlyn asked.

"I have to go," Allison said, abruptly rising to her feet. "I don't want to do this. I've been down this road already, and I would just as soon not travel it again. I've got to go," Allison said as she made a straight dash for the door.

"Allison, wait!" Kaitlyn called out, walking briskly after her. "I'm sorry. I didn't mean to ... "

Allison walked to the car and gave Kaitlyn a backhanded wave before pulling out of the drive.

"Damn it!" Kaitlyn quietly yelled out to no one as the door shut behind.

Feeling a mix of emotions, Kaitlyn began cleaning up in a fury. Taking her irritation out on the dust cloth and broom, angered energies came through her hands as she wiped the kitchen table in a frenzy. Afterwards, the floor felt her hostility through the broom. She swiftly went through the house cleaning whatever needed to be until there wasn't anything left to be done.

Not wanting to be alone with her thoughts, Kaitlyn did what she had done so many years before — she curled up in her now torn quilt on the couch, allowing only the top of her head to be seen through her cover.

Thoughts stomped through her mind in torment, and Kaitlyn was thankful to be saved from her own fervor by the ringing of the phone. She rose to her feet in an angered state and answered the phone, with an annoyed "Hello."

"Mom, you okay?" her daughter Rose asked, sensing Kaitlyn's distress.

"Hi, honey," Kaitlyn replied. "I'm fine."

"No you're not ... Mom," Rose said disagreeing. "I'm coming over."

Kaitlyn's daughter, Roselyn Howard, was Kaitlyn's only child and also her friend. She looked quite similar to Kaitlyn, having light brown hair and friendly facial features. She was a couple inches taller than Kaitlyn, and when Roselyn was younger, she had always made sure that her mother was aware of this particular fact. Roselyn was trim, but not overly thin, and she carried the same sparkle in her eye that Kaitlyn did.

Roselyn, nicknamed Rose, married Robert Howard, a native of Edmund Falls, Massachusetts. They met when he was in Winter's Crest visiting mutual friends, and they immediately fell in love. Their courtship was brief, the two became engaged, and an even shorter engagement preceded their marriage.

Robert didn't struggle with leaving his native state as he found Winter's Crest to have the same New England feel. It also didn't hurt that he was wealthy and had the freedom to leave, doing so for Rose. Robert knew Rose didn't want to leave Winter's Crest or her mother. He understood their special relationship.

Rose and Robert have been married twenty-five years and have raised two grown children. Robert, Rob to his friends, continues to work with his business, and Rose helps out with the paperwork and attends community and social events.

Before now, Rose had stayed home raising their children, tending the house and helping out at the schools, much like her grandmother had. She'd led a comfortable life, and although to others it might have seemed perfect on the outside, inside it was full of relationship turmoil. Rose never disclosed this fact to her mother, but Kaitlyn suspected it.

Kaitlyn tidied herself and tried to conceal the fact that she'd been upset. Fixing her hair in the hallway mirror, she heard Rose coming through the front door, calling to her.

"I'm right here," Kaitlyn said, walking towards Rose and hugging her hello. "How are you, honey?"

"I'm fine," Rose replied. "More importantly, how are *you*?"

"I'm fine," Kaitlyn said, trying to reassure Rose and convince herself. "Allison and I had a little argument, that's all."

"About what?" she questioned.

"That's not important right now," Kaitlyn replied. "Here," she said, handing the letter to Rose.

Rose had a questioning look in her eyes and on her face before she studied the letter. "Oh my God," she cried out, turning the letter over and asking at the same time if she'd opened it.

"Not yet," Kaitlyn replied, wondering herself why she hadn't.

"Why not?"

"To be honest, honey," Kaitlyn answered. "I think I'm scared to. I'm afraid to see what it says. What if he's dying?"

Rose was quiet while staring at the little envelope. "I see," was all she muttered.

"Would you like some tea?" Kaitlyn asked cheerfully, changing the subject.

"Yes, that'd be great," Rose replied, offering to help.

"I see your cup's still holding up?" Rose asked.

"Yes," Kaitlyn replied as she traced her fingers along the edge. "A little worn though now. Do you still have the one I gave you?"

"Yes," Rose replied smiling. "I use it every day."

"One day, this will be yours," Kaitlyn said thinking ahead. "I was supposed to give this to you a long time ago, but I just haven't been able to part with it. At the rate I'm going, you'll get it after I'm gone."

"Mom, don't talk like that," Rose replied. "You're going to be around for a long time."

"I thought you felt I should be in a home?" Kaitlyn asked with a whimsical raised eyebrow, not sure if she wanted to hear the answer.

"You know, I've been giving that a second thought," she confided seriously. "You're fine here at home. This is where you belong."

Kaitlyn motioned for Rose to come with her. "I want to show you something."

Kaitlyn brought her to the living room and took the cover off the old box, taking out the yearbook. They sat down while Kaitlyn strummed through it, showing Rose pictures of John, Ray and Allison.

"Wow, look at them," she said. "It's hard to believe they were that young once."

Kaitlyn turned the page and showed Rose her own high school photo.

"You were beautiful." Rose looked at her mom, studying her face, hair and eyes. "You still are."

Kaitlyn smiled.

Kaitlyn continued showing Rose some of her other friends and then came to the end. "This is Ray's mother, Jaycee," Kaitlyn stated as she pointed to the picture. "This is the woman John killed."

"She was beautiful," Rose said as sorrow fell upon her face. "She looks like she was a wonderful person."

"She was," Kaitlyn whispered under her breath, lowering her eyes.

"What happened to John?" Rose asked after a moment of silence.

"That was one of the hardest times in my youth, Rose. Ray and I had a wonderful evening the Friday night before John's inquest, and then Saturday night, after he visited his father, the mood between he and I changed.

"Also, during that Saturday afternoon, Allison and I had an argument. Then John and I had an argument. It was dreadful.

That's part of what Allison and I had a falling out about today. But enough about that," she said with a dismissive sweep of her hand.

"Ray started to become aloof late Saturday night and was intermittently detached on Sunday, too. Then Monday came, the day of the inquest, and Ray turned into someone I didn't know. I knew he was struggling, and I wanted to be there for him, but he wouldn't allow me to be. He wouldn't talk to me or even acknowledge me. It was the first time he hurt me," Kaitlyn ended briefly.

"The first time?" Rose asked, questioning how many other times there were.

"Yes, Rose," Kaitlyn replied. "It was the first time. There were other times too."

Kaitlyn and Rose settled in on the living room couch with their tea as Kaitlyn went on to explain the following events that took place, letting her know each and every detail of what happened with John, Ray and Allison.

*   *   *

October 12, 1950, at 1:30 p.m., was John's inquest date.

Tensions were high in the Frost household that morning as the reality of a possible trial for John stared them in the face. Feeling torn between what John did, and knowing he should be punished, and then adding in that they'd known him since birth, weighed heavily on Jim and Kathryn, as well as Kaitlyn and Alex.

Ray, on the other hand, had only known him briefly. And although the two had been friends, it was *his* mother who died and *his* father who was still recuperating in the hospital.

Ray was filled with emotions ranging from vehemence to anguish. And as his feelings battled inside his head, he paced back and forth as if he were a male lion protecting his den from the enemy, ready to attack any and all that got in his way. He became short in his responses, only heightening the thickened tension.

Everyone sat at the table stabbing their eggs, chewing with silent frustration. Words were kept to a minimum, with Kathryn only giving Kaitlyn and Ray instructions as to where and when to meet her at the school. When breakfast was over, the three walked to Mackey High, with Ray's pace two steps ahead of Kaitlyn's and Alex's. Ray's inner war was released by the aura he exuded as they walked, and if Kaitlyn or Alex crossed his unnamed line, he would stare them down with burning eyes.

Alex stayed to himself, keeping all words unspoken, as Kaitlyn fought back tears. Alex stole fleeting looks at his sister on the way, checking to see if she was okay — wanting to comfort her. Bewildered glances were shot between the two, trying to make sense of Ray's uncharacteristic behavior.

Kaitlyn felt as if a stranger had taken over the boy she loved, and she didn't care for this *new* person one bit. It was the first time Kaitlyn questioned her love for Ray, wondering if he was the guy she thought him to be. She asked herself if she could love the side of Ray that made her cringe — she didn't have an answer.

As they approached the school, Alex took off running, escaping into the safety of his friends' circle and thrilled to get away. Kaitlyn stayed by Ray, waiting to see what he would do, and then realized he wasn't going to acknowledge her existence. Kaitlyn was devastated, so she began her first class with a tear rolling down her cheek.

Kathryn met Kaitlyn and Ray at the front entrance at precisely one o'clock. They filed into the car and began the short trip to the municipal building.

"Where's dad?" Kaitlyn asked.

"He's at the courthouse talking with the lawyers," she answered, not giving any more information. "Do you understand what will be happening today?" she asked them.

"Not really," Kaitlyn replied.

Ray didn't respond.

"A grand jury will be reviewing the case to see whether John was criminally negligent," Kathryn explained.

"Well, he is," Kaitlyn announced.

"Not necessarily, Kaitlyn," Kathryn replied. "I'll explain further.

There was a long pause.

"Now," Kathryn began, then paused. "What will happen at this inquest is that a group of people, many of whom you know, will be listening to John answer questions about the accident presented to him by the county prosecutor. Then they'll be reviewing the circumstances involving the accident. Two things could happen. One is that John could be found criminally negligent, and he will be kept by the state until a trial date is set. Or two, he could be found civilly negligent, in which case he'll face some other, less ... severe punishment."

Ray was boiling in his seat, his face turning red.

"Ray," Kathryn warned, "you're going to have to calm down, or they won't let you in the room."

Ray replied with a nod.

Kaitlyn, twirling her fingers and thinking all sorts of thoughts she'd like to express, sat next to Ray. She gazed in his direction, deciding to verbalize one important thought. "I want you to have a full life, Ray."

Ray raised his head slightly, looking over towards Kaitlyn and briefly nodding. He didn't bother to speak, knowing that Kaitlyn was referring to the passage in the book, and he knew she was right.

"We're here," Kathryn exclaimed. "Ray, are you okay?"

"Yes," he replied softly.

"Kaitlyn, you're going to see a lot of friends and people you know in there," Kathryn reminded. "But this isn't 'social hour', okay?"

"Yes, Mother. I understand."

The three exited the car and straightened out their clothes before walking up the sidewalk to the hard granite steps of the imposing building.

Flower beds, missing their early fall blooms, lined the walkway before being met by neatly trimmed bushes, decorating the courthouse's stone foundation. Huge white pillars gave grandeur and demanded everyone's respect. Walking under the pillars, they were met by colossal oak doors, leading way to the main corridor.

Their eyes widened as they saw the deep cherry walls and matching stained wooden floors, giving a powerful presence to the atmosphere. Portraits of former and more recent judges were hung throughout the hall, with each portrait having a brass nameplate beneath.

Their entrance was interrupted when Jim Frost came out from nowhere to greet them.

"They're almost ready for us," he said, his hushed voice echoing down the hall.

"Is John here yet?" Kaitlyn asked.

"Yes," he replied. "He's in a conference room preparing with his lawyers."

"Allison?" she questioned.

"No, Allison isn't here," he replied. "She's not allowed to be."

"Oh," was all she could think of to respond. "What about me? Am I supposed to be here?"

"You're allowed to be here, but you will have to sit quietly in the room and try not to be noticed," he replied.

A court secretary opened two massive doors that revealed a magnificent, cathedral ceiling courtroom. "We're ready for you now," he announced.

The courtroom was done in mahogany from floor to ceiling and back down again. The ceiling was decorated with figures of law engraved in plaster, and the raised judge's bench was intimidating and flanked by the state and U.S. flags. Bailiffs stood on either side of the bench, with one stationed at each door.

This was Kaitlyn's first visit to a courtroom, and she was petrified. She felt two inches tall in comparison to the high ceilings and the judge's bench that sat towering above all at the front, announcing the king on his throne.

The Magistrate's name was Martin Byer, or as the townsfolk called him, 'Old Judge Byer.' He was stern looking, but underneath seemed to have a soft side, a minimal one anyway. His hair was dark brown, which accentuated his dark brown eyes. His hair was cut military style, giving him a look of authority, and he demanded respect with his stature and body language. He stood about five foot, nine inches, but up on that bench, he looked ten feet tall.

They all took their seats and waited quietly. John, with his head hung low, came into the courtroom with his attorney. He took the left-hand table before the bench, while the prosecuting attorney was already stationed at the right table. John turned around to look in Ray's direction, and their exchanged looks spoke silent volumes of an unfortunate situation.

Tensions were high in the hushed courtroom as the jury took their seats, ready to hear the circumstances surrounding Jaycee's death.

Kaitlyn peered around the room, taking notice of Mrs. Peterson from the bakery in the jury box. She saw the three gentlemen she had waved hello to on the way to the park back in summertime, and saw Sam the butcher, as well as Tom the hardware guy. She'd known these people for years, and so had John.

John held his head in shame sitting before the judge. The judge's unreadable expression passed like a beacon through the entire room and everyone in it. John's grieving parents sat behind him, looking as if they would have liked to shrink into their seats.

Kaitlyn quietly sat with Ray and her parents in the third bench back from the cordon, waiting for the procedure to begin. The courtroom's deathly calm was broken only by the amplified rustle of a dress or by one or two nervously muffled coughs.

Once the defense lawyer and the prosecuting lawyer were settled in, Judge Byer motioned for the procedure to begin by pounding the gavel once. He instructed the courtroom about the rules before he proceeded to address John's case. The prosecuting attorney stood to announce that he was making a Motion to Discover, followed by John's attorney half-way standing, saying he had no objections.

Judge Byer looked at John sternly and asked him if he understood the proceeding before they continued. "This is not a trial, young man," he said. "This is an inquest to see whether you have committed criminal or civil negligence. You will come to the stand and tell us your recount of the event that occurred, and then the attorneys will question you. The Grand Jury members also have this right. Do you understand?"

"Yes, sir. I do," John replied almost inaudibly, scared out of his mind.

"Please take the stand," Judge Byer demanded.

John rose from his seat while glaring at his attorney in fear, and then looked for a sympathetic face, finding only one from his mother. He stood and walked to the witness box between the judge's bench and the jury.

His hands began to tremble as he placed them upon the Bible to swear in. Sweat glistened on his forehead before forming slight droplets, which rolled down his face. His stomach ached and his heart pounded in his chest when he went to wipe his brow. His lips quivered as he begged for mercy through his tear-welled eyes while his mind and body went into emotional breakdown.

"I didn't mean to do it!" he cried in a garbled sob. "I am *so* sorry!"

Judge Byer asked him to take a moment to compose himself.

John finally settled enough to begin recounting the events of that fateful night.

"It happened two days after my eighteenth birthday, and I went out to O'Rielly's Pub with a few friends. I was finally legal and was drinking beer, becoming drunk, yet not realizing how drunk I actually was. When the party slowed down, I left, not giving any thought that my ability to drive would be hindered. I didn't know. I honestly didn't know.

"I was driving along and found I was going in the wrong direction when I saw headlights coming at me. When I went to swerve out of the way, I ended up doing the opposite, crashing right into the Niles' car.

"I didn't know I had hit them, as everything seemed to move in slow motion, until I was thrown back against the seat, realizing I *had* hit them. I remember sirens and ambulances coming, emergency medics working on freeing Ray, and working on his dad. I remember seeing a white sheet ..."

John stopped, as this was the first time he admitted seeing Jaycee Niles dead. "Oh, my God," he cried.

John composed himself briefly.

"The next thing I know, I'm in the ambulance with Mr. Niles, being driven to the hospital. I was shaken up, but not hurt. I wish I had been the one killed," he sobbed. "Oh, my God, I just want to die."

Judge Byer told John to take a few seconds.

"Once we reached the hospital and I was checked out, I called Kaitlyn Frost to tell her about the accident. Then I called my parents."

"Why did you call Miss Frost?" Judge Byer asked.

"Because Kaitlyn is Ray's girlfriend," he replied.

"Continue please," Judge Byer demanded.

"I was detained for questioning a few days later by the Winter's Crest Police and now, here I am," John finished. "I feel terrible, and I can't tell you how sorry I am. I wish I could take it back."

Judge Byer looked sternly at John. "You can't take it back!" he said.

"I know, your Honor," John replied. "Believe me, I know."

Serious questions were then asked in an orderly, yet casual manner from the members of the Grand Jury. Questions pertaining to why he was drinking and questions that tried to reveal his maturity level were asked, as the jurors tried to decide how responsible he should be for his actions.

When the jurors finished their questioning, Judge Byer asked if John had anything further to add before the jury came to their conclusions.

John said with fear, "Yes. I do, your Honor."

There was a long, silent pause as the room filled with anticipation.

The judge motioned for John to speak. John cleared his throat.

"Please proceed," Judge Byer stated.

John turned quickly to glance at Ray. "I'm sorry."

He turned his attention back to the judge. "There are not enough words to express my deepest and sincere remorse. I was wrong. I thought I was a man, an adult. I wasn't. I acted like a kid. I'm trying to right my wrong to the best of my ability. I'm trying to be a man now. I need to take responsibility for my actions and suffer the consequences of those actions. I deserve to be punished, and I will not ask for leniency from this court out of respect for Jaycee Niles."

John turned his attentions to the group seated with Ray and to his own parents. "I don't know what else to say except that if I could take it back, I would. If I could trade places with Mrs. Niles, I would in a heartbeat. All I can do is express my deepest apologies and keep the promise I made to Mrs. Niles."

John turned back to the judge. "I'm sorry," fell from his lips as he held his head in regret. A tear fell from his cheek as he thanked the judge for allowing him the chance to speak.

"We will take your words into consideration, Mr. Fenderson." Judge Byer said, not without a note of sympathy.

"Is there anyone else who would like to address this proceeding or are there any more questions from the jury?" Judge Byer asked while peering around the room.

A hand was raised.

"Yes, sir," Judge Byer said. "Please state your name and stand."

The speaker slowly lowered his hand and stood.

"My name is Ray Niles, your Honor. I'm Jaycee's son."

Kaitlyn had no idea Ray was going to speak at the inquest. No one did. Shocked eyes stared in Ray's direction, as gasps could be heard echoing throughout the room.

Ray cleared his throat and tried to hold back his tears. "While I was in the hospital, my girlfriend Kaitlyn read a passage to me. It has haunted me ever since. The verse was:

"'If one goes through life with anger and pain, then one has not lived. When one goes through life with forgiveness and peace, then one has led a full life.'"

"I don't want to be angry my entire life, your Honor."

The gatherers in the courtroom all nodded in agreement.

Ray continued. "Don't get me wrong, your Honor. I'm angry, hurt and saddened with the loss of my mother. What John did was inexcusable, and there is nothing he can do to change it. He cannot replace what we lost, and he cannot replace what we would have had in the future."

"My father and I both agree, however, that having John sit in a jail cell for years would not do any of us any good. He was my friend, and I hope he and I can become friends again — someday. I can only imagine what it's like for him having to face himself every day for the rest of his life, knowing that he killed my mother. I feel his remorse is sincere, and I am trying to forgive him, as hard as that may be. I don't want to go through my life hating John. I want it to be over — the pain, the hurt and the sadness. My mom would have wanted it this way, and *I* want it this way."

"With that said, my father and I ask for leniency. We want him to be accountable for his actions, but not have a trial and possibly spend years in jail. We want him to keep his promise to my mother."

Ray took out a small opened envelope and showed it to the judge.

"Please approach the bench," Judge Byer ordered.

Ray went to the bench and handed the note to the bailiff, who handed it to the judge. He then went back to his seat and remained standing.

"Your Honor," Ray said, addressing the bench. "He made a promise to my mother, and we want him to keep it. That is what we ask of all of you. Thank you, your Honor." He took his seat.

Judge Byer sat back and took the envelope in his hands, opening it. He took the note out and began scanning the words. "You wrote this, Mr. Fenderson?" he asked after a moment, looking over the top of the letter.

"Yes, your Honor," John replied at a half-stand.

Judge Byer leaned forward on his elbows and read to himself:

"'I'm sorry, Mrs. Niles, for taking your life. I'm sorry you will never be able to see Ray graduate high school or college or marry. I'm sorry you will never be able to see your grandchildren's smiles. I'm sorry I took you away from your husband and all the things the two of you would have enjoyed. Please forgive me. I make this promise to you:

'I will never drink another drop of alcohol for as long as I live. I will do everything I can to spread the word about drinking and driving. Please know I mean every word, and I intend to keep my promise. Please forgive me.

'Forever in my prayers,
John'"

The Judge handed the note to the bailiff to give to the jury foreman, then called for a recess. Everyone stood as the judge rose and left the room for his chambers, while the Grand Jury went to their anteroom to sort out the entire mess.

The Frosts, Ray and the Fendersons went out to the hallway to await the outcome, gathering on opposite ends of the hall. Already, the high corridor was billowing with cigarette smoke as most of the nervous onlookers lit up at once.

Ray left the courtroom and sought refuge outside, away from everyone. Kaitlyn met up with Allison out in the corridor.

"What are you doing here?" Kaitlyn asked, surprised to see her.

"I couldn't stay in school," she replied. "I know I can't go in, but I just had to be here."

"I'm sorry, Kaitlyn," Allison said. "We shouldn't be fighting over this."

"You're right," Kaitlyn replied as she went to hug Allison. "I'm sorry too."

"How's John holding up?" Allison asked.

"He looks scared, but he's trying to right this wrong," Kaitlyn replied.

"I know he is," Allison said.

"I didn't see it before, but I see it now," Kaitlyn said. "I wish Ray had told me he was going to speak up today."

"What do you mean?" Allison asked, confused. "He spoke on John's behalf?"

"Yeah," Kaitlyn replied.

"He *did?*" Allison asked shocked, not needing to hear it twice. "Wow."

"He's been staying to himself the last few days," Kaitlyn explained. "I thought he was ignoring me, but now I realize he was trying to figure out what to say and do. I wish he had told me though. I'm hurt he didn't."

"Maybe he'll explain later," Allison said, trying to comfort her friend.

"I hope so," Kaitlyn replied. "You know, I'm proud of him today. He did a good thing. I'm even proud of John."

"*You?* Proud of *John?*" Allison queried.

"Those weren't boys speaking today, those were men — our men," Kaitlyn said.

"Wow, Kaitlyn," Allison replied in disbelief. "This is quite a change of heart for you."

"I know. I wish none of this had to happen," Kaitlyn said downheartedly.

"Yeah, me too," Allison agreed. "I never would have expected one split second to change my life and put a wedge between us."

"Let's not let *that* happen again," Kaitlyn said, giving Allison another hug. "I'd miss you terribly."

"Me too," Allison replied almost in tears.

"Allison, I have to tell you something," Kaitlyn confided. "I never wanted to see John rot in jail. I was just angry. Now, after Ray and John's speeches ... I don't know how I feel."

"I know," Allison understood, sympathetically.

"I came here wanting to see John severely punished. Now, after being in there, I feel terrible for him. He really does wish he could take it back."

Allison nodded.

The prosecutor came out into the hall announcing that the judge and jury members were ready.

Judge Byer entered the court without expression and went to his bench. The juror members followed.

The judge addressed all and instructed them not to speak or make noise while the decision was being handed down. Silence echoed in the intimidating room.

"Mr. John Matthew Fenderson," Judge Byer called John's full attention. "Please rise."

John stood with his hands behind his back, joined by his attorney.

"Mr. Foreman," Judge Byer began. "Have you reached your decision?"

"Yes, sir. We have," he said.

"Approach the bench."

The foreman brought the small piece of paper to the bailiff and then returned to his seat. Judge Byer read the jury's decision showing no sign of the outcome. He cleared his throat and began to speak.

"Although we condemn your actions that caused the death of Mrs. Jaycee Niles," Judge Byer began sternly, "we do feel you are sincere in your remorse. Taking into consideration your words and those of Mr. Ray Niles, we have come to a decision. My judgment is as follows:

"You are hereby released from all criminally negligent charges."

John was shaking in his shoes, realizing the judge had taken leniency on him. Sighs of relief were heard from both families until Judge Byer continued.

Judge Byer laid into John, reprimanding his actions and letting him know that if he were caught driving while drinking, he'd be sure to face criminal charges. "This is your first offense. It had better be your last," Judge Byer warned.

"It will be, your Honor," John replied.

Judge Byer continued. "It is my intention to see to it that you keep your promise to Mrs. Jaycee Niles, and from what you have said, that is also your intention?"

"Yes, your Honor," John responded.

"Young man, I expect you to spread the word about the dangers of drinking and driving, and I expect you to be an example to others who face the same decision you did on that fateful night. Maybe if you had known that drinking alcohol *would* impair the ability to drive, maybe none of this ever would have happened. I expect you to let others know. Do you understand?"

"Yes, sir. I do," John said as firmly as he could. "I promise."

"Court dismissed," Judge Byer said pounding the gavel to the block. "Don't let me see you back in this courtroom again!" he said, pointing a finger at John, who nodded energetically.

John shook his attorney's hand, and then went to hug his mother and father.

Ray approached John with an uneasy step. Everyone's eyes locked in their direction as Ray held his hand out to John. John nervously shook Ray's hand and said, "Thank you, Ray. I'm so sorry."

"I know you are," Ray said, still holding John's hand. Pulling him close, he put his other hand on John's shoulder and whispered in his ear. "Just keep your promise to my mother."

John replied, "I will. I intend to." John paused. You didn't have to do what you did, you know."

"Yes, John. I did," Ray said. "I did it for me. I did it for my dad. Most of all, John, I did it for my mom. I didn't really do it for *you*."

Kaitlyn had a blank stare on her face. She had so many emotions that her body didn't know which ones to show. She just sat on the court pew and stared with emotional overload. Ray went to her and offered his hand. "Come with me?" he asked, yet requiring her to do so.

Kaitlyn rose from the seat and took Ray's hand. He and Kaitlyn walked back to the house while Ray explained his recent actions.

"Why didn't you tell me?" Kaitlyn asked.

"I couldn't," Ray replied. "I wasn't even sure if I was going to talk until the judge asked."

"Kaitlyn, my father knew," Ray said. "He knew that John caused the accident."

"How did he know?" Kaitlyn asked shocked.

"The day John came to the hospital," Ray said. "You know the note I placed on my mom's casket?

"Yes," Kaitlyn replied. "The one from your dad?"

"Yes," Ray replied. "Only, it wasn't from my dad. It was from John. I didn't know until my dad told me on Saturday."

"Then how did you get the note you gave to the judge if it was buried with your mom?" Kaitlyn asked.

"John had given my dad a copy," Ray replied.

"I still don't understand why you didn't tell me," Kaitlyn said, still bothered by it. "I don't understand why you kept your distance from me. I thought I did something wrong."

"Kait, you did nothing wrong," Ray explained. "You did everything right. I should have discussed this with you."

"Yes, you should have," Kaitlyn interrupted.

"The thing is, I needed to decide this for myself," Ray explained. "I didn't want to be influenced. You were angry, and you didn't tell me about what happened."

"Yes, you're right," Kaitlyn agreed. "I didn't tell you, did I?"

"What did happen that made you so upset?" Ray asked.

"Allison defended John, and I became angry and said some things I probably shouldn't have," she explained. "John heard me."

"See, Kait," Ray said. "That's why I didn't tell you what I was trying to figure out. Sometimes we all need to work things out for ourselves. I knew you were angry, and I wanted to try to decide if *I* could do this, and if I even *wanted* to. I needed to do it by myself. Then this morning, I became afraid and questioned whether my intentions were good or not. Part of me wants to hate John forever, and another part wants to let it go. I couldn't handle anything else. I couldn't even handle being *me* this morning."

"Okay, I understand," Kaitlyn replied. "If something like this ever happens again, do you think you could just let me know you need to figure things out by yourself? It hurt me. One day we were kissing and loving each other, and the next few days, you were cold and distant. And let's not even talk about this morning."

"I'm sorry, Kait," Ray said taking her hand. "I'm really sorry. I didn't mean to hurt you. There were so many emotions I was dealing with, and I didn't really know how I felt until I walked into that courtroom. I feel good about my decision though. I think my mom would approve."

"I know she would," Kaitlyn said smiling, pulling him in for a hug. "I'm proud of you. That took a lot of courage. You have more than I do."

"That's not so, Kait," Ray said. "You have courage."

"Not like that," Kaitlyn replied. "I will say one thing, though. I listened to what you had to say today, and it made sense. Allison and I talked, and we made up in the corridor. We decided to not let this ruin our friendship."

"I'm glad, Kait. Good friends are hard to come by."

"I'm going to try to resolve things with John too," Ray said. "It's going to take some time, but I'm going to try. I honestly meant every word I said today. I don't hate him. Actually, I miss him. I don't want to lose anyone else."

"Don't ever leave me, Kait," Ray pleaded. "I don't think I could bear it."

"I won't," Kaitlyn said, leaning in for a hug. "I couldn't bear losing you either."

*   *   *

"Ray did that for John?" Rose asked. "That's admirable."

"Yes, Rose," Kaitlyn replied. "He was wonderful. You know, honey," Kaitlyn said. "I'm glad I received the letter from Ray. I'm still not ready to open it, but it's been nice remembering my youth."

"Wasn't there another letter you told me about from years ago?" Rose asked.

"Yes," Kaitlyn replied, heading towards her dusty box. Finding it, she asked Rose if she'd like to read it.

"You don't mind?" Rose asked.

"No, honey. I want you to."

Rose took the old letter in her hands. She carefully removed the thin paper note from its discolored envelope and began reading:

"My Dearest Kait,

I love you today. I will love you tomorrow. I will love you for the rest of my life, forever."

Rose continued to read the remainder of the letter to herself and then read the closure.

"Wow, Mom," Rose responded. "You two were really in love, weren't you?"

"Yes, Rose," Kaitlyn said with a frowning smile. "We were." Kaitlyn looked at her with a tear in her eye. "I still love him, Rose. After all these years ... I can't believe it."

"I know you do, Mom," Rose said. "That's why it's so hard for you to open the new letter."

"How'd you get to be so smart?" Kaitlyn asked, knowing her cover was blown.

"Mom, I'm a grown woman now," she replied laughing. "I can see these things, you know."

"I've never stopped thinking about him," Kaitlyn continued. "He's been in my heart for fifty years. I don't think I'll ever stop thinking about him, or loving him for that matter."

"Why would you want to, Mom?" Rose understood. "It sounds like he was the love of your life."

Rose wasn't looking for an answer. She was thinking out loud and examining her own love, marriage and life. She was wondering if she had that kind of love in her life and couldn't answer her own question.

"Mom, I've got to go," Rose said hurriedly. "It's getting late, and we both have things to do."

"You're right, dear," Kaitlyn replied as she went to hug and kiss her daughter goodbye. "I love you."

"I love you too, Mom," Rose said smiling. "Let me know when you open the letter. I think you owe it to yourself to find out what he has to say."

"I will, honey," Kaitlyn said starting to yawn. "Goodnight. Be careful driving home. Watch out for deer."

"I will," Rose replied smiling, and laughing at her mother's normal goodbye. "Night, Mom."

Kaitlyn tidied up the living room before taking the teacups to the kitchen. She locked up the house and placed the old letter along with the new letter in her pocketbook for safekeeping. She felt an urge to open it, but decided it wasn't time yet. She went upstairs and prepared a soothing late afternoon bath, ready to take on some more memories.

Chapter Twelve

Following the inquest, Kaitlyn and Ray made it home, emotionally drained, but feeling somewhat comforted from their reconnection.

Kaitlyn helped Kathryn get dinner ready, while Ray, Alex and Jim relaxed in the living room in quiet peace. Ray and Jim were preoccupied with their own thoughts of the day's events. Alex kept looking back and forth between the two, champing at the bit, waiting for one of them to fill him in on what occurred. Breaking the silence, Ray apologized for his behavior earlier that morning, but no further conversation took place.

When the evening meal was ready, Kathryn called all to the dining room table, and they all joined hands in prayer. They prayed for Nick's recovery, John and his family, and for Jaycee, as well as asked for strength. They thanked God for the food on their table and for the blessings He had given them. Saying, "Amen," they began their feast.

Alex was finally able to find out what happened at the inquest by putting dialogue pieces together, but felt uncomfortable when the conversation took on a too serious tone. Alex decided to change the topic, bringing up talk of the approaching holiday season. He asked Kaitlyn and Ray about the Halloween party that was to be held at The Fountain.

With a removed tone, Ray said, "I don't think I'll be able to go. My dad ... "

Alex had forgotten that Nick would be getting out of the hospital October twenty-second, so he apologized to Ray for his insensitivity.

"It's all right, Alex," Ray responded. "My dad's more important than some Halloween party anyway."

Kaitlyn nodded in agreement. "That's true. Why don't I come over and help you?"

Ray answered with a simple "Okay."

The tension from the holiday season talk thickened, so they decided to forego any more discussion on the subject, and concentrated on their meals instead.

Dinner ended, and all five pitched in to help clear, wash and dry the dishes before going off to different parts of the house to seek time alone. When yawns seemed to take over the sounds of breathing, they turned in for the night.

Thursday came, and Ray, Kaitlyn and Alex had to go to school. They awakened showing signs of disturbed sleep, and moving slowly, they dragged themselves out of bed. They went through their morning routine in a robotic fashion, without exchanging many words.

Ray had awakened in a strange mood that day. He wasn't himself, and his mind seemed to be wandering. Kaitlyn noticed the change and asked him about it as they walked to school, but Ray didn't offer an explanation, only that he was tired, leaving things at that.

After school, Ray was the same way, and Kaitlyn wasn't sure what to do with it. She didn't know whether to leave Ray alone for a while or whether she should talk to him. Although Kaitlyn knew that the inquest was difficult and Ray had every right to be down, she also thought Ray would let her be there for him. That wasn't the case. Ray was off on his own again, dealing with his problems by himself. Kaitlyn decided to give Ray his space, figuring it would only be for a day or so. She was wrong.

Over the next couple of weeks, Kaitlyn and Ray went their separate ways. They were still together, so to speak, but off in their own worlds. Kaitlyn's heart ached from Ray's evasiveness, and she turned to Allison for a shoulder to cry on.

Allison had her own problems to worry about. She needed Kaitlyn just as much as Kaitlyn needed her. She was struggling with John's issues, and she worried about the harm it was doing to not only their relationship, but to her reputation as well. They spent a lot of time at The Soda Fountain, crying on each other's shoulders and talking out their feelings.

Ray went about his studies and kept his thoughts to himself. He was aloof to all, not acknowledging Kaitlyn's existence, as if she were the cause of all of his problems. It was pure hell for Kaitlyn.

The Tuesday before Ray left, he finally broke through his self-imposed barriers.

Kaitlyn was curled up on the couch warming by the fire. She had retreated within the safety of her quilt, comforting herself with the hug of the pillow. She was depressed, her heart crying with magnified pain. Kaitlyn's eyes were swollen from many tears, her usually radiant face dulled from Ray's treatment. Ray approached Kaitlyn asking if he could sit down beside her, and she nodded without expression.

"What's wrong, Kait?" Ray asked, oblivious to the fact *he* was the problem.

Kaitlyn's eyes glared at him with intense anger and hurt, "You don't know?" she asked in disgust.

"No, Kait," Ray responded. "I don't."

Kaitlyn was beside herself. "Am I still your girlfriend?"

"Yes," Ray answered, "I love you," confused by the question.

"That's not what I asked, Ray," Kaitlyn reprimanded him. "Am I *still* your girlfriend? Because if I am, you sure have a funny way of showing it."

Ray was silent.

Kaitlyn let all her bottled up emotions and feelings come pouring out. She dropped them in Ray's lap and expected him to figure out what to do with them.

"You know, Ray," Kaitlyn blurted. "I'm sorry you were in an accident. I'm sorry your dad's been in the hospital. I'm sorry your mom is dead. I'm sorry your best friend is the one who caused this. But Ray, what did I do to you? I have been here for you and tried to be there for you, and all you have done is ignore me, push me away. As far as I am concerned, you left me two weeks ago."

Ray was dumbfounded. "What are you talking about?"

"Ray, I can't believe you have no idea," Kaitlyn replied utterly annoyed. "You don't realize that you've been ignoring me and staying away from me for almost two weeks now? One day we were hugging and kissing, and the next day, I'm yesterday's news."

Kaitlyn tried to hold back her tears. "Why won't you let me be there for you? Why have you been treating me this way? You've hurt me more than words can say. I hate loving you! Just leave me alone." Kaitlyn buried her hurt eyes into the pillow, not allowing Ray to see her face.

Ray lowered his eyes in shame, realizing what Kaitlyn said was true. He took his hands to her chin and turned Kaitlyn's face towards his. A teardrop fell onto his cheek as he spoke. "Oh, Kait. I'm so sorry. I didn't realize what I was doing to you. I really didn't. I'm so sorry I've hurt and ignored you. I honestly didn't mean to"

"Those are just words, Ray," Kaitlyn said hurt and still angry at the same time. "I want to know why. I want to know why you have been closed off from me. I want to know what has kept you so preoccupied that you couldn't even talk to me."

"I've been doing a lot of thinking and preparing." Ray admitted. "My whole life's going to change in a matter of a couple days. I've been staying here, and it's been like a big slumber party. Reality is starting to sink in, and Kaitlyn, I'm scared."

Kaitlyn brought her attention to Ray as she wiped the tears from her face. "Why didn't you come to me?" she demanded to know.

Ray took her hands in his. "This is something I had to do on my own." He paused. "I ... I've been going over to the house, cleaning it and taking care of the yard work. I didn't realize that walking in my house would hurt so much. Remnants of my mom are everywhere, and I realized I have not finished mourning her death. I still can't believe she's gone. Kait, I miss her, and I feel like a part of me died with her."

Kaitlyn reached her arms out to hold Ray. "I didn't know you were going to the house. Why didn't you tell me? I would have gone with you."

"Because, I needed to go alone, Kait," Ray said, trying to make her understand. "I didn't want you to see me so weak."

Kaitlyn was aghast. "Ray, you're not being *weak* because you miss your mom and because you're scared. You're being *human*. Give me more credit than that. Give *yourself* more credit!"

"I'm sorry, Kait," Ray said. "I really am."

Ray and Kaitlyn embraced, and then he held Kaitlyn back at arm's length. "I don't want to lose you, too."

"You're not losing me," Kaitlyn said, wiping a tear from her cheek. "I thought I'd lost you."

Ray took Kaitlyn in his arms, holding her for dear life as he finally let it all go. "Oh my gosh, Kait. I miss her. I'm so afraid to go home. I wish I'd died with her."

Kaitlyn cradled and gently stroked Ray's back. "Everything will be okay, Ray. It's going to take some time, but everything will be okay."

Ray leaned back against the couch to regain his composure, and began to tell Kaitlyn what else was bothering him. "I'm worried about my dad coming home. It's going to be hard for him to walk in our house, and I'm going to have so much responsibility. I don't know if I can do it."

"Ray, it'll be fine," Kaitlyn said in an affectionate, motherly tone. "You will do what you have to do, because you have to. I'll be there for you and help you with whatever you need. And so will my parents."

"Thanks, Kaitlyn," Ray said. "I'm sorry I hurt you. I really didn't mean to. Heck, I didn't even realize that I was. I'm sorry for that, too."

"Ray," Kaitlyn said in a serious tone, holding him back from her. "Don't ever shut me out again. If you need time to yourself, just tell me. I will respect your request. Pulling away from me will only hurt me, and I don't think I can handle much more hurt. I deserve better."

Ray nodded in agreement.

They sat back on the couch feeling the warmth from the fire, holding each other for hours. They didn't bother moving their position when Jim and Kathryn came into the living room. They were no longer embarrassed expressing their feelings in front of them. Not to mention, it *was* completely innocent.

Kathryn sat down on the couch across from them while Jim placed a log on the fire. "You two okay?" Kathryn asked, taking notice of the swollen eyes and blotchy cheeks.

"Yeah, Mom," Kaitlyn answered. "Ray's been dealing with a lot and trying to do it on his own. He's been to the house."

"Ray, honey, "Kathryn sympathized. "Oh, you should have told me. That is one of the hardest things to do. I know. I've done it. Oh, honey, I know what you're going through."

"I should have told you, Mrs. Frost," Ray said respectfully. "I apologize."

"No, Ray," Kathryn replied. "I'm sorry you didn't feel comfortable enough to ask for help."

"What is there left to do?" Kathryn asked, intending to help Ray with the rest.

"Well, I took care of the yard work and cleaned inside," Ray answered. "The only thing left to do is to get some food and take care of the bills."

"Do you have the bills with you?" Jim interrupted as he went to join Kathryn on the couch.

"Yes, sir. I do," Ray answered. "I'm going to take the checkbook and the bills to my dad tomorrow."

"I won't allow that," Jim replied. "Your father doesn't need that stress right now. Let me have them, please."

"Mr. Frost," Ray said with shock. "With all due respect, I can't let you pay our bills. It's not right."

"I will not hear of it, Ray," Jim lovingly scolded. "I'll take care of the bills, and that's final."

"Mr. Frost, I can't..." Ray began.

"You can, and you will," Mr. Frost interrupted in an authoritative voice, yet showing Ray a sincere smile. "Please get them for me. We want to do this."

Ray got up from the couch and went to his room to retrieve the bills. He came back downstairs to the living room and reluctantly handed them to Jim. "Sir, I don't know what to say ... thank you."

"Ray," Jim addressed him. "You're family to us, son. We want to help."

Kaitlyn, as well as Ray, was shocked by Jim's words. They were delighted, too. Ray had received Jim's full acceptance.

"Okay, now, you need food, yes?" Kathryn asked, going to the end table for a notebook and pen, then making her way back to the couch.

"Yes, I need to get some food in the house," Ray replied. "I plan on getting some groceries tomorrow to stock the kitchen."

Starting to make out a grocery list, Kathryn told Ray she would go to the market tomorrow, and then stop at the house to get things taken care of. "Now, what do you need?"

"Are you sure?" Ray asked slightly embarrassed.

"Yes, Ray," Kathryn replied as she wrote down a few essential food items. "I will tend to the shopping, and then tomorrow afternoon, Kaitlyn and I will start preparing meals for when your father comes home. That will make it easier for both of you as you settle back in."

"I don't know what to say," Ray said. "You've all done so much already. How can we repay your kindness?"

"There's no need," Jim stated clearly. "I wouldn't allow it if you tried. Let us help you out, Ray. All you need to do is say thank you."

Ray went over to Kathryn and gave her a hug. He whispered, "Thank you" and slightly kissed her cheek. He held his hand out to Jim. "Thank you, sir," he said as he took a firm shake of Jim's hand while smiling and making eye contact. "Thank you."

"You're welcome," Jim replied, taking Ray's handshake and turning it into a fatherly hug. "You're a nice young man, Ray."

"You two should get to bed," Kathryn commented, still making out a list, not bothering to ask Ray what was needed again. "It's getting late."

Kaitlyn rose from the warm position on the couch and hugged her mother and father goodnight. Ray said goodnight as well, and the two went upstairs to get ready for bed. Reaching the top of the steps, Ray took Kaitlyn in his arms and kissed her, telling her again how sorry he was. "Please forgive me, Kait. I couldn't stand losing you."

"I do, Ray," she replied. "Please don't shut me out anymore, though. My heart can't take it."

"I won't, Kait," Ray said. "I promise."

"The only thing is, Ray," Kaitlyn replied. "Your promises are beginning to be empty ones."

Kaitlyn turned away from Ray and went to her room. She knew what she said was hurtful, but she couldn't keep it in any longer.

Ray knew she was right, but all the same, it did hurt. He watched Kaitlyn shut the door behind her and went to his room for the night, his face still stinging from the *slap* to the face.

The next morning, they awakened to a beautiful Indian summer day. The forecasted high was supposed to reach seventy, which is reason to celebrate during October.

Kaitlyn woke up cheerful, yet still felt the pains of the past twelve days. Trying to brighten her spirits, she dressed in her finest poodle skirt and cream cashmere sweater. She met Ray outside in the hallway just as he exited his room.

"Hello, beautiful," Ray greeted, smiling, unsure of what reaction he'd get.

"Hi, babes." Kaitlyn whispered. "I'm sorry for that comment."

"That's okay," Ray replied. "I deserved it."

"Yes, Ray," Kaitlyn said, giggling. "Yes, you did."

"Come on, let's go down for breakfast," Ray suggested as he took her hand to lead downstairs.

They had a quick and joyful breakfast before heading out the door hand in hand. They felt alive and awakened with vitality on their walk to school. They were together, and life was good.

Ray squeezed Kaitlyn's hand. "I've got to tell you something."

Kaitlyn looked at him with questioning eyes. "What?"

Ray answered and filled her in on one aspect they did not discuss the previous eve. "You must promise to keep this to yourself."

Kaitlyn responded and looked to Ray with pride. "I promise." Looking away for a brief second, she chimed in with, "And I keep my promises," before she broke out in laughter.

"Ahh, come on, Kait," Ray replied. "That was a cruel."

"Yup," Kaitlyn said smiling and letting Ray know she was teasing.

Hoping Kaitlyn would say yes, Ray asked if she wanted to visit their tree that afternoon after school.

"Yes, I'd love to," Kaitlyn replied. "I've missed you," she said grinning.

" ... a lot. Oh sugar."

"What?" Ray asked.

"I have to help my mother prepare meals after school."

"How 'bout we go for just a bit," Ray begged. "We won't stay long."

"Okay," Kaitlyn said as her eyes lit up. "Yes, let's do it."

They made it to school and parted their separate ways for the day. They met up for lunch as usual, and Allison joined them. Kaitlyn was dying to tell her the secret, but didn't, even though it was killing her not to.

Ray glanced over to Allison. "How are things, Allison?" Ray asked, genuinely concerned.

"They're okay, Ray," Allison answered, grateful that he'd asked.

"Where's John, and how's he doing?" Kaitlyn inquired.

"He's at the eye doctor's today," Allison replied. "He's doing alright. He's been doing some self-evaluation, and we've actually had some interesting conversations. He seems to be doing okay."

"I'm glad to hear it, Allison," Kaitlyn said.

Ray stayed out of the conversation altogether, avoiding a discussion about John at all costs. He just wasn't ready to travel down that road quite yet.

"When are you going home, Ray?" Allison asked, knowing the day was approaching.

"Tomorrow, actually," Ray answered. "My dad comes home tomorrow."

"Today's the last day Ray's with me in the house," Kaitlyn pouted. "Of course, we could've had a more enjoyable time, if *someone* hadn't been so — What's the word? Removed," Kaitlyn said as her eyes slanted in Ray's direction.

Ray shook off Kaitlyn's guilt trip, but he was, nonetheless, irritated.

The bell rang, ending lunch, and they went to their next assigned classes.

"I'll meet you at your locker after school, Ray," Kaitlyn called out as he walked down the hall in the opposite direction.

Ray gave Kaitlyn a backhanded wave, letting her know he'd be there. He was angry from Kaitlyn's cruel, off-handed comment, and they were beginning to irritate him, actually *sting*.

When school ended, Kaitlyn did as she said and met Ray at his locker as planned.

Ray glared at her, "Why do you have to take shots at me?" he asked.

"I was just teasing, Ray," Kaitlyn replied, knowing she was guilty as charged. "I'm sorry."

"Well, they hurt, Kait," Ray claimed, looking her straight in the eyes. "They really hurt!"

"I'm sorry, Ray," Kaitlyn replied. "I guess I'm still angry. It won't happen again."

"Good," Ray said. "Want to go kiss and make up?"

"Yes, sir," Kaitlyn said, standing at attention with her hand raised to the side of her forehead. Lowering her hand, she stuck in an, "Oh, yes," with a sneaky tone. The two hurried off to their tree.

Kaitlyn reached the tree first and leaned up against it, giving Ray his own trademark *come here* gesture as she let out a playful laugh. Ray walked towards her with a 'maybe I will, maybe I won't' attitude, and the two embraced laughing.

"I've missed you, Ray," Kaitlyn said as the familiar feelings began exploding in her body.

"I've missed you, too," Ray said, giving her a tight squeeze.

Ray released his embrace and bent down to pick up a sharp rock by his feet. Bringing it to the bark, he pressed hard and carved: "Kaitlyn and Ray Forever," encircling it with a heart and an arrow. He tossed the rock down when he was done and took Kaitlyn in his arms. Pressing his lips against hers, they engaged in a deep kiss. Bringing his forehead to rest against hers, he spoke. "I miss you! Remember, I will always love you."

Kaitlyn pulled away from Ray and looked at him. "I'm right here, how can you miss me?"

"I miss you already, Kait," Ray confided. "Just remember, I will always love you."

Ray put his soft hands to Kaitlyn's cheek and looked into her eyes. Bringing her lips to touch his, the two engaged in another passionate kiss. Ray held Kaitlyn as if he were trying to emboss every scent, every breath, and every feeling he had for her into his soul.

They released from their hug and slightly kissed each other. With their hands held together, they touched the engraving and smiled, releasing their hands only to begin their walk home.

They went back to Kaitlyn's house, and Kaitlyn immediately began helping her mother plan dishes for Nick and Ray. Ray went about his studies with Alex in the living room.

Kaitlyn was in deep thought.

"What's got you in a cloud?" Kathryn asked her.

"Nothing," Kaitlyn replied, not wanting to divulge information. "Just thinking about things."

She didn't want to tell her mother that she'd miss Ray, nor did she want to tell her she was bothered by Ray's words. Kaitlyn knew she couldn't explain it to her since she didn't quite understand it herself.

Kaitlyn and Kathryn finished the meals and then prepared their own food. When Kathryn and Kaitlyn had fixed dinner, all gathered in the dining room and began their meal with a prayer.

When Jim started to speak about Ray going home, Kaitlyn burst into tears. Unable to conceal her emotions, Kaitlyn excused herself and went to the comfort of her room, once again, finding solace in the pillow.

Ray excused himself and went upstairs to check on her. "What's wrong, hon?"

"I don't want you to go," she replied in broken syllables. "I'm going to miss you."

"Kait, I'm just going home," Ray said. "I'm not going anywhere."

"I know, it's just that ... " Kaitlyn began crying harder, "I won't get to see you as much. It's going to be so hard."

"Come here, Kait," Ray comforted, motioning for a hug. "I'm not going anywhere. I love you."

"I love you, too, Ray," Kaitlyn replied. "That's why it hurts so much. I don't want you to go."

"Come on, Kait," Ray urged her on. "Let's go back down to dinner. We'll snuggle on the couch together later and talk about things. This is going to be hard for both of us."

Kaitlyn wiped the tears and went back downstairs with Ray to finish dinner. She apologized for her outburst, explaining that everything had hit her at once. "I'm okay now," Kaitlyn said, making sure her father was aware of her stability. "It's just been a hard few weeks."

"That it has been," Kathryn agreed, figuring out the real reasons behind Kaitlyn's behavior.

"It's definitely been a tough few weeks," Jim also agreed. "Let's try to enjoy this evening though."

After dinner, Ray and Kaitlyn spent some time in the living room together. Kaitlyn rested her head on Ray's shoulder as she sat next to him, and they read from their book, discussing some of the more pertinent passages. Kaitlyn as usual, went off on her tangents, explaining her views with seriousness and total confusion for others who happened to hear.

By this time, Ray had become accustomed to such blabber. He went along with Kaitlyn, pretending he understood what she was saying, as a smirk would escape from his face every so often — out of her view.

Kaitlyn stopped in mid-sentence and looked up to Ray. "I love you," She said plainly and from nowhere.

"I love you, Miss Kait," Ray said as he donned a grin. He wrapped his arm around her and gave Kaitlyn a side hug. "I miss you already," he said.

"Me too," Kaitlyn said, understanding why he had said that earlier.

When the fire died down, Kaitlyn and Ray called it a night. After putting the book away, they headed upstairs for bed. Kaitlyn went to her room to dress in her evening attire. Just as Ray was settling into bed, he heard a knock at the door followed by a sweet voice. "May I come in?"

"Of course you may," Ray answered, glad that Kaitlyn knocked first.

Kaitlyn entered the room and slid over to Ray, "I love you. I need a hug."

Ray brought his arms up and out to Kaitlyn, inviting her to come to him. She did without hesitation. They grasped each other in an intimate hug before Ray pressed his lips hard against hers. Kaitlyn let out a slight moan, wanting more, and Ray with his arms wrapped around her, squeezed her tight against his chest.

Kaitlyn whispered a crying moan. "I got to go."

"I know," Ray said before he gave her a small kiss and said goodnight. "You always *got to go*," he replied with a laugh.

"I love you, babes," Kaitlyn said as she was leaving the room.

"I love you, too, Miss Kait," Ray replied, getting back into bed. "Goodnight."

Boy she says, 'I love you' a lot, Ray thought, letting out a chuckle.

Ray went to sleep with a smile on his face, as did Kaitlyn.

The day Kaitlyn dreaded so much had finally come. Ray was leaving, and things were going to change. As to how much they would change, Kaitlyn had no idea.

Kaitlyn woke, showered and dressed. She went to extra lengths to brighten herself up hoping it would cheer the somber mood. Her plan, although a good one, failed miserably. A frown graced her pretty face as she walked downstairs for breakfast. However, that frown turned to smiles when the sweet smell of the morning meal whispered its invitation.

Kathryn and Jim, Kaitlyn, Ray and Alex all joined together for a big family breakfast. The smell of fresh pancakes on the grill, tangy sausage and the sweet smell of pure maple syrup filled the dining room with welcoming scents. Smiles were on everyone's faces as the sun shone through the windows, welcoming the day.

"We're going to miss you, Ray," Kathryn said as Kaitlyn's eyes peered in Ray's direction saying *me too.*

"If you need us for anything, please ask," Jim said firmly. "You and your father are family now."

"Thank you," Ray said as he smiled at both Mr. and Mrs. Frost. "My father and I can't thank you enough. You've been wonderful to us — to me."

"It's been a pleasure," Jim replied. "We're glad we could help."

"Now, Ray, after school you are to go home, and Kaitlyn will go with you," Kathryn instructed. "I will be picking up your father and bringing him to your house shortly after you arrive there."

"Okay," Ray replied, still attentive to her.

"I will have the meals Kaitlyn and I prepared at the house ready and waiting," Kathryn continued. "Then I will help get you situated, and Kaitlyn and I will be on our way."

"Okay," Ray said with a little fear in his voice.

"It will be okay, Ray," Kathryn assured, detecting Ray's uneasiness. "We're not far away and can come over anytime you need us to. Just call."

"Okay, thank you," Ray said as he took a deep breath.

"Alex, I'll be home once you get back from football practice," Kathryn said including him.

"Okay, Mom," Alex replied. "Good luck, Ray! It's been nice having a *brother* around, taking a quick glance at his sister.

"Thanks, Alex," Ray replied. "Same here."

Kaitlyn and Ray excused themselves from the table and left for school, while Alex stayed behind to have a second helping.

Kaitlyn and Ray made a detour on the way, stopping at their tree. Ray leaned up against it, and Kaitlyn cuddled into his chest. A teardrop began running down her cheek as she looked up to Ray. He held her close in comfort while his own teardrop escaped.

Kaitlyn cried out, "I don't want you to go. I don't want to go to school. I want to run away with you and stay in your arms forever."

Ray put his fingers to Kaitlyn's chin without speaking. He brought her lips to his and kissed her while grasping his arms around her. "I'm scared, Kaitlyn. I'm so scared. What if I can't do this? What if I can't take care of my dad, do my studies, and take care of the house? I don't know if I can do this. When am I going to get to see you? *How* am I going to be able to see *you*?"

Kaitlyn looked at Ray. "We'll manage, Ray. We'll be okay."

"How?" Ray asked as tears multiplied.

"I don't know how, but we'll have to," Kaitlyn replied. "Just don't shut me out again. We'll get through this, *together*."

"I love you, Kait," Ray said through choked up words. "I don't know what I'd do without you."

"I love you, Ray," Kaitlyn said, wiping a tear from his cheek. "More than you'll ever know."

They took each other in their arms. "We'd better get going or we'll be late," Ray said as he held on a bit tighter.

"No, I don't want to go," Kaitlyn announced as she shook her arms and feet in a tantrum manner. "I'm going to miss you too much. Let's stay here forever."

Ray looked at Kaitlyn knowing exactly how she was feeling. It's just that she had the guts to say it out loud. They held onto each other, feeling like they were drowning. Their lifeline was slipping away. With one last intimate exchange of love before leaving their tree, the two left hand in hand with Kaitlyn burying her head into the side of Ray's chest in sadness.

They both met school with uneasiness and had trouble releasing their hands from one another. Kaitlyn couldn't look at Ray, for fear of breaking out into a full-blown sob. She turned away and walked to her first class choked up with emotion. The gut feeling she had was beginning to feel like a stabbing dulled knife.

Allison saw Kaitlyn and went to hug her best friend. She didn't need to ask what was wrong. She already knew. "I'll help you get through this, Kaitlyn," Allison comforted in a loving way. "It's all going to be okay."

Ray made it through the day and tried not to show his true emotions, but this did not hold true for Kaitlyn. She struggled through the entire day holding back tears, becoming choked up at the mere mention of Ray's name. She stayed to herself, feeling lost and empty, as if her heart had a huge hole in it. She wasn't so sure she would be able to fill that hole for a long, long time.

When the school day came to an end, Kaitlyn met Ray at his locker.

"What happened to you?" Ray asked, bringing his hands to her cheeks, noticing a slight swelling.

"I've had a rough day," Kaitlyn answered. "Let's get out of here."

Ray held Kaitlyn in his arms as they walked out of school towards Ray's house, while she kept her head buried in his chest. "This is going to be so hard," Kaitlyn cried out, not lifting her head. "I feel like I'm losing you. I feel like a part of me is dying inside."

Ray held Kaitlyn in a reassuring grasp. "Oh, honey," he said. "I love you. You're not losing me, and I'm not losing you. We're just not going to be able to see each other as much for awhile."

Just the mention of the reality that Kaitlyn knew existed brought Kaitlyn to tears. Ray didn't speak. He held her tight, feeling the same way, soothing her worry as they finished their walk to his house.

"We're here, Kait," Ray announced with hesitancy.

He slowly opened the door and showed Kaitlyn inside. Once they were in and Ray shut the front door, he wrapped his arms around Kaitlyn in a grip so tight nothing could have pulled them apart. Ray began sobbing, breaking down from a day of hiding emotions. He brought Kaitlyn's hand to his chest saying: "Feel this, my heart hurts."

They collapsed to the floor holding each other while letting the anxiety, the worry, and the ache spill out through their eyes.

Kaitlyn and Ray were able to compose themselves enough before Kathryn showed up with Nick. They all helped Nick get settled in, and Kathryn and Kaitlyn made sure they were set before leaving.

Kaitlyn welcomed Nick home, giving him a hug and a slight kiss on the cheek. She then turned to Ray and hugged him with ache penetrating every cell of her body. She whispered her love to Ray in his ear as she felt a teardrop escape her eye. "If you need anything, *anything at all*, you'd better call!"

"I will, Kait," Ray said, trying to be strong. "I will."

Kaitlyn and her mother left.

As Kaitlyn seated herself in the car, she began to cry. Her body shook with overpowering sadness as tears multiplied. Kathryn could only try to comfort Kaitlyn with gentle touches, but there was no consoling her.

It took everything Kaitlyn had to make it through dinner that night. She picked at her food and moved it around the plate, until she finally asked to be excused, finding solace in her room once again.

She made a notation in her diary as tears welled, ready to fall.

"October 27, 1950
"I miss my Ray."

That was all Kaitlyn could enter that evening. The moment she wrote the words, her eyes flowed with tears, and her heart filled with pain. She knew what lied ahead. She couldn't admit it to herself, just yet.

Chapter Thirteen

Over the course of a few weeks, Kaitlyn and Ray were barely able to see each other. Sure, they would see each other in school, and talk here and there, but their conversations had taken on a new tone. They were short, diplomatic and, well, boring without meaning.

Kaitlyn had offered to help out numerous times, but Ray always replied with: "Thank you. We're okay," not continuing the conversation.

Eventually, Kaitlyn stopped asking. Eventually, Kaitlyn stopped talking to Ray altogether. Little by little, she began to retract. She withdrew from Ray first, then Allison, and then the social scene entirely. Nothing in her life had the same feel, and everything in her life had become dismal and gray.

She walked around in a cloud of hurt, a cloud Ray had put there. She had given her heart and soul to Ray, and that didn't seem to matter to him. She didn't seem to matter to him. Kaitlyn didn't matter to Kaitlyn anymore.

The holiday season had come, and Kaitlyn just went through the motions. She never bothered going to the Halloween bash at The Fountain figuring, "What's the use?"

That mood carried over into late November.

Ray and his father were invited for Thanksgiving at the Frost's, but they declined, claiming it was too hard for them. Kaitlyn was relieved. As far as she knew, she and Ray were over. The boy Kaitlyn would know as her first love was no longer in her life. Or was he?

Nothing was the same or had the same excitement during their Thanksgiving feast that year. The turkey was just that — turkey. The dressings, the stuffing, and the breads didn't have the same flavor or aroma of past celebrations. And the cranberry sauce was just a brilliant crimson color of mush. It was just another dinner to her.

After Thanksgiving, the Christmas season came, including Christmas shopping. Kaitlyn continued to go through the motions, choosing gifts for family and friends, even though she had kept her friends at arm's length. And then there was Ray. Kaitlyn couldn't keep herself from putting him on her list, even though it brought with it a solemn sigh.

Kaitlyn picked out each gift for every person she intended to buy for by December nineteenth, except Ray's. She wasn't even sure if she should buy him one. Kaitlyn was desperately in love with him, and even though her head fought with her heart, she just couldn't help herself.

Carefully going through the bundles of merchandise, Kaitlyn never found the right gift — the one that popped out and made her feel like *this is the one*. She saw so many things she wanted to give him, but second-guessed herself when thinking of how it might be received. Kaitlyn finally crossed Ray's name off the list, adding one more painful memory in her heart. She had wished Christmas would not come that year, but Kaitlyn knew that wish would not be granted.

Christmas did come, and it also went without a word or even a card from Ray. Kaitlyn was hurt. By that time though, she had used up all her tears, and the hurt she had been holding onto turned to anger and hate. She made a notation in her diary on Christmas Day, 1950.

"I hate loving him. How can I love him when he has treated me like dirt swept under a rug? Why do I love him? I could scream with anger. I love him. I hate him ... I miss him! How could he do this to me? Merry Christmas, Ray."

Kaitlyn tried to come up with all sorts of reasons why Ray was treating her with total disregard. She thought about the fact that he had had his father to tend to, the housework, schoolwork, yard work, and everything else he had going on. None of her conclusions made any sense though. "He could at least take a few minutes to call me," she thought angrily. Kaitlyn vowed never to speak to Ray again. That promise was broken a week later.

New Year's Day arrived, and Kaitlyn heard a knocking at the door. Her heart pounded in hopes she would view Ray standing on the other side. She argued with herself for even wanting it to be him. "Arghh, I hate loving him!" she screamed silently. "Why do I do this to myself?"

She opened the door and there, in front of her eyes, was a dozen bright yellow roses. The boy peered out from the large bundle of flowers. "Are you Miss Kaitlyn Frost?" he asked.

"Yes, I am," Kaitlyn answered.

"Then, these are for you," the delivery boy said as he handed her the roses.

"Thank you," Kaitlyn replied, accepting the bouquet while taking in its divine scent.

Kaitlyn shut the door behind her as she peered into the flowers searching for a card gently with her fingers — there wasn't one. "That's strange," she thought. "Hmm."

Kaitlyn brought the roses to the kitchen and began cutting the stems to place in a bud vase. Carefully, she arranged them as she tried to think of whom they could be from. "They've got to be from Ray," she thought. "He's the only one who knows I love yellow roses, right?"

Kaitlyn raised her eyebrows, questioned herself, and tried to remember if anyone else knew. She couldn't recall. As Kaitlyn began to fix some tea, she heard the door again. She went to open it with a puzzled look on her face.

"Sorry, Miss," the delivery boy said, handing her a wet piece of paper. "I dropped this on the sidewalk. This goes with it."

"Thanks, I was wondering why there wasn't one," Kaitlyn replied. "Thank you."

Kaitlyn stared at the card as she closed the door. Her hands trembled with fear of opening it. She walked back to the kitchen with her attention focused solely on the card. She bumped her head into the side of the entranceway as she re-entered the kitchen. Shaking off her clumsiness, Kaitlyn put the card on the table, unsure of why she couldn't bring herself to open it.

She turned away to finish fixing tea and then turned back to the card as if it were calling her. Kaitlyn dismissed the strange pull the card had on her and carried on with the tea preparation.

"Oh, no!" she cried out. "Shoot!"

Kaitlyn studied the cup, checking to see if there was damage from her nicking it on the side of the cupboard. Her most treasured teacup now had a small chip in the rim. It was still useable, but tainted. Kaitlyn was devastated.

"Arghh, that Ray," Kaitlyn yelled, blaming him for the carelessness as she began rinsing the cup out. "Great, just great! Here I am, trusted with this cup, dating back to the eighteen hundreds, and I go and nick the darn thing, not to mention, bang my head on the stupid frame. Why does he do this to me?!" Kaitlyn lowered her eyes and shook her head with disappointment, wanting to go into a full-blown tantrum. "I wish I was two!"

Pouring the steaming water over a fresh teabag and then returning to the table, Kaitlyn viewed the card again. She took a sip of her too-hot tea and set it down to cool in front of her, continuing to shake her head in disgust.

Kaitlyn picked the card up in her hands and began unsealing the envelope. She was afraid of what it would say and hesitated for a moment before pulling it out from its concealment. The card simply read:

"We need to talk. Please meet me at The Fountain today, at three o'clock. Ray"

"What does *that* mean?" Kaitlyn asked herself out loud, ready to burst into tears.

Kathryn came into the kitchen just as Kaitlyn put her head in her hands. "What's wrong, honey?"

Kaitlyn couldn't talk. She handed Kathryn the card and returned her hands to her head.

Kathryn read the card and gave it back. "You need to go, Kaitlyn. You need to get this over with, once and for all."

"I know, Mom," Kaitlyn replied through tears. "I'm scared to see him. I'm angry. I'm hurt. I love him. I hate him. I don't know what I even want with him."

Kathryn pulled up a chair and sat down beside her daughter. "I know, honey, but you can't keep moping around. You've been sulking for almost three months now. You haven't seen any of your friends, and you need to live your life."

"I know," Kaitlyn replied.

"No, Kaitlyn, I don't think you *do* know," Kathryn replied back, sick of seeing her daughter hurting. "Go and get this thing figured out. Go talk with Ray. Maybe there's a good reason for his … whatever you want to call it."

Raising her eyebrows, Kaitlyn asked, "You think?"

"I don't know, Kaitlyn," Kathryn answered. "That's what you need to find out. He obviously cares for you if he sent you roses. Not to mention, they're your favorite color."

"You're right, Mom," Kaitlyn replied. "He can't buy me back though."

"No one said he was trying to," Kathryn answered. "Now go upstairs and shower. Put on something that makes you feel good, and go meet Ray."

"Okay, Mom. I love you."

"I love you, too. Now get a move on!"

"Mom." Kaitlyn spoke fearfully.

"Yes, dear?"

"I chipped my cup. I was nervous, and I hit it on the side of the cupboard when I took it out."

"Don't worry, Kaitlyn. It's just a cup. Maybe it'll be a remembrance of when you got your life back. Who knows, just be more careful next time. Now get going."

"Thanks." Kaitlyn headed out of the kitchen and then ran back in to hug her mother.

"You have to do this, honey."

"I know. I'm just scared. I don't want to lose him."

"Well, you can't go on like this either, Kaitlyn. Go. Go," Kathryn said with a few waves of her hands. "Settle this once and for all!"

Kaitlyn braced herself for the meeting with Ray, knowing it could be the end of their relationship. Even though she felt like it was already over, Kaitlyn still had a thread to hold onto, and she held onto that thread with all her might.

She showered and let the hot water fall upon her face, enjoying its massage. When she was done, Kaitlyn chose a warm cashmere sweater to wear with a matching skirt, picking out a floral print scarf to go with it. Tying the scarf in a perfect knot, Kaitlyn encouraged herself in the mirror. "You can do this, Kaitlyn," she said to her reflection. "You have to do this."

She nodded in agreement with her words and went downstairs, stopping by the kitchen to see her mother for a little support.

You look nice, honey," Kathryn complimented. "You'll be just fine."

"Thanks," Kaitlyn replied, taking a deep breath. "Wish me luck?"

"You don't need any, Kaitlyn," Kathryn replied. "All you need to do is listen, and then tell him how you feel. You'll do just fine."

"Okay," Kaitlyn said with uncertainty. "I'll be back in awhile."

Kaitlyn put on her coat and took the walk to The Fountain. It was chilly outside, but Kaitlyn wanted the time walking, to clear her head under the bright winter sun.

Freshly fallen snow covered the trees and small bushes that lined the parkway, and the blue sky showcased a few scattered clouds. She passed by kids making snow angels and trying to build snowmen out of the light flaky stuff, without success. Regardless, the children didn't seem to care. They were having fun. "Boy, I wish I were a young kid again," she thought. "No worries. No heartache. No Ray to break my heart."

Up ahead of Kaitlyn, she spotted her destination: The Soda Fountain. She felt her heart beating faster, and her pulse race as she approached the door. Putting her hand on the doorknob and taking a deep cleansing breath, Kaitlyn walked in.

There he was, more handsome than he had ever been. When Kaitlyn's eyes met his, she turned to putty. While Kaitlyn's common sense argued with her heart, telling her to be angry, her heart wanted to escape into Ray's arms.

Kaitlyn, with a half smile and a half frown, took a seat opposite Ray. She went to speak, but her mouth could not utter a single word. Kaitlyn trembled in fear of what Ray might say. She brought her hands to her face as if to take cover. "I can't do this," slipped from her tongue. "I got to go."

Ray looked at Kaitlyn and then lowered his eyes. He peered back and pleaded with her to stay. "No, don't, please."

Kaitlyn became angry. "Tell me why I should stay?!"

Ray looked hurt as he said, "Because, I love you."

With grave disgust, Kaitlyn looked at Ray. "You *love* me?" she questioned, "You sure have a funny way of showing it. Or is that how *love* is supposed to be? Forget it!" she said, throwing her hands in the air. Kaitlyn turned away and headed towards the door. She stopped one foot before it, overcome with emotion.

Ray went to Kaitlyn and extended his arms.

Kaitlyn spoke angrily, pushing him away. "Leave me alone. You've really hurt me this time, Ray. How could you have done this to me?"

Kaitlyn rushed to the door and scrambled to open it.

Just as Ray reached Kaitlyn, she opened the door, breaking free in a runaway cry, her tears freezing in the brisk winter air.

"Come back!" Ray called out in desperation. "Please Kait, come back ... "

Ray went into The Fountain to retrieve his jacket and keys. He got into his car and drove to the one place he thought Kaitlyn would have gone to. He hoped he'd catch her on the way, but didn't. Arriving at Crestview Park, Ray stationed the car and took off running as fast as he could to their tree. He spotted Kaitlyn curled up underneath it, with her head lowered in her lap, just as it had been the first time they'd met.

Ray quietly went to Kaitlyn and stretched his hand out to her as he tried to peer into her eyes. "I'm sorry, Kait."

Kaitlyn resisted his offer before letting into temptation. She allowed Ray to help her up and then buried her face in his chest, with tears streaming down her cheeks. She was shivering from the cold and trembling from the pain in her heart. She punched his chest screaming "How could you do this to me?! I didn't do anything to deserve this!"

Ray put his fingers under Kaitlyn's chin and lifted her head so their eyes could meet. "I know you didn't."

Kaitlyn stared with the pain in her eyes piercing him. "Why then, just tell me why?"

Ray leaned up against the tree and brought Kaitlyn with him, still holding her. "I don't know."

Kaitlyn continued to keep her head buried in his chest. "Not good enough," she pouted, yet reprimanding.

Ray took a deep breath. "I've never known anyone like you before, Kait. You've awakened feelings in me I'd never knew existed. I can't describe it. You scare me."

Kaitlyn stood up straight and glared at Ray. "*I* scare *you?*" she questioned.

Ray lowered his eyes to look closely into hers. "Kait, I love you so much that it hurts. The pain is so severe that it's easier to run from it than allow it to hurt me."

Kaitlyn brought sarcasm to her voice. "Oh yeah, okay. Well, *that's* a lame excuse."

Kaitlyn began to turn away and Ray pulled her back by one arm, speaking seriously. "It's not an excuse, Kait. It really hurts. I was trying to take care of my dad, the house, the yard, and my schoolwork. All I could think of was you, and it was driving me insane. So, I stayed away, hoping it would ease the pain of not being able to see you. A phone call here and there just wouldn't have done it. I wanted to be with you every second of every day, and I couldn't."

Kaitlyn looked at Ray as she began wiping the tears from her eyes. "*And*?"

"I knew it was hurting you not being able to see me, too. I figured it would be best if I made you hate me. I figured it would make it easier on you."

Kaitlyn looked at him angrily. "No, Ray. It made it easier on *you*," she replied, turning away. "Your plan didn't work. You hurt me, and you broke your promise. How can I ever trust you again?"

Ray didn't have an answer.

Kaitlyn looked at Ray with frustration in her facial cast. "I don't understand why you didn't ask for help or accept my help when I offered it. Why wouldn't you allow me to help you? At least that way, we would have been able to see each other."

"Pride," Ray replied.

"Pride? Your *pride*?!" Kaitlyn screamed in question.

"Kait, you and your family had already done so much," Ray said, feeling guilty about their help. "I couldn't allow you or your family to do anymore. It just wasn't right."

"Ray," Kaitlyn began. "I almost understand that. But I helped because I love you. My family helped because they care. There is no payback or limit to that help. Didn't you hear my dad? You're family."

"Where I come from, Kait, there is," Ray replied. "We pay back our debts, no matter how big or small. My father and I just couldn't accept anymore help."

"That's sad," Kaitlyn said. "What's even more sad is that you've broken my heart trying to keep your stupid pride."

Ray looked at Kaitlyn with sincerity in his eyes and in his heart. "I'm sorry. I really am. I was wrong, Kait," Ray said without hesitation. "I don't want to lose you."

"I don't want to lose you either, Ray," Kaitlyn replied, adding, "but I feel like I already have. And, Ray ... you've already lost me."

Ray looked at her. "I'm right here, where I want to be, with you — if you'll have me back."

Kaitlyn knew she wanted Ray back, but was held back from all the hurt and empty promises he had made. She looked into his eyes with uncertainty. "How do I know you won't do this to me again? I haven't been able to count on you so far. What makes things so different now?"

Ray stared back at Kaitlyn, begging. "You're going to have to try to trust me."

Kaitlyn lowered her eyes. "I don't know if I can."

"Can you try?" Ray asked. "Will you give me the chance to prove to you that you *can* trust me?"

Ray knew this was an end all or a beginning question. He wasn't sure if he could bear to hear the answer. He also knew that whatever decision Kaitlyn made, it was her choice. Ray knew he had done wrong by Kaitlyn. He knew he had hurt her, but he also wanted to make it right again. Nonetheless, he was afraid of the answer.

Kaitlyn hesitated before making her verdict. "If you ever do this to me again ... "

"I won't. I promise," Ray interrupted with pleading eyes. "I will keep my promise, Kait."

Kaitlyn finished. "If you ever do this to me again or treat me the way you have treated me, I will never forgive you, and we will be done forever."

Ray embraced Kaitlyn. "I will never ignore or stay away from you again."

Kaitlyn continued on with what she wanted to say. "Ray, you must promise to work through your feelings with me. If you're hurting, tell me. If you're angry with me, tell me. If you're having a hard time, tell me. You have to promise that you will include me in your life and never run from me again. And one more thing: don't keep things from me. No more secrets!"

"I do promise you that, Kaitlyn," Ray said with happy tears. "I hate myself for hurting you. I wish I could take it back."

"That's the sad thing, Ray. Words or unspoken words can never be taken back. They hurt, they sting, and they last forever."

"I'm sorry, Kait," Ray said sincerely. "I love you."

"I love you, too, Ray. I have since the minute I met you," Kaitlyn replied while wrapping her arms around him. "I've missed you so much."

Ray took Kaitlyn in his arms and looked at her. "I loved you yesterday. I love you today. I will love you tomorrow. I will love you for the rest of my life."

"Me too," Kaitlyn replied, giggling with dried up tears. "Me too," she whispered softly in his ear.

Ray took off his class ring and offered it to Kaitlyn. "Will you go steady with me?"

Kaitlyn's eyes widened with a smile. "Yes." Kaitlyn leaned in to Ray. She pressed her lips against his, embracing in a passionate, heart felt kiss.

They released, and Ray took Kaitlyn by the shoulders and looked her square in the eyes. "I'm really sorry, Kait."

"I know you are. I am, too."

Ray was puzzled. "Why are *you* sorry?" he asked.

"For taking shots at you and because I stopped talking to you too," Kaitlyn admitted. "I could have tried harder. I guess I also ran. Hey, Ray ... "

"Yes, Kait," Ray answered.

"Thank you for the yellow roses. I love them."

"I'm glad, Kait," Ray replied. "I'm very glad. Let's get you out of this cold."

Ray escorted Kaitlyn to the car. "Let's go back to my house and sit by the fire."

"Okay," Kaitlyn said through clattering teeth. "I'm freezing."

Ray and Kaitlyn drove to Ray's house as they discussed what they've been doing over the past couple of months. Kaitlyn broke a silent moment asking about John.

"Have you been seeing him?" Kaitlyn asked.

"A couple times," Ray admitted. "How about you?"

"No," Kaitlyn said ashamed of her behavior.

"Why not?" Ray asked.

"I don't know if I want to," Kaitlyn replied. "I've basically stayed away from everyone lately, including Allison." As Kaitlyn finished her sentence, they pulled into the driveway.

Nick was putting a log on the fire when they entered. Kaitlyn greeted him with a warm hello hug. "You're looking good, Mr. Niles. How are you feeling?"

"Getting better every day, Kaitlyn," Nick replied. "How wonderful it is to see you. Would you like to stay for dinner?"

"I'd love to," Kaitlyn answered. "Let me call my mom."

Kaitlyn called Kathryn and told her briefly what happened. She then told her of the invitation, and Kathryn gave the okay. Hanging up, Ray had Kaitlyn warm by the fire while he fixed hot cocoa for the three of them. They sat and talked. Ray and Nick shared memories of Jaycee with Kaitlyn, making her wish she had known her longer. Soft music of yesteryear played in the background as they all laughed, giggled, and shed a few tears. They had a most enjoyable time relishing in a nice meal together.

After dinner and cleanup, Ray brought Kaitlyn home. On the drive back, Ray stopped the car for a brief moment at the curb. "Kaitlyn, remember what I told you before?"

Kaitlyn nodded.

"That will be happening soon."

"Thanks for telling me."

"I'm not going to keep anything from you again," Ray pledged sincerely. "We're a team. Two apples from the same seed."

"I believe you, Ray."

Ray gave Kaitlyn his private gesture, and she leaned over to Ray. They embraced in a loving kiss. "I love you, babes." Kaitlyn said.

"I love you more," Ray replied. "I love you with all my heart, more than you could ever know."

Ray and Kaitlyn exchanged smiles before Ray started the car out towards her house. They pulled in the drive, and he stole one last kiss before Kaitlyn got out. Just as Kaitlyn went to shut the car door, Alex came outside in a rage. He ran up to Ray's window and began yelling at him.

Kaitlyn scurried over to Alex trying to calm him down. "Alex!" Kaitlyn screamed. "It's okay. We worked things out. I'm to blame as well."

Alex, unsettled by the news, did not believe it, "If you ever hurt her again, I'm going to punch your lights out."

"I'm sorry, Alex," Ray said. "I was wrong for breaking my promise to you and to Kaitlyn. Please forgive me. It won't happen again."

"It'd better not, Ray," Alex warned. "It'd better not!"

Ray got out of the car and looked at Alex. Extending his hand, Ray said, "I'm sorry."

Alex, still fuming with anger, took his hand and shook it. As Ray went to release his grip, Alex held onto it. Pulling Ray in close to him, Alex looked Ray dead straight in the eyes. "You do it again, and I *will* kill you."

Ray nodded, understanding that Alex meant what he said. He also knew he deserved it. Ray got in his car and waved goodbye to Kaitlyn as he started the car. As he pulled away, he waved his hand to Alex saying, "I'm sorry" and waved his hand again to Kaitlyn saying, "I love you."

Kaitlyn yelled at Alex and gave him a sisterly slap. "What'd you do that for?"

"To protect you," Alex replied.

"Oh, well thanks. But I don't need protection."

"Yes, you do, Kaitlyn," Alex replied. "You most certainly do. He paused. "You back together with that snake?"

"He's not a snake, and yes," Kaitlyn answered, "we're back together," as she showed him Ray's ring. "Everything has been worked out and talked through."

"Well, well ... " Alex stumbled. "If he ever hurts you again, he's going to have to deal with me."

"Okay, Alex," Kaitlyn replied. "Fine. Come on, silly, let's get inside."

Chapter Fourteen

*   *   *

Kaitlyn smiled as she relaxed in the tub and even let out a slight giggle when she recalled Alex sticking up for her. The hurt Ray caused so long ago was prevalent in her mind, but she also remembered how good it felt when they made up.

Letting out a joyful sigh, Kaitlyn lay back and let the warm water swirl around her. Deciding to rest her head on a towel against the tub's wall, Kaitlyn closed her eyes while memories traveled back to January 03, 1951.

*   *   *

Kaitlyn and Ray looked forward to each moment spent together. It wasn't so much what they did, but how they felt when they were with one another. They could be walking down the shop-lined streets of Winter's Crest, not speaking a word, and passerby's could see how much in love they were as their body language announced it.

Kaitlyn's eyes always lit up while in Ray's presence or from hearing his name, and Ray had a certain glow about him, too. He looked serene and happy, and when the two were by each others' sides, they radiated like two kids madly in love. Remembering their own first loves, older people couldn't help but smile when they saw them.

Kaitlyn and Rays' time spent ice-skating and visiting The Fountain or hanging out by fires at their homes were magical. They would cuddle up to one another and read from their book while relaxing in each other's arms. The two could have been in 'Timbuktu' for all they cared. As long as they were together, Kaitlyn and Ray felt like they were at home.

They always seemed to have a need to touch in some small way or another. If they became a bit too close in view of Jim or Nick, they would hear an authoritative clearing of the throat. Pleasing their fathers' eyes, Kaitlyn and Ray would inch away, but eventually, they would slide their way back to their previous positions — only to hear the throat clearing sounds again. This always left them chuckling, hiding their mischievous grins from their fathers.

Kaitlyn and Ray talked about everything and anything. They no longer kept secrets from one another, and they helped each other solve dilemmas as a team. They were inseparable, *two peas in a pod*. So much so, they could finish each other's sentences or thoughts. Sometimes, the two would become annoyed, as they were never able to complete their own sentences, but they usually ended up laughing about it, even if they were fed up from the ongoing intrusions.

Kaitlyn and Ray were finally back where they belonged — together. Their love grew with each passing moment, as well as their respect for one another. And Ray had finally earned back Kaitlyn's trust, even if at first she had her guard up.

*   *   *

Kaitlyn gleefully smiled from her reminiscing as she wet her hair one more time. Resting against the towel again, she put the memories of her reunion with Ray aside and began recalling Monday, January fourteenth, 1951.

*   *   *

All of the kids and teachers alike talked about John's scheduled assembly taking place at nine o'clock. Chatter, along with nervous sighs, echoed through the high school in anticipation. They wanted to hear John's side of things, but feared the unknown at the same time. The district itself had never had such an event and met the entire program John planned out with uneasiness. However, the schools were going to have to get used to it because this assembly would be the first of many to come.

John was scared, but ready to keep his promise to Jaycee and his community.

Kaitlyn couldn't help think the day was going to be hard on Ray, John, Allison and herself. She kept wondering how they would react, their peers, and how *she* would react. At this point, Kaitlyn was still weary of John and had not completely found peace with his actions. "If I feel this way," she thought. "How are the others feeling?"

By the time the bell sounded its five-minute warning, all of the kids had filed into the auditorium, with a few straggling faculty members filing in behind.

The auditorium had a certain aura to it, like no other. An excitement seemed to grab one as he walked in, as if something magical was in the air. It was a place where plays and musicals were held, along with some not so joyful events. And it was as if the laughter, the tears, and the cheers remained — a spirit, if you will.

The deep navy carpets were surrounded by oak stained paneled walls, and the chairs were lined up in rows, with an aisle separating them into two sections. The floor angled at a slant. Not too many people had to crank their heads to see, which made attending the events there so much more enjoyable.

The oak stage had deep blue velvet curtains hanging from the stage encasement, which matched the carpet. Velvet backdrops were rolled into the ceiling, able to be used at any point by the pull of a rope. Large speakers for the sound system hung from the corners of the auditorium, and four smaller ones were placed on the stage front. It was definitely a special place and something magical was about to happen there.

And it did when John walked on stage.

A heart-stopping silence took over the echoing room as John stood briefly before all, silent. As pulses raced and anxiety heightened, John screamed: "I KILLED JAYCEE NILES!"

The stagger from hearing John shout those words filled the air. He instilled a fear in each person there. A murderer now stood before them.

John took a deep cleansing breath and softly began reading the promise note he had written to Jaycee Niles. A falling leaf could have been heard in that large room as John read out loud, while eyes stared as if they were glued in one spot. Hands grasped the side arms of their seats in preparation for what was to come.

After reading the note, he looked up at the audience of his peers, pausing briefly. And then, in a loud, authoritative tone, John continued.

"How would you feel if *you* killed your best friend's mom?" he questioned, pointing his finger wildly at the onlookers. "How do you think Ray feels knowing I'm the one who killed his mom?" again questioning, pointing to himself, adding in a tight slap to his chest. "She'll never see him graduate high school. She'll never see him graduate college or serve his country. She'll never see Ray marry. Jaycee Niles will never be able to see her grandchildren's faces light up when she comes into the room. 'Why?' you ask. Because I took that away from her!"

John paused and peered down to his feet, regaining his composure. He gave the audience a chance to regain theirs and to contemplate his questions.

He looked up with teardrops escaping his eyes. "I have to live with this for the rest of my life. It's *my* fault. The sad thing is — all I can say is "I'm sorry, and *that* is *not* good enough."

Everyone choked up with emotion imagining what it would be like to be John, Ray, and Nick. Then they thought about the sadness of the words spoken about Jaycee, and what she'd be missing out on. Their gulping throats weren't able to hold back the disconsolation, and tears filled their eyes. Those tears flowed and cries wailed when Ray walked on stage. Gasps echoed through the air as if a storm had suddenly appeared, bringing with it a confrontation between Ray and John.

People were on the edges of their seats as if they were watching a western flick at the local theatre not knowing what the next move would be. Clenched fists with white knuckles screamed silently while tensions thickened. Facial expressions froze as angry words exchanged between Ray and John. John begging for mercy.

Words ceased, bringing a long pause.

Ray walked carefully towards John, and gulps of suspense infiltrated the air. Ray raised his arm as if he was about to throw a punch. The audience gasped. Alleviated breaths could be heard when Ray extended his hand to John instead.

"I forgive you."

Relieving sighs bounced off the walls, and all cried with such intensity that their bodies didn't know which emotions to show, as if they all had nervous ticks. Half of their hearts wailed with the sadness, and the other half roared with the joy that they had just witnessed. They were so wrapped up with their emotions that they almost didn't see Nick come on stage.

Nick, not being as dramatic as his son, approached John, again leaving all in suspense, until Nick offered John his hand.

"I forgive you, too."

John fell to his knees overcome with joy, sadness, regret and shame. He thanked them both with his eyes as his voice became paralyzed with emotion.

After a brief interlude of exchanging hugs, Ray turned to his classmates with a serious stare and began to speak.

"I forgive John, but I'll *never* forget!"

Ray motioned for Kaitlyn to come on stage with his eyes and a quick nod. He hesitated in short and peered around the room looking for Allison. When he found her, he gestured for her to come up as well.

Ray continued. "Don't think for one second that what John has done is okay. It isn't! However, my father and I will not go through life with hatred and anger. That would *not* honor my mother, and it is *not* what she would want. My father and I are here today to heal and to let you know it's okay to forgive, just *don't* forget. This whole ordeal has been a heart wrenching experience for my father and I, Allison, Kaitlyn and her family, as well as John and his family. Learn from this tragedy. Learn from our forgiveness. Learn to use kind words and actions. You never know when your day will come, and you don't want to have any regrets."

Kaitlyn and Allison made it up on stage as Ray was finishing his speech.

Kaitlyn neared John and opened her arms, mouthing, "I'm sorry."

John embraced Kaitlyn as he said, "I'm sorry I let you down, Kaitlyn."

Kaitlyn stepped back and wiped the tears from her eyes, a half-smile on her face, hands held together at arm's length. "I forgive you, too."

Then, John turned his attention to Allison, who had followed in behind Kaitlyn. John held onto her as if she were his lifeline and voiced his affection, as well as his heartfelt gratitude for sticking by his side. John released his hold and straightened himself, getting enough control of his emotions to continue.

Ray, Nick, Kaitlyn and Allison moved to the side of the stage as on-lookers, allowing John to complete his mission.

John explained his actions and made sure everyone knew how regretful he was, and that he could not fix what he had done. He told about the events that took place. He told about how he couldn't face up to his terrible mistake with Kaitlyn, nor with himself. John talked about his feelings and what he intended to do to make things right.

John called Ray to his side and looked him square in the eyes. "I have every intention of fulfilling my promise to your mother. I wish I could take it back, Ray. I *really* wish I could take it back."

Ray held out his hand to John. "I trust you will keep the promise, John."

Ray and John embraced in a manly hug.

Tears of joy rolled down peoples' cheeks as they stood up, clapping in unison. It was beautiful. It was sad. It was peaceful. It was closure for all.

Ray, Kaitlyn, John and Allison made plans at the end of the assembly to meet at The Fountain after school. It was a time for them to heal, a time for them to reconnect, and a time to start over.

After school, the four walked to The Fountain while trying to sing Kaitlyn and Allison's favorite Perry Como song. By then, Allison and Kaitlyn knew all the words to *Some Enchanted Evening* and had figured out how to actually sing it in tune. Ray and John were totally off key and scrambled through the words laughing at the silliness of it all.

They entered the shop and sat down to some cherry colas and ice cream sundaes.

"John," Allison questioned, "did you and Ray plan that?"

John wasn't sure if he should reveal the truth to her, but decided to tell Allison "yes."

"You mean, that confrontation between you two ... was staged?" Allison asked, thinking it was clever.

John and Ray nodded in unison.

"Did you know about this, Kaitlyn?" Allison asked.

"Yes I did," Kaitlyn said, hoping she wouldn't be mad for not telling her.

"Why didn't you guys tell me?!" Allison asked Kaitlyn, John and Ray together as her eyes stared down each and every one.

John replied first. "I didn't know Kaitlyn knew. Ray and I weren't going to tell anyone."

Ray replied, "I had to tell Kaitlyn. We made a pact that there would be no more secrets."

Kaitlyn replied, "I'm sorry Allison, but I promised Ray I wouldn't say anything. I wanted to, but I also wanted to keep my promise."

"Thanks, guys. Thanks a lot," Allison replied. "I understand though, but don't do that to me again."

"We're sorry, Allison," Kaitlyn said as Ray and John chimed in too.

"Let's make a pact between all four of us," Allison suggested. "For now on, none of us will keep secrets from each other."

"Agreed," Kaitlyn said first.

"Agreed," Ray said with a smile.

"Agreed," John said, starting to chuckle. "Let's go dance and have some fun."

The four went to the dance floor, and Ray dropped some nickels in the jukebox. They swayed to slow dances and then *cut rugs* to some faster ones. Intermittently they would go back to their seats to quench their thirsts, and then head back to the dance floor, finally able to just be teenagers again.

Kaitlyn, Ray, Allison and John reconnected that day. They talked things over and just had a wonderful time being together. Ray and John were able to put aside their differences and enjoy being friends again, although still somewhat guarded. Kaitlyn and Allison enjoyed having smiles back on their faces. All were delighted that a terrible situation had finally been put to rest.

*   *   *

Kaitlyn's bath became cool. She exited the tub and threw on a robe and went downstairs to make her evening tea. Before taking the special teacup out from the cupboard, she opened the front door, allowing the summer night winds to flow inside. With her mission accomplished, Kaitlyn returned to the ever so important preparation of the tea. Kaitlyn loved her tea.

Taking notice of the small chip on the edge of the cup, Kaitlyn smiled, thinking, "Fifty years, I've had this cup ... a lot of memories."

The rose design had begun to fade, and the gold rim was not so gold anymore, the ivory base showing through. Regardless, Kaitlyn's teacup had more memories and more value than any material item she'd ever owned.

The kettle whistled, signaling her tea could now be made, with Kaitlyn doing so before sitting down at the kitchen table. Tracing her finger over the chipped rim, she remembered her feelings when she and Ray had come back together, recalling how their love and bond grew. Kaitlyn closed her eyes momentarily, reliving Ray's kisses and hugs, and how good they felt against her body, her lips. Kaitlyn spoke softly to no one. "I'd like to feel *that* again," knowing it was wishful thinking.

She enjoyed going through this sentimental journey. Though some of the memories were painful, she was glad it could still be recalled. "I've still got my mind, thank God," she thought while sipping her tea. "I can't be all that old yet. Well, I'd better not be."

Kaitlyn felt a chilling breeze come through the porch door. A cold front had moved in and brought northern air to her midsummer's eve. As she went to close the front door, the sudden cool winds reminded her of February in 1951.

*   *   *

Winter's Crest was hit hard by chilling, below zero winds. Roads were blocked with the heavy snowfall and school was cancelled, allowing Kaitlyn, Ray, John and Allison time to play.

The brisk temperatures brought John's backyard pond to a freeze, making it perfect for wintertime activities. During one of the cancelled school days, the four met at John's house for some fun, deciding to take advantage of the warmer twenty-degree weather, and bright shining sun — something they hadn't seen in awhile.

Once they were bundled up in jackets, scarves, gloves and ice-skates, they traveled outside of John's home to meet the depths of the snow.

Each step they took was met with resistance, as their legs became buried knee deep. Eventually, they made their way to the pond, using up half their energy to get there. They ice skated, joked around, and snowball fights popped up every once in awhile.

They did find the snowball fights to be a little difficult to do on skates and usually ended up on their bottoms laughing.

Foregoing the ice-skating, Kaitlyn and Allison decided to make snow angels. Finding some undisturbed snow, the two created their masterpieces. As they lay on the snow moving their arms and legs, they looked at each other with their special sneaking grins.

Allison motioned to John that she needed help getting up, as did Kaitlyn to Ray. And when the boys extended their hands out to help their forlorn gals, Allison and Kaitlyn pulled them face first down in the snow with them.

Ray laughed. "I'll get you, Miss Kait."

Kaitlyn tried getting to her feet and replied, "You'll have to catch me first." She tried to hop away as fast as she could, but the deep snow kept her basically in one place. Ray, being taller and stronger, and quite the 'man', was able to catch up to her in no time. But as fate would have it, they both ended up right back in the snow, together.

Giggling through their playfulness, Ray stole a kiss. "I got you, Miss Kait."

"Yes you did, sir," Kaitlyn replied, pulling him back into the snow. "You sure did," she said laughing with victory.

Allison and John frolicked in the snow together, hugging, kissing and enjoying the innocence of the day.

"Boy, this feels good, Allison," John commented.

Allison looked at John and then hugged him, knowing exactly what he meant. "Let's go get some hot cocoa," Allison suggested as she felt a chill overcome her.

"That's a good idea," Kaitlyn chimed in, shivering at its mention.

Ray and John took their ladies in their arms and tried to help them back to the house — unsuccessfully. They all ended up falling back in the snow. Trying to walk through it was like walking in molasses; *you get nowhere fast.*

Eventually, they made it back to the house with their laughter, smiles and drenched clothing. The gentlemen helped the ladies off with their coats and wrapped them both up in separate blankets, and instructed them to warm by the fire. With the girls' needs tended to, Ray and John excused themselves to prepare the cocoa.

When the young men came out from the kitchen and handed the girls their drinks, they asked them about the Valentine's Dance that was going to be held at the school, and Ray and John each knelt down on one knee. In unison, they asked, "Would you do me the honor of accompanying me to the Valentine's dance m' lady?"

Giggling from the role-playing, Kaitlyn and Allison accepted their offers.

Kaitlyn replied, "Yes, sir. I'd love to," as she gracefully bowed, while Allison looked at John and replied, "I'll have to think about it," putting her finger to her forehead as she let out a sassy grin. "Okay, she said, lighting up her eyes."

Continuing to warm and relax by the fire, they all talked about the dance. Ray asked Kaitlyn to join him for a Valentine's dinner date beforehand. Kaitlyn's eyes gleamed with an over anxious yes.

John couldn't ask Allison for a dinner date because he had an assembly to give beforehand. Allison knew this, and therefore knew there would be no invitation for her. Besides, she had begun to accompany John at the assemblies in support. She didn't need a fancy dinner date. She was happy being there for John.

Finishing their Valentinc's Day plans, the four decided to meet at the school gym when the dance began. Finding that their chills had ceased, they parted their separate ways for the day. Because they were at John's, Ray drove Kaitlyn to her house and then took Allison home to save John a trip out.

Allison and Ray had never spent any time alone together in close confines, and at first, they weren't sure what to say, but once they began talking, it was hard for them to stop. They found out they had a lot in common and enjoyed many of the same activities. It was the first time they'd really come to know each other, and both of them liked what they had discovered.

When Ray dropped off Allison, Ray took her hand and told her to take care. Allison smiled and thanked him for the ride, enjoying the attention she received from him, maybe a little too much. She could see why Kaitlyn was so much in love with Ray. A little jealousy showed its face as well as a tingling sensation when he touched her hand goodbye.

Allison thanked Ray for the ride again and shut the door. Ray drove off and waved good-bye as her mind went wild with forbidding thoughts.

Kaitlyn walked into her house smiling from ear to ear. She had such an enjoyable time with Ray, John, and Allison that she was absolutely ecstatic. Kaitlyn walked into the library interrupting her mother's reading to say hello.

Kathryn looked up to Kaitlyn and could see the jubilance written all over her face. "Had a good time, I see?" she said, smiling at Kaitlyn.

"The best," Kaitlyn replied. "We're all going to the Valentine's dance together. I need to check my closet and see if I have something to wear."

"I remember my Valentine's dance when I was your age," Kathryn recalled with a reminiscent smile. "I went with your father, you know?"

Kaitlyn made herself comfortable in the chair beside her mother. "You did? Tell me more about you and Dad."

"Well," Kathryn started as she switched her position. "Your father and I have been together since tenth grade."

"Really?" Kaitlyn questioned. "I thought you didn't become pinned until twelfth grade?"

"That's true, Kaitlyn. But, I've been in love with him since tenth grade." Kathryn paused as she looked to Kaitlyn's interested eyes. "Your father and I got off to a rough start, similar to how things have been for you and Ray."

Kaitlyn perked up hearing that and wanted to know more. "Yes, continue."

"I met your father at a winter carnival. He was standing by some ice sculptures, and I couldn't take my eyes off him. I was intrigued and had this spellbound feeling as I looked at him and watched him. My friend Jane grabbed my hand and pulled me over towards him, and then she pushed me in front of your father, saying, 'This is Kathryn.' All I could do was mutter 'Hi.' I had *butterflies* in my stomach, and my heart was pounding. It took all I could do to stay standing."

"Wow, Mom," Kaitlyn replied. "I never thought of you and dad *that* way. Tell me more."

Kathryn leaned back in the chair and spoke as she recalled the fond memories of her and Jim.

"We dated on and off for a couple years. We'd be together and then break up over something stupid. Of course, back then we didn't realize how stupid the arguments were. We made it, though, and eventually stuck it out through our problems. And well, here we are — married with two kids and still in love."

Kaitlyn's eyes lit up understanding her mother was just like she is. She looked at her more as a woman and not just as *Mom* or a housewife. She realized her mother was a woman with feelings and desires, just as she had felt with Ray. Kaitlyn smiled and took a seat by herm other. With Kaitlyn's full attention, Kathryn began telling her daughter more about the high school relationship between she and Jim.

When their conversation took a long pause, they went into the kitchen to prepare dinner. Kathryn told her daughter not to bother looking through her closet. "Let's get you something new for the dance. This is a special time in your life, and I want you to feel wonderful, just as I did so many years ago."

Kaitlyn leaned into Kathryn and hugged her. "Thanks, Mom. I love you. Oh, Ray's going to be taking me to dinner beforehand, too."

"That's wonderful, honey," Kathryn replied. "Do you know where?"

"No, he didn't tell me," Kaitlyn replied, then changed the subject back. "So what happened with you and Dad?"

"Would you like to hear more?" Kathryn asked.

"Yes," Kaitlyn eagerly replied.

Kathryn continued on with stories about her and Jim. Some were shocking to Kaitlyn, and she began to see her father in a new light, especially when Kathryn brought up romantic things he had done and still did. Kaitlyn couldn't believe her ears. All she could think about was this rigid, regal type man, *her father*, and think: "He did that?" She was shocked that her father could be so sweet and romantic.

The idea of it blew her away. "Wow! Really? You two used to dance in the living room? Alone? And sometimes without any music playing? Wow!" Kaitlyn expressed complete shock. "Mom," Kaitlyn questioned, "It's hard to believe Dad was that way. What made him change so?"

"The war," Kathryn answered simply. "People change, honey. Your father saw a lot of dying, pain, and suffering. The things that your father had seen and experienced affect how he is, what he believes in and what he cares about. He's still the man I fell in love with, just with a rough edge to him now. Underneath, he's still a romantic and loving man, with whom I am still madly in love with."

With Kathryn's last sentence, she announced dinner was ready to Alex and Jim, who had been in the living room listening to news about Korea on the radio. They all sat down to their evening meal.

Throughout dinner, Kaitlyn kept staring at her father, trying to see past his rough exterior. She found what she was looking for. Although it had been there all along, Kaitlyn was too self-absorbed to see it. Kaitlyn took notice of the warm glances and gentle smiles her father would send Kathryn's way. As Kaitlyn sat there eating with an occasional slight smile showing up now and again, she realized Ray was a lot like her father. "I've got myself a good man here," she thought, pleased with the newfound discovery.

After dinner, Kaitlyn and Alex excused themselves to work on their studies. While they were in the living room, Alex asked Kaitlyn about Ray. Actually, he interrogated her. Alex wanted to know how things were going. He wanted to make sure he was treating her right and that Kaitlyn was happy.

"He hasn't hurt you, has he?" Alex questioned Kaitlyn in an overbearing, almost fatherly tone.

"No, silly," Kaitlyn replied, looking at him with sweetness. "Thanks, Alex."

Alex nodded with a serious stature. "I just want to make sure. You'll let me know if he does hurt you, yes?"

Kaitlyn let out a smile. "Yes, Alex, you'll be the first to know."

"Okay," Alex replied. "That's settled then."

Kaitlyn smiled to herself and peered over to Alex. "You know, Alex. I never thought I'd see the day when my little brother was sticking up for *me*."

Alex looked at her. "I'm not so little anymore."

"I know," Kaitlyn said, understanding what he meant. "I can definitely see that. Thanks, Alex. You're sweet."

Alex didn't say anything to Kaitlyn. Instead, they exchanged caring smiles and went about their studies until it was time for bed. The whole conversation was a bit too mushy for Alex's manhood.

The next morning, the roads were cleared, and the snowfall had tapered off. School was in session that day, but because it was the last day before the weekend, school was bearable.

After school, Kaitlyn and her family had plans to visit with some of Jim's colleagues. So, Friday night had turned into family night instead of date night for Kaitlyn. Ray spent time with his father, while Allison and John hung out at The Fountain.

Saturday came, and Kaitlyn and Kathryn made plans to go shopping for a dress while Alex had plans with his friends. Ray was helping his father with the household chores, and Allison and John were busy with preparations for the assemblies. The Valentine's dance was one week away, so Kathryn took Kaitlyn to the little boutiques in town. One particular shop that Kathryn liked was called Ribbons and Bows.

Ribbons and Bows, the perfect place to find a dress for a young woman, was adjacent to The Soda Fountain. They had every kind of dress imaginable and in every color. The shop was set up in a uniformed storefront, lined up on Main Street. The entranceway was white with touches of mauve, enhancing the wood detail. Inside, there were rows of dresses lined up against the walls. A large, mauve carpeted open area adorned with full-length mirrors allowed Kaitlyn to view the dresses from all angles.

She tried on a red one, a green one, a pink one and a blue one. Some had floral prints, and some were solids. Some had ribbons and bows, and others had simple fabric designs. As she was trying on a pink floral her mother had found, Kaitlyn spotted a deep burgundy, three-quarter length cocktail dress in the far corner of the store. "May I try *that one* on?" she asked weary of her mother's answer, pointing to it.

"Yes, Kaitlyn," Kathryn replied with an uneasy tone.

The dress shop employee retrieved the garment and handed it to Kaitlyn. Kaitlyn smiled as she put it up against her body and viewed it in the mirror, taking notice of the daintily buttoned bodice. She knew that this particular dress was the *one*.

Kaitlyn brought it to the dressing room and slipped into it. She loved it immediately. It made her feel sophisticated and a little bit sexy, too. She came out of the room, and Kathryn's eyes lit up. "It's beautiful on you, Kaitlyn. Let me see the back."

Kaitlyn turned around, and the swing bottom skirt swirled with her. Kaitlyn liked the feel of the dress and began twirling as if she were a young girl playing dress up with her mother's clothing. "I love it," Kaitlyn exclaimed, begging for it.

Kathryn nodded, letting Kaitlyn know she had approval. "My little girl's all grown," she thought, bringing her fingers to her lips.

"Thanks, Mom," Kaitlyn said with a wide grin. "Thank you. Thank You. Thank you," she replied while bouncing up and down in childhood delight.

"Okay, maybe she isn't completely grown," Kathryn giggled under her breath.

The dress did look beautiful on Kaitlyn. It was quite basic, but on Kaitlyn, it looked glamorous, accentuating her natural beauty. Kaitlyn was overjoyed with the new dress, and when they arrived home, she went directly upstairs to hang it up in the closet and to pick out the right shoes to match. Of course, having to share the news, she called Allison to tell her all about her latest purchase. Allison was almost as excited as Kaitlyn. Continuing their talk about important fashion matters, they brought up talk about the upcoming dance, their boys, and how much fun they were going to have the following weekend. Their conversation was one big giggle fest.

Kaitlyn, Ray, Allison, and John all did their normal weekend things. They helped with chores in the house, shoveled drives and sidewalks, and they met at The Fountain. They went to church on Sunday and had their quiet family day, playing cards, listening to the radio, and playing board games.

The week before the dance, they all went about their normal activities at school as well as after school. Kaitlyn had taken another babysitting job to earn some extra cash so she and Ray were unable to get together much. But when the school week was over, Kaitlyn made final preparations for Saturday's Valentine's bash, figuring she and Ray could make up for lost time then.

Friday night, Kaitlyn was so excited, and had burst with anticipation that she couldn't sleep. She tossed and turned all night as dreams about her dancing with Ray played out in her mind. When she finally did fall asleep, it was already time to wake up, and she was exhausted. The bags under her eyes showcased this fact. Still though, she got up and did her daily weekend chores, and took care of anything else she needed to do.

After Kaitlyn had lunch, she went upstairs to nap, as she didn't want to be yawning all night with Ray. Kathryn woke her up at four o'clock and told her to start getting ready, knowing it would take her at least two hours.

Kaitlyn sprung from the bed and hopped into the shower, allowing the warm water to revive her tired body. When she heard her father yelling at her for taking too long, she quickly finished and stepped out of the tub. Kaitlyn draped a towel over her back as she glanced over her nude body in the mirror.

She felt good as she studied herself, and then dropped the towel to trace her fingertips over her delicate skin. She smiled as she turned her head to the side, imagining Ray touching her.

Alex came knocking at the door. "Kaitlyn, get out of there. I need to get ready. You're taking too long."

"Okay, okay," Kaitlyn replied, briskly wrapping her body in the dampened towel.

Kaitlyn came out of the bathroom with Alex staring her down. "What you doing in there anyway?"

"Nothing," Kaitlyn replied, disturbed that her privacy had been invaded.

A miffed Alex reminded her: "I have to get ready for the dance with Amy."

"It's all yours," she said with a roll of the eyes, while sweeping her arm grandly as though laying out a red carpet for the heir apparent.

Alex crinkled his brow in annoyance as he stalked past her, closing the door behind him with a bang. Kaitlyn knew he was anxious about the dance and smiled to herself knowing that this was his first real date with Amy — or anybody else for that matter.

Amy was a petite girl and was positively adorable. She had one of those bubbly personalities that made people smile and giggle when they were around her. She was kind, warm hearted and perfect for Alex. Her hair was a golden blonde, and her eyes of blue shined with exuberance. Alex was a nervous wreck.

Kaitlyn was in her room carefully sliding on the burgundy stockings. She felt sexy and attractive as she gently slid her fingers up towards her creamy thighs and attached the stockings to her garter belt. After the stockings were in place, she stood up and allowed the dress to fall against her legs. She walked over to the vanity and sat down to apply some soft make up and brush out her hair. When Kaitlyn was finished dressing, she cascaded down the stairs feeling like she was Ginger Rogers.

Jim took immediate notice of his daughter with a gasp. "You look beautiful, Kaitlyn," he complimented as he glared at his baby girl. "You're the spitting image of your mother when she was your age."

Kaitlyn smiled remembering the conversation she and her mother had. "Thank you, Dad," Kaitlyn replied, walking towards him.

Jim sat in his chair, shaking his head with the memory of Kathryn and when they had *their* Valentine's dance. "I can't get over how much you look like your mother. It's like I just traveled back in time."

Kaitlyn smiled, as her father had never complimented her so much, thoroughly enjoying it. She felt as if their relationship had changed right then and there. Jim saw his little girl was *not* so little anymore. He saw her as a young woman, just as he had seen Kathryn so many years before.

Chapter Fifteen

*   *   *

It was seven p.m. and Kaitlyn still had not opened the letter. She wanted to, but just couldn't bring herself to unseal that envelope. Fear kept her from finally bringing an end to fifty years of wonder.

Kaitlyn stood in the kitchen, forgetting the reason for being there, until it dawned on her that she had forgotten to eat. Her stomach reminded with its growls. She fixed a grilled cheese sandwich with chicken noodle soup, and then she sat at the kitchen table eating dinner alone — something she had grown accustomed to. She did, however, have her thoughts from the day keeping her company.

As she ate the last bite, she felt an inexplicable urge to check her old memory box. Kaitlyn wanted to see if Ray's 1951 Valentine's Day card to her was still around. She didn't recall seeing it when she went through the box with Allison, and then Rose, but decided to check it more thoroughly, especially now that she had something she was actually looking for.

She put her plates in the sink and headed into the living room, settling on the couch with the box by her side. Kaitlyn rummaged through each piece of paper and each card before viewing the corner of a red envelope sticking out from underneath an old photo album. Excitedly, she grabbed the card and brought it to her chest in a long lost hug. "Yes, I found it." she rejoiced out loud as she carefully began removing the card from its seal. Reading what Ray had written so many years ago melted her heart, bringing her memory back to February 14, 1951, the first *real* date with Ray.

*   *   *

Ray, dressed in his finest double-breasted black suit with a country blue shirt underneath, picked up Kaitlyn. His eyes were mesmerizing and his smile — radiant.

He had made plans to take Kaitlyn to *Chateau L'Amore,* a quiet up-scale French restaurant in the heart of Lake George. *The Chateau,* as it's referred to, is known not only for its delectable menu, but also for its ambiance.

Kaitlyn ran upstairs to powder her nose right before Ray arrived. A few minutes later, while exchanging small pleasantries with Jim and Kathryn, Ray's eyes were summoned to the top of the stairs by Kaitlyn's sweet greeting voice.

His lips separated in awe, and he grew speechless when his eyes were met with breathtaking beauty. Kaitlyn looked elegant, sophisticated and held the grace of a young woman. She stepped down to meet him with a sophisticated hug.

Ray courteously helped Kaitlyn with her coat — not taking his eyes away from the woman who stood before him. Ray was completely enthralled with Kaitlyn's appearance, not to mention — her scent was divine.

This was a big night for Kaitlyn and Ray. It was their first Valentine's together, first intimate date, and two of many *firsts* yet to come.

The half-hour drive to Lake George was splendid. They talked casually about little things, which sometimes added up to a lot. And when they were still, their silence spoke for them. They arrived at The Chateau, and Ray helped Kaitlyn from the car before the valet took it for parking. Ray escorted her to the front entrance, where an usher met them and opened the door.

Now, Kaitlyn was no stranger to this type of scene. She had been to many functions where valet parking and ushers at the door were, well — expected. It was different this time, though. This time it was for her and Ray. This time it wasn't because *Daddy* was the president of the bank; it was because Ray wanted to make Kaitlyn feel special — his plan worked.

After their coats were removed and placed with a coatroom attendant, the hostess showed them the way to their table. Kaitlyn and Rays' eyes took in the breathtaking scenery on the short stroll there.

Set back on a wooded lot, the log cabin style restaurant exonerated what one would expect. Complete with wooden logs showing on the inside and beautiful Vermont green area rugs, the restaurant looked like a hunter's hideout, except this hideout was elegant.

Each table, holding two to four chairs each, were strategically placed, allowing each dining couple privacy. Soft classical music played in the background. The candle-lit lanterns placed in the middle of the table, along with two complimenting bud-vases that were put on top of the matching green cloths, brought romance to the milieu. The black iron candleholders set on the walls glimmered with the essence of bayberry and the brisk fire burning in the open-hearth fireplace only added to its ambiance.

As Kaitlyn and Ray were guided to their dining area, Kaitlyn took notice of their table. It was a little different from the others. Instead of a simple Valentine's Day red carnation, their vases had single yellow roses with a speckle of greenery enhancing their beauty. Kaitlyn glanced fondly at Ray, smiling. Pointing ever so gracefully to the flowers, she asked, "Did you have something to do with this?" already knowing the answer.

Ray smiled back as his eyes directed Kaitlyn to the envelope lying beside one of the vases. Kaitlyn reached for the card wearing a sneaking grin and opened it, reading it out loud.

"Happy Valentine's Day! A perfect yellow rose for my perfect gal. I love you, Miss Kait."

Kaitlyn smiled, even chuckled at the silliness of his words, but nonetheless, she absolutely loved it! Kaitlyn loved the mushy stuff.

Ray helped seat Kaitlyn while draping the cloth napkin over her lap. Sitting down beside her, he took the menu and held it out in front of them to view and make sense of, without much success. Trying to pronounce the selections, their words came out as if they were speaking a foreign language — only a language no one had ever heard before.

Laughing quietly, Kaitlyn suggested, "Let's get something we can actually pronounce."

Ray chuckled. "That's a good idea."

They looked over the menu again, deciding to try the Chateau *Brig-Non*, *Breeg-noon*, Brignon.

As they waited for their attendant to come, they held hands and played with each other's fingers while enjoying one another's company. Ray's plans for the future came up in conversation.

Ray applied to colleges and planned to major in engineering, in case things didn't work out for the Army. His knee was still giving him some trouble, so he wasn't sure if they would accept him or not. Being level headed, Ray decided he had better have a back up plan. He hoped that if the Army didn't work out, he would get into The University of Southern California.

Kaitlyn, hearing the news, secretly hoped he wouldn't. Yes, Kaitlyn wanted Ray to be happy, but she didn't want him to leave the state, let alone, go clear across the country. Heck, she wasn't too thrilled about his wanting to join the Army either. She would miss him terribly.

Ray had become Kaitlyn's world. She had come to depend on and need Ray, and he had become a part of her. He was not only her boyfriend and her friend, but also her best friend, her soul mate — even over Allison. Kaitlyn was not ready to share him with the world, just yet.

The waiter, Andrew, came to take their order and present the entrees of the evening. When Andrew began pronouncing all the menu choices, Kaitlyn and Ray looked at each other in confusion. For all they knew, he was offering frog legs or snails. The mere thought of eating these *delectable* entrees grossed them out to no end. Respectfully, they let him continue before trying to pronounce their choice of Chateau Brignon, deciding to just point to it instead. Finding the correct word for the shrimp appetizer, they ordered two of those, along with two colas, then passing on a dinner wine.

Andrew thanked them for their order and went to the kitchen to place it. As soon as he was out of site, the two broke out in laughter feeling like total idiots, but enjoying their ignorance at the same time. Idle chitchat took place before their delicious appetizer arrived, going along with the *delicious* theme of the evening.

Kaitlyn seductively hand fed Ray while trying to maintain some sort of innocence. A couple of times, Kaitlyn gave him the shrimp and purposely became playful with it, smearing the sauce, (just a little), over his mouth. She wanted to see his tongue slide over his lips as he tried to catch the sauce before it fell to his lap. Then, Kaitlyn placed an entire shrimp in her mouth, only to pull it out — sucking off the sauce with a flirtatious smile.

Ray looked at her, smirked and said, "You're cruel," as he let out a polite laugh. They grinned while trying to maintain some sort of adult behavior. It was funny, and it certainly kept things interesting.

Kaitlyn enjoyed seducing Ray, (just a little), and smiled in the fun. Of course, Ray would always get her back, somehow — somewhere, she just never knew when.

"Ahh, the chateau *breeg-noon* is here," Ray announced as the two of them made room on the table for it, laughing. "Now, this is exquisite dining, my lady," Ray said with a sweet charming voice, while Andrew served their plates.

Potatoes were baked to perfection — perfectly crisp on the outside and mouth-watering on the inside. Au jus sauce was placed beside each plate for dipping ease, and their side of broccoli, smothered in cheese sauce, looked positively enticing.

Andrew asked if everything was to their liking, and both nodded in appreciation and awe.

They couldn't wait to dive right into their meal and held back their urges to just start cutting and chewing. In a respectful manner, they both used proper etiquette, with Kaitlyn trimming her meat with a knife, holding her pinky in the air as if she were the *Queen of England.* Ray chuckled at her royalty-like ways.

Oh, the food was delicious. Smiles adorned their faces as they chewed their first bite of their Chateau Brignon, with some of the au jus escaping their lips. Their tongues tried to catch it, not wanting to miss one drop of their palatable cuisine.

Just as they were about to take the last bites of their meals, Andrew brought over their requested after-the-meal salads, offering each a choice of dressings. They both chose Italian and asked if the restaurant would be offended for not choosing French. Andrew laughed quietly and said, "No."

Their meal came to an end, topping it off with chocolate mousse for dessert.

Ray gazed at Kaitlyn as he went to reach for the spoon. "Let me help you with this," he offered as he dipped it in the mousse.

Kaitlyn looked at Ray and knew exactly what his plans were. "No, that's okay, Ray. I can feed myself, thank you."

Ray got a nice spoonful of the smooth chocolate and brought it to Kaitlyn's lips. "Don't worry, I'm more mature than that."

Famous last words — he did it. Ray managed to get the sweet cream all over Kaitlyn's lips, chin, and nose. Ray laughed. Then Kaitlyn laughed while trying not to spit the mousse all over Ray. She leaned in and gave him a great big, chocolate mousse kiss, flat on his lips. Yet they still *tried* to maintain some sort of *mature mannerism.*

They laughed and cleaned themselves off, deciding to curtail their playfulness and get back to some more *adult* conversation.

In the middle of their serious discussion, one would start giggling out of the blue, and then the two would be laughing all over again — not quite clear as to why. Calming down just a bit, they took their colas and toasted the evening, toasted each other and their love, and started to break out into laughter again as they sipped from their glasses.

With all seriousness though, Kaitlyn told Ray to close his eyes and give her his hand. Ray did as he was told. As he sat with his hand out, Kaitlyn gave him a gift. He opened his eyes to a small present, wrapped in red paper with a white bow, cupped in the palm of his hand. She had put a tiny Valentine's card with it that read:

"I am in love with you. I was in love with you when I first met you. I am in love with you now, and I will be in love with you tomorrow. I look forward to being in love with you for the rest of my life."

Inside the package were two fourteen-karat gold necklaces. One had a small gold key, and the other had a small gold heart. A note inside said: "You hold the key to my heart."

Kaitlyn rose from the chair and stepped behind Ray. She put the chain holding the key around his neck, while she leaned over to kiss his cheek. Ray stood up smiling and shared his gratitude, then turned Kaitlyn around to place the necklace's partner around her neck. With necklaces secure, he wrapped his arms around Kaitlyn's waist, and when Kaitlyn turned to face him, they kissed. Taking her arms and tossing them around Ray's neck, Kaitlyn reached up for another kiss. He looked her in the eyes and said, "I have something for you."

Ray nervously put his hand in his pocket, and as he pulled out the small box, he got down on one knee.

Kaitlyn started shaking, and tears welled as her heart trembled. "Oh my God," went through her mind repeatedly.

Ray took a moment before speaking.

"Kaitlyn Marie Frost, I love you. I want to spend the rest of my life with you."

Kaitlyn felt her knees begin to buckle as she brought her hands to her mouth in disbelief.

"I know we're young, and I know we have college yet, but I want to marry you someday."

He opened up a tiny, black velvet box, holding a small diamond pre-engagement ring.

Tears trickled down Kaitlyn's cheeks, while Ray swallowed his own emotions. Kaitlyn held out her hand, and Ray removed his class ring, replacing it with the new. He stood up, and they held each other tight. Kaitlyn's trembling lips whispered, "Yes."

She held her hand out, palm up, and asked Ray for his class ring back. With his ring between her thumb and index finger, Kaitlyn completed the symbolic circle, placing the class ring on his left fourth finger.

They smiled. They loved. And they had no concept of the commitment they had just made.

After paying the bill and leaving a hefty tip, Ray and Kaitlyn left Chateau L'Amore hand in hand. Kaitlyn was sure to grab the two yellow roses on their way out. Bringing the roses close to her face in a graceful fashion, Kaitlyn took in their sweet scent. She smiled softly, knowing how lucky she was to have Ray's love.

Ray couldn't believe how lucky he was to have found such a wonderful young woman to love and to love him back. In a small way, he felt almost as if he didn't deserve her.

The two would glance in each other's direction as they walked to the car, with their walk seeming to take thirty minutes with all their lingering thoughts — taking only one.

Ray opened the car door and helped Kaitlyn get in. "You ready for the dance?" he asked.

"Yes, and you?" she replied eager to get there.

"Yup, let's go," Ray said. He smiled and shut the door, making it over to his side of the car. Turning on the engine, he gazed in Kaitlyn's direction, and in his lowered private voice said, "I love you."

"I love you, too."

Kaitlyn inched closer to Ray, as the one-foot of distance between them was more room then she could bear. He smiled knowing what she was up to, but continued keeping his eyes on the road.

Kaitlyn rested her hand on his knee, checking out Ray's body language to see if *that* was permissible. It was. She slid her hand up a little higher approaching the lower thigh area, again checking to see if she had crossed any unspoken barriers. She hadn't. Kaitlyn was pleased.

Kaitlyn's eyes began to twinkle, and as a sneaking grin came to her face, she moved her hand just a little bit higher, now to his mid-thigh area. She glanced in Ray's direction, catching Ray squirm just a bit. She didn't see any behaviors from Ray that said she couldn't proceed with the now engaged plan, so she slithered her hand up to his upper thigh, letting out a slight proposing chuckle as she did.

Ray was doing all he could to concentrate on the road, but the rise in sensations made it somewhat difficult to do. Again, though, he didn't fight it. He liked it. No, he *loved* it! His pants slightly tightened, and he had to switch positions to make things more comfortable. Kaitlyn giggled at the *power* she now felt she had.

Kaitlyn had removed her hand when Ray changed positions, but was sure to put it right back where it was once he was *situated*. She rubbed her hand up and down his thigh before making a direct jump to his uppermost thigh area, feeling the hard flesh through his pants; the softer flesh beneath his pants stroking the back of her hand.

Ray took a quick, shortened breath when Kaitlyn lay her hand on him. He liked it. She liked it. Hell, they both *loved* it. It was naughty. It was *forbidden.* It was so — *improper* and completely out of character for *Miss Innocent.*

Kaitlyn enjoyed feeling Ray's body pulsate with want and grow harder and harder. Ray moaned with pleasure as his eyes became blurred from the excitement. He swerved. Screams took over the car from inside and out as Ray tried regaining control of it and clear his fogged vision. They swerved to the right, then to the left, then back to the right again, until finally coming to a full stop and facing in the opposite direction of where they were headed in the first place.

Kaitlyn, in a panic, was screaming, "Oh my, God," over and over again, till she could say it in a whisper.

Ray screamed, "You okay?" in between Kaitlyn's "Oh my, God" cries.

Kaitlyn took her hands and rested them with straight arms on the dashboard. She put her head down and took deep breaths, trying to get a hold of her fear. Ray put his arm around Kaitlyn and leaned to kiss her, asking again if she were okay. "Are you hurt?"

"No," she replied in a scared tone. "I'm okay, just a little shook up." She took a few cleansing breaths, as did Ray. "I guess I'd better not do that again, huh?" she said giggling, tilting her head to the left to gaze at him.

Ray looked at her not wanting to have to answer yes to that question, but said, "Yeah, best not to."

Kaitlyn situated herself next to Ray, but kept her hands folded in her lap like a *good girl*. Ray put the car back in gear, placing the steering wheel in the correct direction and stepped lightly on the gas. "Whew, that was close," he said, adding, "And I do mean, *that* was close," as he let out a disappointed laugh.

"I'm sorry," she said, feeling quite naughty.

"Well, Kaitlyn," Ray replied, "just think of what a great story this will make to tell our children when they're old enough to hear this sort of thing."

"Oh, Ray," Kaitlyn exclaimed, "I'd never tell *anyone* about this. It's too embarrassing. Not to mention, it'd kill my image," she said in afterthought, laughing.

"You are a *naughty innocent* girl, Kait," he said chuckling. "I'll give you that."

They re-entered Winter's Crest, and you would've thought that everyone went to high school. People lined the streets walking towards the school, all dressed in their red and white. Up ahead, Kaitlyn and Ray could see the school grounds lit, and the windows shined with welcome as they pulled into the parking lot.

Ray, in a gentleman-like fashion, helped Kaitlyn from the car, and as he helped her out with one hand held, he whisked her into his arms for a hug. He brought his mouth to her ear, kissed it gently and whispered, " We'll have to continue that little escapade a bit later ... hmmm?" He gave her a squeeze and laughed. "C'mon, let's go," with a shrug of the shoulder.

Kaitlyn didn't say too much, as she had her own plans, figuring he would find out the specifics of her schemes when he needed to know them. She wasn't the type to give way to what she was up to or what she planned out, way before anything ever took place. Tonight, for instance, it may have *seemed* to be spontaneous, but in Kaitlyn's mind, it was a well-carried out, chartered plan — well, except for the *almost accident part.*

Friends came to join them as they walked towards the front entrance of Mackey High. The guys were playing macho, patting each other hard on the backs — *playing* the role.

The girls came up to Kaitlyn giggling and complimenting each other so much that each compliment thrown towards the other was basically a way to get one for themselves. All the teenagers, especially those in the *accepted* crowd, were so full of themselves. It was enough to make an onlooker sick. Nonetheless, that's how it was in high school, and Ray and Kaitlyn's experiences weren't any different in that aspect.

Once each couple got closer to the school, the guys started to back off a bit from their dates. They needed to be cool and not seem like *lovesick puppies*, so holding their girl's hand just wasn't, well — *cool*. Sad, but true.

However, that is what separated Ray from the others. He didn't need to hide behind a facade. He wasn't ashamed of loving Kaitlyn. Heck, he had just asked her to marry him — three to four years down the road. But, nonetheless, he did ask.

Ray held Kaitlyn's hand, opened doors for her and the other girls. He made Kaitlyn feel special, not realizing that was what he *was* doing. He paid attention to her, talked with her and her friends, and even embraced Kaitlyn in front of the guys. *Oh, the thought.* One of those guys happened to be John.

John wasn't looking too good. Even the bright lights, balloons, and red and white streamers in the background couldn't bring any sort of festive mood to his face. The music played the popular hits, leaving many tapping their feet or swaying to it, but not John. John stood there as if he'd just seen a ghost.

All the loud chatter, laughter, and giggles from the numerous flighty girls and the roaring banter of young men in the background seemed to float around John, not infiltrating his seemingly private world.

Kaitlyn eyed Allison approaching from behind John and excused herself to go see her. Ray stayed with John, even though he was uncomfortable with the situation, not knowing what *that* situation was. They stood about a foot apart, not saying a single word. John stood quietly to himself, staring straight ahead with a sharpness that could slice through glass.

Kaitlyn caught up with Allison, and they gave each other a hug, throwing more compliments around — like the two of them hadn't received enough already. Although, most of their compliments were from hopeful courtiers, hoping something would go amiss in their current relationships. As soon as the two got their formalities out of the way, Kaitlyn presented Allison with her hand.

"Oh, my God, Kaitlyn!" Allison bellowed in utter shock, drawing the eyes of others in their direction. "When did this happen?" she asked quietly, trying to redirect attentions.

"Tonight," Kaitlyn replied. "At The Chateau."

"Congratulations … I think."

"Thanks, Allison. Hey, did something go wrong tonight at the assembly?"

"No," Allison answered. "It went very well actually."

"Then, what's up with John?"

"What do you mean?" Allison questioned, confused.

"He looks like he's seen a ghost … " Kaitlyn replied, interrupted by Allison taking off towards John. Kaitlyn followed in quick steps behind.

Allison approached John carefully and put her arms around him as gently as she could. She looked up to him and asked what was wrong.

John looked down at her, replying something about the punch.

Ray stepped in. "What about the punch?"

"I had some," John answered.

"So," Ray said, confused as to why John would be in a stare after drinking *punch*.

"Someone spiked it," John replied shamefully.

"Did you know someone spiked it?" Ray questioned in a lawyer-like tone.

"No, but ... "

"John, it's not your fault," Ray responded maturely.

"My promise — I made a promise," John replied remorsefully.

"Well, I know how to take care of this," Allison abruptly broke in the conversation before briskly walking away with her head held high on a mission.

Allison approached the punch table, and people seemed to know to get out of her way. She placed both hands on either side of the bowl, picked it up and headed straight for the door. She opened the door as she balanced the punch on her hips, went outside, and threw that punch out, turning the white fluffy snow to a pink mush. Allison walked back in, swiped her hands in a *'that's done with that'* motion, walked up to John, grabbed his hands and said, "Let's dance," as she pulled him on to the dance floor.

John, at that point, was in a stupor so he did as he was told. He wasn't about to mess around with *her*. Kaitlyn and Ray looked at each other, letting out a slight chuckle at Allison's uncharacteristic and quite bold behavior, deciding to join them and doing as the lady said.

John tried to come back to reality as Allison cradled her head in John's chest, swaying back and forth. Allison eyed Kaitlyn, who also had her head cradled into Ray's chest, and the two began to smile, then snicker, then burst out into a roaring laughter, bringing tears to their eyes.

Ray and John were brought into their hilarity, realizing how funny Allison's action was. Then the boys couldn't stop laughing because the girls wouldn't.

Finally, they settled down enough to go sit and take a breather from the chortle. John and Allison sat on one side of the table holding hands, while Kaitlyn and Ray sat on the other, doing the same. Kaitlyn sensed Allison eyeing the pre-engagement ring and noticed a somewhat disturbed look on her face.

"What, Allison?" Kaitlyn asked.

"What?" she replied innocently.

"You're staring at my ring."

"Oh."

"Alright, let's hear it," Kaitlyn demanded.

"Let's hear what?" Allison replied. "Let's hear that you're too young? Let's hear that you haven't been together long enough? Let's hear that you're making the biggest mistake of your life? Or how about, let's hear how stupid you are?"

"That's it," Kaitlyn said. Ray, I want to go ... now!"

Ray stood up, joining Kaitlyn, who had already risen from the chair. Ray looked at John and told him not to worry about the punch. "You didn't break the promise to my mother. That wasn't your fault. How were you supposed to know it was in there? Okay? I'm not upset at all."

"Thanks, Ray," John replied gratefully. "Hey, congratulations!"

Just as John finished the "...tions", he received a nice kick in the shin from Allison. John glared at Allison like *did I say something wrong?*

Ray helped Kaitlyn with her coat, and the two left the dance for the night, still having some time before Kaitlyn's curfew. Taking a slight detour, the two drove to a secluded spot near Crestview Park to *talk*.

On the way there, Ray told Kaitlyn not to worry about Allison, telling her she was probably jealous. Kaitlyn agreed whole-heartedly, and then turned their discussion to more important, immediate issues.

She inched her way closer to Ray, but this time, Ray gave Kaitlyn a cautionary look with a raised brow. Kaitlyn succumbed to his warning, but as they drew closer to the secluded area, she began to re-start what had brusquely ended before.

Ray was able to be more involved in the fun this time around. He now had his two hands free, deciding to tease little Miss

Kaitlyn in the manner she teased him. She was not as accepting, having the *tables now turned.*

"Oh, I see how it is," Ray said sarcastically. "You can do it to *me*, but I can't do it to *you*. Controlling aren't we?" he declared, letting out a slight chuckle.

Kaitlyn jumped from the seat, did a half turn mid-air, hitting her head on the car ceiling before landing in a straddle on his lap. "Yup," she said, answering his already known answer to the question. She then brought her hand to her head and said, "That hurts," before she lay her head into Ray's neck, needing a little *caring for.*

When she decided her *injury* no longer needed attention, she brought her lips to Ray's neck and let her hot breath fall on him. Ray, quickly becoming excited, held Kaitlyn tight as she brought her hands lower, and then lower again. She caressed him, feeling his want grow. *"Oh, the power,"* Kaitlyn mockingly laughed.

Her giggling smile turned serious when Ray began unbuttoning her dress, allowing him to see her erect nipples through her brazier. They craved his touch, and he soothed their hunger, bringing pleasure to her loins as she felt herself become wet with want and hard with pleasure.

Breaths grew heavy as they moved their hands urgently all over each other's dressed bodies while kissing with incredible passion. Kaitlyn manipulated her hips in a circular frenzy, pressing hard against Ray's desire. Their kisses and petting grew even more intense as their faces became flushed and their heads feeling dizzy.

Kaitlyn inched her hand back down towards Ray's hardened wants while continuing to rotate her hips faster, making the bondage of clothing and her grasp rub harder and harder, 'til ... "Ahh ..." came from Kaitlyn's quivering mouth. Ray moaned in pleasing agony.

Ray leaned back slightly, allowing both to feel the strong pulsation's run through them separately. The throbbing continued as Kaitlyn kept rotating her hips ever so lightly, like the sections of trains as they reach the track going over the road — steady, evenly spaced, slowly fading moments of pure pleasure.

Words cannot describe how much in love they were at that exact moment. They were happy and emotionally fulfilled. The expressions upon their faces showed unconditional commitment, not to mention complete satisfaction.

Chapter Sixteen

February seemed to fly by for Kaitlyn and Ray, with the two of them being closer than ever. They were inseparable. The special night they had had brought them to a better understanding of each other's wants, needs, and weaknesses. They had both allowed themselves to be vulnerable to the other, securing a trust like nothing else can. There were no limitations to their undying love and devotion.

Come the middle of March, their friends started to become annoyed as the two stayed within their own little world, forgetting that other relationships were important too. It was as if the two had become one person, completely full of themselves. And as time went on, their close friends began to disperse — even John and Allison. Kaitlyn and Ray didn't take notice. They were two kids in love, and nothing else seemed to matter. Boy, were they wrong.

Allison and John were doing well with their relationship during this time. Allison was extremely supportive of John's efforts in keeping his promise, and she, herself, helped spread the word about drinking and driving. She even took part in the assemblies, roll playing a skit with John. Allison had begun to earn respect back from lost friends as John began earning the respect of others — something he never truly had.

Kaitlyn and Ray spent time together either finding secluded spots to explore their *feelings* or curled up on a couch warming by a fire. They would read or have long talks about anything from apples to world peace, with Kaitlyn a little lost on some of the conversations. They hung out at The Fountain, and sure, their friends surrounded them, but they were *always* together. Their cast away friends would tease them with comments like: "You two joined at the hips?" or "You two Siamese twins or something?"

Kaitlyn and Ray would laugh and shrug it off as immature behavior, since they *knew more now* and had more experience. Eh, it didn't matter. They were together. They were happy. They were in love. The world revolved around *them*.

Unfortunately, it had come to the point where all they had were each other, and that is when both woke up. Kaitlyn and Ray finally realized they had lost who they were — separate individuals.

Spring came, bringing blooming crocuses, warmer days, and small creatures scurrying about, making up for their long winter's nap.

"Must be nice to hibernate," Kaitlyn commented when she and Ray were visiting Crestview.

"Where'd that come from?" Ray asked, knowing he was in for one of Kaitlyn's on-going conversations.

She looked at him thinking he should know what she meant, but decided to expand his knowledge anyway. "Imagine what it'd be like to sleep all winter. Think of all the things we wouldn't have had to deal with."

"True," Ray began, "but then we wouldn't have had that night together and all those other nights. I think I'd prefer to have been awake for that."

Kaitlyn laughed. "Okay, you got me there," she said in between chuckles. "You mean, some of *this*," Kaitlyn said wide-eyed and with a sneaking grin, giving him little kisses.

"Oh yes," Ray answered pleasantly. "Some of *that*."

Kaitlyn and Ray were in their private world, hidden away from the park visitors in their own haven in the woods. That is until Bob walked by and *stopped*.

"Oh my," Kaitlyn said, trying to hide herself from Bob Westman. She tidied herself up a bit, but it was too late.

"What ya up to, lovebirds?" Bob said laughing along with his female friend.

"Hi, Bob," Kaitlyn replied, red-faced.

"Hi, Bob," Ray replied all manly. "Nice to see you again."

"Nice little spot you got here, you two," Bob said. "Our *spot* is over on the other side," he said with a sarcastic smile.

"Ha ha," Kaitlyn said, not sure if she should believe him or not, then changed the subject. "What are you doing home from school?"

"Spring break," he replied. "Can't have all work and no play. Oh, but I guess *you'd* know that, wouldn't you?" Bob joked.

Kaitlyn didn't know what to do. She couldn't tell if Bob was treating her like an adult or treating her as if she was that thirteen-year-old flirting girl. She looked to Ray for help.

Ray smiled. He knew Bob was just kidding. Bob confirmed to Kaitlyn what Ray already knew.

Bob turned to go. "You kids have fun. We're going to finish our walk. Good to see you."

"Good to see you, too," Kaitlyn mouthed, barely able to pronounce her sentence.

"Bye, Bob," Ray said, giving a slight wave to Bob's friend.

As Bob walked off, Kaitlyn and Ray could hear the friend complain to him for not introducing her to his friends.

Kaitlyn and Ray looked at each other, sing-songing, "Someone's in trouble," then laughed at poor Bob's expense.

Kaitlyn and Ray decided they'd better curtail their affections before someone else caught them. After they situated their rather ruffled attire, the two began to walk back towards the car. Talk of the upcoming prom came up, and Ray, of course, asked her.

"Would you like to go to The Chateau again?" Ray asked. "Or would you like to try out The Vineyard?"

Kaitlyn didn't need to think about her response. "Definitely, The Chateau," she replied, smiling a certain remembrance."

Ray smiled back. "The Chateau it is then."

The beginning of May came, bringing with it sunny days, warm spring showers, and blooming buds. It brought romance, love, and cheer to the once winter darkened days. It also brought with it Mackey High's Senior Prom — the theme being *Love Is In The Air* — appropriately enough.

Although love had been in the air for Kaitlyn and Ray since after the first of the year, the mid-spring made the air even thicker. One thing that did change was that Kaitlyn and Ray weren't as closed off from everyone like they were. The newness of their love had finally come to an even keel, and they realized they could still love each other as much as they did and still have time apart with their own friends.

By the time the prom had come around, they had patched things up with the neglected· friends and had begun to spend time on a regular basis with Allison and John.

Allison and John were to join Kaitlyn and Ray for dinner at The Chateau, then proceed onward to the prom. As they had done nine months before, the two girls dressed at Kaitlyn's house, and the boys met them there.

John and Ray played the prom down, trying to be cool about it. Yet, they were excited that this was their senior prom — *the best night of their life*.

Kaitlyn and Allison were all *girl*. Excitement burst from their eyes at the mere mention of it. Having it actually at their doorstop, brought bubbles of giggling laughter and anticipation.

Now, since this was their second to last appearance as high school kids, Kaitlyn and Allison were careful in their prom dress selections. Kaitlyn chose a taffeta deep emerald green, spaghetti-strapped dress with a tight fitting bodice. It allowed her to look innocent, womanly and yes, even sexy. And Allison chose a similar style. Only hers had a scooped neck with short-cuffed sleeves. She usually went for the lighter shades of color, opting for a deep mint green and touching it off with silver jewelry. Kaitlyn chose gold.

It was to be a magical night. It was to be the kind of prom one dreams about and one expects, but usually doesn't happen. Kaitlyn and Ray knew their prom would be the most magical night of their lives.

The boys arrived right on time, 6 p.m., so they could make their 6:45 dinner reservation. Both boys' mouths dropped when they viewed their ladies descending the stairs. Elegant is the only way to describe them. Their hair was done professionally, with cascading curls caressing their cheekbones, and their eyes were done in a soft green shadow, accentuating their already dazzling emerald eyes. Allison wore a soft pink lip-gloss while Kaitlyn wore dark. They were stunning, breathtaking, and enjoying every single second of the attentions received.

Now, Ray and John weren't looking too shabby themselves. Ray wore a black double-breasted tuxedo, with a deep emerald green shirt to match Kaitlyn's dress. Regardless of the color, his eyes still burned bright, melting her. He had even rented a cane to go with the outfit for the night — just for the fun of it.

John decided on wearing a charcoal gray tux, fixed with all the decorations, right down to a matching frilly cummerbund of mint green.

Ray presented Kaitlyn with a single yellow rose corsage, adorned with greens, babiesbreath, and a couple of small mini-white carnations, which added more sentiment to an already sentimental gift.

You see ... Kaitlyn loved the smell of white carnations. Some may have argued with her that there wasn't one, but she insisted that if you took a deep breath when smelling their scent, you would undoubtedly pick up on their fragrant aroma. "Once you have smelled their sweet scent, you don't have to try so hard to find it." she always said. "Take The Fountain for instance. When those fans swirl high above and they've replaced the old carnations with new — oh trust me, they have a scent."

Ray would always respond with, "Okay, yes. I believe you, honey."

Kaitlyn would just roll her eyes. She knew the truth.

John presented Allison with a similar corsage, since he and Ray purchased them together — except that Allison was partial to light pink roses.

Once the men pinned the corsages on the ladies with Kathryn's assistance, and the picture taking was over and done with, the boys escorted their girls to the car — pulling out all the stops when it came to being gentlemen.

Ray drove with Kaitlyn seated next to him, and John and Allison were seated in the back — rather closely, too. At first, conversations were at a high on their drive there, and they talked about all sorts of stuff. Then, quiet fell in the backseat. After a few moments, Kaitlyn peeped in the back, catching John and Allison in a full-blown, all out kissing frenzy. Kaitlyn let out a chuckle, catching Ray's attention. Ray glanced at Kaitlyn with a *what* look on his face. Kaitlyn gaped at Ray sharply, then away, with eyes that beckoned him to follow. Kaitlyn looked beyond as Ray trailed her gaze.

"Enjoying ourselves, we see," Ray commented, glaring in the rearview mirror at the two, letting out a roaring laugh as Kaitlyn joined in.

"Ha ha," Allison said, then replied with: "As a matter of fact, we are ... " and continued on with her mission.

A few minutes passed, and they pulled into The Chateau's parking lot, a valet ready to take the car.

Ray and John let themselves out and then dutifully helped their ladies from the car, making sure they were treated like princesses. Handing the keys over to the valet, Ray took Kaitlyn's arm as John did Allison's, and the four headed to the door, ready to be seated at their table.

Even knowing the ambiance of The Chateau, Kaitlyn still couldn't help but take in the romance and tranquility of the place. It was new to Allison and John. They took in all the fine scents as they peered around the room and noticed the Vermont green color scheme and roaring fire. Even though it was May, in this neck of the woods, a fire was still needed to keep warm when evening strolled in.

Everything was the same with the exception of the flower vases. Each table except theirs was set with soft pink carnations, sprinkled with babiesbreath and greenery. Ray had done it again. At the reserved table, the restaurant had placed one yellow rose in a vase for Kaitlyn and one pink rose in another vase for Allison. The girls looked at each other and smiled a *gotta love it* smile.

Dinner went off without a hitch as they sat down to Chateau Brignon, jumbo shrimp appetizers, and delightful salads dressed in Italian, again asking the waiter if he'd take offense. Things felt back to normal for all of them. They weren't uneasy being around each other and conversation flowed as if there had never been any tensions between them. They actually had a lovely dinner, wonderful intellectual and not-so intellectual conversations, with plenty of laughs to go around.

By the time dinner was finished and topped off with delicious chocolate mousse, it was time to head to The Lake George Mansion for their *Love Is In The Air* prom.

On the way to the car, Ray pretended to be an old man, wavering around on his cane, gaining many laughs from their private party and a few on-lookers. An older couple walked by them and smiled — surely remembering their own proms and seeming to step back in time for a brief moment.

On the way to the mansion, only a few minutes away, John mentioned that he feared someone might spike the punch again. Kaitlyn and Allison took it upon themselves to be the punch wardens for the night, not wanting John to go through *that* again. John thanked them for caring and looked to Ray for approval, receiving it, just as they pulled into the parking lot.

The ballroom was decorated with themes of yesteryear's love, full of class and elegance. Posters of famous couples from the twenties hung on the walls, and ribbons were used in place of streamers. Bouquets of colorfully abundant fresh flowers hung in place of balloons, making the air smell sweet with love. The punch tables were decorated with pink linen cloths, replacing paper ones, and china cups and pure silver replaced the typical boring glass and metal wear.

The band called *Twilight* played music from the past as well as popular hits of their time. And as the four settled themselves into a round table away from the crowd, Kaitlyn and Allison's ears perked up when they heard their song.

Grabbing their men/boys' arms, they dragged them in an almost run to the dance floor as the two sung their hearts out, getting others to join in the fun. Before they knew it, they had most everyone singing *Some Enchanted Evening* and having the time of their lives. They even got the shy, conservative kids to join in. Oh, the *power* those girls had.

After the Mackey Seniors gave their rendition of the song, they found themselves lined up ready to do some line dancing. When that finished, it was time for a few slow songs, causing each and every couple to embrace lovingly on the dance floor, embossing those very moments deep within their memories, and leaving those without dates to sway to the music at the walls, looking uncomfortable in their own situations.

Ray's body felt good next to Kaitlyn's, and the closeness awakened sensations in her she wished to explore further. Their eyes were locked in a stare as they both felt their bodies crave more. They knew it was possible and decided to hold off their affections until later. They smiled knowing this particular fact.

Meanwhile, the music picked up in pace as did the conversations taking place between everyone on the dance floor. They all laughed, played, and cried, while they enjoyed group dancing with their friends. Ray would walk around like an old man with his cane, catching a few laughs. He then tried dancing with Kaitlyn as if they were seventy years old, pretending his body wasn't working quite right. It was funny, and Kaitlyn found it interestingly humorous and imagined him being that way when he was older.

It was an enjoyable evening, one with fond memories — not so much of what happened, but of how they were feeling and how it was a turning point in their relationship.

Kaitlyn and Ray left the prom early and intended to catch up with John and Allison at 11:45 p.m., since 12:30 a.m. was the girls' curfew. John and Allison knew what was planned, but neither one gave their opinions to Ray or Kaitlyn, deciding it was none of their business. Besides, they had issues of their own to worry about.

Kaitlyn and Ray reserved a room at an upscale hotel, just on the outskirts of Lake George — five minutes from where the prom was held. Ray had stopped to pick up the key earlier in the day when he dropped the flowers off at the restaurant, so everything was in place. They had a room with a private entrance. They had their undying love and lust. They had their alibis worked out to a tee, and they had each other.

Hesitancy showed on their faces as they entered the room, knowing this was it. This was the *big* event. Kaitlyn began having doubts about going any further than they had in the car. She had her father's voice in her head reprimanding her as if she were psychotic and arguing with an invisible being.

Ray could see her struggling and at first shrugged his shoulders, thinking she was being her strange self. He then realized that she was apprehensive and approached with a loving hug. "We don't have to, you know," he said, reassuring Kaitlyn. "I only want to be able to hold you and kiss you without having to worry about someone catching us. That's good enough for me, Kait."

Kaitlyn looked at Ray and then placed her head against his solid chest and folded her arms around his waist. "I love you, Ray," she said as she leaned up for a kiss, then another and then another. Slowly, they found themselves embraced in deep passionate kisses, and their smiles in play turned to smiles of serious want for one another.

Ray slowly removed his tux, draping it carefully over one of the soft velvet chairs. Asking for help, he then removed his necktie. Kaitlyn turned him around, reaching with one hand to place the tie on the tux, while slyly unbuttoning his shirt with the other. Ray smiled as he reached around to slowly unzip her gown. Sliding the straps off her shoulders, the gown fell to the carpet in a billow of satin, revealing an emerald green slip, garter belt and hose, while exposing her cleavage.

He whisked her into his arms and felt the smooth slip against his hands as he massaged her back and clasped her bottom, enjoying the sliding of the fabric. Each caress sent shivers through Kaitlyn, with the negligible material covering her adding to the thrill.

She leaned back a little to finish with his shirt, uncovering his fine biceps. Grabbing hold of them and squeezing, she rejoiced in his strength, and it excited her even more. She couldn't wait for Ray's strong arms to envelope her, she pulled him in close to quench that longing.

Again, taking control, Kaitlyn began unbuckling Ray's belt, loosening the top button of his trousers, then insisted he go to the bed.

Kaitlyn, still in the garter, hose and slip, slithered over Ray's form, settling astride him, something she enjoyed, and felt he did too. They gazed into each other's eyes for a momentary forever before their lips tangled, kissing. Warm hands explored, strong arms embraced, and before long, Kaitlyn was swirling her hips ever so slightly.

She felt her own excitement grow with Ray's obvious want nestled so close against her, heating the mounting desire. She kissed his neck, his ears and traced her lips slowly downward, finding herself tasting his chest, his stomach, his navel and lower. Ray's breath became short in the awareness of Kaitlyn intent, not in his life dreaming she would actually perform this, but hoping to *God* that she would follow through.

Kaitlyn carefully unzipped his pants, pulling them away with ease, then sensuously removed his last piece of clothing, bringing

Ray to freedom. Kaitlyn liked what she saw and even more what she savored. She enjoyed feeling Ray's love grow within the warmth of her mouth and loved the power of the act.

Ray soon felt as if he were about to leave his body, but stopped her, pulling her close. "It's your turn," he whispered with a smile.

Kaitlyn stood and went to the light switch, dimming them low, all prompted by a rising insecurity about Ray seeing her naked. No one except the doctor had seen her naked before, not even Allison.

"Why the lights?" Ray asked.

Kaitlyn didn't answer; she just crept slowly in his direction while unveiling her body, beginning by removing her slip and tossing it towards the velvet chair.

Ray stood and moved close, helping undo the garter. Sliding his fingers gently under Kaitlyn's hose, he delicately removed them, enjoying the sensuality of the act. One last article of clothing remained, and Kaitlyn slipped off her emerald satin panties by bending over in awkward seduction before releasing them from her legs. Ray studied Kaitlyn with appreciative eyes and wordlessly asked her to come to him as he slipped back onto the four-poster bed.

A chill came over Kaitlyn as she went to join Ray, and he swathed a soft blanket over her shoulders. Secure in their homemade warming tent, Ray traced his fingertips over the outline of her silhouette. He drew her in and brought his mouth to her breasts, suckling them as Kaitlyn straddled Ray's lap.

Her hips moved in a slow circular motion as she felt him pressing against her, wanting to enter. She could feel her body respond, desperate for joining, but was afraid, and Ray sensed the apprehension.

"Do you want to?" he asked sincerely.

"I ... want to, Ray. I want you so much!" she confided. "But ... I'm scared."

"We can try, Ray offered. "We'll take it slow. If it hurts too much or you want to stop, we will."

Kaitlyn leaned into him for his reassuring hug. They entangled in kisses as they slithered their bodies against one another, and

Kaitlyn kept her hips moving, enjoying the sensations the motion caused. She felt her body open wider, allowing the excitement from the mere touch of his body.

Ray grew more excited at the moment of penetration, both gasping in unison with the thrill. Letting nature take its course, he allowed Kaitlyn's body to take all the time it needed. She responded by swirling her hips with him partially inside, heightening the sensation even more. She felt him slip deeper, until there was no longer two of them alone, but one together.

While savoring the moment, Ray soon began to move his hips in an inward and outward motion, just enough to keep things going, but careful not to hurt his girl.

Kaitlyn rested her head into Ray's neck, concentrating on what sensations were running through her body, kissing his neck every so often, with Ray kissing her back. Feeling sensations rise further, Kaitlyn nuzzled into Ray's neck as she felt the tips of her toes begin to tingle, finding their way in a rush through her entire body as she rotated her hips faster, now pressing hard against Ray. With quick short breaths, she gasped as her body and mind expanded into a fearfully delicious bloom of love and release.

Eventually, Kaitlyn's breathing settled and the pulsing of her heart slowed into ever-diminishing intervals. Ray now moved in and out of her in small, quickened, gentle motions until his breaths too became heavy. She felt his body tense and freeze for a moment, just before the powerful release of his love flowed into her.

It was at that moment that Kaitlyn instinctively knew that Ray was the One — forever and always. She also knew Ray was the one with whom she was to give the present of herself to. They had made love, and in sharing their bodies with caring sweetness and gentle touches, bonded that love. They held each other and cuddled, lying side-by-side, smiling with joy. It was a beautiful experience for both, and they would never forget how they made each other feel that night, or how much in love they were at that moment.

When 11:30 p.m. came, Kaitlyn rose from the bed, only to notice the blood stained sheets. Instantly panicked, she rushed to the bathroom and took a half shower, having no idea why she was bleeding. Ray came to check on her, asking if she was okay, with her showing a little fear, but saying she was fine. He decided to take a half shower as well to wash away any evidence.

They dressed, fixed their hair so it looked similar to when they arrived at the dance, made sure they had everything, and left.

"We forgot about the hymen," Ray said as they strolled hand in hand to the car.

Kaitlyn nodded and then chuckled uncomfortably. She didn't know what a hymen was.

Ray put his arm around Kaitlyn, whispering that he was glad she was his first.

"Me too," Kaitlyn replied happily.

Ray helped Kaitlyn into the car, asking if she was okay before he shut the door.

Driving back towards the dance, they found John on the roadside walking aimlessly with his head bowed. Ray slowed the car to a near stop beside him, catching a glimpse of a tear trickling down John's emotion filled face. When Ray asked him what was wrong, he muttered, "Allison dumped me. Just leave me alone, please," he begged, not wanting Kaitlyn to see him cry.

As Ray began to pull away from the curb, Kaitlyn turned around and watched John out of the back window. Her heart reached out to him.

They pulled up to the Mansion's grounds, finding Allison sitting on the steps with her head held in her hands. Kaitlyn got out of the car and seated herself beside Allison, and wrapped her arms around her best friend.

"You okay?"

Allison nodded. "Let's go."

Kaitlyn helped Allison to the car and asked Ray about John. Ray glanced over to Kaitlyn with a *what do we do* look, and Kaitlyn shrugged her shoulders. He reached for the door handle, saying, "I'll be right back."

Ray approached one of John's friends and asked him to give John a ride home, filling him in on the situation and where to find him. John's friend accepted, and Ray went back to the car, letting the girls know he had found John a ride.

It was the longest ride back to Winter's Crest.

Ray dropped the girls off at Kaitlyn's, being careful to not get too mushy in front of Allison, but let Kaitlyn know his love before he kissed her goodnight. He waved to Allison and wished her well before he drove off towards John's house.

Ray waited for John to arrive home. He wanted to make sure his friend made it there safe and sound. He did. John looked at Ray and said only one thing: "You're a lucky man, Ray." John turned and walked towards his front door — never looking back.

Kaitlyn and Allison walked into Kaitlyn's house, meeting her parents in the living room. Kathryn picked up on something being amiss with Allison and left her questions for another time, telling them that it was late and they should get to bed.

Kaitlyn hugged her father goodnight, kissing him slightly on the cheek before turning her attention to her mother. "Thanks, Mom," Kaitlyn whispered in her ear. "I'll fill you in tomorrow, goodnight."

Kaitlyn and Allison put on their pajamas and then settled on top of Kaitlyn's bed. They wrapped up in blankets and began talking about the night. Allison wasn't ready to discuss what happened between she and John, opting to find out about Kaitlyn's night instead.

"Well, did you?" she asked with quiet smirk on her face.

Kaitlyn nodded with a smile.

"Did it hurt?" Allison asked, cringing.

"A little," Kaitlyn replied. "You'd better not tell anyone!"

"I won't, Kaitlyn," she replied. "That's between you and Ray."

"I want details!" Allison demanded.

Kaitlyn laughed quietly as to not be heard by her parents or brother. Kaitlyn and Allison huddled together, while Kaitlyn filled her in on some of the important details, leaving out the extreme graphics of losing her virginity. She did, however, ask Allison what a hymen was, with Allison's comment being: "I should've warned you about that. I broke mine riding a bike."

Allison explained to Kaitlyn what it was, while Kaitlyn told Allison what making love was like, peaking her interest. "Well, it isn't going to be happening for me anytime soon," Allison sarcastically remarked, not going any further with her comment. "You think you'll do it again?" Allison asked.

Kaitlyn stirred her head and shrugged her shoulders with uncertainty as to how to answer that question, then left it with a simple "Maybe," as she smiled.

"Not to change the subject, Allison," Kaitlyn said, intending to change it. "What happened? Why'd you break up with John?"

"It was time," Allison said. "Besides, there's no future for us, why waste his or my time?"

"Why now though? Kaitlyn asked confused. "Why prom night? Especially with the way you two were in the car tonight."

"If you must know the truth," Allison said. "Bob asked me out."

"Bob Westman?" Kaitlyn asked. "Really?"

"You know I've always had a crush on him," she replied. "He's done with school, and he's so cute."

"I thought he knew about John though?" Kaitlyn asked, trying to understand it all.

"He does," she replied. "But, he also knows that there hasn't really been anything there. John and I are basically friends that kiss. Besides, Kait, I can't compete with you."

"What do you mean?" Kaitlyn asked, thinking Allison was nuts.

"Oh, come on, Kaitlyn," she exclaimed. "You can't tell me you don't notice the way John looks at you?"

"Honestly, Allison," Kaitlyn replied. "I don't know what you're talking about. He's been like that with me since we were kids."

"Yeah, well," Allison continued, "he's not a kid anymore, and kids don't look at other kids that way."

Kaitlyn didn't know how to take the news. She knew that John would playfully say things, and he did have that one outburst at

The Fountain when he confessed his love for her, but John? "John and me?" she thought. The mere thinking of such a travesty brought chills to her already grossed out thoughts.

"We're just friends, Allison," Kaitlyn stated firmly.

"Oh, I know," Allison said. "I just think John would like it to be more than that. "Kaitlyn, it's okay. I feel bad that I hurt John, but I still like the guy. I'm just not in love with him, nor have I ever been. And, you know what, he's not in love with me either. You wait and see. He'll be looking girls up and down, right and left, always keeping one eye directed towards you. You watch and mark my words. Then, maybe you'll see what I'm talking about."

Kaitlyn wasn't sure what to make of this particular conversation, deciding it best to leave it alone.

"Kaitlyn," Allison called her. "John will be fine, and I'm fine, too. This is all for the best."

Both girls started yawning and decided to turn out the lights. As Allison lay her head to the pillow, she looked up with a smirk briefly to Kaitlyn saying, "I guess you're a woman now, huh?"

"Oh, shut up," Kaitlyn giggled, throwing a pillow at her. "Goodnight, silly."

Chapter Seventeen

The day after the prom, Allison thought she should pay John a visit. She didn't want to lose him as a friend. Besides, she was feeling a tad guilty.

When John opened the front door to find Allison there, he was not too eager to have words with her. He wasn't depressed, but he was upset with her for ruining his second to last hurrah as a senior. He thought it was heartless of Allison to choose prom night as her stage.

Allison asked John if he would like to take a walk, as she wanted to clear the air and allow closure for both. John was hesitant with accepting the invitation, but did so. He didn't want to lose their friendship either.

They walked closely, but did not hold hands or become playful with one another. John expressed his resentment towards her for ruining the prom, but gave Allison the chance to explain.

"John," she said, "we're better friends than we are boyfriend and girlfriend. You know it, and I know it. We're friends that kiss — and kiss well, I might add."

John nodded in understanding. He knew she was right, but hated admitting it.

"We," Allison continued, taking her finger and gesturing between the two of them, "weren't meant to be together as boyfriend/girlfriend. It's just not there — for either one of us." She paused. "Okay, except for the kissing part," letting out a tension relieving chuckle.

John continued listening in agreement.

"John," Allison got his attention. "You know that I have always had a crush on Bob Westman, and I know you have always been in love with Kaitlyn. Why were we together in the first place?"

John stopped walking and turned to her. "I don't know … 'cause it was fun?"

"Yes," she replied. "And convenient. John, you're cute and I really like you, but I just don't have the romantic feelings that I should have for you, and you don't for me. So, doesn't it seem like it's best we move on and stay friends?"

John glanced in Allison's direction and smiled. "When did you get to be so smart?"

Allison laughed and threw her head back, tossing her hair in the air. "I've always been smart. My flightiness is just a cover," she said laughing, with John joining her.

Allison extended her hand to John. "Friends?" she asked.

"Friends," John replied, pulling her handshake into a *friend* hug.

John, I have to tell you something," Allison said meekly.

"What?" he replied, not sure he wanted to hear more.

"Bob asked me for a date," Allison admitted. "I've seen him around town lately, and we keep eyeing each other. I figured if I was having feelings for him, it wouldn't be fair to either one of us if I strung you along — even if we are good at kissing."

"Oh, so that's the real reason," John replied with faux hurt.

"No, actually, it's not," she replied. "I've thought this for a long time, but I was afraid I'd lose your friendship. But, John, if it's not there for us, it's not there. I can't control my feelings for Bob any more than you can control your feelings for Kaitlyn."

"I know," John replied. "I saw your face light up when you saw him at the birthday party. I guess I've always known, just … never wanted to admit it."

Allison clasped her hands together and began swaying back and forth as if she were a young child vying for some candy. "May I still help you with the assemblies?" she asked. "I really enjoy being a part of them and helping you, too."

John took her hands and replied, "Of course," telling Allison, "I wouldn't have it any other way."

"So, John," Allison began. "What do you think about Kaitlyn and Ray, and well ... you know?" she asked, changing the subject.

"Honestly?" he asked.

"Yes, honestly," she replied. "We're friends, you can tell me anything."

"I kind of wish it was me and not Ray," John answered.

"See," Allison said laughing. "I knew it. I just knew it," she said hitting him playfully, with both laughing.

"We okay?" Allison asked.

"Yeah, we're okay," he replied.

"Maybe some day you'll have your chance with Kaitlyn," Allison said, surprising herself. "But, whomever you end up with, John, she'll be one lucky lady. You've really turned out to be a wonderful man. And, John ..." she said, looking at him sincerely, "I'm proud of you."

John's eyes lit up and his chin dropped. He was shocked those words came from her mouth, yet enjoyed hearing them. "Thank you, Allison," he replied. "That was really nice of you to say that."

"I mean it, John," she replied. "Come on, let's go to The Fountain."

By the time John and Allison made it to The Fountain, it was well after church hours, and Kaitlyn and Ray were there. Surprised to see them come in together, Kaitlyn rushed towards Allison and scurried her away to the ladies' room.

"What happened?" Kaitlyn asked. "You two back together?"

"No," she replied. "We worked things out, and we both agreed we're better at being friends than a couple."

"Oh," Kaitlyn replied, unsure of how to respond, but glad the two were at least talking.

The girls returned to the dining area, finding Ray and John in deep discussion about something. They couldn't make out what it was even though they had tried hard to eavesdrop. They ordered some sodas and decided for old time's sake to get those yummy sundaes they had enjoyed on their first double date.

After devouring their ice cream, John got up and put a nickel in the jukebox, pushing C-4. He turned around and said, "Come on up here, girls. I'm playing your song." The girls didn't need to be talked into it, hopping out of their seats and rushing to the dance floor before John could finish his sentence.

Ray joined them, and the four, along with their fellow *non-shy* restaurant patrons, got up and did their rendition of *Some Enchanted Evening* once again. They laughed, played, and hugged each other in frolicking fun. As the last note faded, Bob Westman came into the restaurant, and Allison's eyes lit up with fire.

She looked sidelong to John, then back at Bob, only to glance back to John again. John nodded telling Allison he was fine with it, realizing it didn't bother him. The only thing that *did* bother John was that he wanted a girl to look at *him* that way, and he wanted *that* girl to be Kaitlyn.

The five then sat together conversing, with John feeling like an outsider. Even though it was a bit awkward for John seeing Allison with Bob, he was okay with it. It made him realize that he didn't truly love Allison the way a romantic couple should. He loved her as his friend, and he was glad to see her smile with her eyes aglow.

The hours flew by, and it was getting time for all to go their separate ways. Just as they were getting ready to leave, the waitress called out for Ray, telling him he had a phone call. Ray quickly went to the phone questioning why he would receive a call there. Nick was on the extension asking him to come home, saying he wasn't feeling too well. Ray told him he would be right there and asked John if he minded taking Kaitlyn home.

Ray gave Kaitlyn a quick kiss goodbye and then dashed out the door. As John helped Kaitlyn with her coat, he asked her what that was all about.

"Nick's been sick lately," she replied. "Some sort of flu, or something like that."

"Really?" John asked, not sure if he believed her.

"Yes." Kaitlyn said, lying through her teeth.

Kaitlyn didn't want to tell John that Nick had been having trouble with his heart. The heart attack caused damage to the lower part of Nick's heart, but the accident was just a tool to bring the attack on. His heart wasn't in good shape before the accident, and he definitely wasn't in good health after it. But Ray hadn't let anyone in on Nick's condition — except for Kaitlyn. Ray didn't want John to feel guilty about something he hadn't caused. Nick would have had the heart attack regardless of the accident, and Ray wasn't so sure John would accept that as truth.

John and Kaitlyn had a pleasant walk to her home. They talked about their childhood games, the mistakes they have made, and the breaking up between he and Allison. They also discussed how happy Kaitlyn was with Ray. John tried to come across delighted for Kaitlyn, but the whole time he felt crushed. His dream someday of being with Kaitlyn had gone from a glimmer of hope to doused flame.

They arrived at Kaitlyn's, and John escorted her to the door, briefly saying hello to Jim and Kathryn before heading towards his own house in grave introspection.

They all had four weeks left until graduation, and most of that time was spent hanging out at The Fountain or going off on their own secret excursions.

Allison and Bob were an item now, hanging all over each other every chance they got. Kaitlyn and Ray were inseparable as well, taking many planned or unplanned trips to their tree, getting in as much alone time as they possibly could. Having tasted the fruits of desire but once, they craved it each time they were together, but held back in resistance. Ray didn't want to just have sex with Kaitlyn in a car or at the tree. He wanted to make love to Kaitlyn and treat her like a lady. She didn't worry about such *trivial* matters.

Kaitlyn spent many afternoons begging Ray with her pouting lips, hoping he would take her up on the offerings, but he didn't. Ray had too much respect for her. She respected herself too, but the temptations overrode her sensibility. Kaitlyn secretly liked Ray respecting her; she just couldn't get enough of him. Now that she knew what lovemaking was and how it made her feel, she craved it as if it were air to breathe. Our good little girl Kaitlyn was not such a *good little girl* after all.

Everyone thought so though, all but Ray. She left her wild side for his eyes only, and no one else would've ever had a clue that Kaitlyn could be so, well ... *wild* in her wants. Ray liked it though, and so did she.

John went on a few dates with a girl named Mindy Patterson. Mindy was petite with a heart that made up for her physical size. Her hair and eyes matched that of John's, making them look like they could be sister and brother. Their relationship, if you can call it that, was simple and just for fun. It was a passing of the time for both, enjoying what was left of their senior year together.

School would be out soon and graduation was just around the corner. Ray received the okay to join the Army, if he wished to do so. He also was accepted to The University of Southern California to major in engineering, as he wanted. At that time, Ray had not decided as to whether or not he would enlist or go to school first, so he decided to take the first month of summer off to make that decision.

John, on the other hand, had planned on joining in August, but ran into some difficulty with his plans when he had his final physical. His eyesight had gone terribly awry, and not only did he need to get strong glasses, but also he was no longer able to serve. This devastated him momentarily. Being no stranger to disappointment, John quickly pulled himself together and made new plans. He decided to go to a nearby college and find work in town once school was over, figuring there had to be a reason for his forced change of plans.

Kaitlyn and Allison didn't have any plans to further their education, although they had both toyed with the idea. Their dreams were to get married, have kids, and run their households. They had even talked about having homes in the same neighborhood, getting pregnant at the same time, and having their children grow up being friends, too. Wishful thinking, they knew, but girls can dream can't they?

Kaitlyn and Ray spent much time together talking and discussing how their lives would change. Kaitlyn was happy for Ray that his dreams were coming true, but simultaneously, she was saddened. She didn't want him to go. Kaitlyn still wasn't ready to share him with the world. They knew they didn't have much time before Ray left for one of his possible destinations, and they cherished each and every moment, breath, and detail of their time together.

Ray's hugs grew strong as time grew closer to graduation, and when Ray held Kaitlyn, he held her as if he were trying to remember her every scent, every touch, and every sensation. It scared her. She felt as if she were being visited by a past haunting ghost, and all Kaitlyn could think was that this was going to be it. "He's going to do it to me again," her inner voice told her, choosing to ignore it.

Graduation plans were all set by the morning it arrived June 25, 1951, closing the doors to Kaitlyn, Allison, John, and Rays' high school days, with a new door opening, welcoming the future.

Kaitlyn didn't mind this door being shut, and she welcomed the open window. She knew what was ahead for her.

Decked out in their blue caps and gowns, they all met the day with excitement and fear twirled into one as they approached the school grounds for opening ceremonies. As all the parents, friends, students and faculty alike settled themselves on the white wooden chairs placed on the front lawn of Mackey High, Principal Petry spoke. Applause for his opening words of welcome roared through the air, and when the cheers dwindled, he introduced Mackey's 1951 Valedictorian: Ray Niles.

Ray stood up to a grand applause. Being sure to find his father in the crowd, Ray smiled lovingly before beginning his speech. He spoke of dreams, hope, love, and forgiveness, and having the guts to go after your dreams, no matter what the outcome, saying that the fact you even tried is success in itself. "No one can ever blame you for trying," he said. "Dream it. Do it. Live it!"

A roar of acceptance showed its face with applause before Ray's face became somber. He cleared his throat a few times and tried to find the courage to go on, then looked for the one support he needed by his side: Kaitlyn. Eyeing her in the crowd towards the front, Ray motioned for her to come on stage with him, Kaitlyn doing as he asked. As she joined Ray on stage, he signaled for her to come closer with his private gesture, and Kaitlyn giggled going to his side.

Ray put his arm around Kaitlyn and spoke of his love for her, confessing it to all. He then expressed his feelings about how the Frost family had been there for he and his father, and how much compassion he had received from all that were in attendance. Ray looked out to his father and said, "I love you," before he reached his hands in the air and looked up to Heaven saying, "This one's for you, Mom!"

The entire school body burst in a celebrating ovation, with many knowing just how lucky they were to have their own mothers and fathers with them. Hugs were the order of the moment.

Ray grabbed a hold of Kaitlyn and embraced her with such intensity that time stood still once again. Wrapped up in their own world, the sounds of laughter and applause came to them through a clouded distance, and as they held tight, the realization that they were at a life-changing crossroad began sinking in.

When the cheers and cap throwing slowed down, and all hugs were exchanged, everyone parted their separate ways to attend private family parties and gatherings. But the graduates all knew they were to meet at eight o'clock for the one celebration held for all at The Soda Fountain.

The Fountain had decorated the restaurant in a graduation theme and offered the traditional free pop and music for the festivity. It was their way of thanking the students for their patronage, and because they just loved those kids.

At eight sharp, scores of people took over the small restaurant, with one of the football players taking over the Wurlitzer too, cranking up the sound a few notches and announcing, "Let the party begin!"

Shortly after, Kaitlyn and Ray, along with Bob and Allison, and John and Mindy showed up at the door. The six were met by an onslaught of fellow friends and graduates, some parents and siblings, a few local townsfolk, loud laughter and chatter, along with plenty of jubilant faces. The music throbbed through the chatter, and they could barely hear themselves speak, let alone hear what *they* were saying when they spoke.

Peggy the waitress dashed to and fro in her red poodle skirt, with her usually perfect coif askew, indicating her frantic workload. A blue cloud of cigarette smoke hung overhead, with the fans above hard-pressed trying to keep up.

As people walked by Kaitlyn's group, their senses were assaulted with an overdose of perfume. Some smelled like roses, while others had a scent of something that had been in a bottle far too long — or should have *never* been in a bottle to begin with.

Lively attempts at dancing to 'How High The Moon' by Les Paul and Mary Ford were made comical by the lack of elbowroom, making it look as if all the partygoers were dancing a push and shove number instead of swaying in one another's arms.

After observing the craziness that they chose to be a part of, the men politely shoved their way through the maze of people towards The Fountain to get colas for the girls. While Ray stood waiting by one of the vases filled with white carnations, he unconsciously admitted that he smelled their sweet scent Kaitlyn always insisted was there. He smiled.

The tight knot gave the appearance of trying to hear one another, but they were actually picking up snippets of their own conversation while hearing a few trailed words from others around them. After an hour of yelling and trying to have *some* sort of conversation without getting nudged or having a foot squashed, Ray called in a drowned whisper to Kaitlyn, "Let's get out of here!"

Kaitlyn's only true smile of the evening couldn't have agreed with him more.

They made their hasty farewells to the group along with their other friends and acquaintances, and winnowed their way out the door. Escaping into the night air, the two swung around as if just released from prison.

"I'm free ..." Kaitlyn sang while twirling in the moonlight. "Come on," she said holding her hands out to Ray. "Let's get as far away from here as we can." She pulled him in the direction of Crestview Park. "Once-you-have-found-her," she trilled, "n-e-e-v-e-r-let-her-go."

"What is it with you and that song, Kaitlyn?" Ray chuckled.

She shucked her shoulders coyly and hugged her arms across her chest. "I just love Perry Como. Oh, he's just so, *dreamy*! She batted her eyes. "Oh, but I love *you* more," she confirmed sarcastically.

Wanting to be alone, Ray and Kaitlyn escaped the crowd. The beautiful moonlit night was still young, and the sun had begun to set, allowing for a vast array of colors to grace the skies. They walked towards their one special spot while the twinkling stars hovered above with the sounds of crickets playing their songs, which added to the romance Kaitlyn and Ray felt in their hearts. Reaching the tree, the two embraced in desperate measure.

Ray pulled Kaitlyn in close and began to ravage her lips, his hands grasping her back and bottom. Kaitlyn's fingers hurriedly massaged Ray's hair while their tongues entwined as if they were couldn't get close enough. He pulled back and stopped.

Ray picked Kaitlyn up in his arms as if they were newlyweds and carried her over to a small patch of soft green grass hidden behind the brush. He laid her down ever so gently and joined by her side.

Ray wanted her, and Kaitlyn wanted him. The two entangled in deep passionate petting and kissing until Kaitlyn rolled Ray over to bestride him and began unbuttoning his shirt in an urgent fashion. With Ray's shirt out of the way, Kaitlyn began to undo her clothing, allowing her breasts to expose their delight to Ray as the warm night air caressed.

He traced his fingers over Kaitlyn's soft skin before pulling her in closer, wanting to savor her longing bosom. And after a few moments of shared enjoyment, Kaitlyn laid down facing Ray, wanting to slide her tongue over his chest, nipples and neck. Ray moaned in pleasure, feeling deep urging desire.

Kaitlyn slid her tongue downwards and teased at his waistline, sliding her tongue under, just below his pant's buckle. Looking to Ray, she smiled and slid her fingers under the fabric in a playful manner before unclasping the belt in a seducing manner.

Carefully unfastening the top button of his trousers, Kaitlyn unzipped his pants with her teeth, her hands helping a bit — smirking as she did so. Ray liked the animalistic feel of the act and helped her finish the mission. Both let out nervous giggles.

Pulling slightly away from Ray, Kaitlyn hiked her skirt, allowing herself to remove her panties while checking Ray's facial cast to see if he would succumb to her advances. With her eyes and pouting lips, Kaitlyn asked Ray to become one with her.

Giving into temptation and letting out a playful dreading sigh, Ray held out his arms, and Kaitlyn knew she had the okay. Enjoying the act of straddling Ray, she ever so gently worked her hips, allowing both to feel each other's cravings. Kaitlyn's desire grew wet and hard, while Ray's desires had already hardened with want.

Allowing their bodies to sail at their own paces, Kaitlyn slowly maneuvered her hips in a mutually satisfying rotation as their lips locked together in lust. Ray's love slipped slowly into Kaitlyn's longing loins, making her gasp as sensations overtook their bodies, leaving the two moaning in great pleasure.

Kaitlyn massaged her breasts against Ray's chest, and her hips flowed with the rhythm. She felt her love expand as Ray shared his with her, and gradually and softly, the two loves combined. They smiled.

Ray kissed Kaitlyn overpoweringly, and they rolled over, still engaged as one. He kissed her and slid his tongue over her lips, neck and cheeks as he gently entered her, deep. And as Ray would start to leave their single being, Kaitlyn, in a whisper, would beg him to stay as her hips followed his movement upwards, her loins aching for his return, and her legs trying to keep him near. Ray gave into Kaitlyn's begging and entered her once again, pushing deeper — harder. Staying for a few moments, he'd then retreat again, leaving Kaitlyn's body crying out for him to stay. Kaitlyn desperate for release.

Their breaths shortened with anticipation and excitement, and they felt their bodies' awakenings take over. Their motions had grown faster and harder until both, in unison, shared their love — with Ray's overflowing into her, allowing Kaitlyn to share twice.

When the last pulsation sailed away, Kaitlyn and Ray cuddled side by side, catching their breath and gazing satisfied into the night sky. Caressing each other lovingly, the two exchanged smiles, both knowing how much they enjoyed sharing their love. Their bond was stronger than it had ever been before — they didn't think *that* was possible.

"Wow," Kaitlyn whispered.

Ray smiled, "You just had to make me do this, didn't you?" and laughed, ecstatic that he had given in.

Realizing it was getting late and they couldn't account for their time, the two did their best to clean up and straighten their attire before heading towards Kaitlyn's home. They walked away from their tree with their arms wrapped around one another, feeling love like they never thought they could. It was a beautiful and sensual night for both. They had no idea how much this night would come to mean to them.

Arriving at Kaitlyn's home, they were met by Kathryn on the front porch, having a worried and frantic look on her face. She didn't even notice that Kaitlyn was in disarray — or Ray for that matter. Kathryn had one thing on her mind and that was getting an urgent message to Ray.

"Ray, your father ... "

"Where is he?" Ray interrupted.

"He's at the hospital. We've been looking all ... "

Kathryn couldn't finish her sentence as Ray and Kaitlyn high-tailed it to the car and headed for the hospital. Ray backed out of the drive, slammed on the brakes, then quickly turned the wheel and spun off, leaving tire marks behind.

Honking his horn through town like a mad man and going through red lights and stop signs, they made it to the hospital in one minute flat. Jumping out of the car without concern for Kaitlyn, Ray ran into the emergency room, only to be met with somber faces.

Kaitlyn, a few steps behind him, heard a blood-curdling scream.

"NOOOOOO! NOOOOOOOOO!" Ray screamed, collapsing to the floor. "Oh my God, NOOOOOO!"

Kaitlyn brought her hands to her mouth in disbelief as she scurried to comfort Ray. Bending down beside him, he shooed her away, not wanting any consolation.

Kaitlyn took a few steps backward, deeply saddened and hurt all in one. She stood quietly watching Ray, wanting to help him, but she couldn't. He wouldn't let her. Not sure of what to do or say, Kaitlyn called her mother, wailing for help and breaking the news.

"I'll be right there," Kathryn cried into the phone, dropping it as she flew out the door.

By the time Kathryn arrived, Ray had pulled himself together enough to ask what happened. Alice happened to be doing emergency room duty and came over to talk to all three.

"He had a heart attack," Alice said, looking at the floor. Looking up, she tried to comfort. "We did everything we could for him, but his heart wasn't strong enough. I'm so sorry, Ray."

"May I see him," Ray asked, not real sure if he wanted to see his dead father.

"Yes," Alice replied, gesturing for him to follow.

"Do you want me to go with you, Ray?" Kaitlyn asked quietly.

"No," Ray answered in a short tone.

As Ray walked away from Kaitlyn and Kathryn, they heard Ray murmur, "I didn't get to say goodbye."

Ray stayed in the room with his father until the funeral director came to escort Nick's body. Kaitlyn and her mother stood idly by, not knowing what to do or what to say, or whether they should even be there. They both felt that somehow they were intruding, but knew Ray needed them at the same time. When the funeral director took Nick away, Ray came out into the hall with an expressionless, numb look on his face.

"Come home with us," Kathryn invited.

Ray stared at her for a brief second, then stared at Kaitlyn. "I can't," was all he could say. "Thank you. But I can't." He paused. "I'll be fine. I'm going to go home and call my grandparents and my family in Georgia. I'll be fine."

Mrs. Frost and Kaitlyn tried to encourage Ray to come home with them again, but he wouldn't have anything to do with it. Ray wanted to be alone, and he got what he wanted.

Ray found himself alone in this world, without parents and without hope. Tears consumed him the entire evening as he sat isolated in his house with pictures of his mother and father surrounding him. Looking at his parent's wedding day photo, he cried. "You're together now."

The next morning Ray went into survival mode. He made more phone calls to family members, and they insisted they come to him, but he insisted they not. One was on her way regardless. He called a realtor to put the house up for sale, and he spent time packing his parents items to donate to the needy, keeping treasured items for himself. He made necessary arrangements, and then made arrangements for himself.

To ease his pain and suffering, Ray kept the funeral for immediate family only, inviting just the Frosts from outside that circle. The funeral held a few days after Nick died was brief as Ray couldn't go through the painstaking agony of a long interment again.

After the funerary service and after Nick's casket was placed next to Jaycee's, Ray invited Kaitlyn back to the house. As they sat amongst the many boxes waiting to be picked up by The Salvation Army, Ray broke the news.

"I'm leaving," he said quietly, knowing it would send Kaitlyn into tears — which it did.

"I don't belong here anymore, Kait," he said, feeling misplaced. "I'm going home to Georgia."

Kaitlyn was still stuck on the "I'm leaving" part and was not able to comprehend all he was saying. Her tears cried out in agony as she begged him to stay, telling him her family was his also.

Ray shook his head no, saying that the only good thing that came from his move to Winter's Crest was her, and the rest had all been hell. "I have to get out of here, Kait," he said convincingly. "I love you, but I no longer belong here."

Kaitlyn, in a full-blown sob, wrapped her arms around Ray in a death grip as if she were trying to stop *her* nightmare. "No," she cried out. "No, don't go!"

Ray held her tight confessing his love, assuring Kaitlyn he'd be back.

Kaitlyn's tears began to settle hearing that, and she looked up to Ray as the last tear fell from her reddened eyes. "You're coming back?"

"Yes," Ray replied. "I just need to get away for awhile and get my head together. I'll be back near summer's end."

"I'll miss you, Ray," Kaitlyn said, starting to cry again. "No, no! I don't want you to go. You can't go. I won't let you!"

"Kait," Ray said in a reprimanding tone. "I have to. I just have to. Please try and understand. This doesn't have anything to do with you. It has to do with me. Except for you, this place has brought nothing but heartache to me and my family, and I just need to get out of here."

"I understand," Kaitlyn replied, eyes lowered. "I don't like it, but I understand. Will you write me?"

"Every day," he replied. "That's a promise!"

"Good," she replied, nodding once firmly, having tended to that matter. "When are you leaving?"

"The sooner the better," he replied apprehensively. "Tomorrow."

"Tomorrow?!" Kaitlyn questioned madly. "And you're telling me today?!"

"I just made the plans today," he replied. "I'm going back home with my mother's sister and stay with her for awhile."

"What about school or the Army?" Kaitlyn asked.

"I've decided on the Army and will get in touch with a recruiter in Georgia," he replied.

"Well, it seems you've got this all figured out then, don't you, Ray?" Kaitlyn said with an angry tone.

"What am I supposed to do, Kaitlyn?" Ray asked sarcastically. "Sit around here until I die or get killed, too?"

Kaitlyn didn't know how to answer that, as she knew Ray had every right to feel the way he did. "So, I guess I don't mean that much to you. To stick around here?"

"That's the thing, Kaitlyn," Ray answered saddened. "You're the *only* reason for me to stick around. I don't want to leave you, but I don't know what else to do."

"Marry me," Kaitlyn suggested.

Ray smiled. "Someday, Kaitlyn, after the Army, we'll get married. We are engaged you know."

"I know *this*," Kaitlyn said. "I just thought *you* forgot."

"I could never forget that, Kait," he replied smiling, and taking her into his arms. "I loved you yesterday. I love you today. I will love you tomorrow. I will love you for the rest of my life."

Kaitlyn closed her eyes and cradled her head into Ray's chest. She squeezed him as tight as she could. "I love you, Ray. I don't want you to go, but I understand this is something you must do, even if *I'm* not happy about it."

"Thanks for understanding, Kait," Ray said, pulling her away from him. "I'll be back," he said, giving her a promised eye.

Kaitlyn and Ray spent the rest of the day together, with Kaitlyn helping him tend to last minute details before they settled into a cuddle on the couch, holding one another in saddened reality.

Kaitlyn arrived home far after curfew, only to be met by her angered parents.

"Where were you, young lady?" Mr. Frost's deep authoritative voice echoed through the house.

"Ray's," Kaitlyn answered meekly.

Jim and Kathryn stood there, waiting for an explanation.

Kaitlyn began to cry and tried to voice out loud that Ray was leaving, but her words came out in broken gasps.

"What?" they questioned. "What about Ray?"

"Leaving ... tomorrow ... Georgia," she was able to get out as tears magnified.

"Oh my," Kathryn said as she changed her disposition and went to comfort her daughter, knowing exactly how she felt.

Jim joined his wife in hugging their daughter, remembering the look on Kathryn's face when he left. All he could do was hug her. He didn't know what to say, and worse yet, Jim couldn't make it all better for his precious little girl.

Chapter Eighteen

Kaitlyn had not slept well the night Ray told her he was leaving "tomorrow". She went to bed with tears, only to wake up with them June 29, 1951. As soon as she had awakened, all Kaitlyn thought about was getting to Ray.

As depressed as Kaitlyn was, she had no choice but to face reality; Ray was leaving, and there was absolutely nothing she could do about it. She wiped the sleep from her eyes, catching her morning tears in a tissue, and dragging her unwilling body to the shower. Strangely, soon after Kaitlyn began her shower, she went into high gear.

Feeling as if *someone* were telling her to race, Kaitlyn began to go through the steps of showering in a speeding motion. This imagined, or unimagined, *inner voice* badgered Kaitlyn to hurry, walking her through the steps of washing her hair, while the whole time the voice yelled at her to go faster, with Kaitlyn's conscious voice doing the same. She quickly lathered her body, only to rinse the suds off as soon as the soap touched her skin. Kaitlyn crossed the finish line when she stepped out from the tub, only to continue with a second race in the same motion as she dressed.

Throwing her wet hair back in a ponytail, she ran downstairs and out the door, not bothering to say good morning — let alone goodbye, and ignored when Kathryn called her name.

Kaitlyn had no intention of eating breakfast or even having tea; her priority was seeing Ray, and her frantic spirit was telling her to get to him as soon as possible. Kaitlyn's quickened walk turned into a desperate run, making it across town in record time.

As she stopped to catch her breath in the middle of Ray's street, Kaitlyn saw a car pulling out from a driveway and saw a figure in the car she thought was Ray. It was. Her heart sunk.

Ray looked at her, then looked away and then turned back towards her in shock, not expecting to see her there. The car came to an abrupt halt, the door swung open, and Ray, still unsure if it was Kaitlyn, got out of the car and started walking towards her, with that walk turning into a run.

Crying and in an emotionally overloaded shaken state, Kaitlyn fell to her knees, realizing he was going to leave without saying goodbye. Cries wailed out from under her bowed head, as she lay against the cold paved road. Ray tried to get her to stand.

As he went to touch her, Kaitlyn backhanded him away, screaming, "How could you?!" as she carried on with the outburst.

"How could I what, Kait?" Ray asked so innocently.

"Leave without saying goodbye," she answered in angered hurt.

"I wasn't, Kait. We were just about to come over to your house. Didn't your mom tell you?"

Kaitlyn tried to pull herself together. "I ran out the door and never said a word," Kaitlyn replied, feeling like a fool, crying and totally out of breath. "I didn't even see my mom this morning, let alone tell her where I was going. She did say something to me, but by that time, I was out the door."

"Oh, honey," Ray replied, embracing her. "I'm sorry I scared you like that. I'd never leave without saying goodbye. I love you," he said while bringing her chin up so their eyes could meet. "I love you, Kait. With all my heart."

Kaitlyn pouted through her tears, "I love you, too," then began to cry out, "don't go! Please, don't go."

"Kaitlyn, you know I have to," he replied, feeling terrible that his decision was ripping her apart. "Honey, I'm sorry, but I have to do this. I have to do this for *me* right now."

Kaitlyn looked up to Ray, continuing to keep a firm grasp of his body to hers.

"I'm going to miss you so much, Kait," he started. "This has been the hardest decision I've ever had to make in my life. And

Kaitlyn, I hate what it's doing to you, but ... I don't know what else to do." Ray lowered his eyes.

"I know, Ray," Kaitlyn replied. "I really do understand, but damn it, what am I going to do without *my* Ray? I can't imagine life without you!"

Ray squeezed Kaitlyn tight. He brought her hand to his heart and said, "Feel this, it's broken."

"This hurts to damn much, Ray," Kaitlyn said, taking his hand to hers, allowing him to feel each thump of her aching heartbeat. "If it hurts this much, it can't be right," she cried out, grabbing him.

Ray coupled Kaitlyn's face into the palm of his hands. With a serious look of love and trust, he confessed his love while staring intensely into her eyes. "I'll be back. I promise, Kait. I love you. I'm just going to be gone for a short time."

"I know," she replied as a tear trickled down her cheek. "I love you too."

"This hurts too much," she said again. "I can't do this. I can't handle this. Go, Ray ... please, just go. Oh, God, I think I'm going to be sick," she cried as she collapsed back to the ground. "Oh, God," she cried out. "Help me. Please, help me. Oh, God, please don't go!"

Ray crouched down beside her and held Kaitlyn, trying to console her as he himself broke into tears. He held Kaitlyn on the pavement for a long time comforting her until she felt a little better. "Come on, honey. Let's get you home."

Ray helped Kaitlyn to the car and cuddled with her in the backseat, as his aunt drove her home. The whole time there, Kaitlyn rested her head into Ray's tranquil chest, trying to emboss in her mind every scent, every breath, and every detail of their last few minutes together.

Ray held her tight, doing the same ... smelling the scent of her hair as he traced his fingers through it, loving her, caressing her, and caring for her.

Kaitlyn's house came in view, and Kaitlyn began sobbing again, once more feeling as if she were going to be sick. "This is killing me, Ray," she confided.

"It's tearing me apart, too, Kait," Ray revealed. "But, everything's going to be okay. Just 'cause I'm leaving, doesn't mean I don't love you. I don't think I could love anyone as much as I love *you*, Kait."

With that, they pulled into the drive, and Ray brought Kaitlyn inside. He thanked Kathryn and Jim for everything they've done and said goodbye to Alex.

Alex was not too happy with Ray for breaking his sister's heart, but he too understood why Ray had to leave. Alex shook Ray's hand and wished him well, telling Ray to remember what he said.

"I do, Alex," Ray replied, giving him a firm word with a look of his eyes and a hold of his shake.

Kathryn, Jim, and Alex left the front corridor, giving Ray and Kaitlyn one last chance to say goodbye.

Ray took Kaitlyn in his arms and held her in sadness. The two confessed their love for one another before breaking out into a soft, longing kiss.

"I got to go, " Ray said quietly.

"I know," Kaitlyn replied. "Don't!"

"Kait, Ray replied. "Please, don't make this harder than it already is."

"You're right," she replied. "I'm sorry."

"I love you, Kait," Ray said one last time before he left.

"I love you, too," Kaitlyn replied, hiding her hurt face in her hands.

He pulled her hands down and asked to see her smile. "I want to see your smile, so I can take it with me."

Kaitlyn smiled, being unable to resist Ray's charm. "I love you, babes," she said, giving him one last hug. "Be safe and take care of you," she was able to say, trying to be brave.

"I love you, too," Ray replied back with a smile and shining cobalt eyes. "Yub yub."

"Yub yub," Kaitlyn said with a crying giggle.

"Goodbye, Kaitlyn," Ray said somberly.

"Don't say goodbye, Ray," she said. "That sounds like it's forever. Let's just say, 'So long for now.'"

"Okay," he said with a shortened smile. "So long for now."

Giving each other one last hug and turning that hug into a handhold, Ray slowly backed away from Kaitlyn until their last fingertips touched. Just as their touch faded away, Ray bowed his head and turned towards the car on his heels. Kaitlyn brought her hands to her mouth, trying not to burst into tears.

Ray situated himself in the car and looked out the window at Kaitlyn with tears falling from his eyes, only to find rest upon his cheeks. He waved and mouthed, "I love you," as they drove away.

Looking out the back window, Ray saw Kaitlyn running after him with her hands out, crying in desperation to keep her one true love from leaving, her attempt — unsuccessful. His car went out of sight. Ray was indeed gone.

Kaitlyn was out of breath and emotionally exhausted she fell to the ground in defeat. She couldn't stop Ray from leaving any more than she could stop her heart from hurting.

After a few moments, Kathryn came running out to her, only to have Kaitlyn run away, telling her mother to "just leave me alone."

Kaitlyn took off in a confused state, running to where she could be alone — the tree. The whole way there she kept asking, "Why," beating herself up senseless to find the answer. Yes, she knew *why* he had to leave, but *why now, why today — why ever?* She was lost and completely dumfounded, not knowing whether to cry, scream, or curl up and die. When Kaitlyn reached the entrance of the park, she entered in a state of confusion and denial, full of pain and excruciating heartache. She didn't know what she was supposed to do with herself. Lost and scared, she approached the tree and collapsed by its trunk — onto the dewed ground, reminding herself to breathe.

With Kaitlyn's legs curled into her chest and her head resting inside her knees, she sat alone in the woods absorbing the pain, the loss, and the feeling as if her whole life had just come crashing down on her. "Happy Independence Day, Ray," she said to herself. "You sure got your independence ... and five days early, too."

As time went by, Kathryn grew more worried and called John to ask if he'd seen Kaitlyn. John told Kathryn that he hadn't but thought that he might know where she was. He offered graciously to help find Kaitlyn, as he was just as worried as she was. He also thought this might be his chance to be Kaitlyn's 'knight in shining armor'.

Ray had told John about their tree and how special it was to both of them. John didn't know its precise location, but he did know its *approximate* one. He drove to Crestview Park, parked, and got out of the car, keeping his eyes and ears open for any sign of Kaitlyn.

He walked towards Sweetheart Lane, still keeping his eyes peeled, and as John approached the wooded area, he began searching left and right, and up and down — not that Kaitlyn would be in the trees, but John was nervous and wasn't exactly thinking straight.

He walked down the lane towards the wooded area and heard a faint cry coming from just beyond the brush. Walking in its direction, John found Kaitlyn hidden away from the world, alone and crying. Unsure of what to say or do, John approached Kaitlyn with a careful step, trying not to scare her with his intrusion. She felt his presence, but ignored his advancing footsteps, until she couldn't ignore them any longer.

John took a seat beside Kaitlyn and didn't say a word. Respectful of Kaitlyn's need to be alone, John stayed with her anyway, knowing *someone* should be with her. They didn't speak, and John didn't try to comfort Kaitlyn with a hug. He just sat down beside the girl he'd always loved and stayed by her side. He spoke without words, letting Kaitlyn know he was there for her — when *she* was ready.

After a long while, Kaitlyn glanced towards John and begged for help with her eyes. She held her arms out in a cry for comfort, finding John's arms reassuring and strong. With her head buried

into his chest and John encouraging her to let it all out, Kaitlyn
went into a full-blown sob, bringing John to tears as well. He hurt
for her.

John quietly spoke, telling Kaitlyn that he hated seeing her like
this and again told her to let it all out, adding that he was there for
her. Kaitlyn did 'let it all out'. John's shirt was covered in
crocodile tears, and it was just a slimy mess. He didn't mind
though. Kaitlyn needed *him*, and John was happy to oblige. After
an hour passed, Kaitlyn's tears had all been cried, and she gazed
up to John and said, "I thought he loved me?"

John looked at Kaitlyn with compassion and love. "He does,
Kaitlyn."

"How do you know," Kaitlyn asked meekly.

John knew Ray loved Kaitlyn because Ray looked at her the
way *John* has always looked at her, but Kaitlyn never noticed. That
is until John said, "I just know," lowering his eyes.

Kaitlyn gazed sidelong at John and felt an eerie sense. For the
first time, she noticed what Allison had talked about. Kaitlyn
didn't run from it though. She kept what she now knew to herself
and even took comfort in it.

John suggested that he take her back to the house, telling
Kaitlyn she could rest at home.

"Kaitlyn," he spoke with concern. "Your mother and father are
worried sick about you. Please ... let me take you home."

Kaitlyn nodded, acknowledging that John was right. "I need to
face reality," she said, with John in agreement.

"Kaitlyn," he called to her. "I'm here for you. I hope you know
that."

"Yeah," she replied as she wiped her face. "I know. And, John
... thank you."

John put his arm around Kaitlyn and walked her to the car. He
opened the door and helped her get situated before getting in
himself.

"John," Kaitlyn said, "I'm really sorry."

"For what?" John replied in question.

"For treating you the way I have," she said. "I'm truly sorry. If it helps matters, I was very proud of you during the inquest. You've really turned out to be a nice, responsible man."

For the first time, John felt proud, and he felt pride for himself, hearing such a compliment from Kaitlyn. It was *her* views of his actions and *her* perceptions of him that drove him bonkers as he vied for her attentions. Now, *she* noticed *him.* And for the first time, John didn't feel like he had to compete for Kaitlyn's care. He realized that all he had to do to get it was to be the *real* John. He liked this new discovery and felt a glimmer of hope that maybe — someday, he'd get his chance to be Kaitlyn's guy.

Arriving home, Kaitlyn invited John to come in with her. She didn't understand why she wanted him to, but felt compelled to ask. John accepted the invitation, then opened the car door for her and led Kaitlyn to the house. As they took one step onto the porch, Jim and Kathryn came out, happy to see their daughter was okay and embraced her in family hug. Kathryn walked Kaitlyn inside, while Jim walked in with John, being sure to thank him for bringing their daughter home.

Kathryn settled Kaitlyn in the living room and offered she and John tea. Kaitlyn curled up on the couch with a throw blanket, and John sat beside, facing her. At first, it was a bit awkward for the two, finding themselves in a strange circumstance, but after awhile, they began to talk.

Kathryn interrupted them when she brought out the tea, and then quickly excused herself to join Jim in the library — probably to go read another one of her sappy romance novels. Kathryn knew Kaitlyn needed someone her own age to talk with, and that when Kaitlyn was ready to let *Mom* help her, she would.

As Kathryn turned to walk away, Kaitlyn told her mother she was sorry.

Kathryn smiled at her daughter with a look that said, "It's okay. I understand more than you know."

Quiet fell in the living room as John and Kaitlyn carefully sipped their tea, trying not to let the hot steam burn their lips. Out of the blue, Kaitlyn broke the silence.

"I feel like dying, John," Kaitlyn confessed. "I wish I was ... dead. That seems like a pretty good option right about now."

John was floored by her comment and wasn't sure how to respond. His mouth dropped, and his eyes widened as thoughts brought him to imagining the world without Kaitlyn in it. He didn't like *that* world.

Kaitlyn could see that John's imagination was going wild with her statement and settled it, letting John know that she felt suicide was a permanent solution to a temporary problem.

"I know this is transitory, John," she soothed his worries. "I just don't like how it feels right now. I know it will get easier in time, but right now, it just hurts so bad that I have no idea what to do and where to be. I feel like I suddenly don't belong anywhere."

Again, John being unaccustomed to such deep conversation, he didn't really know what to say in response. But he did remember a saying he had heard once and decided to share it with Kaitlyn.

"I don't know who wrote this, but I think it fits this situation."

Kaitlyn looked at John in question, asking him to go on with her eyes.

"The saying goes: *'If you love someone, set them free. If they come back to you, it was meant to be'*, or something like that."

Kaitlyn tried to hold back her tears, but couldn't. She reached her arms out in desperation to John as she cried in a whisper, "That's a hard gift ... " She couldn't finish. Her throat filled with exasperating tears, not allowing her to breathe one more syllable.

John took Kaitlyn in his arms and held her. Kaitlyn held onto him in pure fright, then backed away, feeling as if somehow she was cheating on Ray. Putting a bit of distance between them by placing a pillow in her lap, Kaitlyn settled enough to start talking through her feelings. Kaitlyn started out by telling John that she felt like she was dealing with a death, "but no one's died."

"You know," Kaitlyn continued. "It would probably be easier knowing he wasn't around anymore, instead of knowing he's alive and well. And only a few hundred miles away. Damn," she whispered, so her parents wouldn't hear her swear. "This hurts."

John extended his arms, inviting Kaitlyn to find protection in them. Kaitlyn thought briefly about accepting the invitation before giving into her primal needs. She allowed John to be there for her, and John accepted his newfound role with an open heart and a huge *Grinch*-like smile.

John stayed with Kaitlyn until the evening turned to night. Time had come for him to go home and for Kaitlyn to get some rest. Kaitlyn thanked John for his friendship and just said a simple thank you with her eyes and a smile. She thanked John for everything he said, didn't say, did, or didn't do. He knew what the *thanks* was for.

A few days passed, and Kaitlyn continued to stay in a depressed state. She was unwilling to spend time with family and friends, unwilling to go look for a job, and unwilling to live. She hadn't heard a word from Ray, and as each second and each minute passed, Kaitlyn fell into a deeper depression. Feeling sad, angry, unworthy, betrayed and abandoned, Kaitlyn sunk into a world of her own — allowing no one in.

In desperation, Kathryn called John, asking him to come and stay with Kaitlyn while she did some errands. She was concerned for Kaitlyn's well being and didn't think she should be alone. Kathryn knew Alex would not be the right person to leave with Kaitlyn, and she was hopeful that Kaitlyn would open up to John, since she already had the day Ray left.

John rushed right over, almost leaving the receiver dangling from the phone. John felt as if there were nothing he could do, and he hated the fact that he couldn't fix this for Kaitlyn. But John did know he could be there for her, and he did know *that* would mean something in Kaitlyn's eyes. By the time he finished those thoughts, John was at Kaitlyn's front door.

John joined Kaitlyn in the living room, and they sat in silence for what seemed like forever. Noticing a small red book in the magazine rack, John walked over to it and began to strum through its pages. He sat and read quietly to himself and then began to read softly out loud. Kaitlyn didn't let on to John that she was listening until John stopped reading. She asked him to continue.

He recited passages from the book, while Kaitlyn sat listening, absorbing the spoken words into her thoughts and feeling a connection to them. She started to heal, just a little, but it was better than not.

The afternoon rolled around, and John noticed the mailman outside. He offered to get the mail, and Kaitlyn nodded, allowing him to do so. John went out to the mailbox, and there it was — a letter addressed to Kaitlyn.

The *old* John wanted to rip the letter up and never let Kaitlyn know about it, but the *new* John came in and told her what he had. Kaitlyn's eyes lit up as John handed her the letter. She grabbed it and tore it open it as if she were a three-year old child receiving a huge birthday gift. Kaitlyn's eyes smiled as she read the letter; then sank with disappointment. She put the letter down and eyed John, implying that he should read it. John picked it up and read:

"Dear Kait,
I miss you and love you very much. I'm doing okay and it feels good to be back in Georgia. I'll be up in a few weeks to visit before I go to basic training. I love you, Kait, and I wish you were here. I hope you're doing okay. I'll see you soon.
Love Always,
Ray"

"What's so bad about this," John asked.

"It just doesn't have the same tone," Kaitlyn said. "And he didn't put his usual."

"His usual?" John queried.

"Never mind," Kaitlyn said, "It's personal."

"Oh," John replied as if hurt that Kaitlyn felt she couldn't share this one aspect, but sort of relieved she didn't. "You feel better now?" he asked.

"A little," she replied. "I miss him, John."

"I know," he replied, "But moping around the house isn't going to bring him here any faster. Come on, Kaitlyn. Let me take you to The Fountain for lunch and get you out of this house."

Kaitlyn let out a deep sigh and agreed to John's invite, and went upstairs to try and freshen up first.

John waited patiently downstairs and kept busy by reading the letter over and over again. Even though he didn't know the kinds of things Ray would write or say to her, he could tell that the letter was not exactly affectionate.

Kaitlyn came downstairs, looking as good as she was going to. John handed her the letter, which she swiftly put in her pocketbook, and the two headed out the door. A summer's afternoon walk to the teen hang out of Winter's Crest was just what the doctor ordered. Or wasn't it?

Arriving at The Fountain, they bumped into Allison and Bob, and then a few of Kaitlyn's other friends came to say hello. She was bombarded with questions about Ray. "Did you hear from him? When's he coming back? You must really miss him?" came thrashing at her from all directions. Kaitlyn needed to get out of there.

John sensed it was too much for Kaitlyn so he suggested they take a walk in the park. Kaitlyn liked the idea, knowing that she could relax there and be left alone from the invasion of unsettling questions. She knew her friends meant well, but she wasn't prepared for the onslaught.

Although John and Kaitlyn didn't speak much on the way to the park, or at the park for that matter, their non-verbal communications were loud and clear. John was being Kaitlyn's friend. He allowed Kaitlyn to share her feelings without having to hide her true thoughts. And although some of Kaitlyn's true feelings were tough for him to hear, John kept his own turmoil to himself. This was just the beginning.

Kaitlyn's trust grew for John during their short interactions, and she began to see John in a new light. She found that she actually did like the guy and felt him to be a good friend as well. She wondered why she had never seen it before.

Since Kaitlyn didn't feel the need to impress or win John over, she could be herself with him. Kaitlyn took comfort in knowing John was there for her and that he cared about her. John just enjoyed being around Kaitlyn, because being with Kaitlyn in any shape or form was all John had ever truly wanted.

When they went back to Kaitlyn's house, she was feeling better and thanked John again for his friendship, as did Kathryn. She said goodbye and gave him a friendly hug and a kiss on the cheek. John blushed. He smiled and walked away, waving his hand in the air and telling Kaitlyn to call if she needed him.

Kaitlyn went inside and chatted briefly with Kathryn, telling her she was going to write Ray a letter. Kaitlyn went upstairs and propped herself up on the bed while taking out a piece of notepaper, and she began to write.

Kaitlyn told Ray how much she loved him, cared for him, and missed him. She told Ray how much she wished he was with *her*, and that she'd been having a rough time of it. She begged Ray to come *home*, telling him she wanted to marry him and be his wife. She signed it with: "*I loved you yesterday. I love you today. I will love you tomorrow. I will love you for the rest of my life,*" and then signed her nick-name, "*Kait.*" She folded the letter and placed it in a perfume scented envelope, addressing it to the corresponding return address on the letter she had received from him. She went downstairs to put it in the mail pile.

"Is that you, Kaitlyn?" Kathryn called out from the kitchen.

"Yes, Mom," Kaitlyn replied.

"Come join me for some tea," she invited, yet requesting.

"Okay," Kaitlyn agreed while walking towards the kitchen.

Kaitlyn joined her mother at the breakfast table, while Kathryn poured fresh tea in Kaitlyn's now special cup. Not wanting to distract from its flavor with cream and sugar, Kaitlyn liked her tea black, enjoying the aroma and flavor of English Breakfast Tea by itself. Although, sometimes, she liked it with a slice of lemon. She sipped carefully, detecting its too hot temperature and tried cooling it down by blowing on it gently.

"I need to finish my story," Kathryn said, sitting down, thinking a diversion would be good for her daughter.

"About what?" Kaitlyn asked.

"The tea cup. I never did fill you in on the entire story.

"Oh yeah, that's right," Kaitlyn replied, getting situated into a more intrigued listening position.

Kathryn began by reminding Kaitlyn that the teacup originated from the 1800's, with Kaitlyn recalling their first conversation.

"My great, great, great, well you get the idea, grandfather and grandmother were coming to America on a ship from England. Their son, Sebastian, who would be my ... uncle, I suppose ... was with them, too. On their long voyage here, the ship ran into heavy storms and was rocked so hard that people were thrown into the sea."

"Oh my," Kaitlyn replied, while Kathryn agreed with her reaction.

"Sadly, my great," waving her hand in the air expressing multiple 'greats', grandmother Elizabeth was one of those people violently tossed into the sea. My grandfather Maurice tried to throw out a lifeline to her, but his strength was no competition for the high winds and waves. The ship drifted away from Elizabeth as the current carried her out towards the horizon. And with their arms reached out to one another, they stared in agony, screaming out their love for one another before Elizabeth was swallowed by the depths."

Kaitlyn brought her hands to her lips. "Oh, Mom. I can't imagine. This is so sad."

Kathryn nodded and took a moment of composure.

"I didn't know this part until later. But as Maurice was staring out to his soon to be lost wife, he felt as if time stopped. To him, the waves and winds weren't rocking the ship, and all was still, except for his beating heart. It was just Maurice, his wife, and the bond of love between them that existed at that very moment. With their eyes in a locked stare showing fear and love jumbled together, he saw Elizabeth go under. Maurice jerked forward as if to jump in after her, and Sebastian lunged forward and grabbed my grandfather back. My grandfather tried to free himself from my uncle's grip, but Sebastian kept pulling Maurice back and wouldn't let him go. Sebastian knew that if he did, he'd lose his father, too."

"Wow," Kaitlyn replied in a mourning voice. "He truly loved her."

"Yes, he did, Kaitlyn."

"Sebastian wrestled Maurice over to safety and wrapped his arms around his father as he held onto one of the sail's poles for both their lives, knowing Maurice didn't have the emotional or physical strength to hold on — nor the want to. When the storm abruptly ended, just as it had begun, there were thirty-seven survivors, all in shock, all in a state of numbness, and overwhelmed with agonizing grief. Sebastian, Maurice, and the remaining survivors all came to America with a dark cloud over their heads with their hearts broken in two.

"When they docked in New York City, they were able to retrieve what was left of their possessions, but did so in a robotic state. One of Maurice's possessions that survived the trip was a China set. My grandfather fell to his knees as he went to open the box, and he became overwhelmed with emotion when he did. Elizabeth's favorite china was in there, but almost all of it was broken into tiny pieces. He sifted through the rummage with tears rolling down his cheeks to see if any part of the set was salvageable until his eyes made out a recognizable piece. Carefully moving the broken pieces of china away from the shape, he discovered this teacup, and searching further, he found this saucer right below it," Kaitlyn said, pointing to them. "There wasn't a scratch, a nick or anything on either piece. It was almost as if it were a *sign*."

"Oh great," Kaitlyn responded not-too-thrilled with herself. "And then I have to go and chip it. *Sure*, the cup and saucer make it through a storm out at sea, but *no, Kaitlyn* can't even keep it safe in her *own* kitchen!"

Kathryn looked at Kaitlyn with a look that said *stay focused*. The last thing she wanted Kaitlyn to do was to start getting depressed again, or getting upset about the chipped cup for that matter.

"Well," Kathryn continued, trying to ignore her daughter's outburst. "He wrapped up the cup and saucer in his shirt and protected it against all odds, holding on to it as if it were his wife's ashes. And no matter where Maurice lived, he always kept it in a special place. It was a memorial for him and a constant reminder of the love he had lost.

"On his deathbed, Maurice passed the treasured teacup and saucer to Sebastian, who later passed it on to his own children, and so on, and so forth, until it ended up in my mother's cabinet safe and sound."

"Yes," Kaitlyn commented, "I remember seeing it there."

Kathryn nodded.

"Some time over the course of the years, a tradition for 'the passing of the teacup' was born. The cup is supposed to be passed on to your child when something important happens in their life, or in yours. So, when it came time for my mother to pass it to me, she chose the day you were born to be that special day.

"Now, I originally chose your eighteenth birthday to be the day, but decided that remembering your first love should be the special day for you, as you already know."

"I wish you hadn't," Kaitlyn meekly commented. "Look what I've already done to it. Besides, he left."

"Now, Kaitlyn," Kathryn replied. "You knew he was going to leave at some point for the Army or college. Of course, he never expected to have his mother and father both die in a year's time. He'll be back. He's just trying to get his life together. And besides, Ray will always be your first love and those feelings are always worth remembering, they're good feelings."

Kaitlyn knew her mother was right, but still didn't find comfort in it.

"Anyway," Kathryn finished, "so, now, when you have a child, you will decide when the right time is for 'the passing the teacup'."

Kaitlyn understood her mother and now knew the significance more clearly. "That's sad, Mom," Kaitlyn said. "I can't imagine what it was like for Maurice and Sebastian — seeing Elizabeth thrown into the sea like that, knowing she was going to drown and not being able to do anything about it. Gosh, it's terrible!"

"Yes, Kaitlyn, it is," Kathryn replied. "But the part that I haven't shared with you is this. Maurice never married again. He knew that Elizabeth was his one true love, and he never opened up his heart to another woman. He died saying his last words. 'I'm coming for you, Beth.'"

"Was he lonely," Kaitlyn asked.

"From what I understand, he was," she replied. "He spent his whole life reliving the last seconds with Elizabeth, feeling as if he too were drowning. He could have found a lifeline with someone else's love, but chose not to. He grew to be a cold, heartless, angry old man. Now you tell me? Do you see any smiles on his face?"

Kaitlyn shook her head.

"One of the reasons I told you this story is that we can have the love of our life and there's no guarantee that they're going to be with us for the rest of our lives. And if things don't work out with Ray for some reason, then it's okay to love again. Look what happened to my grandfather. He didn't allow himself to open his heart to anyone else, and he lived a lonely, closed-off life. He just existed, Kaitlyn, going through the motions of living. Do you think that Elizabeth would have wanted him to be unhappy? I think not. Just keep things in perspective, Kaitlyn. If things do not work out for you two for some reason, it's not the end of the world. It just means that it wasn't meant to be. And, honey, no matter how much in love you are with Ray, there's never a guarantee. Look at his parents. They died in the prime of their lives. Do you think they ever thought that would happen? Were they guaranteed it wouldn't?"

Kaitlyn knew her mother meant well. Nonetheless, she wasn't too thrilled with hearing there was a possibility she and Ray wouldn't work out. Kathryn wasn't telling her that, but the mere thought of it drove Kaitlyn over the edge. Having heard enough of her mother's wisdom, Kaitlyn told her she was tired and was going to take a nap. She wanted to avoid the 'no guarantee' rule as fast as she could. It wasn't a place she wanted her thoughts to visit — not now — not ever.

Kaitlyn dutifully thanked her mother for sharing the story with her and promised to give some thought to what she said, but had no such intentions. She retired to her room for an afternoon slumber, trying to put every word Kathryn had just said out of her mind, but she couldn't.

Kaitlyn wrestled with swarming thoughts about she and Ray never being together, until her mind had exhausted all avenues.

Chapter Nineteen

Kaitlyn was able to bring herself around the following day. Having heard from Ray helped to brighten her spirits, and even though she missed him terribly, she felt she could at least function again.

She and John had begun to spend a lot of time together, hanging out with Bob and Allison at The Fountain, but purely on a friendship basis. Seeing Allison with Bob so much made Kaitlyn understand how it was for Allison when she and Ray were inseparable. Kaitlyn apologized, knowing how it felt to have the 'tables turned'.

It was strange for Kaitlyn to spend time with her friends. Even though Kaitlyn did enjoy her time with friends, she always felt like something or *someone* was amiss. She tried to move on and forget about how much pain she was in from missing Ray, but found that hard to do. Subconsciously, Kaitlyn created a pretend world to live in — one *she* could face every day.

Sure, she would laugh at good jokes and dance with John, Bob, and Allison. She would even get into deep conversations with her new clique, but Ray was always in the back of her mind. She couldn't shake her feelings, no matter how hard she tried nor how good of an actress she was. She couldn't fool anyone — not even herself.

Somehow, she made it through each day, remembering to breathe, remembering to wake up each morning and put one foot in front of the other. But it was all an act   an existence.

A week had gone by, and the time for Ray's visit moved closer. Kaitlyn was excited, and she began to act like the *old* Kaitlyn again.

She and John had become close friends by this time. They shared their thoughts, their dreams and their deepest, darkest secrets with one another — all but one. Although their relationship was strictly platonic, John was in his glory having Kaitlyn by his side, and Kaitlyn enjoyed having someone, *anyone* around that loved her.

When John wasn't with Kaitlyn, he was working down at the sawmill on the outskirts of town earning a decent wage for his age. This particular job was not what John had in mind for a career. It was a part-time gig to help him save for college come fall.

Kaitlyn knew that she too should get a job and knew she could have had one at Daddy's bank anytime she wanted. Actually, Kaitlyn had been expected to start work there when she was more stable emotionally. It was a comfort for her knowing she had a job at any time she wanted, but Kaitlyn wasn't ready to commit to anything. Heck, she wasn't even sure what she wanted to do with her life. The only thing Kaitlyn knew was that she loved Ray. She wanted to be his wife, bare his children, and be by his side for the rest of their lives.

Three weeks before Ray was to arrive, Kaitlyn's dreams all but died. Hoping she'd have one more letter from Ray before his visit, Kaitlyn fetched the mail with hope in her eyes and in her heart. A huge smile came to her face when she recognized the handwriting on an envelope addressed to her. Excited and feeling on top of the world, Kaitlyn rushed inside, simultaneously ripping the letter open.

A blood-curdling scream echoed through the Frost's house, and a thump to the floor sounded. Kathryn rushed from the kitchen to find her daughter in an uncontrollable crying and angered rage.

"What is it?" Kathryn bellowed scared out of her mind — not sure what to do or how to help, or what happened.

"Oh my God...Oh my God...Oh my God," Kaitlyn wailed over and over again, curled up, rocking back and forth on the floor and pounding her fists on the hardwood floors, with the letter as her target.

When Kathryn tried to get near Kaitlyn, in an effort to help her daughter, or find out how to help her, Kaitlyn shooed her away. Continuing to rock back and forth, Kaitlyn brought her "Oh my God" to an "I can't believe this. This isn't happening!"

Scared for her daughter and not knowing what to do, Kathryn called John at work, frantically crying into the phone. "Something happened ... She got a letter ... Please help..."

John not only heard the fright in Kathryn's voice, he felt it. Urgently explaining the situation to his boss, John left work immediately and high-tailed it over to The Frosts, finding Kaitlyn still in the same position.

Just as John arrived, Alex came in, seeing all. "That bastard!" he yelled. "What'd he do now?"

Kathryn, appalled at her son's language, reprimanded Alex. "Watch your mouth, young man."

"I'm sorry, Mom," Alex replied. "But he is a bastard! That's it. I've had it. Kaitlyn, I forbid a relationship with Ray. I forbid you to talk to him, see him ... *anything* with him!"

Kaitlyn snappishly stood up and stared Alex down with a look that made him feel as if knives were being stabbed into his eyes. Shaking, crying and angrily, Kaitlyn threw the letter at Alex. "Ray's already seen to that," she hollered and took off running to her room in a heart-wrenching cry.

Kathryn looked to John, and with her eyes, instructed him to get upstairs with Kaitlyn.

Alex picked up the note that had fallen to the floor, opened it, and began to read. Kathryn looked over Alex's shoulder and then boldly took it from him. They both sharply glared in each other's direction. "Oh-my-God," they slowly said in whispered unison.

Looking at the note again, they re-read it to make sure what they were reading was for real.

Dear Kait,

I received your letter and I have been doing a lot of thinking. With everything I want to do in my life, it wouldn't be fair to you or me to continue on with our relationship. I want to see the world and build an empire. I don't want to live in Winter's Crest and settle down, not having the chance to see my many dreams come true. I'd be miserable, and I'd make a terrible husband, as I would always be thinking about what opportunities I've missed out on. I do love you, Kait. I love you so much that I have to let you go.

You'd be happy living in Winter's Crest, raising a family and settling down; I wouldn't. The more I think about it, the more I realize that we both want different things, and our relationship doesn't fit into that equation. I will not be coming back to Winter's Crest and have no plans to in the future. I want you to be happy, and I want you to have the chance to have your dreams come true. I'm not the right guy to help make that happen. I'm sorry.

I loved you yesterday. I love you today. I will love you tomorrow. I will love you for the rest of my life, from afar.

Loving You Enough To Let You Go,

Ray"

Kathryn and Alex both shook their heads in disbelief.

"You'd better go show John," Kathryn told Alex. "I'm going to call your father."

Alex went upstairs and caught John's attention through Kaitlyn's opened door. John stepped out into the hallway and read the letter quietly. His mouth dropped as he too shook his head in disbelief.

John had a mix of emotions. He felt terrible for Kaitlyn, knowing how much in love she was with Ray. But on the other hand, Ray was now out of the picture, leaving the door wide open for *him*. John was torn between slyly rubbing his hands together while devising a plan to be Kaitlyn's 'knight in shining armor' or just being a good friend and giving Kaitlyn 'a shoulder to cry on'.

Kaitlyn stayed in her room for the remainder of the day and into the night, with John by her side trying to comfort her, with little success. His actions were appreciated though, and not only by Kaitlyn, but also by Mr. and Mrs. Frost. Eventually, it came time for John to leave, doing so against his heartstring's pull.

The sun still came up the next day, and the clock hands still moved in time as Kaitlyn opened her eyes to meet the day. It was hot outside, and the sun shone bright, but to Kaitlyn, her welcoming of the day was dimmed and gloomy. It may have been eighty degrees, but Kaitlyn's heart was stone cold. She was angry. No, she was beyond anger. She didn't know what she was, but whatever it was that she was, that is what she was.

In a world of confusion and despair, Kaitlyn got out of bed, taking her frustration out on the covers and violently throwing them aside — the same way she felt Ray had treated her. She couldn't understand how one day Ray was loving her and the next, made her feel like an interruption to his life — a bother and a waste of his time, all in one breath.

She was too angry to go back over the previous conversations they'd had. All she wanted to do was figure out what was going on and more importantly — *why*. The more Kaitlyn thought about the answer, the more she didn't have one, deciding to go directly to the source.

Kaitlyn went to the phone and began dialing Ray's number. Her hands shook, and her body quivered. Ray answered.

Breaking out into a painful cry, Kaitlyn yelled, "How could you do this to me?!"

Ray swallowed his nerves back down his throat. "Kait," he said. "I will always love you, but I can't be with you or near you right now ... or ever."

"What?!" Kaitlyn replied, and then thought, "What am I supposed to do with *that* answer?"

"Kait," Ray said. "I want you to forget about me and go on with your life. I'm not coming back, Kait. I'm sorry, but it's for the best."

"The best for *whom*?!" Kaitlyn questioned, knowing the answer.

"For me," Ray replied meekly. "I love you, Kait. I'm sorry, but it's over."

"What happened to forever?" Kaitlyn cried in a last attempt to save the relationship with her first love. "What happened to us? What did I do? What did I say? What did I do wrong?"

"Nothing," he said. "You did nothing wrong. I'm sorry for hurting you. Please, just forget about me. It's time to move on."

Kaitlyn hung up the phone after hearing the reality of her situation. It *was* time to move on, but she didn't know how. She didn't want to move on without Ray, but knew she had no choice. Ray had made *that* perfectly clear.

Deciding to shower and let the sound of running water drown her cries, Kaitlyn headed for the bathroom. With tears clouding her once shining face, Kaitlyn undressed in front of the mirror, studying her body and tracing her fingers over her aching skin. Placing her hands on her navel, Kaitlyn looked up, just as a teardrop fell to her cheek. She wiped the tears away and had a good long talk with herself. Staring at her reflection, she knew what she had to do.

Now, don't take this wrong. Kaitlyn was hurt, saddened, depressed and angered, but she knew she had to move on, and she now knew *for sure* there was no hope of Ray ever coming back.

Putting on a cheerful face for family, Kaitlyn went downstairs, shocking her mother and Alex as she sat down for breakfast.

Kathryn greeted her. "Hi, honey," but did so in a questioning, surprised way.

"About time you came out of that room, " Alex said.

Kaitlyn just glared and smiled. "I love you, too, Alex."

Alex smirked back in her direction, realizing his cover for being a bratty kid, didn't cover up the fact he was showing concern; he'd been caught.

Kaitlyn was uncharacteristically talkative during breakfast. She talked about moving on and getting her life straightened out. She talked about how she didn't want to end up alone for the rest of her life and how it was time to start venturing out, looking for the next love of her life.

"Hmm, maybe I'll give John a try," she said sarcastically, yet half meaning it. "I don't want to end up like Grandfather Maurice."

Alex looked at Kathryn at the same time Kathryn looked at him — both thinking Kaitlyn had lost her mind. Alex mouthed to his mother, "Kaitlyn and John?" as he furled his brow. Kathryn raised her eyebrows and scrunched her shoulders with an *I have no idea where that came from* look.

"Yes," Kaitlyn said, thinking out loud. "I *will* give John a try. He's matured, and he's turned into a nice young man. Besides that, he loves me, and it's nice to be loved."

Kathryn shook her head. "Kaitlyn, don't you think you're rushing it a bit? Sure, John is a nice young man, but you haven't even begun to get over Ray."

"Well, Mom," Kaitlyn began with her newfound sense of strength, "Ray's not coming back. He has no plans to come back. He told me to forget about him, so I will do him that last honor."

With that, Kaitlyn stood up, took her dishes to the sink and left the house, and told her mother she was going to visit John.

Mrs. Frost tried to stop her, but there was no stopping Kaitlyn; she had gone into some kind of survival mode. Her mother figured if this is what Kaitlyn needed to do to get through this horrible time in her life, then she should allow her to do it. Even if it broke her heart to see Kaitlyn ignore and bury her pain. "This will come back to haunt her," Kathryn thought, being sure to make a note of talking to Kaitlyn later.

Boy, was John surprised to see Kaitlyn on his doorstep so early in the day. Not that he minded, but he was shocked, nonetheless.

"John," Kaitlyn said. "Ray told me to forget about him and move on with my life. So that's what I'm doing. Want to go to the park with me?"

"Sure," John said jumping at his chance. "You want to drive there or walk?" he asked.

"Lets' walk," she replied, grabbing his hand as John hopped, trying to finish getting one of his shoes on.

With shoes in place, John's eyes grew wide. "Wow, Kaitlyn's holding my hand," he thought. "Whatever brought this on ... I like it." He was careful not to show too much excitement and only smiled gently at Kaitlyn. She smiled back.

"You love me, don't you?" Kaitlyn asked matter-of-factly.

John looked away and looked down, only to look up to the sky asking if this was for real. Looking back down to Kaitlyn, he grinned childishly and said, "Yes, Kaitlyn. I've always loved you. Ever since we were five years old."

Kaitlyn half-smiled. "I think I love you, too, or ... well, I think I could fall in love with you. You're a good person. You're kind to me. You've never hurt me personally and if you had or will, it wouldn't be intentional. Yeah," she said trying to convince herself, "I guess I've always loved you and just didn't know it."

John couldn't believe his ears. "Kaitlyn loves me?" he thought. "No, this can't be real," he questioned himself, literally pinching his forearm.

"You ever made love before, John?" Kaitlyn asked quite out of the blue and quite bluntly.

John swallowed his disbelief in Kaitlyn's question, answering it with a shaking of the head, looking down, like he wasn't a man because he was still a virgin.

"Come on!" Kaitlyn called, pulling on his hand as they approached the park's entrance. "I'll race you to The Lane."

Kaitlyn and John raced towards The Lane and picked back up on their walk. Once they reached the trail, Kaitlyn took a hold of John's hand again.

John wasn't sure how to take Kaitlyn's behavior and felt that somehow, someone had taken over her. But, he enjoyed Kaitlyn's affections and wasn't going to argue with her, especially when she was in this type of mood.

"Come with me," Kaitlyn demanded, and John followed her directions like a lost schoolboy.

She brought him to the opened grass area, hidden behind the trees and brush. John questioned Kaitlyn's actions, but that didn't stop him from enjoying the situation she had put him in. Kaitlyn sat down and patted her hand on the grass next to her, signaling for John to sit. He did so, and they sat together viewing the blossomed trees, watching the birds fly by, and enjoying the sun's warming rays in silence.

Suddenly, Kaitlyn leaned into John and kissed him flat on the lips. John didn't have time to respond back, leaving his lips straight — but his eyes *popped* out of his head.

"What was that for?" John asked, not complaining.

I just wanted to see what it was like kissing you, John," she replied, surprising him with another. This time he could respond.

As she planted her lips on his, John grabbed Kaitlyn around her back and brought her close to him, and with eighteen years of build up coming through, his responding kisses were passionately powerful and sensual, leaving Kaitlyn spellbound.

It felt *so* good to Kaitlyn having *someone* hold her, play with her and kiss her again, that Kaitlyn found herself escaping into the reality of John, fantasizing she was with Ray.

"What are you doing?" he asked excited, out of breath and scared all at once.

"I want to see what it's like," she replied innocently. John just said, "Oh," while his mind was saying, "Oh, baby."

What else could he say? He had been dreaming of this forever.

"Relax, John," Kaitlyn said, then nodded and opened her eyes wide asking if she could continue.

He, of course, nodded with eager want.

Kaitlyn knew she was with John, but the line between reality and fantasy was a bit blurred for her. It felt so good for her to have someone touch her, hold her, and love her, that she was able to escape *her* reality even more, bringing a sense of subconscious completed revenge to Ray.

Kaitlyn was delighted. She knew what she had just done, and knew it wasn't with Ray. The thing is, is that she liked it. She now knew that she could have the same kind of enjoyment and love

311

from someone else, even if she didn't feel as strongly about the other person. Regardless of Kaitlyn's reasons and choice, she loved it, she needed it, and she just plain wanted it.

John, on the other hand, sat bewildered, wondering what the heck just happened — exuberant, but confused, too.

After the reality of what had just occurred set in, the two decided to leave, making a small detour to The Fountain before going home.

John brought Kaitlyn to her front porch, thanking her for a wonderful day. He kissed Kaitlyn and hugged her, then set a date for the following day. With a click of the heels, John turned and walked home, a little lighter on his feet.

Kaitlyn continued to accept John's invitations, and after a couple weeks of fun and frolicking, Kaitlyn and John had become a real couple. Kaitlyn was no longer stuck on Ray, even though she had just buried her feelings deep inside and threw away the key. She was happy with John, and he was flabbergasted being with her. Things were going well. Things were going *very* well indeed.

Bob and Allison were still hot and heavy, with plans to marry in the future, and John and Kaitlyn were both happy together. Kaitlyn had again found peace in her heart. She enjoyed spending time with John, and he treated her like a queen. Life was good.

Two days before the end of August, the day Ray was originally scheduled to visit, Kaitlyn surprised John at work with a picnic lunch. She waited a few moments for his scheduled lunchtime, and then the two sat under an old Oak tree on a blanket to eat. Kaitlyn leaned into John and kissed him, right after he had taken a bite of his sandwich. John smiled, trying not to show the chewed food in his mouth. Kaitlyn stared at him with a hurt love before announcing she was pregnant, a tear escaping her eye. John choked and spit his food all over her, before giving her a reassuring hug. "That's wonderful news ... I think."

"No it's not, John," Kaitlyn insisted. "I'm not married. I'm the bank president's daughter, and I'm having a baby whether I want to or not."

John hugged her again. "It'll be okay, Kaitlyn. Trust me, it'll be okay. Listen we'll work this out together."

Kaitlyn and John made plans to meet at The Fountain after he got off of work, doing so precisely at 5:15 p.m. While discussing the issues at hand and enjoying their pops, John smiled incessantly.

"What are you smiling about?" Kaitlyn asked somewhat perturbed. This isn't something to smile about!"

"I love you, Kait," John replied. "Come with me."

Kaitlyn and John left The Fountain and headed towards Crestview Park. As they reached the arced entrance, John bent down on one knee and asked Kaitlyn for her hand in marriage.

Kaitlyn smiled, appreciating the gesture, but knew what she had to do. As emotions battled it out in her mind and heart, Kaitlyn's eyes directed towards her fourth left finger. Ray's pre-engagement ring was there, and tears fell from Kaitlyn's face as she removed Ray's ring. Slipping the ring into her purse and extending her hand to John, he placed a *true* engagement ring on her finger. John and Kaitlyn were now officially engaged, with baby in tow.

Asking his boss for an advance in salary, John was able to leave work early to stop by the local jewelers. Not having a wealth of money, he did find a suitable ring that was good enough for his Kaitlyn. Although the circumstances called for marriage to Kaitlyn sooner than he would have ever imagined, John was in his glory. He had Kaitlyn, and he would soon be her guy, and she — his gal, forever.

After taking a brief walk to let things sink in, Kaitlyn went home with John and made the announcement to her parents together. In a matter of fact way, Kaitlyn confessed their love and explained that even though the engagement was sudden, they wanted to marry in two weeks.

"What? Are you pregnant?" Jim demanded to know, not liking the answer.

"What am I supposed to say, Kaitlyn?" he asked.

"How 'bout, 'Welcome to the family'," she replied meekly.

Jim extended his hand to John, and even though he wasn't too thrilled with the situation that brought this to a quick engagement and marriage, he was thankful Kaitlyn was with John. He knew she'd be well taken care of.

"We need to go tell John's parents," Kaitlyn said. "I'm sorry if I've disappointed you two, but I *am* happy, and we're doing the *right* thing."

"I know," Kathryn agreed sympathetically, ready to break out in tears. Jim didn't reply.

Kaitlyn and John left to go to his house. They broke the news to his parents in a similar fashion and received a comparable reaction. John's parents knew how much their son loved Kaitlyn, and they knew John was happy. It was a little easier for them to take the news than it was for Kaitlyn's parents. Kathryn and Jim knew John was a rebound flame. They also knew they couldn't have their daughter walking around town with an illegitimate child. Societal pressures gave them no choice but to bless the impending marriage.

There was one last thing Kaitlyn had to do. Kaitlyn told John she needed to take care of something and left for her home. Arriving there, Kaitlyn went up to her room and wrote Ray one last letter.

Kaitlyn told Ray almost everything. She told him how he made her feel and how much he had hurt her. She told him what she thought of him, calling him some *not so nice* names, and she claimed that she no longer needed him, wanted him, and could live without him.

"I am returning your ring. Even though we will never be together or probably ever see each other again, I love you, and I will continue to love you for the rest of my life and hate every minute of it. Kait."

She enclosed the ring in the envelope by wrapping it inside the note with a piece of tape holding the ring in place. Kaitlyn didn't

314

tell Ray about she and John, figuring it was none of his business. She did feel some closure though. Kaitlyn spoke the final word, finally feeling back in control.

"Goodbye, Ray," Kaitlyn whispered softly as she dropped the letter into the mailbox on the way back to John's house. "I'll always hate loving you."

*   *   *

That was Kaitlyn's last contact with Ray, until today.

Kaitlyn sat back quietly on the couch with a painful smile. She placed the Valentine's Day card back into the box and let out a whimper as she pulled the letter out from her pocketbook. Kaitlyn decided to have one last cup of tea before evening's end, and with the letter held securely in her hands, Kaitlyn went into the kitchen.

Placing the now worn envelope on the kitchen table, she put a tea bag in her special cup and waited for the water to boil. Her eyes trailed in the direction of the letter as her frightened anticipation grew.

When the water came to a boil, she poured the tea and went out to the porch, being sure to take the tea and note with her. Placing the cup on the table beside her and resting the letter in her lap, Kaitlyn sat back in the rocking chair and let out a deep breath.

"You can do this, Kaitlyn," she said, convincing herself. "Yes, I can," she confirmed, the letter now in front of her. The moonlight danced through the trees of her front yard as the stamp echoed its light. It was time.

As the crickets played their songs of a summer's eve, Kaitlyn unsealed the envelope with caution and slipped out the crinkled letter. Unfolding the page and bringing Ray's handwriting to plain view, Kaitlyn simply read:

"Dear Kait,

Please join me at The Fountain, June twenty-seventh, 2000 at three o'clock. We need to talk.

Ray"

*   *   *

The woman brought her fingers to her mouth as a tear rolled down her cheek. An eerie déjà vu encapsulated her, leaving her to feel even more vulnerable on that beautiful June evening in the year 2000.

Chapter Twenty

*   *   *

Mom called me shortly after opening the letter. She was happy, scared, sad, confused, and everything in between. Recalling her time with Ray had taken its toll, but she was happy to find out he was in town — scared he wanted to see her though.

Mom read the short note to me and commented. "I don't know what to do, Rose," before she paused and in a faint whisper, said, "Yes I do."

I simply told Mom to do what she felt was best.

Her reply: "I still love him."

I simply told her I knew.

I'm working at my mom's house today packing up her things in the attic and cleaning out the many boxes of treasures she'd saved over the years. Mom was quite the 'packrat'.

I've had many unanswered questions since Mom and I chatted the day she received Ray's letter, and I finally have my answers. The reason I say 'finally' is because it feels like I've been trying to put together a puzzle with a few missing pieces.

Today though, a year later, I came across Mom's meticulously kept diary. When I glanced at it, it didn't seem like it had been packed away for years. The diary looked like it had been shaken of its dust a few times. Intrigued, I opened it, and turned to the last few pages, noticing the entry dates.

All the intricate details were there as if they'd been wrapped up in a bow and placed on my lap as a gift. I sat quietly and read her most recent excerpts. The first one dated June 26, 2000.

*   *   *

Kaitlyn's Diary

June 26, 2000

I never received a reply from the last letter I sent to Ray, and I haven't seen nor heard from him since my last phone call. Not until today that is, and after all these years. I still can't believe it.

There's always been a place in my heart for Ray, and I've never stopped loving him. I just hated loving him.

I've often pondered about Ray. I've wondered what he looks like and how his life's been. I've questioned what it would've been like if he and I had married.

I want to see him, but I'm scared. So here I sit, curled up on my bed like I did when I was young, pen in hand, writing and sorting out what I want to do.

Oh, I wish there were an easy answer.

Am I ready to see Ray again? Am I ready to open those old wounds? Can I handle opening those wounds as well as opening all those familiar feelings? Well, I just did that today, didn't I?

I'm frightened. Here I am, sixty-eight years old and feeling like a schoolgirl. What should I wear? Will he still think that I'm beautiful? Does he still love me? That's the big question, the real big question. Why do I care so much? I'm talking like I'm going to accept his invitation.

Think, Kaitlyn … think!

My heart is racing with anticipation. My stomach is in my throat ready to explode. My heart aches. Everything's come back to me: the love, the sharing, the words exchanged — the words never exchanged. The pain he has caused me, and the hurt I continue to carry with me. I remember all the feelings as if it were fifty years ago right now! I was so much in love with Ray, and I guess, I still am. No, I don't guess — I know I'm still in love with him.

I have questions. Some I know the answers to, but others have never been explained. Why does he want to see me? Is he ill? Is he coming to peace with me, an old love? Does he miss me? Okay, that's a little vain. It was always about what I thought or my thinking that Ray's life revolved around me. I see that now. Maybe that is why he left me. Maybe, I was always thinking of me, and not giving him the right attention — or the choice. No, I admit I was a tad vain, and I admit that I made everything revolve around me, but Ray never gave me the chance to find out what it was that made him leave, especially the way he did. He never gave me any closure. He never said goodbye — well, not to my face.

Wow, it's been fifty years since I've seen my Ray. What am I doing calling him 'my Ray'? He was only 'my Ray' for a short time.

First, I want to know what happened, and then I want to know everything about him. I want to know what he's done with his life — whether he married, whether he succeeded with his dreams. I want to see if my pain was worth it.

Oh gees, there I go again.

I can't wait to see what he looks, feels, and smells like. I wonder if it will be the same as it was back then. Oh listen to me. This is unbelievable. I just can't believe I'm going to see Ray again.

From just re-reading my sentence, it looks like I've made my decision. Yes, I will go and see Ray.

Breathe, Kaitlyn. Breathe.

I've had a good life. I married someone who became a good friend to me first, and then I fell in love with him as time went on. I don't want to say that I settled for anything, because I didn't. John was a wonderful husband who treated me well. He was a terrific father, and he supported his family with love and pride. John set a good example for Rose, and I was extremely proud of him.

I lost John a little over a year ago to cancer. He was a strong man, and I watched him whither away to a skeleton of himself. I was there every minute suffering through the chemotherapy and radiation with him, the endless surgeries, and the long nights, as if I were going through it myself.

The night had come when it was time for John to go Home. I held him in my arms as we curled up in our bed and read passages from the book that Ray and I once held so sacred. I read this verse:

'I see the light. It's calling me. It warms my heart and fills my soul.
A time to live ... a time to die ... pain dispersing ... peace.'

I gazed into my husband's eyes and told him that I loved him enough to let him go. He looked at me, smiled, whispered, 'I love you,' and went to be with

God. I held John and cried. Not so much because he was gone, but because he was finally at peace. No one deserved the agony he went through trying to survive. His body had had enough. Although I have not had John with me physically, he's been with me in spirit, and that to me has been a great comfort.

John and I had held a small private wedding ceremony two weeks after our engagement. It was quick, and yes, rumors flew all over Winter's Crest, but people were soon forgiving.

John was a good friend to me when I felt like the world was ending. He knew I was devastated from the break up with Ray, yet he still asked for my hand in marriage knowing that the baby wasn't his. How could it have been? We never made love until months after we were married. John and I never had a baby between us, but he raised Rose as his own. And whether he planted the seed or not, John was and always will be her father.

John knew of my feelings for Ray, and he allowed me to work through them. He gave me a shoulder to lean on, cry to if I needed, and gave me both quiet and unspoken advice.

John and I up-kept Jaycee and Nicks' graves after Ray had left, and I still tend to them. John, not only finished his community service, but also kept on going after his time was served. Later, he founded a youth center for children and teens to go to, keeping them out of trouble. He also gave lectures all over the country on drinking and driving, with many of the lectures given when he went out of town on business trips for Crestline Insurance Company.

At first, John just worked for Crestline as a representative, but as time went on, he was promoted into management, and eventually, he ended up taking over proprietorship when the first owners retired.

One thing about John that I admired the most was that he kept his promise to Jaycee. Except for that misfortunate night at the Valentine's Dance, John never drank a drop of alcohol. I could count on him, trust him, and he was a man of his word. He really did turn out to be a wonderful man and father. I was proud to be his wife.

He was there for me when my mother was dealing with her first bout of Breast Cancer, and he was there for me when she died twenty years later from the same disease. He also gave me a shoulder to cry on when my father passed away a few years later.

We never knew what Dad died from, but Alex, John, and I suspect he died from a broken heart. Even in their old age, my parents shared their secret smiles and loving glances. My mother and father were truly in love. Oh, how I admired them.

Alex ended up serving proudly in The Korean War. It was a difficult time in all of our lives, as we worried about his safety. But we were fortunate enough to have him come home. War did change Alex, not only emotionally, but physically as well. He may have lost his left leg overseas, but he didn't lose his fighting spirit, although it was lost for a few months upon his homecoming.

When Alex came home from the war, he was greeted with a hero's welcome. He had earned the same caliber of respect my father had had, which was something he had always strived for. We were all proud of Alex, and still are.

After Alex served, he worked as an apprentice for my husband, and since John's death, he has taken over the business. He ended up marrying Amy, his date from the 1951 Valentine's dance, upon his return to the states, and they've been married for over forty years now. And they, as well as their grown children, now run the family insurance business.

Oh boy, I wonder what Alex is going to think of *this*.

You know, I miss John, but I wouldn't want him back in this life suffering the way he did. I have him in my thoughts, my memories, and I hold him dear to my heart every day. I thank the Lord each day for allowing me to have had John in my life and for having him love me.

Our marriage was not perfect by any means. We had some real tough spots, but somehow we muddled through. John was my security in this world — my one true constant.

Even though I've had a happy life, there's always been a part of my heart closed off to anyone — except for Ray. It's been as if I've kept a vacancy sign hanging outside my door, just in case one day Ray would want to fill it. The thing is though, I'm not sure if I want him to. But then again — hmm… Oh, I just don't know. Maybe he doesn't even want me back. Maybe he's come to break my heart again. Oh, God, what if he's dying?

Stop it, Kaitlyn. Stop.

The scent of white carnations, the beauty of yellow roses and their divine scent, songs, and just everyday things always bring Ray to the forefront of my mind, but I just push them down to where they belong. The one ongoing reminder of Ray is every morning when I have my tea. The chip on the rim stares back at me as I take my first sip, continuing to do so until the last drop reaches my lips. Usually, I'd just push those thoughts right back to where they came from, buried away and locked up with a key. I couldn't do that today — not with Ray's handwriting staring at me.

I don't think I ever told John the story behind the chip in the cup. No, I don't believe I ever did.

You know, that's another thing, what about John? How would John feel about me meeting up with Ray after all these years? I believe he'd be pleased knowing I had the chance to find out what happened, and he'd probably be disappointed with me if I didn't find out.

I wish I could ask you, John.

Part of me really wants to see Ray. The other part is, well — apprehensive. Part of me wants revenge, wants to stand him up. Part of me wants to hurt him as he hurt me. It's almost as if I feel like here's my chance to get back at him — somehow even the score. Oh this is crazy! We're two adults now, having lived the majority of our lives.

I can do this. I really can.

Well, here I am in my room staring at my closet door as I did so long ago. Same thoughts, same feelings, same 'what am I going to wear'.

I am still attractive, although some of the beauty has faded. Regardless, I'm still a reflection of my younger self. My hair is now frosted with silver, and the supple skin I once had is now withered in time. My eyes though, they still have that glow, and inside this wrinkly old body is that eighteen year old girl — full of hopes and dreams.

I enjoy being sixty-eight. I may not have the bounce of a young lady, but I'm in charge of my life. I know who I am, and I'm at a point in life where I have no problem discussing my views. I'm not worried what people say or think of me either.

With Ray on the other hand, I'm eighteen years old. And since things were never settled, it feels like we would be starting from where we left off.

I opened the closet door and searched. I came across the old dress my Grandma had made for me that I wore my first day of twelfth grade, sealed in a plastic dress-cover. I tried it on for old time's sakes, but knew I couldn't wear it. Heck, it wouldn't even go past my shoulders. I couldn't resist giving it a try though.

I searched further and found a nice rayon pantsuit. Of course, it was black, my favorite color — although, over the years the reasons have changed — for instance: black is slimming. I tried it on and found it to be the perfect outfit, casual, yet a tad alluring. It speaks maturity, wisdom, class, and seduction all in the same unspoken sentence. I've decided to wear the pantsuit with my black heels. Now it's just a matter of waiting for tomorrow to come.

Hmm, I wonder if I should wear a girdle with it.

I wonder what life would have been like had I married Ray, had he not hurt me, had he not left me. Then though, I never would have had the chance to get to know John and have a comfortable life with him. Still, I wonder ...

Well, tomorrow's the big day, the day I get my answers, the day I am reunited with Ray, the day I hope Ray will look me in the eyes and say, 'I am so sorry!'

It's off to bed for me for some beauty rest. I will tell you all about it in a few days. Oh boy, I knew it would happen some day. I'm just not so sure I'm ready for that day to be tomorrow.

June 30, 2000

The day came whether I was ready for it or not. It arrived with soft summer breezes, and the sun shone through the scattered clouds, adding a glimpse of hope. It was a day for fresh beginnings.

I woke up and began my preparations for meeting Ray for lunch. I paced back and forth, the way Ray and I had done when we waited for his father's arrival home. My stomach was full of 'butterflies', and my heart was full of anticipation. The minutes seemed to drift by ever so slowly, making the hour of noon seem so far away.

I decided to look through 'our book', which had become John's and my book also. I hadn't picked it up since John's passing, but for some reason, I felt compelled to read it. As I settled in a cozy chair, sipping hot English Breakfast

Tea from my wonderful chipped cup, I thumbed through the pages to see what saying I wanted to read. To my surprise, I came across a handwritten note, tucked within the pages, written by John. It said:

'My Dearest Sweet Kaitlyn, I love you more than words can describe. I have known for a long time that my time left with you is short, and my wish for you is to find peace within your heart. I wanted to leave you one last present of my love, and that gift is Ray. Don't be surprised if you hear from him. I've asked him to come.'

I began crying as I realized how much John truly did love me — enough to sacrifice his own feelings, knowing how much pain I was still in. And after all these years, he still knew. I continued to read.

'If you ever get the chance to meet up with Ray again, take it. This has been my dream for you, that you would have your questions answered and find peace. Please thank him for giving me the chance to spend my life with you. I hope you find your answers. I love you. I love you enough to let you go.

Goodbye my love, until we meet again in Heaven, John'

I sobbed reading his passage over and over. I'm a lucky woman to have had two wonderful loves in my life. And I'm lucky to have married the one who showed the most love for me. My love for John grew from reading that, and I no longer felt the need to see Ray, knowing I already had everything I needed here in my heart. John was truly a special man.

John brought me to the tree shortly after we were married, and he said something that I will never forget.

'I know Ray is going to be a part of your heart forever. I accept this, as Ray is as much a part of you, just as much as he is a part of us. I'm not asking you to forget about Ray or to even stop loving him. I'm asking you to love me, too. I brought you here because this is where I first held you in comfort, and I'm hoping this is the place where we will bond as a couple. I love you, Kaitlyn Frost Fenderson.'

324

I remember looking in his eyes as tears welled, and I smiled. I held him tight while many thoughts popped in my head. One being that I had to accept the person I was married to was *not* Ray. The other being, I had deceived my parents into thinking I was pregnant with John's baby.

I think my parents, as well as everyone else, always had the gumption Rose was not John's natural daughter. I think they probably knew for sure, but chose to look the other way. You see, Rose's eyes are a dead give away. She has the deep cobalt eyes of my Ray. Regardless of Ray fathering Rose, John was her father. He raised her, he loved her, he provided for her, and he'd 've given his life for her.

There are a few things I regret the most in my life. I regret never having told my parents the truth about Rose. I regret not telling Rose that Ray was her father until I called her after opening the letter, and I regret not telling Ray about Rose.

Ray said he was never coming back, and I couldn't see the point in telling her, or him, for that matter. In retrospect, it's probably two of my worst mistakes. I hope Rose will forgive her mother's frightened selfishness, and I hope Ray will forgive me for not allowing him to have a relationship with his daughter. I never gave him that chance, and I was wrong. I was very wrong.

My last regret is not having saved myself for my husband, even though at the time I thought it was right. I thought Ray and I would be together forever — foolish really, but then again I was a foolish kid in love. If I had to do it all over again, I'd wait until my wedding night.

However, I do *not* regret my Rose. I wouldn't trade her for the world!

The time had come. I dressed and wore light-enhancing make up — a little more than when I was younger, as there are a few more things that need fixing these days. The clock was nearing noon, and it was time. Just as I was ready to head out of my bedroom, I stopped short and went to my jewelry box. Removing the charm bracelet from the soft velvet pouch I put it in after finding it, I fastened it around my wrist. I smiled. It was back where it belonged. Feeling as ready as I was going to be, I went downstairs and looked in the hall mirror one more time, checked my hair, make-up, and said, 'Here we go.'

My pulse raced, and my heart pounded. I became nervous and scared, yet, exuberant all at the same time. I parked the car, walked up to the door, took a deep breath, exhaled and entered. My heart was beating so fast that I thought I was going to have a heart attack.

The Soda Shop was exactly the same way it was fifty years ago. Different owners had taken over, but nothing had really changed — right down to the white carnations on the table. The scent of those flowers brought a sweet smile to my face.

I glanced to my left, and there he was — just as beautiful and as charming as he was the day I met him. Ray's hair glistened with silver shine, and his eyes of cobalt were more intense than I ever remembered them being. He looked up at me, smiled, and gave me his famous 'come here' gesture. I approached him with a careful step, and Ray rose from his chair with the help of a cane and gently took my hand to kiss it.

He had turned into a fine man. He was handsome, classy, and carried himself with grace.

At first, it was awkward. I wanted to yell at him, but how could I yell at *this* man? Yes, it was Ray. But this was an old man, not a young kid about to embark on his future. I felt eighteen, but Ray was *clearly* not eighteen. I looked at him, then down at the table, then up again, not knowing what to say. Well that's a lie. I knew what to say. I just wasn't sure if it was necessary at that point.

Ray, with his arm shaking, reached for me. He put his fingers under my chin, pulled me up to look me in the eyes, and said, *'I'm so sorry.'* Tears formed in his eyes as he cried for my forgiveness.

I couldn't do anything at that point but cry myself. I couldn't even look at him, as I knew I'd go into a full-blown sob. I wanted to hold him, kiss him, and pop into a fairytale, and have my prince whisk me away to fantasyland. I wanted him close. He reached for my hands to draw them near, and I pulled away.

Honestly, I would have liked to keep them there, but couldn't. I couldn't without answers to my questions. I had slipped back into the eighteen-year old Kaitlyn when I saw him, but after he tried to take my hands, I turned back to my present day self: a sixty-eight year old woman of class, dignity and self-assurance. I plainly stated, 'Ray, you hurt me, and I don't know whether you even realize how much, or whether you ever even cared. And, Ray — I'm still hurting.'

Tears fell to Ray's cheeks, and he cried out to me.

'I do care. That's why I've asked your presence today. I'm hurting, too.'

The awkwardness brought an uneasy silence, and I was thankful that the waitress came over to take our orders. (I laughed when I saw her name was Peggy). I ordered tea, to no surprise, and Ray ordered the same. Eating at that time was not possible, as we were both nervous wrecks. I was scared of what he'd say. Ray was scared of what he had to say. I decided to let him begin.

I was wrong. I treated you terribly, and you didn't deserve it. I have spent the last fifty years trying to put it all together, and I have come to a point in my life where I need to explain my action, and hope for your forgiveness.

I was, to say the least, bothered, thinking, 'How could he have the nerve to say *he* was ready? What about me all of these years not knowing why he left me that way — what about me? You're damn right you have a lot of explaining to do.'

I didn't say what I was thinking, choosing to be the bigger person. I just kept my mouth shut and prepared to listen, giving Ray the opportunity to make it right — so that I had the chance for final peace. Not just for me, but for John also, to see his wish for me come true, too. I settled myself in a listening mode, and without interrupting, I heard Ray explain.

'I was a coward, a spineless coward — selfish, mean, unkind and just a plain bastard,' he admitted.

'Okay, yeah, you're on a roll. Keep going,' I thought.

'I did need to go home to Georgia to clear my head. Losing my mother and then my father, it was too much to bear. I needed to get away from Winter's Crest. Except for you, it had become my hell on earth.

'When I was away from you, I missed you terribly, but found that as time went on, I could cope better with it. I knew if I came back to visit when I said I would, that I would just be right back to where I was

when I left — devastated. I knew I was hurting you, but I didn't see any other option. It was the weakest time of my life. I knew things would change drastically when I went into the Army, and I knew if I came back, the pain I had from being away from you would drag out even more, or increase.

'It was hard, Kaitlyn. I was torn between what my heart wanted and what my head was telling me to do. Without realizing what I was doing at that time, I began to disconnect from you, figuring that it would lessen the hurt. I wanted to get away from you quickly, without much pain. I didn't want to have to leave you again, but I also knew it was inevitable. I wanted to get away and stay away, and I thought it would be easier to handle what I thought was reality by escaping from you.

'I tried to make you hate me so it would be easier on you. I wanted you to hate me because I hated myself for what I was doing. You came after me with a love that just devoured me. I didn't want you to love me, so I was mean to you and called everything off.

'My plan backfired, as I have spent the last fifty years trying to work up the courage to see you — to apologize, to explain what I was trying to do.

'I wanted to see the world, sail around it, and place my stake in the ground. I had big dreams and fantasies of making my mark on the world. I was selfish for thinking I couldn't go after those dreams with you, and I left you behind to do it. But I thought loving you would keep me from doing those things, so I ran. I ran like a spineless coward. What I didn't realize is that I couldn't run away from my love for you, and I still can't.

'I loved you then. I've loved you over the past fifty years. And I love you now, Kait. I will love you for the rest of my life. I know I don't deserve your love, nor do I even deserve your forgiveness. I do know you deserve to know why I did what I did.

'I know it wasn't right. I know it was terrible, and well basically, it didn't get me anywhere except for a lifetime of regret and pain. I hurt you so badly, and at the same time hurt myself. I was wrong, Kait. I was stupid, selfish, and I was terribly wrong.'

I sat back in my chair trying to understand what had just occurred. Emotions from rage to understanding were fighting within. I wasn't sure whether to cry, laugh at the craziness of it all, or just plain out punch him. That eighteen-year old girl in me stared him down and said, 'You've got that right!'

To tell you the truth, I was disappointed with his reason, but none-the-less, it made sense to him at the time. I just never thought that Ray, this wonderful boy that I was so madly in love with, was a coward. I thought that he could handle anything. I guess I had him pegged wrong back then.

'Ray, I have something to tell you,' I confessed. 'I married John.'

'I know,' he replied.

'What?!' I screamed, turning attentions of the patrons in my direction.

'I came back, Kaitlyn,' Ray told me. *'Didn't Bob tell you? I came back to make things right and to ask for your hand again in marriage. I wanted to marry you before I went to Officer's Training Camp, and then take you with me overseas to where I would be stationed — which ended up being Frankfurt, Germany.'*

I shook my head. I was hurt that Bob didn't tell me something so important. But more importantly, I had just realized that the one dream I had back then was in my grasp, and I missed my opportunity.

'I came back in November after my basic training before heading to O.T.C.,' he told me. *'I stood by a lamppost, out of view, and Bob saw me. He came over and talked with me briefly, and then I saw you walking with John, pregnant. Bob told me you were married, and I knew then that I had lost my chance. Besides, I saw you smiling and you looked happy. I didn't want to have all the hurt I brought you upset your new life, and the beginning of your new family. I so wanted to see you and talk to you, but instead, I thought of you first — deciding it was best to fade into the evening skies.'*

'Why didn't you try and see me again? Why didn't you come a year later, five years later, ten years later — anything would have been better than having this burden for fifty years?!' I screamed, adding in as a spoken thought: 'Allison knew all this time?!'

'I couldn't. I owed it to you not to interrupt your life. You were so happy when I saw you, and the last thing I wanted to do was upset your life. And no, Kait. Bob never told Allison.'

I didn't know what to do. I was hurt that Bob has kept this from me for so long, but at the same time, Ray was thinking of me. Damn! It sure would have been nice to have the answers to all these questions. I excused myself from the table and went to the ladies room to compose myself, look in the mirror for some self-encouragement, and freshen up. All I could think of is that I could've been Ray's wife. God knows I would have considered taking him back. But he's right. It was too late.

I returned to the table and there was Ray, head in his hands and a yellow rose placed in the vase. The friendship rose. My favorite, and he remembered. I smiled my gratitude.

'Ray,' I said. 'Tell me everything, please. Place it all on the table, and give me the chance to handle it my own way. I'm a big girl now, and I can take it. Just please tell me everything, the entire truth or I will never be able to forgive you.'

Those were some pretty strong words and some words that an eighteen-year old Kaitlyn may not have had the courage to say, but with my years and experience, I was much better at handling life's disappointments. Not to mention, I had nothing to lose that I hadn't already lost.

Taking a sip of tea, Ray put the cup down on the table, while his hands played with the handle and explained everything.

'Well, I received a letter from John when he found out his cancer was terminal. He explained that his final dream for you was to have peace, and that you needed that peace from me. He asked me to gain the courage to come and see you and to explain myself, so that you could let it all go. He had said it was his dying wish for you, but he gave me one stipulation. He told me to wait at least one year after his death. He wanted you to have one last year with just you and his

memory before opening your heart to new beginnings. He really did love you, Kaitlyn.

'As for how he got a hold of me, John asked Bob to find my address at the post office. John also asked Bob not to tell you, as he was afraid it would hurt you too much, knowing that he knew where I was and that I had not come sooner.'

'You're damn right,' I cried through my tears. 'It does hurt.'

'Kait, John did it for you. It was his way of giving you a surprise gift, only a surprise gift of a lifetime. During the last year of his suffering, John would write me every so often. He shared photos of your wedding, your daughter, and through these photos I have been able to see you turn from a beautiful young lady to a sophisticated beautiful women. You know, after I saw the wedding picture, I squirmed with jealousy.' Ray paused. *'Kait, I have to ask you. Am I Rose's father?'*

I didn't know what to do or say. I felt so guilty for not telling him. My face turned to a guilt blush, and I answered with a nod.

'I'm so sorry, Ray. I should have told you. But you said you were never coming back. I didn't see the point. I felt like I was an interruption in your life, and figured if I was, than surely a baby would be.'

Ray took my hands and told me it was okay, and that he understood my reasoning. But I still couldn't shake the guilt of not telling him. I will regret not telling him for the rest of my life. Ray looked me in the eyes and told me, 'It's okay, Kait. I don't blame you,' then continued with his explanation.

'John told me about your mother and father, and I felt terrible. I wish I could have reciprocated their kindness. I really would have liked to have been there for you. I wasn't though, and I will have to live with that for the rest of my life.

When the last letter came, it was from Bob, telling me of John's passing. I wish I could have come to comfort you, but I gave John my word, and I wanted to keep it. So as the seasons have passed, I have been counting down the minutes until my time to come here arrived.

Anyway, that leads me to my letter. I didn't know whether I should call you or stop by some day, or write you. I decided to write you to give you time to adjust to seeing me, and to let you decide whether you even wanted to see me.'

Ray paused waiting for my reaction. I didn't really have one, and I'm not sure why.

'I never married, Kaitlyn. There was no one who could measure up to you. There just wasn't room in my heart for anyone else. I have held a torch for you for all these years. Silly, I guess. I brought this all upon myself trying to make it easier on me, and I'm the one who's ended up suffering from my decision, and I hurt you so deeply in the wake of my self-centeredness.

So here I am, on my hands and knees, begging for your forgiveness, asking for your friendship, asking you to understand my childish behavior of the years past, and years present, and letting you know that I am still in love with you. Please forgive me. Can you forgive me, Kait?'

Those were four words that I didn't have an answer to. 'I want to. I really want to,' I said. 'I'm going to need some time to gather my thoughts.'

Ray nodded, showing me he understood and smiled.

As I went to say goodbye to Ray, I leaned in towards him, brought my face to his, and kissed him gently on the cheek. I thanked him, and then I gently tweaked his nose for old time's sake. I helped Ray from his seat, and we walked out of the restaurant chuckling at the craziness. I then looked up to him and asked if the cane was the same one from the prom. We both started laughing.

He looked just like he did that night when he was playing around at The Chateau and at the prom, although this time it was for real. The injury from his youth had come back to haunt him, settling in as arthritis in his knee. Ray walked me to my car and gave me the number of his hotel room. He told me I could call, but only if I wished to. He said he would understand if I didn't.

It was awkward saying goodbye. We didn't know whether to kiss, hug, or shake hands. I went for the hug. I wanted to see if those feelings were still there. They are.

I arrived home this afternoon, feeling relieved — I guess, feeling some closure. Still though, I was angry that he'd known where to find me for the past fifty years, and that it took this long for him to come and see me.

I suppose I was a little upset with John for going behind my back, but at least I understood his reasoning. As for Bob, well, I'll have to deal with him later.

Ray, on the other hand, his reasons were not, well, good enough. I suppose him not leaving me for something I did wrong or for another girl is a good thing. I just don't know. I suppose it could be construed as a 'forgive and forget' thing, or a 'forgive and move on' thing. He was only eighteen at the time, and back then, small things seem so large. I can see his reasoning, I guess. Hmmm … And well, also, it was considerate of him to think of how his coming back into my life after I was married to John would affect me, and that he had had the foresight to figure out that it would have caused more hurt for both of us. And then on top of that, he did keep his word to John.

I don't know. Considering our age, (his age), and considering that I have had a good life, a good husband, and much love shown and given to me by him, I have not lost anything really, and maybe I have even gained a better life from it. Yes, that's the answer. I've had a good life. I didn't lose out on anything.

That's it, Kaitlyn! You go girl! (Oh, such phrasing.)

I've decided that it's time to let it all go and allow Ray to be a part of my life again, allow him to enter my heart one more time, and for the last time.

I took the number out of my purse and called Ray. I felt eighteen again as I dialed his number for the first time. 'Here we go again,' I thought. I took a deep breath and let it out as I dialed the last number. It rang a few times, and then he answered. 'Ray, hi, I'm ready to move on, can you come over for dinner tonight?'

Ray accepted my invitation and planned on coming over at six o'clock. I hung up with a smile, and with a slight click of my heels, I prepared myself a nice bath to relax. I just needed to think about what I wanted to say, what I needed to say, and what had to be said, as well as what I had just heard.

I prepared a wonderful dinner, complete with white wine and folded napkins. I had candles lit, as we did during the special night at my house when my parents went to the social function. And I filled my home with music of yesteryear, opening my heart for Ray.

He, with a smile that could melt you, arrived on time, wearing a blue cardigan and holding fifty long stem yellow roses. I invited him in and we embraced. I hugged him close and whispered in his ear, 'Ray, I have always loved you.'

He made himself comfortable and poured us a couple glasses of wine while I put the roses in water, and then we joined in the living room. There was a chill in the air that night, and the fire warmed the air, not to mention the atmosphere. Music was playing softly, and Ray and I sat together, just enjoying the reality of it all, actually being together after all these years. We sat next to one another, taking it all in. And every once in awhile, we'd start laughing.

When dinner was ready, he and I served the dining room table, and then sat for our meal. We held hands and said a prayer, remembering John, Jaycee, Nick, and my mom and dad. We thanked God for bringing us together again. We also asked God to help us move past the pain.

Ray and I had a lovely conversation. We talked about our fond memories, our lives over the past fifty years, and we talked about the matters at hand. I told him how I felt about how he had just abandoned me. I told him how he had hurt me, but that I was ready to forgive him. I let him know that although I was not thrilled with his reasoning, I could understand him thinking that way at the young age of eighteen.

I told Ray that I have always been in love with him. Even when he hurt me, I still loved him. I told him the struggles I went through, what I did to get through them, and what John had done to help me. I talked of my struggles with my mom's Breast Cancer and how much I miss her and my dad. I also told him that I have tended to his parents' graves since he left. I apologized again for not letting him know sooner that he had a daughter and that I was wrong, too.

I told him I was sorry for everything, but that mainly I was sorry because we never had the chance to explore our love further and never allowed it to be a part of our lives. Our eyes met when I said that, and he whispered simply: *'Never say never, we can still enjoy each other with the time we have left.'*

And he's right. He has come back to me at a time when I am lonely and need a friend to share my life with.

After dinner, we settled in by the fire, held each other as we did before, and read from our book. We sat there in peace, two friends coming back together, reminiscing and enjoying one other's company. We read a few passages and smiled with fond memories, and we came across one that pertained to us, in the situation we're in right now. It said, 'Life goes by with loss and despair, only to bring back joy in the later years.'

I am taking the chance at love again with Ray. I realize that I could get my heart broken all over, but I also realize that there's no sense in running from it. I don't have fifty years to wonder, and neither does he.

Ray was able to make many of his dreams come true. All but one … the one of true love and marriage, and sharing his life with someone.

He became an engineer and had his own company out on the West Coast. He traveled around the world, and he even got to sail around it. Ray explained that he had sold his business and was quite well off financially. He wanted to come back and spend his remaining years here, enjoying the one aspiration he never was able to achieve — sharing his life with me.

I would think that it would be great to have all the exciting adventures Ray had, and it was. What was missing for Ray, was someone to share it with. Although some people choose to have their lives not be complicated by marriage and such, Ray wanted that and missed it in his life, even though it was the path he had chosen.

We finished dinner and washed the dishes together, and then we settled by the fire, holding each other, talking, and playing catch-up. We put everything on the table by allowing ourselves to be vulnerable with one another, sharing each and every emotion, each hurt and sadness. We worked everything out. We both felt as if fifty pounds had been lifted from our shoulders, and we were finally at peace with ourselves and with one other.

I have my Ray back. I have my wonderful, cobalt-eyed friend back.

Ray and I held one other and fell asleep in each other's arms.

Morning came on the twenty-eighth, and we were a little stiff from sleeping curled up on the couch together. I guess we aren't 'spring chickens' anymore. That's okay though. I kind of like our new relationship — our new beginning.

That morning, we had some tea and some of my own strawberry-jam on toast. Ray went back to change and shower at his hotel room, and we planned to meet up later. He asked me to join him for an afternoon stroll, and I immediately accepted his invitation.

Ray met me at my house, and we took off down the road, right towards 'our tree'. Our walk took a little longer than it had in the early years, but the feelings that surrounded us were the same — the smells were the same. Everything was the same, except our bodies. We walked up to the tree, still holding the engravings of he and I, and touched it with fond remembrance.

Ray looked at me, raised his hand to my chin, and said, *'I love you, Miss Kait. I will never leave you again. I can't lose you twice in one lifetime. Marry Me.'* He proceeded to bring out a small black velvet box from his pocket, and I opened it to find my pre-engagement ring from years past.

Tears were in his eyes asking me. Tears were in my eyes when I said, 'Yes'."

*   *   *

Epilogue

Mom and Ray married. They held a small wedding consisting of close friends and family members on a hilltop, so they could be as close to Heaven as possible. Ray and Mom wanted their parents and my father to have the best seats in the house — a completed circle if you will.

They married on a beautiful summer day. The skies were as blue as Ray's eyes, and the heavens shone down upon them. A few clouds danced above as the winds whistled through the trees, singing sweet melodies of never-ending love. The birds chirped with the sounds of the breeze, as if they were in celebration of a love that was meant to be.

Mom's dress was made of soft cream satin, and it flowed and swished as she walked. Her hair was done in soft curls with a few cascades gently caressing her cheeks. Mom looked radiant as she walked down the grass aisle, the few rows of white wooden chairs created.

Ray looked distinguished in a black double-breasted suit, similar to the one my great-grandma had bought for him years ago. His smile shined with peace and happiness, and his eyes glowed with love. Ray's hair shimmered in the sunlight, enhancing his already glowing ambiance. And a boutonniere holding two small yellow sweetheart roses adorned his suit, matching my mom's bouquet.

Allison stood up as Mom's matron of honor, while her husband, Bob Westman, Mom's long time friend and mailman, stood up as Ray's best man. They were both equally radiant.

Mom and Ray were so happy, so much in love, and so devoted to each other. It was nice to see my mother smiling again.

It was a lovely wedding, although Ray had a little trouble climbing the hill. I remember Mom joking with Ray, telling him to walk like he did at the prom. Of course, I didn't get it then, but they laughed with fond memory.

After the wedding, there was a small reception held at The Soda Fountain. Every table was decorated with white mini-carnations and each held one bright yellow rose. The fragrance was divine, and I've found myself going into The Fountain just to sit down and remember their wedding day.

I can picture my mom and dad, and Ray and Allison frequenting the restaurant when they were younger. I can see them dropping a nickel into the jukebox and cutting a rug to the latest seventy-eight and singing, "Some Enchanted Evening," by Perry Como. I can visualize my mom sitting at a table with Ray or having talks with Allison, as well as with my dad.

I'm smiling to myself as I sit here in the cobwebs, cleaning out her attic, while she and Ray are on their honeymoon. I sure hope they're having a good time.

After the wedding, Mom had one last detail to attend to: 'the passing of the teacup'. Handing it to me, she said, "Remember this day, June 26, 2001 as the day your mom got a second chance at love and learned to forgive. I know this isn't your special day, but I hope that not only will it bring back fond memories of my wedding, but that it will be a reminder to you, that you always have a second chance."

With that, she hugged me and whispered in my ear, "My whole life has changed with a stroke of the pen."

Afterword

With A Stroke Of The Pen has been a joy to write, and I hope you were able to feel that emotion come through the written words.

Although many first-time writers write more of an autobiographical story, I have to say that this novel is not. I wish I could tell you where it came from, but all I can say is that each character and each scene developed at its own pace. I watched and grew with my characters, and I became each one as I wrote what they felt, did and saw. (Well, *not* the romance scenes.) The words just seemed to take on a life of their own, sometimes keeping me at the computer for up to fourteen hours in a day.

The town in my novel, Winter's Crest, is an imaginary town that grew from my love for Lake George, New York. However, one of the readers from *The Vinland Journal* commented that my illusory town could be a dead ringer for Wells, New York. Additionally, the character of Winter's Crest is derived from the charming rural town in which I live, as well as its surrounding townships.

Some of the exciting things I have found with writing this book are the e-mails or talks I have had with strangers. I was telling one lady about it at The Alley Cat Hair Shop, and it was amazing to find out that her life was similar to that of my main characters. I could see her mind churn, as she too wished to catch up with her first love. I have had many similar conversations, but this one sticks out clearly in my mind.

I hope you have enjoyed reading *With a Stroke of The Pen* and the story brings you memories of first love, leaving a smile in your heart. Remember, you always have a second chance.

If you wish to keep updated on the current happenings with this book and the one that is in progress, please visit my website at: www.KimbraLeigh.com

Sincerely,
Kimbra Leigh

About The Author

Living in Pennsylvania, Kimbra has volunteered extensively in the community from coaching kids in various sports to working as a teacher's aide in her children's classrooms, to helping out in various community activities.

Currently, she is working behind the scenes and on stage for her local community theatre while raising three kids with her husband, and writing her second novel. She is also the web master and editor of *The Vinland Journal*, www.VinlandJournal.com, a free literary e-zine co-founded with ND Wiseman, author of *The Seven Waiting Worlds*.

Ever seeking new avenues to express her boundless energy, Kimbra turned her hand to writing in March 2000. Immersing herself in the craft, she began, not long afterward, to frame and write *With a Stroke of The Pen*.

Kimbra is publishing her first completed novel with the intention that there will be many more to come.

Readers' Reviews

"*With a Stroke of the Pen* is a warm, well-paced romance novel that transports the reader from the present to the past with seamless agility. Ms. Leigh succeeds in creating the tension and anticipation we've all come to expect from novels of this type, and I have to say that in this, her first venture into the publishing world, Ms. Leigh's efforts have paid off well. From cursory perusal to in-depth examination, *WSP* stands up to the scrutiny. Kudos to her, in the hopes that there will be more well-crafted novels to come!" N.W. (40+ male)

*　*　*

"WOW to your book! You really did something special there, Kim! It seems to start slow, but as I went along, I got HOOKED! I kept sneaking in a few minutes of reading whenever I could. Finally, I just gave up and sat down and finished it on Sunday! NOT GOOD, only 9 days before Christmas!! I've been paying for it ever since! I sat there SOBBING twice! You really did a masterful piece of work, Kim! Still today, I find pieces of the story flitting through my mind. And such creativity! In all my years of reading, reading, reading, I never remember hitting a storyline even remotely similar to this one!" B.F. (50+ year old woman)

*　*　*

"I loved it! It's excellent! I stayed up 'til one in the morning to finish it. You've got to read this book!" K. D. (30+ year old woman)

*　*　*

"I loved your book. I had all these chores to do and all I wanted to do was just read your book. I couldn't wait to see what happened next! I really enjoyed *With a Stroke of the Pen*. It is a wonderful story of first love and second chances. It shows that life is not always what it appears to be, and that we have to work at it and sometimes move on. Your first love is always special. It's something you never forget. It stays in your heart forever. This book reinforces that even if your life takes a different path than you expected, live it to its fullest. You never know what will happen." L. B. (43 year-old woman)

*   *   *

"*With The Stroke of a Pen* is a tender book about lifelong friendships, love and happiness. I re-read the book a couple of weeks later, and was even more fascinated the second time around. The author writes with understanding and a joyful heart. This book is a 'must read'." M. B. (80+ year old woman)

*   *   *

"I just finished reading *With a Stroke of the Pen* and was truly impressed with its ability to keep me not only on the edge of my seat but also with its ability to pull me in ... in anticipation to what each additional page would bring. I began on a Wednesday afternoon, and before I was less than halfway through the 1st chapter, I was hooked. I put everything else on hold (television, lifting weights and even eating) to complete the book. I finished at about 12:30 Friday evening. Wow! Now I'm not a man who normally reads stories of this type, but I couldn't believe how much I enjoyed it. It even choked me up on more than one occasion. Ask anyone who knows me and they'll agree that this is a feat in itself. My recommendation -BUY THE BOOK! READ THE BOOK! You won't be disappointed!" J.R. (40 year -old man)

*   *   *

"By far the best book I have read in awhile. I couldn't put it down. I highly recommend this book. It's a romance unlike the usual, predictable, paperback romances out there." Anonymous

* * *

"My daughter and I just finished reading "With a Stroke of the Pen," and it was excellent! We can't say enough about this book. We enjoyed it so much. It brings back so many memories of having tea with my mother, sister, brother and the talks we had. This is the kind of book that you can read again and again, and still love it. Which is why we are going to keep it and read it in a couple months, a year, and so forth. We feel that you did an excellent job and we can't wait for your next book. We loved it. We absolutely loved it!" E.C. (40+ and 17 year old females)

* * *

"You did it!!
"What? You made me cry!!! I never thought I'd get teary-eyed and mushy reading a book of all things!! But it happened last night when I read up through and completed chapter 8 of *With a Stroke of a Pen*. That last chapter was gripping and pulled me in. Your writing captured the emotions of the moment, and you put realistic, human hearts into your characters, unlike anything I've ever read before. You captured the thoughts that fly through people's minds in situations like that, and you captured the imagery that makes it possible to close my eyes and envision the situations unfolding in front of me, not unlike a movie or a play. I honestly have trouble escaping from the imagery. I actually had a snippet of a dream about that story last night, like my mind was trying to picture it like it were a movie. But then maybe it will be a movie one of these days, maybe a television movie!!! You never know." E. L. (late forties male)

Remember to go after your dreams
with a smile on your face and in your heart.
Life's too short not to.

Thank you, my readers, my friends,
for being by my side as I go after mine.